Kate Ellis was born and brought up in Liverpool and studied drama in Manchester. Keenly interested in medieval history and archaeology, she lives in Cheshire with her family.

Kate has been twice nominated for the CWA Short Story Dagger and her novel, *The Plague Maiden*, was nominated for the Theakston's Old Peculier Crime Novel of the Year in 2005.

Visit Kate Ellis online:

www.kateellis.co.uk
@KateEllisAuthor

Praise for Kate Ellis:

'A beguiling author who interweaves past and present'
The Times

'[Kate Ellis] gets better with each new book'
Bookseller

'Kept me on the edge of my seat'
Shots magazine

'Ellis skilfully interweaves ancient and contemporary crimes in an impeccably composed tale'
Publishers Weekly

The
Shining Skull

Kate Ellis

Piatkus
An imprint of
Little, Brown Book Group
Carmelite House
50 Victoria Embankment
London EC4Y 0DZ

An Hachette UK Company
www.hachette.co.uk

piatkus
www.littlebrown.co.uk

PIATKUS

First published in Great Britain in 2007 by Piatkus Books
This paperback edition published in 2007 by Piatkus Books
Reissued in 2017 by Piatkus

3 5 7 9 10 8 6 4 2

A CIP catalogue record for this book
is available from the British Library.

ISBN 978-0-349-41896-4

Typeset by Phoenix Photosetting, Chatham, Kent

Printed and bound in Great Britain by Clays Ltd, Elcograf S.p.A.

Papers used by Piatkus are from well-managed forests
and other responsible sources.

MIX

In memory of my mother Mona Ellis (1924–2005) who loved crime fiction and who was a constant source of encouragement to me.

'We have your son.'

Anna Fallbrook found it hard to focus on the words as her eyes filled with tears.

As her heart pounded in her chest like a warning drum, she closed her eyes and gulped air into her lungs. But the intake of oxygen had no effect. She felt as though she could pass out at any moment and sink to the ground like some Victorian invalid.

A warm tear ran down her cheek, tickling the flesh. She wiped it away with the back of her hand and tried hard to concentrate on the letters swimming before her eyes behind a film of tears. 'We have your son. If you obey our instructions to the letter, he won't be harmed. But if you tell the police we won't hesitate to cut his throat. Await instructions.'

It wasn't real. It couldn't be. Things like that happened to somebody else ... to stars ... to celebrities ... to multimillionaires. Not to families like the Fallbrooks. Marcus – her little Marcus – would be with Jenny. He would be on his way home now from his prep school with his nanny, Jenny. Someone was playing a joke on her. A nasty joke in very bad taste.

Anna didn't know how long she'd sat there in the cool shade of the late summer garden staring at the words neatly printed in black ballpoint on the sheet of pale yellow paper. She felt as though her body didn't quite belong to her. As if she was in some cruel and frustrating dream.

She could see the river through the trees at the end of the garden; the sun reflected on the rippling water like sparks of silver fire. That sort of thing didn't happen in a place like this. Derenham was a refuge from urban life; somewhere you could leave your doors unlocked without fear of being robbed. Perhaps that's why they had been off their guard. Perhaps their complacency had made it easy for a snake to slither unseen into their Eden.

But she took another deep, gulping breath, trying to convince herself that it was all a sick joke. When Marcus and Jenny returned she'd laugh about it. And then she should really mention it to the police.

She walked round the house to the drive and waited by the front door, watching for Jenny's Mini to appear at the gate. For the next ten minutes she paced to and fro, swinging between hope and despair, between telling herself it was all a wicked hoax and battling a crushing, trembling fear that the note might be genuine.

Then when Jenny's Mini sped up the drive and the nanny emerged from the car with tears streaming down her pale, pretty face saying that Marcus hadn't been at school since lunchtime and nobody knew where he was, Anna realised it was for real.

Marcus was gone.

Thirty years later

It was so familiar, the view of the low, stone house through the overhanging branches; the open French windows giving a glimpse of a comfortable, slightly old-fashioned interior; the manicured lawn stretching down to the wide fringe of trees at the water's edge; and the small paned windows twinkling in the weak September sun. The smell was familiar too; the damp scent of undergrowth after the rain, the faint salty tang of the river.

Marcus staggered up the bank, ignoring the nettles and thorns that snatched at his legs and stung the flesh exposed by the tears in his tattered jeans. He had reached the top of the bank now and he stood perfectly still, shielded by the leafy oak trees.

This was it. This was home. He hadn't seen it for three decades but it had hardly changed, as though it had been waiting for him, frozen in time.

Slowly and reluctantly, he retraced his steps and made for the wooden jetty where he'd tied up the small motor boat he'd hired in Tradmouth. He'd have to think. He couldn't just barge in and announce his return as though nothing had happened.

He knew he'd have to face it soon – but he dreaded seeing the disbelief, the bewilderment, on their faces as he tried to explain.

Returning from the dead is never easy.

2

Chapter One

TO BE HELD AT THE GEORGE INN, DUKESBRIDGE
ON THE 24TH DAY OF APRIL 1814

A MEETING AT WHICH WILL APPEAR
THE AMAZING DEVON MARVEL
WHO, BEING BUT 10 YEARS OLD, WILL ASTOUND
ALL PRESENT WITH HIS PRODIGIOUS
CALCULATIONS

Admission 1d

Leah Wakefield was in full view now.

Watching from the shelter of the trees, the stalker shifted from foot to foot. The time had to be right. The conditions had to be perfect for the operation.

The little bitch was strutting down the green velvet lawn behind the house, making for the azure rectangle of the swimming pool wearing a bikini that left little to the imagination. There was a fixed scowl on her lightly tanned, baby pretty face and she kept throwing contemptuous glances at the older woman trotting beside her, trying to keep up.

The stalker recognised the woman, the small, plump blonde with too much make-up on her hatchet face and a skirt too brief for her years. Leah's pushy mother, Suzy Wakefield – a face that had graced every tabloid and celebrity magazine in recent months. And for once it looked as though the newshounds at the lower end of the market had struck a rare and rich vein of accuracy. The body language and the never-ending barrage of carping from the older woman targeted at the half naked girl with the California tan and the gym-honed body said it all.

The rift between mother and daughter was deep. As deep as the cut the stalker would make in the victim's throat if the family didn't come up with the goods.

The girl was in the pool now, floating on her back, her bronzed limbs spread out like a sacrificial victim. She was vulnerable; oblivious to the outside world. And completely unaware of what lay ahead.

'There's been another taxi attack. That's the second in two weeks.'

Detective Constable Steve Carstairs looked up from the open copy of the *Daily Galaxy* he was reading underneath his desk and saw Detective Sergeant Rachel Tracey looking down at him.

'Sorry, Sarge. What was that?'

Rachel pushed her blond hair back off her face, trying to conceal her impatience. 'Another woman's been abducted by a bogus taxi driver . . . same as before.'

Steve looked at her blankly.

'Forget it. Everyone else seems to be out so I thought you could come with me to interview the victim. But if you're busy . . . ' She said the words with heavy irony as she stared down at the newspaper. 'Anything interesting?'

Steve felt his cheeks reddening. 'Er . . . I was just reading about that singer Leah Wakefield. She's a right little slapper by the sound of it.'

Rachel unfroze for a second and allowed herself a grudging grin. She too had followed the musical career and personal life of the teenage singing sensation, Leah Wakefield, with some interest – along with a substantial proportion of the population. But she was hardly ready to admit this weakness to Steve.

'If I were you, Steve, I wouldn't believe everything you read in that paper of yours. They usually make it up as they go along.'

By the time Steve had opened his mouth to protest, Rachel was heading towards DI Peterson's office with the determination of a guided missile. Steve watched her retreating back and saw her hesitate for a second by the office door to smooth her hair. Any excuse, he thought, to talk to Peterson. Sometimes she made it so obvious.

4

As his office door opened, Wesley Peterson looked up. 'Anything new?'

'Another taxi abduction,' Rachel began as she made herself comfortable in the visitor's chair. 'Early morning this time, would you believe. Woman on her way to Neston Station to catch the London train. She rang for a cab and one turned up. Then after a while she noticed the driver wasn't taking the right route for Neston. She told him but he just carried on and parked the taxi in an isolated country lane somewhere – she wasn't sure where. Anyway, it was exactly the same MO as before. He took out a pair of scissors and cut off her hair.'

'The boss thinks he fancies himself as a hairdresser. Or he used to be a hairdresser and he got the sack.'

Rachel shook her head. 'I don't think even a defrocked hairdresser would make the sort of mess this bastard does. I've seen the other victims. He just hacks their hair off. No marks for artistic merit.' She looked up. 'The papers are starting to call him the Barber. Do you reckon it's sexual . . . a power thing?'

Wesley shrugged. 'I think it's a distinct possibility. But we won't know for sure until we catch him. Where did he drop off his latest victim?'

'Just like the others. He dropped her off at the station. He leaves them wherever they've asked to go.'

'Description?'

'Nondescript. Middle aged. Baseball cap pulled down over his face. Droopy moustache. Average build. Average height. Average everything.'

'Last time it was a clean-shaven man with long mousy hair.'

'Perhaps he's disguising himself . . . or it's a different man?'

Wesley looked up. 'Surely there can't be more than one of them. What about the taxi firm she booked?'

'Again the bona fide cab arrived to find the client already gone. Our friend's listening in to the taxi frequency for likely victims and getting in there first. All the victims swear that the car bore the name of the correct taxi company and a licence plate. It all looked kosher.'

'He's organised. I'm just worried that he's going to move on from chopping his victim's hair off to doing some real harm.'

Rachel looked at Wesley. 'I wondered if you'd like to come with me to see this latest victim.' She felt herself blushing. 'She might have seen something the others didn't. I mean, as you said, he's got to be stopped before someone gets hurt.'

'Where does she live?'

'Stokeworthy. Next to the village school.' She hesitated, the mention of schools bringing something uncomfortable to mind. 'How's your wife by the way? Has term started yet?' She couldn't help asking the question, like picking at a scab.

'She went back last Tuesday.' Wesley smiled. 'And she's looking forward to half term already.' Pam Peterson taught in a primary school and Rachel had worked out long ago that Wesley's domestic life tended to follow a pattern – agreeable in the school holidays and strained in term time.

Wesley stood up and looked at his watch. 'The DCI's in a meeting with the Chief Super which means he'll be like a bear with piles when he gets back. I think we should make ourselves scarce, don't you?'

Rachel smiled. Wesley's assessment of DCI Gerry Heffernan's mood was probably all too accurate. She followed Wesley Peterson out of the office. It looked as if it was her lucky day.

The stalker watched Leah Wakefield disappear into the house. A big house. Neo-Georgian. Vulgar as its residents and built on the outskirts of Neston in the days before the South Hams became an area of outstanding natural beauty and the planning authorities became too fussy.

He felt he knew the house. The interior was familiar from a four page spread in a well known celebrity magazine. And then it had featured on the TV series *Star Homes*. Cameras had followed the scantily clad Leah around the house ... to the gold and cream lounge with the massive plasma TV occupying one wall like a cinema screen; to the sumptuous bedroom with its walk-in wardrobe and en suite with corner spa bath with solid gold taps; to the kitchen with its acres of polished wood and granite. The stalker had played the video through again and again until he knew the layout of the house and the contents of each opulent room off by heart.

He'd seized the opportunity to have a good look round when the house was empty during Leah's last nationwide tour and he'd paid particular attention to the security system, noting each PIR detector and every lock on the doors and windows. Emboldened, he had called at the house pretending to sell alarm systems and struck lucky with Leah's cleaner. She was a garrulous woman who, in her pride at being connected with a celebrity, had talked far too much. When the stalker had feigned the excited interest of a genuine fan, Mrs Cleaner had played to the gallery, impressing him with her intimate knowledge of the Shining One, bathing in her reflected glory. As far as she was concerned it was only natural for someone to be awed and fascinated by someone who had appeared regularly on the TV and whose every action was reported in newspapers and magazines.

Leah and her mother had been staying in Devon for a week now and the stalker had watched her from his well-concealed hiding place in the woodland – in the wild area between her grounds and the adjoining farmland. There had been a close shave when a brace of paparazzi came stamping through the undergrowth in hope of capturing a shot of the star off her guard and doing something that might be worth a headline or two. But they had given up after a few hours. If they'd stuck it out, they would have got an eyeful.

The weather forecast for tomorrow was good. She would be in the pool again. Half naked and vulnerable.

If he was to take her, it would have to be soon. But the moment had to be right.

It was a strange symbol, one Dr Neil Watson of the County Archaeological Unit had never come across before. Seven boldly carved rays radiated from a seven-pointed star with a flower, possibly a rose, at its centre.

'It's on several graves ... all dating from the early nineteenth century.' The Reverend John Ventnor, Rector of St Merion's church, Stoke Beeching, gave a nervous smile. 'I've no idea what it means. Do you ... ?'

Neil shook his head. 'Contrary to rumour, archaeologists don't know everything. I've never seen anything like it before in my life.'

'There's been quite a bit of opposition, you know.' The Rector saw that Neil looked puzzled. 'To the church extension ... the new parish room. A lot of people don't like the idea of disturbing the dead.'

Neil assumed what he considered to be a suitably solemn expression. 'No. I suppose some people are squeamish about ... '

7

'They'll be disinterred respectfully, of course, and reburied in another part of the churchyard but . . . '

'Yeah.' Neil gave an impatient smile, trying to think of something intelligent to say. He just wanted to get on with the job. The authorities had insisted that the delicate work of disinterring the old graves and digging the foundations for the new parish room at the north-west end of the church should be supervised by an experienced archaeological team, due to the thirteenth-century church's historical significance. And now it looked as though part of his job would be to soothe the nerves of a jumpy clergyman.

The Reverend John Ventnor leaned towards him confidentially. 'To be honest, this has caused so much ill feeling in the parish that I almost wish Miss Worth hadn't specified that the money she left should be spent on building an extension to the church. Half the parish think it's the best thing since sermons were cut from three hours to the requisite fifteen minutes but the other half seem to imagine that we've hired Beelzebub himself as the architect. You just can't win, can you?'

Neil smiled, suddenly finding himself sympathetic to the man's predicament. 'Don't worry,' he said. 'It'll all be done as discreetly and quickly as possible. We're erecting screens today so nobody'll be able to see what's going on. I presume all the relevant families have been informed? It's not going to come as a nasty surprise to anyone that Great Uncle Albert's being shifted to another part of the churchyard?'

John Ventnor nodded earnestly. 'That's all been dealt with. Fifteen burials will be disturbed and only one family couldn't be traced . . . a burial dating back to 1791. Of course there's the Bentham family vault – the tomb you were looking at before with the odd symbol – but that's not a problem.' He leaned forward confidentially. 'Miss Worth was their only surviving relative.'

'And she suggested that her nearest and dearest be shifted to make way for the parish room.'

'Miss Worth was a very practical woman,' the Rector said with a twinkle in his eye. 'Sentimentality was hardly her forte. She lived till she was ninety, ran a smallholding single handed and rode to hounds until she was eighty-two. Salt of the earth.'

'A formidable lady.'

'You didn't argue with Miss Worth,' said the Rector with feeling. Neil suspected he'd had one or two altercations with the formidable lady in his time.

Neil looked around. The contractors were arriving to erect the screening, their thoughtlessly parked lorry blocking the main street through the village. Some of the archaeological team had already turned up in an old camper van and they'd started to unload equipment from the back. John Ventnor turned and gazed upon this scene of industry but showed no sign of moving and leaving Neil to his work.

Neil had never considered making conversation to be one of his strengths but, as he wasn't in a position to do much else just yet, he thought he'd give it a try. 'Do you know the new Vicar of Belsham?'

'Mark? Yes, of course.'

'I was at university with his wife's brother.'

The Rector's eyes lit up. 'Really? I've met Maritia a few times ... lovely lady. She told me that her brother's a policeman in Tradmouth.'

'That's right. Wes studied archaeology with me at Exeter before he joined the force. He's a detective inspector now.'

'Did you go to the wedding?'

Neil nodded. Then he turned away. The mention of Maritia Peterson's wedding conjured uncomfortable memories.

His eyes focused once more on the strange carving that adorned the Bentham family tomb. The past, to Neil, was a safe and comfortable country ... unlike the present. 'Odd symbol that. Wonder what it means.'

'I'll have a look through the church records if you like ... see if there's any mention of it.'

'Thanks,' said Neil as the builders were making their way noisily up the church path carrying various unrecognisable pieces of equipment.

It was time to make a start.

The Barber's latest victim lived in the increasingly pricey village of Stokeworthy, in a cottage straight off a chocolate box. Pink cob and thatch, it stood next to a small village school which, unlike many such schools in the area, was still open for business, just. It seemed like every town dweller's dream of rural living And Sienna Calder had acquired that dream. But now, maybe, her idyll had turned into a nightmare.

Rachel Tracey lifted the heavy knocker, formed in the shape of a Cornish pixie, and let it fall. As she waited for her knock to be answered she turned around and gave Wesley a shy smile which he returned automatically.

After half a minute the door opened, just a little at first as though the resident was a nervous old lady, terrified of bogus callers. After Rachel had done the introductions and poked her ID round the door for examination, the door was opened wider to admit them.

As they stepped straight into the low-beamed sitting room, Wesley caught his first glimpse of their hostess and what he saw shocked him. Sienna Calder had an attractive face, mature but, as yet, unmarked by the ravages of age. Wesley guessed she was in her thirties and the clothes she wore had a well-cut simplicity that marked them out as expensive. But the sleek image was marred by her hair, hacked inexpertly almost to the scalp like some Victorian workhouse child who'd been found to be crawling with lice. He averted his eyes, feeling that it would be rude to stare.

'How are you feeling?' Rachel asked sympathetically.

Sienna slumped into a brown leather armchair. 'It was a bit of a shock but at least he didn't . . . .I suppose it could have been worse. A lot worse.' She put her hand tentatively to her head. 'I expect it'll grow back.' The words were brave but Rachel could detect a tremble in her voice.

'Can you tell us exactly what happened?' Wesley said gently.

Sienna nodded and invited them to sit.

'My partner, Guy, works in London during the week. I work from home here for two days – I'm in IT – and I go up to London on Wednesdays and stay in the apartment with Guy. Then we both come down here on Fridays.'

'Rather a lot of toing and froing,' said Rachel with a hint of disapproval. Her family had farmed the Devon earth for generations and she felt the native's resentment of wealthy Londoners who bought up weekend places and priced local youngsters out of the housing market. But she tried to concentrate on the matter in hand. The woman had been attacked and her attacker had to be caught.

Either Sienna hadn't heard Rachel's remark or she'd chosen to ignore it. She carried on. 'I was catching the London train from Neston and I ordered a taxi from the firm I usually use. A cab turned up, no problem. Everything seemed normal then . . . '

'Go on,' said Wesley quietly.

10

'He started driving towards Neston. Then he turned off down a little lane . . . very narrow. Only room for one car.'

'That could describe most lanes round here,' said Rachel sharply. 'Did you notice any signposts or . . . ?'

'No, I was sitting on the back seat reading some business papers so I wasn't really concentrating. I assumed he was just taking a short cut.'

'Then it became clear he wasn't?' said Wesley.

Sienna nodded. 'It seemed to be taking rather a long time so I said something like, "I did say Neston railway station, didn't I?" But he said nothing. He just kept on driving down these lanes. That's when I started to get really worried. I kept asking him where he was going. I was going to tell him to stop the car then I thought better of it. We were in the middle of nowhere.'

'Go on,' Wesley prompted gently.

Sienna glanced at Rachel, as though for support, but Rachel avoided her eyes. It would be up to Wesley to do the tea and sympathy bit.

'He stopped the car. Then he got out. I tried the back doors but the child locks were on. I was trapped. I really started to panic then, believe me.' She looked Wesley in the eye. 'Well, you can imagine what I thought. It's amazing how everything you learn at self-defence classes goes out of the window when you're faced with . . . '

'You thought he was going to rape you?' Wesley was surprised at the lack of sympathy in Rachel's voice.

'Of course. I saw he had something in his hand. I thought it was a knife but now I know it was a pair of scissors. I remember crouching on the floor of the car thinking that if he couldn't drag me out, he wouldn't be able to . . . But he was stronger than me. I tried everything . . . biting . . . hitting out. But he dragged me out of the car onto the ground and pinned my arms behind me and bound them with tape – I think it was that brown tape you use on parcels. I was so terrified that I couldn't even scream. Then I saw the flash of a blade and I thought, "this is it. He's going to kill me."' She took a deep breath. Wesley could see her hands were shaking. 'I closed my eyes and prayed. I'm not religious but I prayed.'

'Go on,' Wesley said quietly.

'Then I just felt my hair being pulled and I heard . . . All I heard

11

was cutting. He was cutting my hair off. It seemed to go on for ever and . . . '

Rachel leaned forward. 'Did he say anything?'

'Not till it was over. He must have used the scissors to cut the tape round my wrists then he just told me to get back in the car. To tell you the truth, I was so relieved that he hadn't raped me and that I was still alive, I just did as he said.'

'Did you get the impression the motive was sexual?'

Sienna thought for a few moments. 'I honestly don't know. It might have been but he never tried to . . . ' The sentence trailed off.

'What happened next?'

'He drove fast and before I knew it we were on the outskirts of Neston. When we reached the station he got out and opened the door and I jumped out. Before I had a chance to think about alerting anyone, he sped off.' She gave Wesley a shy smile. 'But I did get the registration number.'

Wesley and Rachel looked at each other. The other victims had taken the number too but when it had been checked out, it had become clear that the attacker used a variety of false number plates along with his selection of false taxi stickers. But the car was the same each time; an old dark-blue saloon, possibly a Ford – common as seagulls on Tradmouth waterfront.

'What did he do with the hair,' Wesley asked suddenly, although he knew the answer already from interviewing the other victims.

Sienna frowned and put her hand to her head, as though trying to conceal her attacker's handiwork. 'It was strange,' she said slowly. 'He had a plastic bag . . . one of those self-sealing ones. He picked it up very carefully and put it in.' There was a long pause while she tried to find the right words to explain. 'It was as if it wasn't an attack on me personally. It was as if there was some purpose to it. Does that make sense?'

Wesley smiled, reluctant to say that it didn't make any sense to him. And, from the puzzled look on Rachel's face, it perplexed her too.

'You've already given a description to the officer who took your statement. Average height, average build, baseball hat, droopy moustache . . . '

She nodded.

'The other victims have given us different descriptions. It could be that he changes his appearance every time. Please think carefully: is there anything else you can remember? His accent, for instance?'

Sienna shook her head. 'He didn't say much but I'm sure he wasn't local. I'd say he sounded northern.'

Wesley leaned forward. 'What sort of northern? Manchester? Liverpool? Yorkshire? Newcastle?'

'I'm not sure. I'm sorry. Just northern.'

'Well, that could be very helpful,' said Wesley with an optimism he didn't feel. 'Do you think you could find the place where he took you again?'

Sienna shook her shorn head vehemently. 'It could have been anywhere around here. All these narrow lanes look exactly the same, don't they?'

'You don't remember passing any houses or crossroads or farms?'

After more negative answers, Wesley and Rachel took their leave with a plea for Sienna to get in touch if she remembered anything more.

'What do you think?' Wesley asked as they climbed into the car.

'I haven't a clue,' Rachel replied.

'That makes two of us.'

Marcus returned his hired boat early that afternoon. The rain had held off, which was lucky, and as he sat on the quiet quayside watching the car ferry scuttle to and fro across the river in the fading light, he wondered whether he should summon the courage to go back there. It was late now and it would soon be dark. But there was no right time for something like this.

He wasn't sure whether it was fear of rejection that was holding him back, or the simple possibility that nobody would believe him in the first place. He had been out of their lives since 1976. How could he just turn up and say, 'Hi, I'm home?' Perhaps he should send a letter. Or make a phone call. But that would be just as bad as turning up in person. However the news was broken, it would come as a shock.

He had to face his return to life some time.

His guesthouse was up one of the steep streets that led away from the river front to the higher part of the town and the uphill walk made him breathless. He decided not to go in – the landlady was the nosey type. Instead he climbed into his battered red car and backed it out of the front drive before heading for the main road out of Tradmouth.

Having studied the maps over and over again, he knew how to get to the house by road. He drove slowly down the narrow, unfamiliar lanes. Last time he had been down them, he had been far too young to drive and he barely recognised the cottages and farm gates that lined the route. The signposts to Derenham told him he was on the right road and as he pulled in to let a tractor squeeze by, he realised he was on the brow of the hill that overlooked the village. Soon he'd be heading down the steep streets past the church and down to the glittering ribbon of the River Trad. Then he'd branch off and head out of the village towards the house. He remembered it best from the river of course – the river had been part of his life all those years ago. But he thought he could find it from the road. He had to find it.

He drove through Derenham's barely remembered streets, taking two wrong turnings. He was reluctant to ask for directions, reluctant to involve strangers in this, the most momentous occasion of his adult life. He found himself wondering whether anybody in Derenham would recognise him. But then time changes everything and everyone.

It took him fifteen minutes to find the house. He recognised the gates at once. And the name. Mirabilis. Over the past few weeks he'd wondered whether they would have changed the name to something more sombre in view of what had happened there. But it seemed they had kept it. Perhaps they'd been waiting for a miracle. The one they were about to experience.

He parked the car by the gate. It seemed right to go the rest of the way on foot. To walk back into their lives as he'd walked out all those years ago.

It was dark now. Country dark without the jaundiced glow of street lighting. Instead the full moon and the pin-point stars cast a silvery pall over the countryside. His eyes adjusted to the dimness as he walked up the drive, his footsteps on the gravel crackling like gunfire in the silence.

The doorbell was new, he could tell. Plastic, not like the old brass bell push that had been there before. He placed his forefinger on it and heard a buzzing noise from somewhere within the house. Then footsteps. There was no turning back now.

The door opened and a man stood there in the hallway, holding onto the latch. There was something familiar about his face and Marcus realised that he was looking at himself, only changed . . . different; younger; better groomed; taller; blue eyes rather than his own green. But the same shape of face; the same mouth. The two men stood, staring at each other for a while, weighing each other up, neither wanting to break the spell.

It was Marcus who spoke first. 'Does Mr Fallbrook still live here?'

The man in the hallway gave a brief nod, his eyes never leaving the newcomer's face. 'I'm Adrian Fallbrook.'

The newcomer looked confused. 'No I meant . . . Mr Fallbrook. Mr Jacob Fallbrook.'

'That's my father. Look, I'm afraid he . . . '

But Marcus wasn't listening. His eyes were shining as the words spilled out. 'You must be . . . ' He hesitated. 'My brother?'

Adrian Fallbrook looked confused. 'What are you talking about. I haven't got a brother.'

'You don't know who I am, do you? I'm Marcus. Marcus Fallbrook.'

Adrian Fallbrook's mouth fell open and he stared at the visitor with disbelief.

'I'm back.' He hesitated, nervous. 'I'm back from the dead. You going to ask me in or what?'

15

Chapter Two

Letter from the Reverend Charles Boden, Rector of Stoke Beeching to Squire John Bentham, 7th May 1815

Sir,

It has come to my attention that the boy, Peter Hackworthy, is displayed around the county at halls and fairs like some common sideshow. I have also heard it said that he performs at inns where the company is not fit for one of such tender years.

I put it to you, sir, that you bear some responsibility for this sorry situation for it was at your urging that Matthew Hackworthy did embark upon this unfortunate path of displaying the boy's rare and God given talents as though he were some performing dog or dancing bear.

I beg you, sir, to spare the boy this indignity and allow him to use the gifts the Lord has given him in some respectable manner. A gentleman of my acquaintance from Oxford would be willing to admit him to his school where he would receive an education appropriate to his undoubted abilities. I took the liberty of mentioning this to Matthew and he would have none of it, but I know you to have much influence with him and I entreat you to do all in your power, for the boy's sake, to put an end to this unfortunate state of affairs.

I am, sir, your servant, Charles Boden

DCI Gerry Heffernan feared he'd be late for work.

He had seen Joyce Barnes the previous night: they had visited the cinema and he had consumed more than his fair share of red wine with his meal because Joyce had to drive home. Joyce had had a lot on her mind and it had all come pouring out as they sat

16

drinking coffee after their meal. Joyce's little problem. The thing that was bringing her to the edge of despair. Gerry had listened – he had never considered himself a good listener but on this occasion he could think of nothing to say so he'd had no choice.

Joyce had two options. To struggle on caring for her mother, holding down her full time job at Morbay Register Office and making herself ill or to do as her doctor suggested and find a place where her mother could be looked after by professionals. But it had to be Joyce's decision. Gerry couldn't make her mind up for her, much as he'd have liked to.

Because of his late and rather emotional night, he had overslept that morning. And, after throwing on yesterday's clothes, he'd arrived at the police station hot and bothered even though the September weather had cooled down considerably in the past twelve hours, prompting fears that the Indian summer was at an end.

As he entered the CID office to a chorus of mumbled greetings he looked at his watch. Only fifteen minutes behind schedule and nothing too urgent to command his attention. Only the spate of strange abductions by someone impersonating a taxi driver who seemed to fancy himself as the next Vidal Sassoon. No doubt when they caught up with the joker in question, he'd have some explanation for his bizarre activities. But in the meantime Gerry's chief fear was that the attacks would escalate – that next time it wouldn't only be the woman's hair that got cut.

Before gathering the troops for their morning briefing, he wanted to catch up on the latest news and gossip – official and unofficial. So he made straight for Wesley's desk.

Wesley, who'd been engrossed in his paperwork, looked up, eager for a distraction – any distraction. 'Morning Gerry. Late night last night?'

Gerry Heffernan felt himself blushing. 'Me and Joyce went to the flicks then out for a meal. We got talking and . . . I had to creep in so Rosie wouldn't hear me.'

The DCI's daughter, Rosie, had returned home after finishing her degree course at the Royal Northern College of Music in Manchester. Having made no attempt to secure any sort of permanent job, she had settled to a summer of seasonal bar work combined with a regular slot playing piano in an exclusive Tradmouth restaurant. Although Heffernan was glad of his daughter's

17

company, he hadn't yet told her about his dates with Joyce. It was his guilty secret, his little rebellion against the tyranny of the young.

Wesley sat back in his chair. 'Why don't you just tell her? She won't mind her dad having a bit of companionship, surely.'

'She was very close to her mum. Our Sam reckons she'd think me seeing any other woman was betraying Kathy's memory.'

Wesley said nothing. In his opinion Rosie Heffernan was being selfish but he knew that sometimes it's best to keep your opinion to yourself.

'So what happened yesterday? I was trapped with the Assistant Chief Constable and the Nutter discussing long term community policing strategy and the role of policing amongst minorities in the twenty-first century – at least I think that's what they were discussing. Don't ask me what was said 'cause all I can remember is that all that hot air gave me a splitting headache.'

Wesley assumed a sympathetic expression. Gerry Heffernan, like himself, held the deeply unfashionable opinion that the police were there to protect the innocent and apprehend the guilty. Pam had often hinted at the possibility of Wesley pursuing promotion but if it meant enduring a lifetime of time-wasting meetings when he could be using his energies more usefully, he'd rather stay where he was.

'You know our bogus taxi driver's been at it again?'

'Yeah. The report's on my desk but I haven't had a chance to read it properly yet. The papers are calling him the Barber. They love it, don't they? Putting the fear of God into every woman in the area.'

Wesley decided to give him a brief résumé before the report went the way of most things that ended up on the DCI's desk, buried under a layer of debris that needed someone with Wesley's archaeological skills to disentangle. 'Rachel and I saw the latest victim yesterday afternoon. Her name's Sienna Calder and she lives in Stokeworthy. She works in London three days a week and she called a taxi as usual yesterday morning to take her to Neston to catch the London train. You can guess the rest, can't you?'

'Taxi turns up. Everything seems kosher until he starts taking a strange route. He drives to an isolated spot, drags her from the back of the car and cuts all her hair off. Then he takes her to where she wants to go.'

'She took the registration number.'

'False?'

'Belongs to a minibus up in Yorkshire that's used by a local Scout troop. We've been in touch with the registered owner and he's as puzzled as we are. And the description's not much use – seems to be different every time. I reckon he changes his appearance.'

Heffernan snorted. 'A Master of Disguise! Didn't they go out with Sherlock Holmes? And he must know about listening in to taxi radio frequencies . . . And he's able to either get hold of their logos . . .'

'Or forge them?'

'Whatever he does, he's well organised. Why's he doing it, Wes? What's the point?'

Wesley shrugged his shoulders. 'Your guess is as good as mine. Perhaps it's a power thing.'

'Like rape you mean?' Gerry Heffernan shuddered. 'We'll have to get him before he starts going further. Soon giving them a bad hair day won't be enough for him. That's when he'll become a serious danger. Anything from Forensics?'

'Still waiting. But if it's anything like the first, it won't be much use. He leaves no DNA and takes the parcel tape he uses to tie them up away with him so there's no chance of getting finger-prints.'

'Pity. Surely he must have been caught for something before . . . even if it's only pinching knickers off washing lines.'

'Sienna Calder said he didn't say much but she thought he had some sort of northern accent.'

Heffernan's eyes lit up. 'Maybe there is a link with the Yorkshire minibus after all. Maybe it's someone who used to own it before the Scouts bought it second-hand and he's still using the number. Get it checked out, will you?'

Wesley nodded, putting it on his long mental lists of things to be done.

'These women . . . they all had long hair?'

'Not when we saw them, they didn't,' said Wesley and immediately regretted his flippancy. 'Yes, I think they did.'

'And they were all blondes?'

'You think he has a thing about long blond hair?'

'If he has, we could use our Rach as bait. The tethered goat idea.'

Wesley was about to open his mouth to object but thought better of it. The thought of Rachel Tracey in danger made him uncomfortable. But he knew that she was more than capable of taking care of herself.

His musings were interrupted by a knock at the door. Gerry Heffernan shouted 'Come in' and the door opened to reveal a puzzled Trish Walton standing on the threshold.

'Sir. There's a man at the front desk wants to see you. He says it's important. It's about a kidnapping.'

Heffernan looked at Wesley and they both stood up. Maybe this was the lead on the Barber they needed at last.

'What did he say exactly?' Wesley asked.

Trish frowned, trying to remember the exact details. 'He said his half brother was kidnapped back in the nineteen seventies and they all thought he was dead. But he turned up last night, alive and well.'

Trish's story grabbed Wesley's interest. 'Kidnapped?'

'That's what he said. His name's Adrian Fallbrook. Why don't you have a word with him?'

Wesley didn't need asking twice, even if Gerry Heffernan seemed reluctant to add to his work load. Ten minutes later they were both sitting in Interview Room One, face to face with a tall man, probably in his thirties, wearing a pristine white T-shirt and jeans with neatly ironed creases. He wasn't fat but he had a well fed, prosperous look about him. His clothes looked as though they'd just come out of the packet and his wavy fair hair was longish but well cut. Wesley ordered tea. The man looked as if he needed it.

'I believe you want to talk to us about a visit you received from a man claiming to be your brother?' Wesley began. Heffernan was sitting beside him, listening intently. But he knew it would be up to him to do most of the talking.

'I didn't really know what to do but . . . '

Wesley gave Adrian Fallbrook an encouraging smile. 'Why don't you start at the beginning? Tell us what happened to your brother.'

'My half-brother,' the man said quickly. 'Marcus was my half-brother. My father had been married before, you see, but his first wife – Marcus's mother – died. My mother was a nurse and she looked after her through her illness . . . cancer. That's how my parents met. They married eighteen months after his first wife's death.'

'Does your father know Marcus has turned up?'

'My father died last month. A stroke.'

'I see,' said Wesley. Something, some vague memory, stirred in the back of his mind. Some mention in a newspaper perhaps, of the death of a wealthy retired businessman whose son had been kidnapped many years ago. It had only half registered and now he wished he'd taken more notice. 'Presumably your mother knew Marcus?'

'No. He'd . . . .he was abducted a year before my father's first wife fell ill. I've heard it said that the stress of the kidnapping brought on her illness. They say it can, don't they? Besides, my own mother died last year. She went into hospital for a routine operation and caught an infection. There was nothing they could do.'

Wesley could detect a tremor in the man's voice. 'I'm sorry,' he said automatically.

'Aye, terrible that,' Gerry Heffernan chipped in. It was the first time he'd spoken and Adrian Fallbrook looked up and gave him the ghost of a smile, acknowledging his attempt at sympathy.

'You said your half-brother was kidnapped?'

'Yes . . . in 1976. Of course it was long before I was born and nobody talked about it when I was young. But when I was about eleven, my father . . . I knew he'd been married before and . . . Well, I didn't know anything about my half-brother. I didn't even know I had one until . . . ' He took a deep breath. 'One day my father took me out on the river; on his boat – he had a yacht, you see. It must have been May or June. It was sunny and there was a breeze. Perfect sailing weather.'

Gerry Heffernan nodded. As a sailor himself he appreciated the niceties.

Adrian continued. 'When he took her out to sea he hardly said a word for a while. Then he said he had something to tell me . . . something important. He'd had another little boy a long time ago and he'd disappeared one day. He'd been taken off by wicked people and he'd never come home. I could tell he found it painful to talk about it but he said he wanted to tell me before I heard about it from someone else.' He paused, swallowing hard. 'I must admit, I didn't really understand the enormity of it then. I mean, you

21

don't at eleven, do you? I remember asking why the police hadn't caught the wicked people.' He gave another sad smile. 'The young have a very naive concept of justice, don't they?'

'Simple maybe, but not altogether naive,' said Wesley with a frown. 'How did you feel about your father's revelation?'

'Feel?' He inclined his head to one side. 'I don't know. It was hard to take in at first, I suppose. Then gradually things began to make sense. It explained so much. Why my father was over-protective. And why people – grown-ups – whispered behind my back as though they had some secret that I wasn't allowed to hear. I'd been sent away to school at seven. I suppose it was thought that if I'd gone to a local school I might have found out. Parents gossip and their kids overhear and put two and two together, don't they?'

'You can't keep much from kids,' said Heffernan. 'So this missing half-brother's turned up on your doorstep?'

'Last night.'

'Where is he now?'

'I don't know where he is at this very moment but I presume he went back to Tradmouth last night.' He hesitated. 'If he is . . . if he is who he says he is, there's quite a bit of money involved. My father, understandably, was reluctant to make the final acknow-ledgement that Marcus was dead so his will stipulated that if he was ever to turn up, he would have a half share of the family property. Nobody thought he actually would, of course.'

'Did he know your father was dead?'

'He said he didn't. But there were obituaries in some national newspapers. My father was a very successful businessman,' he added with a hint of pride.

'You suspect this man who's claiming to be Marcus could be an impostor?' Wesley asked. The mention of money had sud-denly added another dimension to the story . . . and not an attrac-tive one.

'When he was with me – when I was talking to him – I believed him. He seemed to remember things that nobody outside the fam-ily could know. And he recognised things in the house. He asked if we still had the pianola – said it had fascinated him as a boy, watching the piano keys move by themselves as if a ghost was playing. How could he have known about that if he wasn't who he said he was? And he asked about Dad's yacht, the *Anna's Pride* –

she was named after Dad's first wife . . . his mother. I told him Dad had sold it shortly before his death. He said he remembered Dad taking him out on it.'

'You didn't ask him to stay with you last night?'

Adrian shook his head. 'No. He said it must have come as a shock to me and that it was best if he gave me some space. And of course I had Carol, my wife, to think of. It's hardly fair on her if a stranger turns up out of the blue like that. He's staying at a guest-house in Tradmouth. He gave me his mobile number and told me to get in touch when I'm ready.' He looked Wesley in the eye. 'He must be genuine, mustn't he?'

Gerry Heffernan leaned forward. 'There's just one problem with your long-lost brother, Mr Fallbrook. Where's he been since 1976? I presume you asked him.'

'Yes. Of course I did.'

'And what was the answer?'

'He said he doesn't remember much about the abduction. It's all a haze. He vaguely remembers being with some sort of commune then he thinks he was taken away from them . . . '

'Officially? By social services?'

'I don't know. It was all very vague.'

Heffernan and Wesley looked at each other. For an impostor vagueness was good . . . the vaguer the better.

'He told me he had an accident fairly recently – he was knocked down by a car and he had concussion for a while. That's when it started to come back to him. He started to remember Devon. Tradmouth. And the name Marcus Fallbrook. He came down here to try and put the pieces together. And he said that when he came to Tradmouth and took a boat on the river everything started to flood back. Just the bit before his abduction . . . what happened afterwards is still a blur at the moment.'

'How old was he when he was abducted?'

Adrian frowned. 'About seven, I think.'

'And is he calling himself Fallbrook?'

'No, Jones. Mark Jones. My half-brother's name was Marcus but it seems that he became known as Mark.'

'You're convinced he's who he says he is, aren't you?' said Wesley gently.

Gerry Heffernan sniffed. It all sounded suspicious to him. But then so did a lot of things. His years in the police force had destroyed much of his faith in human nature. 'So why has he waited so long before trying to find his family?'

Adrian looked a little confused. 'As I said, he didn't remember. People block out traumatic events, don't they? I suppose it took the accident to bring it all back. We didn't talk for that long. I'm supposed to be getting in touch with him again and . . . '

'And you thought you'd just put us in the picture?' Heffernan said, watching the man's face.

Adrian Fallbrook nodded. 'To be honest I didn't really know what to do. But as it's connected with a crime – albeit an old one – I thought I'd better have a word with someone. He'll be a witness to an unsolved crime, won't he? Or . . . '

'Or if he's an impostor, he's committing one.' In Gerry Heffernan's opinion the man sitting there in front of him didn't know what he believed.

It was Wesley who spoke, the voice of reason. 'Perhaps we'd better have a chat with this Mark Jones. If he was the victim of a kidnapping we'll need to talk to him anyway. Kidnapping's a serious offence. And if he won't talk to us . . . '

'Then he's probably an impostor.' Adrian finished the sentence for him. 'But how did he know about the house? The pianola? How did he . . . ?'

'There could be any number of explanations. Maybe he had a relative who worked for the family or . . . '

Adrian nodded. 'Yes. We always had cleaners, nannies, gardeners and what have you. I suppose . . . '

'Just tell him we want a word. That should settle the matter once and for all,' said Heffernan confidently. In his experience most villains never spoke to the police voluntarily.

Adrian Fallbrook looked as though a weight had been taken from his shoulders. 'Yes. I'll do that. Thank you.'

'And of course there's one way to find out if he's who he claims to be. Is he willing to take a DNA test?'

Adrian considered the question for a moment. 'I'll ask him,' he said before turning to go.

'Nice to have a satisfied customer for a change,' Heffernan whispered as Fallbrook disappeared down the corridor.

Moving the dead is a delicate matter. And Neil Watson didn't like it. He didn't like the sight of the soil-covered coffins emerging from the ground. And he was in constant fear that the wood, having been under the damp Devon earth for so long, would disintegrate before his eyes, revealing the corpse within. The previous night he had dreamed that when a coffin was lifted, it fell away and a stinking cadaver had tumbled to the ground on top of him, suffocating him with its terrible embrace. He had awoken sweating with panic, wrestling with his duvet, relieved that the nightmare wasn't real.

He was used to excavating burials but somehow this was different. He knew their names. They were loved ones whose nearest and dearest had recorded details of their lives on the lichen-covered headstones. And worst of all there were the babies and children; death had claimed the very young in those days as regularly as it now claims the very old.

Once the coffins were out of the ground they were reburied, with John Ventnor's solemn prayers, in the place at the edge of the churchyard which had been prepared for them. Neil found himself hoping that the Rector was getting paid for all the extra work . . . but he doubted it.

As soon as Ventnor had done his bit, the ground was Neil's, to investigate as he wished. According to old records there had been an earlier church on the site. But he would have to wait until all the eighteenth- and nineteenth-century burials were moved before he could dig deeper. He knew there might be medieval bones down there still, but somehow they didn't bother him as much.

He watched as a fragile coffin emerged from the ground. The contractors' faces were masks of neutrality, as though they were trying to demonstrate their indifference in the face of death. Neil looked over to the lych gate where his archaeological colleagues were in a huddle, chatting amongst themselves, awaiting his signal to start work.

Suddenly Neil heard a voice at his shoulder which made him jump. 'I've found out what it is, by the way.'

His heart was pounding. He hadn't realised the place was getting to him so much. He swung round and saw John Ventnor standing just beside him, smiling.

'I found an old book on local history in the vestry. Apparently the symbol on the headstones was used by a strange sect who called themselves the Shining Ones.'

Neil took a deep, calming breath. 'So the people buried here were members?'

'It's a possibility. Why else would they go to the trouble of putting the symbol on their memorials.'

'But would members of some sect be buried in the parish church?'

The Rector shrugged. 'Who knows?'

At that moment the coffin, held just above the ground by straps prior to being placed onto something more substantial, began to break up. First one side fell away, and the bottom began to creak and crumble, revealing the bones within, still festooned with fragments of rotting cloth.

Neil stared, horrified, as the bones fell away one by one and tumbled back into the grave.

The Trad View Guesthouse was situated some way away from the river, up one of the steep, narrow streets that wound away from the town centre towards the outer suburbs. It wasn't one of Tradmouth's most sumptuous guesthouses. But although it was short on luxurious trimmings, it was clean, well run and reasonably priced. Wesley walked through the neat front garden and when he rang the doorbell he was greeted by a plump woman with a fixed smile on her face. But her eyebrows shot upwards in alarm when he showed her his ID and when he said he was looking for one of her guests, she began to assure him emphatically that she kept a respectable establishment. The police had never come calling before in all the time she'd been in business.

Wesley was quick to reassure her that her guest, Mr Jones, had, as far as he knew, committed no crime. All he wanted was an amicable chat. This seemed to put the landlady's mind at rest and she became eager to co-operate, telling Wesley that Mr Jones had gone out. He had told her at breakfast that morning that he wasn't sure what he'd be doing that day but, as he'd taken his car, she suspected he'd gone off sightseeing. Some people were like that on holiday, she said. They didn't like to be tied to definite plans like they were in their everyday life.

Wesley nodded in agreement at her psychological assessment of the average holiday-maker and asked her to call him when Mr Jones returned.

He decided to return to the police station. It was high time he found out about the kidnapping of Marcus Fallbrook. Presumably it would have been dealt with by the Tradmouth CID officers of the day. There would be records somewhere. And it would be best to speak to Mark Jones with the facts clear in his mind.

He found Gerry Heffernan at his desk, looking through the statements made by the Barber's victims. Looking for something, anything, that would betray the man's identity before he did more than just hack his victims' hair off. Wesley knew Gerry well and he could sense his fear, his dreadful foreboding that next time somebody might get seriously hurt.

'Anything new?' Wesley asked as he entered the chief inspector's office and sat himself down.

Gerry Heffernan let out a large sigh, like a balloon slowly deflating. 'Nothing. I've had people checking out all the leads and every patrol in the area's been looking out for dark-blue saloons.' He rolled his eyes to heaven. 'Do you know how many dark-blue saloons there are in South Devon?'

'I can imagine.' Wesley was anxious to change the subject. 'Look, Gerry, what do you know about the Marcus Fallbrook kidnapping?'

Heffernan shook his head. 'Before my time, I'm afraid, Wes. I joined the force about eighteen months later.' He blushed. 'While all that was going on I was at sea.' He smiled at the memory. 'Happy days. In fact it must have been around that time I had appendicitis and had to be winched off and taken to Tradmouth Hospital.' Another smile. 'Every cloud has a silver lining, eh.'

Wesley smiled dutifully. He had heard the story of how Gerry had abandoned the sea for the nurse he later married many times before. Kathy had died several years ago but Gerry still thought of her . . . often.

Heffernan continued. 'When I joined the force I remember people mentioning a little lad who'd been kidnapped and never found. But, as I said, it was before my time so I don't know the details.' He thought for a moment. 'There'll be the case files of course. But if I were you, I'd have a word with Barry Houldsworth. He used to have my job in those days and he'd have been in charge of the case. DCI Houldsworth – bit of a legend, he was.'

Wesley leaned forward, curious. 'Why's that?'

Heffernan grinned. 'You'll see. Did you see this man who's claiming to be Marcus Fallbrook?'

'I went to the guesthouse but he was out for the day. The landlady promised to ask him to get in touch when he gets back.'

27

'And if he's genuine he will and if he's not . . . '

'We won't see him for dust.'

'Just a matter of waiting, then.'

'And finding out everything I can about the case in the meantime. Where can I find this ex-DCI Houldsworth?'

'Try the Bentham Arms in Stoke Beeching.'

Wesley didn't reply. He didn't fancy hanging around a country pub on his own, enduring the stares of curious locals just on the off chance someone might be there. 'Where does he live?'

'I told you, try the Bentham Arms. I heard his wife left him a few years ago. Said she couldn't compete.'

'With the job?'

'That and the nation's breweries and distilleries.'

Wesley thought for a few moments. 'If this Marcus Fallbrook business is a hoax, it's a cruel one. What if the mother had still been alive?'

'But she isn't, is she? And the dad died recently. Maybe he knows that. Maybe he's done his homework.'

Wesley stood up. 'It's about time I did mine.'

'Take care,' said Heffernan as Wesley left the room, his words heavy with meaning.

Wesley turned to look at him, puzzled and saw that he was smiling.

The newspapers were calling him 'the Barber'. He didn't like that. They didn't understand. They didn't realise that it was necessary.

He stared at the computer screen. He had hoped there would be something new . . . more instructions. But there had been nothing today so he left the homepage with its image of a yellow beach beneath an unnaturally blue sky and walked over to the window.

He looked out at the row of shabby Georgian houses opposite, their stucco façades flaking with age and the salt breeze from the sea. They would have been there when she walked the earth for the first time. She might have seen them: she might even have stood there on that very street. She had attracted crowds in Morbay back then.

A woman with long fair hair was walking down the street, displaying too much midriff and a lot of leg. He licked his lips. The hair didn't look natural but she would do. If circumstances presented her to him.

28

As soon as she disappeared from sight, he shuffled over to the table which stood next to the computer desk. He had laid out his trophies carefully, having tied the ends with white ribbon neatly – with love – and the hair lay in skeins like newly spun flax. He picked each one up carefully and put them back in their special box. Velvet lined. The best.

He would go to the lock up garage later and take the car out. Tonight he might get lucky again.

Pam Peterson put the local newspaper down on the coffee table. With this Barber about, for the first time in her life she was glad she wasn't blond.

She thought of her husband's colleague, Rachel Tracey – the woman who saw far more of him than she did – and couldn't resist a wicked smile. Rachel was just the Barber's type, she thought before telling herself that jealousy wasn't an attractive quality. And since her ill-advised little fling in the early summer, she had let the moral high ground slip from her grasp.

She remembered it now with a shudder of bitter embarrassment. Flirting with Wesley's future brother-in-law's old schoolfriend, Jonathan, who'd come up for the wedding, had seemed like a great idea at the time – a respite from work, motherhood and a husband whose job seemed more important to him than she did. A bit of harmless fun that lifted her spirits and made her feel attractive again. And what woman doesn't want to feel desirable? But things had gone too far; had slipped from her control like a kite in a hurricane.

Then Neil Watson had caught them together and in that heart-shrinking moment of guilt and regret she had suddenly seen things clearly. Jonathan was shallow and maybe a touch amoral. A purely temporary temptation. She realised then what she could lose and from that time on she'd tried her best to make amends. To be patient and understanding. And not to complain about the hours Wesley spent at work. But it wasn't always easy.

As soon as she heard Wesley's key in the door, she rushed into the hall to greet him, making an effort. He stepped into the house, bending to kiss her. 'How are things? School OK?'

'As well as can be expected with an inspection in a couple of weeks. And my class isn't the easiest I've had. I've got four kids with special needs. And some of my year six girls are right little madams – doing those Leah Wakefield dance routines in the playground. If they put as much effort into their work as . . . '

'Leah Wakefield?' Wesley made a point of not keeping abreast of popular culture.

'She's that tarty teenage singer who writhes about showing all she's got – hardly a suitable role model for eleven-year-olds.'

Wesley gave her what he considered to be a sympathetic smile, hoping that fashions would change by the time Amelia reached that age. 'Kids OK?'

'They'll be glad you're back before their bed time for a change,' she said, then immediately regretted her sharpness.

'I'll make the supper if you like,' said Wesley with just a hint of martyrdom.

'Already done. It'll be ready in five minutes.'

Wesley kissed his wife again before making for the living room to entertain his children who greeted him enthusiastically – almost as though he'd been away for months.

It wasn't until the supper had been eaten and the children tucked up in bed that Wesley made his dreadful confession with the wary guilt of a man confessing to an affair. He would have to go the Bentham Arms for an hour or so to talk to a retired DCI about the Fallbrook kidnapping case but he'd be back as soon as he could. By the time he'd finished his speech, he was aware that he was grovelling like some Victorian servant. But he felt a little grovelling was just what was called for.

He found himself promising that he would find ex-DCI Houldsworth, arrange a meeting at a more congenial time and come straight home. It would only take half an hour. No problem.

'You're not bloody drinking again. Give that to me.' Leah Wakefield's mother snatched the bottle of champagne from her daughter's hands and marched off into the kitchen as the bubble-filled girl sprawled on the white leather sofa emitted a loud burp.

Suzy Wakefield, being naturally thrifty due to an upbringing in which money was in short supply and luxuries like champagne as rare as snow in the Sahara, put a stopper in the champagne bottle and stood it up carefully in the door of the massive American style fridge.

As the fridge door closed with a discreet whisper of rubber meeting rubber, Suzy heard footsteps behind her on the slate floor. She swung round and saw Leah standing there, swaying slightly and reaching for the nearest granite worktop to steady herself.

'Give me that bottle, you old cow.' Leah's words were slurred. 'You've no right . . . '

'I've every right. It's not good for you all this drinking.' She had a sudden flash of inspiration. 'It's not good for your voice . . . your career . . . '

'Fuck my career. I want a fucking drink. You're treating me like some fucking kid. I've got a platinum fucking disc.'

Suzy took a step back as the girl came towards her. 'And if you carry on like this you'll end up in the gutter.'

Leah stopped in her tracks and a malicious smile spread across her painted lips. 'Well, you'd know all about the gutter. That's where you belong, you old slag. That's why Dad left you.'

It was an automatic reaction. Suzy raised her right hand and slapped her daughter across the face, the sound echoing like a gunshot off the tiled walls.

Leah held her cheek, half bent in theatrical agony, her eyes ablaze with spite. 'You'll regret that, you jealous old bitch. If you think you're getting one more penny of my money . . . And you can get out of this house. My house. It was bought with my money. The money I earned.'

Suzy squared up to her, more confident now. 'Until you're twenty-one everything needs my signature . . . and your Dad's. You can't do anything without my say so.'

She looked the girl in the eye. Her daughter. The little girl she'd taken to singing and dancing lessons in spite of her husband, Darren – now her ex-husband – telling her it was a waste of their hard-earned money. The little girl she'd pushed and encouraged. The little girl on whose behalf she'd even slept with men of influence to make the right connections in the business. The little girl for whom she'd sacrificed her dignity and her marriage so that she could reach the top.

Her combination of fierce maternal love and overarching ambition had been a potent one. But now it had turned sour. She had created a monster. One look at Leah's sneering face, at her glazed, drunken eyes, told her that. She felt warm tears trickle down her cheeks.

'I'm calling Brad.'

31

Leah laughed. 'My wonderful bloody manager. Good in bed, is he?'

Suzy ignored the last question. 'He should know what you're doing to yourself . . . How you're throwing away everything we've worked for . . . '

Leah stared at her mother and drew herself up to her full height. Suddenly she seemed to have sobered up. 'Everything you've worked for, you mean.' She turned unsteadily on her stiletto heels. 'I'm out of here. I can't stand this any more.'

'Where are you going?' Suzy asked, trying hard to keep the nascent hysteria she was feeling out of her voice. She had to stay calm. It was the only way to deal with the situation. 'You've got to understand, Leah. I'm only thinking of you.'

The generous lips that had smiled out from the covers of Leah Wakefield's four best-selling albums, formed a snarl as she turned back to face her mother. 'I'm going.' She tossed her mane of blond hair. 'I'll be in touch when I'm ready.'

'But there's that magazine interview coming up. You'll have to . . . '

'I haven't got to do anything. Tell them I'm not well.' She span round. 'Tell them I'm dead.'

She marched out of the kitchen without looking back.

The man driving the dark-blue minicab pulled his woolly hat down so that his bearded face was in shadow. The registration number had been changed again. That was good. And he had the peel-off logos in the glove box ready. He was prepared and there was no way anybody would be able to track him down. No way anybody could halt his mission.

He listened to the radio, crackling on the dashboard. He knew their voices by now, the men and women in the control rooms: he had started to think of them almost as friends as he listened to their banter and their feeble jokes.

He slouched back in his seat. Some nights he had no luck and it looked as if this would be one of them. Then suddenly everything changed. A name. Female. Could Eddie pick her up and she wanted to go into Morbay.

The man's heart started to pound as he started the engine. He had the equipment in the glove box. Everything was ready . . . if she was what he was looking for.

*　　*　　*

32

Leah Wakefield knew that she was in no fit state to drive. Although a drink-driving charge on top of everything else hardly seemed an alarming prospect at that moment. If that happened she'd get someone to drive for her. A chauffeur, she thought, as she tottered down the drive on her precarious heels. A good-looking one – dark with rippling muscles.

She started to laugh and, as the huge electronic gates came into view, she stopped and took a deep breath. She'd been meant to drive to the meeting place – that had been the arrangement – but she didn't think she was capable of putting the key in the ignition, never mind negotiating the narrow Devon lanes. Maybe she'd go back now. She'd made her point to the old bitch, fired warning shots across her bow.

But, after a moment's hesitation, she continued walking. An arrangement was an arrangement and publicity was oxygen to keep the flames of her fame alive and crackling. It wasn't far to the main road. She'd walk it. Pick up a taxi. It'd clear her head.

She looked up at the stars and laughed out loud, the sound breaking the still silence of velvet night, before walking very slowly, towards the road.

Lost in her own thoughts, she was unaware of someone behind her, approaching silently across the neatly trimmed lawn.

When the strong hand locked over her mouth, she collapsed against the warm body of her assailant, unable to scream. Helpless.

Chapter Three

Letter from Squire Bentham to the Reverend Charles Boden, 14th May 1815

I do assure you, sir, that the boy, Peter Hackworthy, has come to no harm on his travels. Rather the lad enjoys the adulation he receives for his performances. I myself have witnessed the generosity of the crowd as they shower him with gifts of money. You will be aware, sir, that the Hackworthy family is large – I myself have taken two of them into my service – and I am not inclined to deprive his father, who was before these remarkable events but a poor working man, of this welcome remuneration.

Were this gentleman of your acquaintance to take the lad and make a scholar of him, I fear for the future wellbeing of the Hackworthys. The door of the poorhouse always stands ready to receive poor families of such fecundity who, by the vagaries of life and through no fault of their own, fall upon misfortune. Yet, through young Peter's gifts, the Hackworthys now enjoy some welcome shelter against the storms of this precarious existence. I trust you would not, sir, expose them to a reduction of their rising fortunes. Unless you, sir, are willing to compensate them from your own pocket for the grievous loss of income that would result from such a course of action.

I remain, sir, your servant. John Bentham

Adrian Fallbrook's heart lurched as the rough jangling of the doorbell shattered the silence of the drawing room. He looked up from the newspaper and caught his wife, Carol's, eye. It could be him.

Carol stood up. 'I'll go?'

Adrian put the paper down untidily beside him, his emotions swinging between anticipation and dread like the pendulum on the oak grandfather clock in the corner.

'No. I'd better . . . '

As he stood up, Carol put a hand on his sleeve. 'If it's him be careful what you say. We don't know anything about him. He could be . . . '

'My brother?' Adrian brushed her hand away and marched into the hall.

'Will you tell him you've been to the police?'

Adrian stopped in his tracks. 'Why not? If he's got nothing to hide, he won't mind.'

As soon as her husband left the room Carol began to bite her nails. This was a habit she'd managed to break a few years before but this new turn of events had made her tense. Not many families had to deal with a long-dead relative – a relative they had never even known – being resurrected, returning to life from some unknown underworld.

She wondered what he wanted of them. Money was the obvious answer of course. But she had a uncomfortable feeling of dread in the pit of her stomach, a premonition perhaps that his return might herald some unspecified disaster.

She could hear the sound of voices in the hall and she froze, trying to make out the words. But they were speaking too quietly; almost, it seemed, in a whisper. She had a sudden sense of conspiracy but she told herself that this was ridiculous. Adrian was just as confused as she was.

A few moments later the two men appeared in the doorway, Adrian leading the way into the drawing room and inviting the stranger who was claiming to be his long-lost half-brother to sit. Marcus sat down on the edge of the faded chintz sofa, as though preparing for a quick getaway if things didn't go according to plan. Carol watched his face carefully but saw nothing there but nervous shyness, which, she supposed, was only to be expected in the circumstances.

'Have you told, er . . . Marcus that you've been to the police?' was Carol's first question. The name Marcus almost stuck in her throat but she didn't know what else to call him.

Adrian nodded.

'Yeah. It was the right thing to do. They had to be told,' said

Marcus quietly, his eyes focused on the carpet. Carol watched him but found it impossible to guess at his true feelings about the involvement of the authorities.

'They'll want to speak to you,' she said.

'Yeah. But I can't tell 'em much. I don't remember nothing about . . . '

'But you remember this house.' Carol stood up. She was a tall woman, thin with a mane of unruly black hair. As she had never been a beauty, she had channelled her considerable energies into being capable, ending up as head girl of her private school. Later she had worked as PA to a millionaire businessman but then she abandoned the world of business for rural domesticity. However, she still organised the local PCC and an assortment of charity events with the same ruthless efficiency with which she'd run her employer's life.

'It's like a sort of fog. Sometimes it clears and I remember things. But sometimes . . . '

Carol pressed her lips together. The snob in her wincing at the man's Manchester accent. She said nothing for a few moments in the hope that the silence would unnerve him.

'So I presume,' she began after half a minute, 'that in time you'll remember what happened when you were . . . abducted.'

Marcus looked wary. 'I hope so.' He looked around. 'I remember this room. French windows . . . and the tree house. Is it still there, the tree house?'

Carol looked him straight in the eye. 'Adrian says his parents always employed help in the house. What's to say that you haven't learned all the things you know about this house and family from someone who worked here?'

But Adrian was seized by a sudden impulse to defend the man who was looking so crestfallen, so confused, like someone who'd been invited to a party to be insulted for the amusement of his host. 'Don't be ridiculous, darling. Look at Marcus. Can't you see how alike we are? There's no question of it . . . '

But Carol wasn't giving up. 'Marcus, are you willing to take a DNA test . . . just to prove it once and for all?'

The look of relief on the visitor's face was unmistakable. 'I was going to suggest it myself,' he said without a hint of hesitation.

'I've looked it up on the Internet and there are several firms who promise results in a few days if you go for their premium service.'

36

She looked Marcus in the eye. 'Have the police contacted you yet? They told Adrian they would?'

Marcus nodded. 'Someone called round at the guesthouse but I was out. I'll give him a call tomorrow.' He didn't sound as if he was looking forward to the prospect. Perhaps, Carol thought, he had had some unpleasant encounters with the police in the course of his mysterious life.

And as far as she was concerned, that was the six-million-dollar question: what had the man who claimed to be Marcus Fallbrook been doing between the time he'd disappeared from his family's lives at the age of seven and the moment he turned up out of the blue at Mirabilis yesterday?

Carol Fallbrook wouldn't rest until she knew the truth.

Wesley Peterson wasn't used to hanging around pubs on his own and when he approached the bar of the Bentham Arms, he felt rather like a lonely child at a party where he knew nobody and nobody wanted to know him.

Clutching his warrant card in his hand, ready to show it to the bar staff if any awkward questions were asked, he looked around the pub. It seemed a cosy establishment; pleasingly old-fashioned with an array of pewter tankards, horse brasses and hunting prints. A country pub with a large fireplace which, being the back end of summer, was filled with dusty pine cones rather than roaring logs. It was in this home from home that ex-DCI Houldsworth reputedly held court and Wesley scanned the lounge bar for anyone who had the tell-tale look of a jaded ex-copper.

But halfway through his search, he spotted a familiar face. Neil Watson was sitting at a battered oak table in the corner of the bar, surrounded by a group of people who Wesley assumed from their appearance were Neil's fellow archaeologists. Neil was sipping beer from a pint glass and looked completely relaxed, a man in his natural habitat.

After a few seconds Neil looked up and spotted him, a smile spreading across his face. 'Hi, Wes. Come and join us.' As Wesley approached, Neil spoke to his colleagues who had all assumed vaguely welcoming expressions. 'You know, Wes Peterson, don't you? He did archaeology with me at Exeter. He's a copper now but don't hold that against him.' The group made noises of acknowledgment and shifted up to make room for the newcomer.

Wesley hesitated. He was there to talk to ex-DCI Houldsworth, not to spend an evening socialising with old university friends. And besides, he had told Pam he wouldn't be long. But temptation was often difficult to resist. He asked if anyone wanted a drink before going to the bar. He'd only have the one, he told himself firmly. Just to be sociable.

While he was at the bar he leaned forward and asked the motherly barmaid whether Mr Houldsworth was in that evening. He spoke in a low voice, not wishing to be overheard. The barmaid looked him up and down suspiciously as though she was wondering what this strange black man wanted with one of her regulars. But when Wesley showed her his warrant card and explained that he wanted to pick his brains about an old case, her expression softened and she pointed out a large man sitting in solitary splendour in the far corner, armed with a pint and a whisky chaser and puffing away heroically on a cigarette. Wesley thanked the barmaid politely and returned to Neil with the drinks. Houldsworth didn't look as if he intended to move from his post until closing time.

'How's the dig going?' he asked Neil, opening the conversation.

'Gruesome,' was Neil's one-word verdict.

Wesley raised his eyebrows.

'The earth's damp and half the coffins are rotten,' said one of his female colleagues, a rosy-cheeked girl fresh out of university. 'When they lift them they keep breaking with a horrid sound of splintering wood. Then the bones fall out,' she added with inappropriate relish.

Wesley nodded sympathetically and turned to Neil. 'You haven't been round for a long time ... not since Maritia's wedding.'

'Is it that long?'

Wesley noticed that Neil was avoiding looking him in the eye. And, as Neil was one of the most straightforward people he knew, this puzzled him. 'Is there something wrong?'

Neil felt his cheeks reddening. He forced himself to smile. 'No, course not, mate. It's just this dig's not as easy as we thought it was going to be, that's all. Look, I'll call round when I've got a moment. Er ... how's Pam?'

'Apart from the fact that term's just started, she's fine.'

'You're sure everything's OK? It's not like you to indulge in solitary drinking in strange pubs.'

'This is business, not pleasure. There's someone I have to see and I've been told I can find him here.' He drank half of his pint and looked round. 'In fact I'd better get on with it. I told Pam I wouldn't be long. See you soon, eh?'

Wesley raised his hand in farewell to the company and carried his drink over to where ex-DCI Houldsworth was sitting. The pub wasn't particularly full but there seemed to be an exclusion zone around Houldsworth, as if he had staked his claim to his own little corner of the pub as people used to own pews in churches and had their own leather armchairs in gentlemen's clubs. He looked up as Wesley approached, his eyes filled with barely disguised hostility.

'That seat's taken,' were his first words. He was looking at Wesley as though he'd crawled out from a sewer.

But Wesley decided to ignore the obvious message. 'Gerry Heffernan told me I'd find you here.' He watched the man's face and saw a flicker of recognition. 'My name's Wesley Peterson. I'm Gerry's DI at Tradmouth.'

Houldsworth smirked. 'I heard something about Gerry being promoted. How's the old bugger doing?'

'He's fine.'

'Sorry to hear about his wife. Tragic that.'

'Yes. Very sad.'

Houldsworth looked Wesley up and down. 'So you're his DI? Bet you stand out like a sore thumb.'

Wesley decided to ignore the racist innuendo. Putting the man straight would hardly make him co-operative. 'Gerry suggested I ask you about one of your cases.'

Houldsworth let out a mighty burp and patted his chest. 'Pardon me.' He held out his empty pint glass. 'I find the memory works better after a pint of best and a Scotch chaser.'

Wesley had no choice but to oblige. And when he returned from the bar with the drinks, Houldsworth looked decidedly more friendly. It's hard to insult the man who buys the drinks.

Wesley decided to come straight to the point. 'I'd like to arrange a convenient time to speak to you about the Marcus Fallbrook case.'

There was a long silence while Houldsworth quaffed his drink with the speed and urgency of a suction pump. It could hardly be good for the man's health, Wesley thought. And the bloodshot eyes and sallow skin suggested a serious drink problem.

'You've kept your notebooks, I take it?'

Houldsworth tapped the side of his nose. 'Nasty case. The nanny had something to do with it . . . never proved it though. Did you see that article in one of the tabloids a couple of months back? Great unsolved crimes of the seventies. Did the police make mistakes and was there a cover up? That sort of thing. Made us look like incompetent idiots it did.' He downed what was left of his beer. The article had clearly got to him.

Wesley glanced at his watch. 'Can we talk about it tomorrow?'

Houldsworth said nothing for a few moments. Then all of a sudden he picked up the small glass of whisky and drained it. 'Better make it lunchtime. In here. OK?'

Wesley would have preferred somewhere away from licensed premises but he nodded. 'What about your notes?'

'I'll dig them out. OK?' the large man snapped.

'Do you live far away?' Wesley asked, unable to contain his curiosity.

'Just up the stairs.' He grinned, showing an uneven set of yellow teeth. 'My sister's the landlady. She split up with her husband a couple of years ago so I give her a hand. It's a convenient arrangement for both of us.'

'Oh,' was all Wesley could think of to say. There was an old joke about every man dreaming about marrying a nymphomaniac who owned a pub, but he supposed a divorced sister who owned one was the next best thing for a man like Houldsworth.

He stood up to go.

'You off already?' Houldsworth almost sounded disappointed.

'I'm afraid so. My wife'll be wondering where I am.'

Houldsworth stared into what was left of his beer. 'Mine always used to wonder that and all. There comes a time when they can't be bothered asking any more.'

Wesley took his leave. The last thing he wanted was for that time to come.

Suzy Wakefield had made the call to the mobile number she had. But she had been told what she didn't want to hear. Leah wasn't where she thought, where she hoped, she might be.

She'd waited an hour before locking the house up. After she'd switched on the alarm she walked as fast as her stiletto heels would allow her to the triple garage fifty yards from the front door, her progress lit by the banks of security lights, bright as theatrical spots, installed by her estranged husband, Darren, when they'd first moved in.

She drove the Mercedes down the steep hill towards the twinkling lights of Neston. She knew where Leah was likely to go: the only pocket of urban sophistication in the town mainly populated by New Age hippies and elderly ladies. She would be propping up the bar of the Castle Top Hotel, the best hotel in town with a Michelin starred restaurant.

The Castle Top was the place where the rich kids hung out – the ones from London whose parents owned second homes in the area. On a few occasions Leah had invited them back and, after one impromptu party, Suzy had had to call in a firm of cleaners. Suzy had never taken to that crowd of rich kids with their arrogant braying and their lack of respect for other people's property but she hoped Leah would be with them now, safe. Although the state she was in, she'd probably be flat on her back being screwed in the back of a Mercedes by now. Suzy suspected that chivalry wasn't their strong point.

But it seemed her journey was wasted. None of the bright young things at the Castle Top had seen Leah that evening and she hadn't booked into that hotel or any other in the vicinity. Suzy wandered through the narrow, winding streets of Neston looking into every pub she passed. But she saw nobody who remotely resembled Leah.

She had to think. Leah must have called a taxi with her mobile – which was now, frustratingly, switched off. Suzy hurried back to the Mercedes and drove back home. That nutcase was about – the one they called the Barber. She had heard about it on the local news. But the possibility that Leah had fallen into his hands was something she didn't like to contemplate.

She had calls to make. Darren. Brad. Any of Leah's ex-boyfriends she could think of. Leah Wakefield had to be somewhere. And she wasn't an easy girl to miss.

At nine thirty the next morning Wesley telephoned the guesthouse and asked to speak to the man who was claiming to be Marcus Fallbrook. He was using the name Mark Jones and Wesley wondered how many other names he'd used in the course of his life. But then he had a suspicious mind. The job had made him that way.

He had ordered the case files and they had arrived on his desk first thing. Glancing through them, he caught the gist of the bare facts. The seven-year-old child disappearing from his exclusive prep school one lunchtime: the nanny, Jenny Booker, driving there in her Mini to bring him home at three thirty and finding he wasn't there.

The school had been criticised for not informing the parents right away that he wasn't in class. They'd said it was a regrettable breakdown in communication – Marcus had been due for a dental appointment that week and the teacher taking the register that afternoon had assumed she'd marked the day down wrongly. And besides, Wesley thought, this was in the days before people saw paedophiles behind every bush – things had been more relaxed back then.

The family had received ransom notes and phone calls from public telephone boxes but nothing had yielded any solid clues. In fact, the file was surprisingly thin. The ransom of fifteen thousand pounds was left in the specified place and it was picked up. But the child was never returned and the pessimistic view at the time was that young Marcus Fallbrook was dead, although a body had never been found.

Reading through the file, Wesley found that, in addition to the bare facts, he wanted to find out about the gossip surrounding the family and the suspicions of the officers working on the case at the time. He knew only too well that not everything finds its way into official statements and reports . . . especially in a sensitive case like the abduction of Marcus Fallbrook.

Mark Jones had offered to meet at ten thirty on neutral ground and Wesley had suggested the waterfront next to the old cannon. He'd been about to quip that he'd be wearing a carnation in his button hole and carrying a copy of *The Times* but he'd thought better of it. This matter was no joke. For the Fallbrooks it was deadly serious.

He looked into Gerry Heffernan's office before he left the police station.

'I'm going to meet this bloke who's claiming to be Marcus Fallbrook. Want to come with me?'

Heffernan looked up and scratched his head. He had the look of a trapped animal. 'Sorry, Wes. Got to go and see the Chief Super – he wants to know how we're getting on with the Barber case. He says we have to reassure the public.'

Wesley rolled his eyes to heaven. 'Reassure them? Surely we should be warning them to be on their guard. Good luck. Fancy coming with me to talk to Houldsworth at lunchtime?' Somehow he didn't relish the prospect of venturing into the Bentham Arms alone again.

Heffernan's eyes lit up. 'Try and stop me. See you later.'

He watched the chief inspector disappearing through the office door. He knew that the boss would much rather be interviewing Mark Jones. And Wesley would have valued his opinion too. He looked around the office and saw that Rachel Tracey was out. She was talking to local taxi firms, trying to trace ex-employees. Everyone would feel relieved once the Barber was caught.

He would have to meet Mark Jones – or Marcus Fallbrook – alone, which was probably for the best. After all, he didn't want to frighten the man off by arriving mob handed. He sat at his desk for a while wondering how to play the situation and eventually he decided that he'd let Jones do all the talking. Awkward questions could wait until he had all the details of the case at his fingertips. And the more people were allowed to talk, the more they gave themselves away.

He left the police station and took a short cut through the Memorial Park. It was almost deserted apart from a couple of council employees sweeping the pathways. The fine drizzle had stopped but a veil of mist hung over the river that rippled, battle-ship grey, in front of him. It was the sort of day the Irish described as 'soft'. As far as Wesley knew, Devonians didn't have a word for it, which was surprising because such days were as common there as sunny ones were in his parents' native Trinidad.

He walked on down the esplanade. Moored yachts bobbed on the river to his left, not as many now as in the height of summer. The town seemed quiet as he carried on past the ferry's landing stage and the harbour master's office.

The streets and waterfront that had been invaded by an army of tourists throughout the summer now belonged once more to the town's inhabitants, to the relief of most except those who made their living by the holiday trade. The local police usually breathed a collective sigh of relief in September. But not this year. Not with the Barber about.

Wesley could see the cannon ahead. It dated from the Crimean War and stood proudly at the end of the esplanade, overlooking

43

the place where the car ferry plied to and fro. In the summer, children swarmed over it but now that part of the esplanade was deserted apart from a solitary figure. A man in early middle age; average height; thin with cropped hair; a pale face and full lips. He wore jeans and a sweatshirt that had seen better days and a pair of scuffed trainers. If this was Adrian Fallbrook's brother, he had slid several rungs down the social ladder.

Wesley slowed his steps, studying the man who was leaning against the cannon, staring at the yachts bobbing at anchor on the high tide. It was him all right. In spite of the differences in height, age and colouring, the resemblance to Adrian Fallbrook was remarkable. The shape of the face, the set of the jaw, the shape of the eyes. Surely no impostor could achieve the subtle family likeness, Wesley thought to himself as he walked forwards, his eyes fixed on his quarry.

'Mark Jones?'

The man swung round, his face wary. Suddenly Wesley's resolution to let the man talk himself out of his inheritance faltered. He wanted to ask questions. He wanted answers.

'Mr Jones, I'm DI Peterson, Tradmouth CID.' He glanced up at the leaden sky. If they stayed there much longer, it would start to rain. 'I know a place that serves a good cup of tea.' He smiled to put the man at his ease and began to lead the way to the Scone and Kettle, a place he judged to be relaxing and unthreatening despite the establishment's reputation as the most haunted café in Tradmouth.

Once they had ordered tea, Wesley studied the man sitting opposite him awkwardly, like a gangling teenager at a family party. He noticed that his green eyes were watchful and wary. But then, if his story was true, that would hardly be surprising.

'I know this isn't easy for you but Adrian Fallbrook had no choice. He had to tell us about your visit. Your – Marcus Fallbrook's – kidnapping was a very serious crime.'

'Yeah. I know' Wesley was surprised that the man had a Manchester accent: somehow he had expected him to be well spoken ... or even to have a faint West-Country twang. 'Look, thanks for meeting me. I didn't know what to do and ...'

'That's OK,' said Wesley. 'Do you feel up to talking about what happened?'

Jones nodded. 'It's all a bit hazy. I had an accident about six months ago. I got knocked down by a car. Hit and run ... just banged my head. No bones broken.'

The words 'how convenient' sprung into Wesley's mind, but he suppressed them swiftly.

'You went to hospital?'

'Yeah. I thought I'd better get it checked out and they said I had concussion and kept me in overnight. I thought I was OK but then I started to have these headaches ... and flashbacks.'

'You saw a doctor about the headaches?'

Suddenly Jones looked uncomfortable. 'Not once I'd left the hospital. The headaches got better on their own, like. No need to bother the quack. Don't like doctors. Don't know why, I just don't.'

Wesley began to pour tea from the white china pot into the cups, watching the man's face while he played mother. 'Look, why don't you just start at the beginning and tell me everything you remember?' he said as he slid the cup towards his companion.

Jones took a sip of tea and sighed. 'I never remembered anything about when I was very young. The first thing I remember was living in a caravan. It was in Ireland. I remember being happy. And climbing trees and that.'

'Do you remember your parents?'

He frowned. 'There were lots of grown-ups. Don't know which were my parents.'

'It was a sort of ... commune?'

Jones looked at Wesley and nodded. 'Yeah. I suppose it must have been. They went round in old caravans ... and old buses. I remember the old buses.'

'Can you remember how you came to be there?'

There was a long silence. Then he shook his head. 'It was only after the accident I started to remember things. Like I said, I started having flashbacks ... dead vivid. I was at this school where we had to wear these shorts and blazers and ties. We had these lessons. Maths. And Latin. Honest to God, I'd never been to a school like that in my life.'

'Then you started to remember more?'

'Yeah. These flashbacks come at any time; when I'm walking down the road; or lying in bed trying to get to sleep. I've been having dreams too ... about this house and these people who had a boat. And I was taken to the school every day by this girl with

45

blond hair. She had a Mini – a blue Mini. And people were calling me Marcus. And there was a piano that played by itself. And I had a tree house. I remember the tree house. Then there was the smell . . . the river and the seaweed. When I hired a boat and went on the river, it all came back. That smell . . . salty, like.'

Wesley noticed that the man's eyes were starting to fill with tears.

'So how did you find out where the Fallbrooks' house was?'

Jones smiled, showing a row of uneven teeth. 'That was the lucky bit. There was this article in the paper about unsolved crimes of the nineteen seventies. There was a picture of a kid and it was like a bell started ringing in me head. I knew it were me when I was little. Marcus. That's who I was. There was a picture of the house and all – Mirabilis. It all clicked.'

Wesley nodded. Houldsworth had mentioned this particular article.

Jones continued. 'Then I decided to come down here and . . . Well, I took a motor boat out on the river and I saw the house on the bank through the trees. And I knew . . . But knocking on that door was the hardest thing I've ever done in me life, believe me.' The man spoke with such sincerity that Wesley's initial scepticism was fading.

'Do you remember anything about your abduction?' Wesley suddenly realised that he was speaking to Mark Jones as though his story was genuine. But perhaps he'd known from the moment he'd clapped eyes on him, from the moment he'd seen the resemblance between him and Adrian Fallbrook, that he was indeed Marcus Fallbrook, the child returned to life.

'I remember the school and living with the travellers but the rest is just all vague. Sorry.'

'You might remember one day.'

'Now I'm down here things are coming back to me all the time. And I want to remember. I want to know what happened to me.' Mark Jones sounded as though he meant it.

'How long were you with the travellers in Ireland?'

'I don't know. It seemed like a long time but . . . I think they were more New Age travellers than the traditional type. One of them – Carrie she was called – took me to Manchester with her. I remember going on the train. She left me there with Aunty Lynne and I lived there till I left school and got a job in a supermarket.

Then I worked at the airport – baggage handling – but I got sick of that so now I work in a garden centre.'

'What about Aunty Lynne? Perhaps she'll be able to throw some light on . . . '

'She died last year.'

Wesley should have known the lead was too good to be true. 'I don't suppose you know where we can find Carrie?'

He shook his head. 'Never saw her again. Never saw any of them again.'

'Did you ever ask about your birth certificate? You must have needed it to apply for a passport . . . '

He shook his head. 'Never needed one . . . never been abroad.'

'Did Aunty Lynne have any other relatives who might help?'

'No.'

'When she died did you find any papers or . . . '

'I went back to the house and one of the neighbours helped me clear out her things. I remember looking for Carrie's address but I never found it.'

'Were you close to your Aunty Lynne?'

Jones's expression gave nothing away. 'She wasn't the sort of woman you got close to. She provided me with the basics but she wasn't the motherly type. I don't think she had anything to do with the kidnapping – or Carrie. I don't know why, but I think they might have found me wandering or something, the travellers that is.'

'Where do you live now?'

'When Aunty Lynne died the house was empty so . . . ' He shrugged his shoulders by way of explanation. 'Look, I don't want all this to mess my life up.' He put his head in his hands.

Wesley poured another cup of tea for both of them. Mark – or Marcus – looked as though he needed it. Wesley watched him sip, nursing the cup as though trying to warm his hands.

Mark Jones took a deep breath and sighed. 'Perhaps I shouldn't have come here . . . I should have left well alone. But I had to know.' He gave Wesley a shy smile. 'I'm thinking of getting married. You wouldn't think all this would matter at my age. But you have to know where you come from, don't you?'

'If you can prove you're Marcus Fallbrook, you stand to inherit quite a bit of money. Marcus's father was a very wealthy business-man.'

47

Mark Jones shook his head vigorously. 'I didn't know about that. And I couldn't give a toss about the money. Finding my real family's more important . . . finding out who I really am.'

Wesley watched him, wondering whether he was protesting too much. But then he thought he might just feel the same if he was in his shoes.

'I told Adrian that I'll take a DNA test, you know. His wife, Carol, is arranging it all.'

Wesley nodded before asking the passing waitress for the bill. It looked as though the man might be telling the truth after all.

It was the largest memorial in the graveyard.

Neil Watson read the inscription beneath the strange symbol that had so intrigued him. Sacred to the memory of . . . There were so many Benthams listed. Two Marys. A Sarah. A George. A Charles. Four Johns. Three Edwards. Two Katherines. And one Juanita, probably a Spanish rose who had withered in the English chill. Neil imagined the exotically imported wife, regarded with suspicion in life by her in-laws but laid to rest beside them when the time came. She was family after all.

The Bentham vault was topped by a tall granite obelisk, an all too solid reminder of their wealth and standing in the community. From the little local research Neil had conducted – mainly by chatting to the Rector – he had learned that the Benthams were the local squires who had lived from the fifteenth century onwards in Bentham Hall. The original hall had been burned down and rebuilt in the fashionable classical style in the eighteenth century. After the Second World War the family had moved out due to hard times and inheritance tax and the hall had been transformed recently into an upmarket hotel. The last of the Benthams, Miss Worth, whose mother had been the family's only daughter, had died childless in a tiny cob cottage with a smallholding attached, not far from the pub that bore her mother's family's proud name. Neil supposed that this turn of events was a blow for social equality.

He found himself staring at the symbol carved boldly in the centre of the obelisk. The seven-pointed star with the seven rays and the rose at its centre. The Shining Ones. He wondered how it had come to dominate the Bentham family's last resting place. Had they been 'Shining Ones'? Who exactly were the 'Shining Ones' and what did they believe? What, if anything, had set them apart from their more conventional neighbours? He resolved to find out one of these days. But in the meantime he had work to do.

He watched as the crane began to lift the Bentham obelisk, slowly at first, then the thing began to rise into the air, swinging to and fro on its chains.

Once the monstrous monument was clear, Neil walked over to the small digger that was waiting to disinter the bones beneath. It was time to start.

Soon the brick vault was unearthed and the workmen, under the supervising eyes of the archaeological team who were photographing and recording the proceedings, began to dismantle the structure revealing two rows of coffins beneath, some stacked on top of others. There seemed to be an awful lot of Benthams down there, some tall, some small, some only babies and children. A family group.

The first coffin to be lifted out of the ground belonged to a Charles Bentham and the dates on the plaque fixed to the lid told Neil that he had died in 1898 aged eighty-two.

After that they came thick and fast. These coffins, belonging to the gentry, seemed to be far better quality than the ones that had split apart so disturbingly the other day. Class distinction even in death.

Neil watched as the coffins were moved and stacked, ready to be reburied in the plot prepared for them at the other side of the churchyard. This was a job for the contractors: when it was finished, Neil's team would look for older remains beneath. And maybe, with luck, they would find traces of an earlier church.

He was musing on the most efficient way of completing the work, watching the hoist swinging the coffins out of the ground, when all of a sudden there was a thud.

A slight misjudgement by one of the contractors had caused one of the coffins to land heavily. As rusted nails gave way, the coffin lid slid to one side and Neil, through a combination of duty and morbid curiosity, rushed over to where it lay.

First he noted the name on the lid. Juanita Bentham. The Spanish bride. According to the metal coffin plate she had left this uncertain and perilous existence in 1816 – at the time when the Prince Regent had ruled England in place of his poor mad father, King George III. And she had been twenty-seven years old when she died. No age at all.

Neil's eyes were drawn to the inside of the coffin, to the grinning skull. He averted his eyes. It seemed almost indecent to stare. But then he looked again. He hadn't imagined it.

He hadn't imagined the second skull tucked beneath the first, grinning out from behind the first in a macabre game of peek-a-boo.

Suzy Wakefield bashed the off switch of the radio with a violence that surprised her estranged husband Darren who was helping himself to a drink from the mirrored cocktail cabinet that stood in the corner of the room.

Darren swung round, almost spilling the contents of his glass. 'Hey, I was listening to that. It was the news.'

Suzy swung round and stared at him. 'It was about that bloody lunatic who's going round assaulting women in taxis. Do you think I want to be reminded of what could have happened to . . . '

'My little girl can take care of herself. No problem. She'll be lying low for a bit to teach you a lesson.' Darren Wakefield smiled in the smug way that had always infuriated his ex-wife.

Leah Wakefield's father was well built with dark hair and a penchant for gold chains and shirts unbuttoned to reveal his tanned chest. He had always fancied himself but his tendency to narcissism had increased with the realisation that he had produced a beautiful and talented daughter who would make them a fortune. He had been lured from Suzy's side by a young PR woman many years his junior and, with the woman Suzy termed 'the Bimbo' in tow, he had developed a taste for the high life. Suzy suspected that it was only a matter of time before Leah pulled the financial plug on his exploits. And that thought had given her a warm glow of satisfaction in her darkest hours.

Suzy began to pace up and down. 'I've been ringing round everyone she knows. Nobody's seen her.'

'And you think they'd tell you if they had? Give the girl some space, will you.'

Suzy Wakefield looked into her former husband's unworried eyes and what self control she had left suddenly snapped. She gave him a stinging slap across the face before launching herself at him and pummelling his chest with her fists.

Darren stood quite still, a smirk of amusement on his face, holding off the assault with one hand as he had done so often during the course of their marriage. At five foot nothing, Suzy was no match for him, a goldfish attacking a shark.

He waited until Suzy subsided to the thick piled carpet in tears of frustrated rage before speaking again. 'This isn't going to bring her home, is it? This is why she left in the first place,' he said before walking out of the door.

'I never particularly liked Barry Houldsworth,' Gerry Heffernan said thoughtfully as Wesley locked the car. 'He was an insensitive old bugger. Once told a woman whose daughter had been raped to pull herself together.'

'Not in tune with the caring, sharing ethos of the modern force then.'

Heffernan chuckled. 'You could say that. I reckon our DC Carstairs would take on the role of his spiritual successor given half the chance.'

'Too right,' said Wesley with feeling. Steve Carstairs was hardly his favourite underling, although he had to admit he'd been behaving himself of late. 'So Houldsworth wasn't popular then?'

'He was popular enough with a certain type – the ones who joined the force to model themselves on *The Sweeney*. The ones who watched more telly than was good for them. There were quite a few coppers like that around in those early days.' He gave a wide grin. 'I had the reputation of being the station softy at one time.'

Wesley raised his eyebrows. 'Really?' It was hard to see the ex-merchant-navy man who had put the fear of God into so many villains as the station softy. Perhaps it said something about Houldsworth's régime back in the nineteen seventies. Wesley was only glad he had only been a tot playing cops and robbers with plastic handcuffs at the time.

'I suppose you could say Houldsworth was one of the old school.'

'Was he at Tradmouth till he retired?'

Heffernan shook his head. 'Nah. He moved on to Morbay. Not sure why. Clash of personalities with his superiors probably.' He tilted his head to one side. 'I sometimes wonder whether me and CS Nutter are compatible, you know,' he added thoughtfully. 'I'm interested in catching villains but the only things that seems to turn him on are meetings and shuffling paper about.'

Wesley smiled and said nothing. They had reached the Bentham

Arms and the door to the lounge bar stood open invitingly. 'Well, here we are. What are you drinking?'

Heffernan looked at his watch. 'As the sun's over the yardarm and you're driving, I'll have a pint of best.'

Wesley made a beeline for the bar and ordered the drinks while his boss went off in search of Houldsworth. Balancing the beer and his own orange juice, he wandered over to the corner where he'd found the ex-DCI the previous night and sure enough, there he was, waiting with a pair of notebooks on the table in front of him. Wesley was relieved that he'd remembered his promise.

Gerry Heffernan had sat down beside him and now the two men were exchanging grunted pleasantries; enquiries about old colleagues and the current goings on at Tradmouth nick. Wesley let them get on with it until they ran out of things to say, which wasn't very long – Gerry Heffernan had never been one of DCI Houldsworth's blue-eyed boys.

The former DCI looked alert and sober, unlike the night before. But the pint of beer in front of him suggested that he might not stay that way for long. They had to make their enquiries while the going was good.

Wesley came straight to the point. 'What would you say if I told you that Marcus Fallbrook's just turned up out of the blue?'

'I'd say someone's having you on. The kid's dead.'

'What makes you so sure?'

'Call it gut feeling. I think that poor lad was dead before the ransom was dropped. Anyway, if he was alive, where has he been all these years?'

'He says he was found wandering by New Age travellers.'

Houldsworth sniggered. 'Away with the raggle-taggle gypsies o. You don't believe that fairy story, do you?'

'He's offered to take a DNA test.'

Houldsworth looked at Wesley as if he was a particularly stupid child who needed everything explaining in words of one syllable. 'Well he would, wouldn't he? If he refused it's as good as admitting he's a fraud.'

Heffernan had been listening intently. 'You've got a point there, Barry,' he chipped in.

Houldsworth prodded Wesley's shoulder with an unsteady hand. 'What do you bet that he'll find some reason not to take the test when the time comes? He'll be called away urgently or develop an allergy to needles or something. You'll see.'

Wesley glanced at his boss. From the expression on Gerry Heffernan's face, it seemed that he didn't altogether consider the scenario Houldsworth described as far fetched.

Wesley tried again. 'But what if his story's true. There are things we can check out. We can ask Manchester police to check out the addresses he talked about. And we can try and trace the travellers who found him.'

Houldsworth snorted. 'Fat chance. They'll be long gone.'

'He said he was knocked down in a hit and run and was admitted to A and E. He had concussion and that's when he started having flashbacks . . . when he began to remember his early childhood. We can check out his story about the accident. The hospital will have records.'

Houldsworth gave Gerry Heffernan a theatrical wink. 'Ah, the naivety of the young. As soon as you start checking this stuff out, he'll be well away.'

'All I'm saying is that we should keep an open mind,' Wesley protested, sensing he was being ganged up on.

'So what do you reckon then, Barry?' Heffernan asked.

'I reckon the kidnappers were in league with the nanny, Jenny Booker. I never trusted her – or that boyfriend of hers – but there was nothing we could prove. The boyfriend – Gordon Heather his name was – didn't have a criminal record but I still didn't trust the bastard. He was odd . . . decidedly odd. And I ask you, would a pampered, protected kid like Marcus just go off with someone he didn't know? Course he wouldn't. He disappeared from the school grounds at lunchtime and nobody saw a thing. What if Booker had arranged to meet him? Said something like, why don't I come to fetch you at lunchtime and we can have a jolly picnic? She had no alibi for the time he disappeared. She said she was shopping in Morbay but she couldn't prove it. She says she didn't buy anything so she couldn't produce any receipts and this was long before the days of CCTV cameras on every lamp post.'

'Any idea where we can find her now?'

Houldsworth smirked and shook his head.

'You seem pretty sure it was her.' Wesley glanced at Heffernan who was giving nothing away.

Houldsworth pushed the notebooks in Wesley's direction.

'Read the notes I took at the time and I'll bet you a night's free ale that you come to the same conclusion.' He leaned forward. 'I'd have liked to see that little bitch behind bars. What she did to that family was ... ' He shook his head, lost for adequate words. 'It killed the poor mother, you know.'

'So I've heard. You know the father died recently. And there's a half-brother – a son by the father's second wife.'

'She still around?'

'No. She died a while ago.'

'Not a very lucky family, are they?' mused Gerry Heffernan as he savoured the contents of his glass. Houldsworth's sister kept a good cellar.

'It was the half-brother, Adrian Fallbrook, who let us know that this man claiming to be Marcus had turned up.'

'At least he's got some sense. This phoney Marcus won't hang round for long if he thinks the police are looking into his story, you'll see.'

'Can I take these notebooks?'

'No use to me now,' Houldsworth said sadly, staring at his empty glass. 'Anyone going to the bar?'

Wesley and Gerry made their excuses and left.

Neil Watson found the Reverend John Ventnor at the vicarage, a detached brick box on the edge of the village, constructed in the nineteen sixties by someone with more interest in cost effectiveness than architectural style. The original vicarage – a gorgeous Georgian pile with a garden that had hosted many a fete – was now occupied by a retired city banker and his gym-honed second wife.

Neil was greeted by Mrs Ventnor, a plump, pretty woman with a couple of toddlers clinging to her long floral skirts. She told him that John was busy writing his sermon, but would probably be grateful for the interruption, so Neil followed her into the house to the small room overlooking the back garden that served as the Rector's study.

'This is a pleasant surprise,' Ventnor said as he rose from his seat, knocking his notes to the ground. 'Found something interesting?'

'You could say that,' said Neil, glancing round the book-lined room. 'One of the Bentham coffins contains two bodies.'

The Rector frowned. 'Really?'

'I wondered if I could have a look at the burial register. One of the skeletons appears to be that of an older child. I'm just wondering whether a mother and child were buried together or . . . '

'It was common for a baby to be buried with its mother. But an older child in the same coffin . . . You're sure it was in the same coffin? One hadn't just rotted away or . . . '

'No, it was definitely the same coffin.'

Ventnor picked a large set of keys up off the desk. 'Tell you what, let's go over to the church and have a look at the registers. They're kept in a safe in the vestry.'

Neil walked down the main village street with Ventnor who greeted people as he passed, making swift enquiries about bad legs and the state of parents' health. Neil envied him his easy manner, the effortless concern he could muster in a split second; and the remarkable memory that allowed him to store all his parishioners' joys, woes and hospital admissions in its data bank. But then he supposed it was all part of the job and it had been acquired with practice, like his own encyclopaedic knowledge of pottery sherds and artefacts.

The excavations at the church were hidden from public view by tall white screens, carefully erected with no gaps for the local teenagers to peep through during their long and boring evenings spent hanging around the village phone box and bus shelter. Neil glanced at them as Ventnor unlocked the church door, wondering if anything was going on behind them that might require his attention. He fingered the mobile phone in his pocket: if he was needed someone would let him know.

He followed Ventnor down the side aisle to the vestry. St Merion's Church, in common with many Devon churches, possessed an intricately carved and painted rood screen between nave and chancel. Neil paused for a moment to admire the medieval paintwork faded to a subtle, muted beauty over the centuries. The heavy peace within the church was unaffected by all the activity outside in the churchyard and the footsteps of the two men rang hollow on the cold stone floor as they made for the vestry.

The vestry itself was a cosy room with monumental cupboards for surplices and choir robes filling one wall and a large oak desk that had been leaned on by many hopeful couples as they signed the marriage register. A large iron safe, an ancient artefact in itself, stood near the door. John Ventnor opened it and took out an old, leather-bound book with the word 'burials' emblazoned in faded gold on its cover.

'Do you know the name and date of the burial?' the Rector asked, flicking carefully through the pages.

Neil nodded. 'Juanita Bentham. 1816.' He took a sheet of paper from the pocket of his combat jacket. 'I've made a note of all the names on the monument, although there were a few infant burials that weren't listed. And I've noted all the names we have so far from the coffin plates. Perhaps if we matched them with the register.'

'Are all the Bentham burials disinterred now?'

Neil nodded. 'It's just a job of matching names to skulls.'

John Ventnor walked to the desk and flicked through the pages of a large diary. 'I'll conduct the Benthams' reburial service after I've finished writing my sermon. Since Miss Worth died there are no living relatives so there's nobody to notify.' He sighed. 'That line keeps going through my head. "The paths of glory lead but to the grave." The Benthams were the village squires. Front pews in church. Forelocks tugged as they rode past in their carriages. They had the power to appoint the parish clergy . . . my predecessors. They even had the village pub named after them.'

'And now they're just a load a mouldering skeletons – exactly like the farm labourers who had to work their fingers to the bone on their estates and bow and scrape . . . '

'Death, the great leveller.' The Rector smiled and looked at his watch. 'Can I leave you to lock up, Neil? Just bring the keys back when you've finished.'

Neil was glad to be left alone in the silent church, alone to think, away from the bustle of the churchyard and the sight of the ground yielding its grim harvest.

He roamed around the church for a while, examining the rood screen and the worn grave slabs in the aisles, each telling a story of a human being who had lived, loved and died in Stoke Beeching centuries ago. He imagined them: the old; the young; male and female; young soldiers killed in far off wars or sailors drowned in tragic shipwrecks off the treacherous Devon coast; young women dying in childbirth; unmarried sons and daughters barely out of their teens succumbing to fevers; loved matriarchs; loathed patriarchs; innocent babies. They had all ended up together in the church . . . a silent congregation of bones.

After a while he wandered back to the vestry and began to poke around absentmindedly in the massive oak cupboards lining the walls of the small room. But there was nothing much of interest, only the usual assortment of battered hymn books and choir surplices that had seen better days. In the bottom of one cupboard he found an oak box, not large, not small and dulled by years of dust and grime. He was about to close the cupboard door when he noticed a pair of initials carved roughly on the lid – JS. Probably a former Rector, he concluded, having noticed a John Singleton on the list of Victorian incumbents hanging on the wall. The box probably contained copies of Singleton's old sermons, he thought as he shut the door and returned to the desk.

He settled himself down in the throne-like chair and began to go through the burial registers, matching each coffin found with its entry. Even the infant burials – the newborn babies who hadn't survived their first night – had been meticulously recorded by the rector of the day in immaculate copper plate handwriting, so it was just a matter of checking and double checking against the list he had made of the names on the coffin plates and the number of coffins.

The task took longer than he'd expected. And two hours later he realised that he had a mystery on his hands.

It seemed that the Bentham family vault had held one corpse too many. Juanita Bentham's coffin had harboured an interloper.

As soon as the phone started to ring, Suzy Wakefield grabbed the receiver. It would be Leah. She was ringing to say that she was all right . . . that she was sorry and she'd be coming home soon. She'd caused a great deal of heartache but Suzy was happy to forgive her everything. As long as she was safe.

But the voice on the other end of the line wasn't Leah's. It was androgynous, metallic. As though it had been processed through some sort of machine.

The caller didn't wait for any sort of acknowledgement. The words began as soon as Suzy put the receiver to her ear. 'We have your daughter. If you do exactly as you're told, she won't be harmed. Further instructions will follow. If you contact the police your daughter will die.'

When the line went dead Suzy was left, frozen with horror, listening to the dialling tone. After her initial panic had subsided,

57

she pressed the buttons. 1471 to get the caller's number. But she heard an electronic voice, more friendly this time, telling her that it was sorry but the caller has withheld the number. And Suzy Wakefield burst into tears.

Chapter Four

Letter from Juanita Bentham to Mrs Sarah Jewel of Brighton, 15th May 1815

My dearest Mrs Jewel,

I thank you for your kind enquiries. My husband is in good health and myself also. I do, however, suffer greatly from this English damp and cold, so unlike my mother's native island. How I long sometimes to be back on Nevis in the warmth and sunshine. I feel on occasions that I shall die of the chill but Sir John chides me for my foolishness.

I trust the girls are in the best of health. I think of them often and miss their good company for they were always the dearest of my charges. You ask if my new life in Devon suits me and I can say with honesty that it does apart from the climate as I mentioned before. Sir John's house is very fine and the servants respectful. The church here in Stoke Beeching is full of antiquity and in Devon they have the habit of ringing the bells of their churches in wonderful tunes that lift the hearts of those who hear them.

Yet I miss you and Mr Jewel and the girls for you were all so kind to me when my dear father died. Be assured you are always in my prayers.

Although I am happy here, there have been certain events in the village that concern me. I fear there might be something evil here. But it may be a foolish fancy of mine. I shall write no more of it.

I have the fondest memories of my stay in Brighton and I have great hopes that circumstances will allow me to visit with you soon. Be assured of my best and fondest love always.

Your loving friend, Juanita Bentham.

*   *   *

Wesley Peterson and Gerry Heffernan hadn't fancied hanging around the Bentham Arms under Barry Houldsworth's jaundiced eye. Besides, they hadn't been tempted by the range of goodies on offer in that particular establishment. The only choice on Houldsworth's sister's menu was between ham or cheese sandwiches. Hardly a gastronomic treat.

They returned to Tradmouth to grab a hotpot in the Fisherman's Arms and by the time they returned to the police station their stomachs were satisfied and their minds relaxed. Wesley had Houldsworth's notebooks safely in his pocket and as soon as he reached his office he placed them on the desk beside the case files. There must be something in that pile of musty paper, he thought, that would catch Mark Jones out . . . or confirm his story.

Both policemen knew that the problem needed to be resolved fairly quickly before Jones's hold on the Fallbrook family tightened and he became part of their lives. It would save a lot of heartache if the true identity of the newcomer was confirmed sooner rather than later.

Wesley had already glanced at the nanny, Jenny Booker's statement and somehow it did seem a little odd. Maybe Houldsworth had been right to regard Jenny as a prime suspect.

Deciphering Houldsworth's spidery handwriting, he could sense the man's frustration at not having enough evidence to charge Jenny Booker. She and her boyfriend, Gordon Heather had been arrested and interviewed but they'd used the tried and trusted tactic of denying everything, sticking to their story, never deviating from their statements. In the end, Houldsworth had had no reason to hold them, other than a hunch. And hunches don't stand up in court.

And there was another problem: the boy's mother, Anna Fallbrook, was adamant that Jenny had nothing to do with it. Jenny loved Marcus, she said. And she would never have harmed him. When Gordon Heather's name was mentioned she refused to accept that Jenny could have been influenced to do anything that might hurt Marcus. And besides, even though he had aroused Houldsworth's suspicions, Heather had no criminal convictions.

Something told Wesley that Anna Fallbrook had been hiding her head in the proverbial sand. But why? Most women in her position would have clutched at any possibility . . . suspecting anyone and everyone. Grasping for hope.

The more Wesley read, the more he wanted to speak to Jenny Booker. It was just a matter of finding her.

He picked up one of the files and a plastic bag slipped out. He picked it up and studied it. Inside was a sheet of thin yellow A4 paper, the type common in offices at one time. He read the words printed on it.

'We have your son. If you obey our instructions to the letter he won't be harmed. But if you tell the police we won't hesitate to cut his throat. Await instructions.'

Pretty standard fare, Wesley thought. Then he opened the file up and saw a second plastic bag containing a second note. Neatly printed just like the first on identical paper.

'If you love Marcus and you want him returned you must pay £15,000 for his continued survival. We'll say where and when. Wait for instructions and don't tell the police. If you do we'll cut his throat.'

The words sent a chill through Wesley's body. He was a father himself and reading these words, these crazy, cold-hearted words, made him feel slightly sick.

He picked up the phone and dialled a number. Jenny Booker must be somewhere.

Suzy Wakefield had sat, shaking with terror, deciding on the best course of action. For the first time in a year she wished Darren was there with her. The bitter words that had passed between them had fled from her mind. All she wanted was support; a shoulder to lean on. And at that moment she'd even make do with an unreliable, treacherous one like Darren's.

She sat there, staring at the phone; willing it to ring; unaware of her surroundings; unaware of the time passing. In her imagination she picked up the receiver and heard Leah's voice on the other end saying it was all a joke, a cruel trick to teach her irritating mother a lesson. But the telephone didn't ring: the only sound in the house was the distant babble of a TV game show drifting in from another room. She was alone there. Alone with her burden of knowledge.

Then, after a few still and frozen minutes, her brain began to clear. The caller had said that the police shouldn't be contacted but he – or she – had said nothing about talking to anyone else.

With a shaking hand she picked up the receiver and punched out the number of Darren's mobile. If this thing was for real he should be told. She shouldn't have to bear it alone. Besides, if there was money to be found, she'd need his help. She had little money of her own and both of them had to sign documents if they wanted access to Leah's considerable bank balance.

She listened as the phone rang out at the other end, tapping her foot impatiently, whispering 'Come on, come on,' under her breath. When she heard Darren's voice, hostile and wary, her mind went blank for a second then she blurted out the words. 'I've had a call. Someone's got Leah. They're threatening to kill her.'

Darren didn't speak for a few moments. Then he asked if she was making it up, his voice heavy with suspicion.

It was a cruel question and it stung Suzy like a slap. 'Of course I'm not. I wouldn't make up something like that.' She felt the hot tears run down her cheek. 'Of course not. I'd never do anything like that. They've got her. They said not to tell the police.'

'It's someone having a joke. You've got to get the cops in. They'll trace the call and . . . '

'No,' Suzy almost shouted down the phone. 'I won't take the risk.'

'So you're going to let someone bleed us white while madam's sunning herself on some Costa.' There was a long silence. Suzy knew Darren was thinking . . . which made a change. 'She'll be behind all this,' he continued. 'She'll have got one of her mates to call. She's been on about getting her hands on more of her money . . . How she thinks Brad's been keeping her short. This'll be her idea of pay day. Either that or it's Brad's idea of a publicity stunt. Tell the cops. Call her bluff.'

Suzy slammed the phone down, wishing she could share Darren's optimistic assessment of the situation. She stared at the phone for a further five minutes, numb and confused, before making the decision to call Brad Williams.

Leah's manager would know what to do.

At four o'clock on the dot, Rachel Tracey wandered into Wesley Peterson's office and sat down.

Wesley looked up and smiled. 'What's new?'

She sighed and flicked her shoulder-length blond hair off her face. The gesture held a hint of invitation, which Wesley studiously ignored.

'The Barber's victims were all regular customers of local taxi firms. I think he's been listening to the taxi frequencies and whenever the taxi's ordered in a woman's name, he follows the cab.'

Wesley caught on quick. 'And he checks if she fits his requirements and next time she calls a cab, he turns up.'

'Something like that, yeah.'

'If you're right, it means he's very well organised. It's a lot of trouble to go to.'

'For you and me maybe.'

'But not for someone who's . . . '

'A weirdo? We've got to get him, Wesley. We've got to find him before he does something worse than chopping their hair off.'

'Maybe that's all he wants to do.'

Rachel looked at him, concerned. 'You really think he'll be satisfied with a bit of rough hairdressing? You think this thing won't escalate?'

'Gerry Heffernan does.'

'Don't you?' Rachel watched his face but his expression gave nothing away.

'To be honest, Rachel, I don't know.' He paused for a moment. 'I hear you've moved out of the farm.'

Rachel felt her cheeks burning. 'Yeah. Trish and I are renting somewhere. It's a holiday cottage so it's only available till next spring. I thought it was about time I got my own place. You have to leave home one day, don't you?'

'What about next summer? Won't your mother need your help with the holiday lets?' Rachel, a farmer's daughter, had been helping her mother with the holiday apartments that kept Little Barton Farm out of the financial quagmire that faced so many local farmers, since her teenage years. Her move would be a blow to her family. Her parents, like Wesley's own, weren't getting any younger.

'My brother Tom's wife says she's going to start doing more,' she said nervously, as though she hardly believed it. 'And I won't be far away. I can still make it over there to change the bedding on Saturdays when the holiday season arrives. We'll sort something out,' she said confidently.

'So what's it like . . . independence?'

Rachel smiled. She thought she saw a glimmer of envy in Wesley's eyes. 'It's good. Really good.' She paused, wondering whether to say the next thing that popped into her head. But she was feeling reckless so she said it anyway. 'You'll have to come round to see the place.'

'I'd like that,' said Wesley quickly, not really intending to take Rachel up on her offer. He was a married man. And cosy invitations led to trouble.

The awkward silence that followed was interrupted by a sharp knock on the office door and Rachel's heart sank when she saw Steve Carstairs's head appear. DC Carstairs was hardly her favourite colleague and he was the last person she would have wanted to catch her alone with Wesley. She knew his love of innuendo and muck-spreading of the sort not undertaken by the farming community.

But she assumed her bravest face and went on the attack. 'Steve, I was just about to ask you if anything's come in from the taxi firms.'

'Not yet, Sarge,' said Steve with a sly smirk. 'Paul's out doing the rounds . . . asking if any of the drivers have noticed someone following them when they've picked up lone women but nothing yet.' He turned to Wesley. 'I've checked with Greater Manchester Police and there is a Mark Jones living at the address he gave and there's a Mark Jones working at the garden centre he mentioned. And the hospital confirm that a Mark Jones was treated for concussion around the time he said. And the story about his Aunty Lynne checks out too. A Lynne Jones living at the same address died last September. It all seems kosher.'

'Thanks, Steve. Well done,' Wesley said, trying his best to keep on the right side of that fine line between encouraging and patronising. From the sour expression on Steve's face, he wasn't sure whether he'd been entirely successful.

'So it looks as though this Mark Jones is telling the truth,' Rachel said softly after Steve had gone. 'If the DNA test he's offered to take comes back positive . . . '

'Then he's who he says he is. Marcus Fallbrook, heir to a rather substantial fortune. And the first person I've ever known to come back from the dead,' said Wesley.

Rachel stood up. 'It can't be easy for the brother . . . for Adrian Fallbrook and his wife. He's due to lose half his property to this stranger who's just turned up out of the blue. I've known people commit murder for less.'

Wesley looked up. This was something he'd never considered before – the fact that Mark Jones himself could be in danger.

* * *

The bodies had been reburied. All of them except the one with no name; Juanita Bentham's companion in death. Something made Neil ask for his bones – for Neil was pretty sure that it was a teenage male – to be taken to Dr Colin Bowman at Tradmouth Hospital mortuary.

The Reverend John Ventnor eventually acquiesced, although he made it clear that he had his reservations. The arrangement had been to give all the bodies the Christian burial they would have expected and deserved in another part of the churchyard as soon as possible after their disinterment. It seemed rather distasteful, he said, to keep one away from his final resting place just because of an administrative error – for that's what he had convinced himself had happened all those years back in 1816. The rector at the time or, more likely, his inexperienced curate, had omitted to enter the boy's name into the burial register.

But Neil pointed out patiently that this theory didn't explain why he was sharing a coffin with Juanita Bentham. He was far too old to be her child. Ventnor suggested that he might be her brother but somehow Neil couldn't see it. A younger brother who had died tragically on a visit to his married sister would, surely, have had a coffin to himself. Sharing already cramped accommodation in this way would surely be taking thrift too far as far as the wealthy Benthams were concerned.

And then there were the marks on the bones. Neil had hardly liked to point them out to Ventnor but he was eager to hear what Colin Bowman had to say about them.

The only time Neil had seen marks like that before was on butchered animal bones. He needed confirmation, of course, but as far as he could tell, the boy had been killed with a sharp implement of some kind. And his throat had been cut to the bone.

Wesley arrived home at a reasonable time – six o'clock on the dot – and he expected some gratitude for this display of exemplary behaviour.

But Pam wasn't alone with the children. As soon as Wesley opened the front door he heard his mother-in-law, Della, her voice rising above the crying of baby Amelia as if vying for Pam's attention. His heart sank but then he told himself that with any luck she'd just called in and would be on her way out any moment. But fortune is rarely that kind.

Wesley took a deep breath and fixed an artificial smile on his face before making his way into the living room where he found his wife frantically tidying up while Della sipped a large glass of red wine slumped on the sofa next to the crying baby in her playpen.

'Where's Michael?' was his first question.

'He's playing with a friend from school. He's been invited to tea. Nice to know he's settling in,' said Pam, still on the move. Michael had just started in the reception class of the school where Pam taught and, so far, things seemed to be going well.

Wesley picked Amelia up and the crying ceased immediately.

'Hello, Della,' he said, thinking he should make the effort to foster good relations. 'How are you?'

'I'm fine, Wesley. How are things at the cop shop? Still beating up suspects and oppressing the innocent?'

Wesley had learned long ago to take his mother-in-law's remarks with a hefty pinch of salt, even though he suspected that she half believed what she was saying.

Carrying Amelia in one arm, he put the other around Pam's waist and kissed her cheek. 'How was school?'

'Could be worse,' she answered, her face serious.

'I'll make the supper,' he said softly so Della couldn't hear. He feared the mention of free food might encourage her to stay.

'You'd better ask my mother if she's staying.'

The question 'Must I?' formed on Wesley's lips but he managed to swallow the words in time.

He turned to Della. 'I expect you've got to get home,' he said hopefully. But Della announced that she'd stay and have something to eat with them as though she was doing them a great favour. Wesley responded by asking her to set the table, a suggestion she pointedly ignored.

Once they were sitting at the table, Wesley looked across at his mother-in-law who was leaning forward, her hooped earrings dangling in the lasagne she was consuming as though she hadn't eaten in days. He sometimes wondered how Della could have produced a sane daughter like Pam. But he had concluded long ago that Pam must have taken after her father, a man Wesley had never met due to the fact that he'd departed to join that great refuge for put-upon husbands in the sky the year before he and Pam met.

The conversation over the meal was sporadic. Pam's new

headmistress; Michael's reading book; the police's progress with the Barber enquiry. During a short lull in the routine chatter, Wesley watched as Della ate in what appeared to be bored silence and made a decision. If she insisted on imposing on them, he might as well make use of the situation.

'Della, you've lived around here for years. Do you remember a little boy being kidnapped? Marcus Fallbrook his name was. His family lived in Derenham.'

Della's mouth was full so she couldn't answer for a few seconds. But the expression on her face and the frantic gesticulation of her hands told Wesley that the case was familiar to her.

'Course I remember it,' she said at last. 'Someone I was working with knew the family – I was teaching at a high school in those days. It was awful. They never found the poor kid, you know. And they never got who did it either,' she said accusingly as though Wesley was personally responsible.

'How well did your colleague know the Fallbrooks?'

'Quite well I think. She went to school with the mother or something.'

'Do you know where I can find her?'

Della looked wary, as though she suspected that her former acquaintance would be dragged to the bowels of Tradmouth police station and subjected to hours of brutal interrogation. 'Why?'

'There's been a new development in the case.' He felt reluctant to go into details. He didn't trust Della not to spread the good tidings about Marcus Fallbrook's possible return to life across the county. 'And I'd just like to talk to anyone who knew the family at the time, that's all.'

Della looked at him suspiciously. Then, after a few moments, she shrugged the shoulders. 'Can't do any harm, I suppose. I've not seen Linda for ages – in fact I think she's retired – but I still send her a card at Christmas. She'll be in my address book – it's in my bag. Remind me before I go, won't you.'

Wesley didn't know why, but he felt a thrill of anticipation as he walked to pick Michael up from his new friend's house a couple of streets away. He was impatient to contact Linda Tranter, Della's old colleague; impatient to speak to someone who'd actually known the Fallbrooks before and during that traumatic time.

There was always the possibility that she might be able to throw some light on the mystery. But then again, said the pessimist inside him, maybe not.

'Anyone free in the Neston area to take a fare to Morbay?' The voice crackled over the radio and the man, about to pop a toffee between his thin lips, froze.

The answer came. Vic could be there in ten minutes.

'It's a lady called Wetherby. Five Weston Place. New flats by the river. OK, Vic?'

'Wilco. Roger and out.' Vic had watched too much television as a child. He had been having a quiet cigarette after dropping off his last fare at one of Neston's better hotels and he threw the glowing stub out of the window before starting the engine.

He drove through the town to the waterfront, to a block of new flats in what had once been a warehouse storing timber from the Baltic. When he got there he parked untidily in front of a BMW and climbed out of the driver's seat.

As he searched the row of steel doorbells for the name Wetherby, he didn't notice the shadowy figure sitting in the anonymous dark-blue Ford in the car park, stationed well away from the bright streetlights that lit the area behind the flats.

Vic returned to his vehicle and a few minutes later a plump young woman appeared in the doorway of the flats. She was dressed in a short skirt that showed too much dimpled thigh and a small top and jacket designed for fashion rather than warmth. As she trotted over the tarmac to the minicab her long blond curls bounced, shining like brass in the sodium light. She opened the car door and as she climbed in, the Barber took a hardbacked note-book off the dashboard and began to write in it.

He made a careful note of the name of the minicab company and the name of the passenger. He had heard her name before. She used that company regularly.

She was just the sort of person he was looking for.

Leah's manager, Brad Williams was on his way down from London and a tiny voice in the back of Suzy Wakefield's brain whispered that it was for her sake that he had dropped everything to drive through the dark and rain to her side.

When Leah's career was budding, Suzy had yielded to Brad's expert advances and ended up in bed with him. She hadn't liked to refuse – after all, crossing him might jeopardise Leah's future. He had been an imaginative and energetic lover – a pleasing contrast to Darren – and she found that, against her expectations, she had rather enjoyed the experience of infidelity. She had come to look forward to 'business meetings' at Brad's apartment overlooking the Thames, where most of the business had been conducted between a pair of freshly laundered Egyptian cotton sheets.

But over the past year there had been no more trips to the bedroom. Brad had taken up with a pouty South American beauty called Maria, fifteen years his junior, and much to Suzy's disappointment, her relationship with Leah's manager had become strictly business.

But now she sat thinking of his anxiety, his eagerness to be down there with her, supporting her. Perhaps, she thought, Maria was fading from the scene. Perhaps she had returned to wherever she came from, leaving Brad thinking fondly of his old love. Not once did it occur to Suzy that Brad Williams had been using her, playing enjoyable power games. And that he was making the trip to Devon to protect his considerable investments.

'What time's he arriving?'

Suzy was shocked from her reverie by Darren's voice.

'He said he'd drive straight down.'

'I don't know why you had to call him at all. We can deal with this ourselves. If we tell the cops.'

Suzy pressed her lips together in a stubborn line. 'I'm not going to risk it. Let's wait to see what Brad thinks, shall we?'

'Bloody Brad,' Darren muttered under his breath. He sometimes wondered about Suzy's exact relationship with their daughter's manager. He wondered why she'd always known things about Leah's career that he'd had to find out second hand. And there were times when he'd wondered what had gone on at those long meetings in Brad's dockside apartment.

The two of them sat for a while in hostile silence until Darren stood up and marched off into the kitchen to get himself a can of lager. If he was going to be stuck there with his ex for the night, he might as well make the best of it.

He had just opened the steel door of the huge fridge when the phone began to ring and he grabbed a can from the top shelf before hurrying back to the lounge.

As he crossed the threshold he saw the expression on Suzy's

face as she held the receiver to her ear. The mixture of anguish and sheer terror.

'Please,' she was saying. 'Please tell me where she is.'

But it seemed that the voice on the other end was ignoring her maternal pleas. After a few seconds she put the receiver down, tears streaming down her cheeks.

'Well?' In spite of his initial assumption that it was some sick joke, Darren was starting to feel uneasy.

'He says I've got to go to some old gibbet at a crossroads – it's a mile outside Derenham at the top of the hill and one road leads to Burnington and the other to Tradmouth. He says the instructions have been left there . . . and proof they've got Leah.'

Darren stood quite still for a few moments, torn between assuring her that it was bound to be a hoax and entering into his ex-wife's state of panic.

But someone had to keep cool. 'We'll go up there. Now.'

'What about Brad?'

'This is none of his bloody business,' said Darren viciously. There were times he wished they'd never met Brad Williams. Who knows, if it hadn't been for Brad, Leah's meteoric rise in the music business might never have happened. And, despite the money, he had found himself wondering in recent months whether celebrity was all it was cracked up to be.

Suzy stood up. She looked pale. And very frightened. 'OK. We'll go now. Brad probably won't be here till eleven anyway.'

He looked at the can of lager, still full, and put it down. He didn't want a drink-driving charge on top of his other worries. 'Come on. We'll take my car.'

He led her out of the house gently, made sure everything was locked up and set the burglar alarm. You couldn't be too careful, even in what the Wakefields considered to be the middle of nowhere.

The lanes were pitch dark and the headlights of Darren's SUV picked out moths and shy night creatures in their merciless beam. A rabbit bounded out of their path into the high hedgerow. It looked as terrified as Suzy felt. She dug her nails into the passenger seat and held her breath.

Once they caught sight of another pair of headlights coming towards them and Darren pulled into a passing place. Suzy swore softly under her breath, furious that someone had the audacity to impede their progress.

'Calm down, will you,' said Darren, sounding as agitated as she was. 'According to this map, we're nearly there. Can you see anything?'

Suzy strained her eyes. They were coming to a T-junction. A signpost stood against the hedgerow. Darren pulled the car over into another passing place and got out, leaving the engine running and the headlights on to light up the black velvet darkness.

His calculations were right. One finger of the signpost pointed to Tradmouth, one to Burnington and the third to Derenham. This was the place.

Then he saw it. The gibbet. Many years ago men and women had been hanged at these crossroads and their mortal remains left there to rot and feed the crows as a warning to others. Darren shuddered. The sudden feeling of dread he'd just experienced suggested to him that their unhappy spirits were still about, watching his every move in the still night air.

He stood for a few moments staring at the gibbet which was illuminated by the headlamps of the SUV. There was something attached to the shaft of the gibbet, an envelope taped to the rough, rotting wood. Gingerly he crossed the lane and pulled at it and it came off with a noise that sounded like ripping paper.

This was a joke. It had to be.

His fingers were trembling as he opened the envelope clumsily, tearing at it to get to its contents.

He stood there in the headlights reading the neatly printed words on the thin yellow paper.

'If you love Leah and you want her returned you must pay fifty thousand pounds for her continued survival. We'll say where and when. Wait for instructions and don't tell the police. If you do we'll cut her throat.'

Darren stared at the note, suddenly paralysed with fear.

Maybe it wasn't a joke after all.

Chapter Five

Letter from Elizabeth Bentham to Letitia Corly, 19th June 1815

My dearest Letitia,

How the bells have been ringing out to celebrate the great victory at Waterloo. I am quite deafened by their clamour.

I pray that all is well with your mother and that her trouble is much relieved. I shall send a servant with a decoction of rosemary in wine which is a sovereign remedy for giddiness and the falling sickness.

The damp weather of late troubles my new sister-in-law. You have yet to meet dear Juanita but I must tell you that her complexion is dark. It is said that her grandmother was a freed slave and her father – a gentleman of London – did meet and marry her mother on the island of Nevis. Who would have thought to have so exotic a flower here in the midst of our little society, but it seems that she pleases all who meet her with her gentle manner and dark eyes.

When my brother met with her, she was governess to the daughters of a Mrs Jewel in Brighton, a person of good standing and great fashion, as are all in that town now the Prince Regent has built his great pavilion there. I have heard that it is the most astounding creation, more outlandish than any other sight on earth.

Tonight I shall attend a meeting in the house of Lord Penworthy. Lady Penworthy has assured me that I shall see strange and wonderful things there. Juanita does not wish to accompany me so it seems that I must go alone.

Your most affectionate friend, Elizabeth Bentham

* * *

Wesley arrived at the police station early that Friday morning. He knew that there was a mound of papers on his desk awaiting his attention. And he wanted to have another look through Barry Houldsworth's notebooks.

He hadn't heard from Adrian Fallbrook for a day or so. Perhaps everything was going swimmingly. Perhaps Adrian was entertaining his long-lost brother, feasting on the proverbial fatted calf. Or perhaps, more likely, he was still uncertain how to react and awaiting developments. Wesley resolved to call him later and ask whether Mark Jones had contacted him about taking the DNA test he mentioned. At least science would settle the matter one way or another. If the test was ever taken.

Progress on the Barber case was slow and in some ways Wesley wished he would strike again; wished he'd make some stupid mistake that would give him away. Not that he wanted anyone to be harmed, but at that moment they had so little to go on and he was hungry for some new clue that would lead to an arrest.

The car he used was a common type and it had no distinguishing marks; no scratches, no broken sidelights. On first glance it appeared to be just another minicab: somebody's car by day, transformed with the appropriate stickers and licence plate to a private hire vehicle at night. But the licence plates and minicab logos were false and so was the registration number.

Then there was the question of his appearance. The descriptions the victims provided had been different every time. That meant there was either more than one of them out there or, more likely he was disguising himself, in which case he was going to a great deal of trouble to achieve his ends . . . whatever they were.

The chief inspector's glass fronted office was still in darkness. He looked at his watch. Presumably Heffernan would still be at home. He'd never been an early riser.

People were starting to drift in, discarding dripping umbrellas in the stand provided and complaining, as only the British can complain, about the vagaries of the weather. Wesley walked over to the window and looked out. The office overlooked the river which was a deep shade of grey under the glowering sky.

The rain seemed to be easing off so Wesley grabbed his waterproof coat, told DC Paul Johnson he and DCI Heffernan were going to talk to a possible witness, and left the office. He half walked, half ran out of the police station and marched past the boat float, down the High Street, making for Baynards Quay. He needed to talk to Gerry Heffernan away from the office; to share his thoughts and ideas before Gerry was summoned on high to report to CS Nutter or Wesley was diverted by the investigation.

He hurried through a narrow street of medieval houses, their top storeys jutting out over the road, keeping the rain off the walkers below, until he reached the cobbled quayside. To his left was the river. The tide was high and the moored boats gyrated violently on the slate-coloured water. Gerry's cottage was at the end of the row of houses, the smallest dwelling, separated from the Tradmouth Arms by a narrow road. Wesley opened the wooden gate, crossed the tiny front garden and knocked at the door.

'Hope the Nutter hasn't sent you to get me out of bed,' were the big man's first words as he opened the door. He was attempting to do up his stained tie with clumsy fingers and he had the haunted look of a man who knows he's late for work.

'Don't worry. I've given you a cast-iron alibi. We're out interviewing a witness.'

'A witness to what?'

Wesley grinned. 'Take your pick. I just thought we needed some breathing space. You look tired, Gerry. You OK?'

Heffernan grunted in the affirmative and led the way into a small living room which was as neat as his desk at the police station was untidy. He closed the door and sat down.

'I had a late night last night, that's all,' he said in a hushed voice. 'I met Joyce for a drink. She needed to talk to someone. It looks like it's inevitable that her mum'll have to go into a nursing home. The Alzheimer's is getting worse all the time. Joyce had to come home from work yesterday because she'd got out of the house and was wandering in the road.'

'I'm sorry to hear that,' said Wesley.

'There's a vacancy at a place in Morbay . . . Sedan House. Joyce is going to have a look at it.'

At that moment Wesley heard a sound outside the door. Heffernan suddenly fell silent and put his finger to his lips.

'What's up?' Wesley whispered as the door opened to reveal Rosie Heffernan, bleary-eyed and yawning, dressed in a long T-shirt. She registered Wesley's presence and raised a sleepy hand in greeting.

'You're up early, love,' said Heffernan, the indulgent father. 'There's tea in the pot.'

'Thanks, Dad. I'll help myself, shall I?' she said as if she half expected her father to wait on her.

'Yeah, you do that, love. Me and Wes have got things to talk about.'

Rosie grinned and turned to go.

'And put the kettle on again while you're at it, eh.' Heffernan said hopefully.

'What did your last servant die of?' She flung the words over her shoulder affectionately before disappearing.

Heffernan leaned forward. 'Look, Wes ... er, don't mention Joyce when Rosie's around. She doesn't know yet and ... '

'You should tell her. She'll find out sooner or later.'

'The job helps. Whenever I'm out I tell her I'm on duty.'

Wesley shook his head. Gerry Heffernan could face down armed robbers and murderers but his five-feet-two-inch daughter was a different question.

Heffernan sighed and changed the subject. 'So what's new?'

'I've been worried about this Marcus Fallbrook business.'

'Why? If he takes a DNA test and he's a match, that'll settle it.'

'Maybe. But there's still the question of who kidnapped him.'

'You want to talk to him again?'

Wesley nodded. 'And I want to interview the nanny, Jenny Booker. Houldsworth's convinced she had something to do with it. If the nanny abducted him, she'd have probably made sure that he came to no harm. Even if the boyfriend arranged it all and wanted to kill him, she'd have put her foot down, I'm sure of it. We're not talking Myra Hindley here ... just a girl who's got in with the wrong bloke and things got out of hand.'

'You could be right. But Houldsworth said they couldn't prove anything against her at the time?'

'Yes. But from reading Houldsworth's notes it seems they went rather easy on her. She was very upset by it all ... almost hysterical.'

'Understandable – unless it was all an act.'

'That's what I want to find out.'

'What about the boyfriend? What was his name?'

'Gordon Heather. I think it's important that we trace him as well.'

'This Mark Jones claims that he remembers nothing about the actual abduction. That's suspicious, don't you think?'

Wesley shrugged. He was no expert on the effects of a traumatic experience on the human memory but he knew that it wasn't uncommon for such events to be suppressed or obliterated. And being snatched from your family at the age of seven is about as traumatic as it gets. 'All we can do is wait for the results of the DNA test and take it from there.' He hesitated for a moment. 'My mother-in-law called round last night.'

'Oh dear. I am sorry,' said Heffernan with a chuckle. 'How is Red Della these days?'

'Still keeping several Australian vineyards in business single handed. But she did have something interesting to say. She used to work with someone who was friendly with the Fallbrooks at the time of the kidnapping – lady by the name of Linda Tranter. She gave me the address. It's in Upper Town. Not far away.'

'Think we should pay her a visit?'

'Can't do any harm,' he answered, trying to sound casual, relieved that his boss seemed to be as curious about the reappearance of Marcus Fallbrook – or Mark Jones – as he was. 'We should ring her first. If she's an elderly lady, it might not be a good idea to turn up on her doorstep out of the blue.'

Wesley pulled his mobile out of his pocket and made the call. But when he had finished speaking Gerry Heffernan could see the disappointment on his face. 'Well?'

'She said she'd see us at four.'

'Pity. That means we'll have to go back to the station.' He looked around. 'Doesn't look as if Rosie's going to bring us that tea. Anything new come in on the Barber case?'

'He's still keeping one step ahead of us.' Wesley's inner pessimist was rising to the surface again.

'Once more unto the breach dear friends . . . ' Heffernan mumbled under his breath as he stood up and reached for his coat.

Brad Williams must have driven from London in record time because he had arrived only an hour after Suzy and Darren had returned from picking up the note. The three of them talked into the early hours and overnight Brad turned from staunchest ally to the enemy within. And the next morning Suzy Wakefield found herself hating him.

'I'm not going to the police,' she said for the umpteenth time. She was exhausted. She'd tried to sleep but had lain awake, the words of the note echoing in her head. Someone wanted to cut Leah's throat. Someone out there had her little girl and he – or she, although she was sure a woman wasn't capable of such cruelty – was willing to kill the daughter she had given birth to and raised; was willing to take a precious life for money.

There was no doubt in Suzy's mind. The ransom had to be paid and paid quickly. Leah had to be brought home safe. Darren hadn't said much but it seemed that now he knew Brad wasn't involved – that this thing was for real – he had come to agree with her. He had changed his mind too about calling the police in. Maybe it was better, he said, to obey the kidnapper's instructions after all. Why take the risk of antagonising the bastard who was holding his daughter?

Brad Williams's was the only dissenting voice. He stated his case clearly and everything he said would probably have made sense to anyone who wasn't emotionally involved. Once the first ransom's paid, kidnappers usually up the ante. They keep hold of their hostage and demand more. They bleed you white and there's no guarantee whatsoever that the hostage will be released while he or she is playing the part of human cash machine. Leah, Brad claimed, would be killed anyway once she had outlived her usefulness. The only sensible course of action was to call in the police. They had experience. They had ways of tracing these people. They'd know exactly what to do.

Brad ignored Suzy's protestations that the note had forbidden any contact with the police. If Suzy and Darren didn't call them, he'd do it himself.

But the combined forces of Suzy and Darren prevented Brad from making the call. The image in the note of Leah's throat being cut was too strong to be overcome by common sense. Reluctantly, Brad agreed to wait and see what happened. The call could come any time. They wouldn't do anything hasty.

Brad had taken charge of domestic arrangements. He had called up the cleaner, the cook and the gardener, saying that their services wouldn't be required that day but they'd still be paid. Then he had made toast, which still remained soggy and cold in the kitchen. Nobody felt like eating. The three of them sat there, sipping coffee they could hardly taste, watching the telephone, willing it to ring.

And when the sound of the instrument finally pierced the silence, it was Suzy who grabbed the receiver, tears in her eyes.

*   *   *

77

Neil Watson gazed down at the bones that had been laid out on a table in the vestry. He had assured John Ventnor that this was a purely temporary arrangement, promising that he would take them to the mortuary as soon as he received the go-ahead from Dr Bowman.

He wondered whether to call Wesley. If the skeleton had been discovered anywhere but in a graveyard – and in a tomb whose date was certain beyond any doubt – he would have notified the police. But in this case, although foul play was almost certain, the fact that the body was more than seventy years old, meant any interest Wesley had in them would be personal rather than professional.

And the same went for the pathologist, Dr Colin Bowman. The St Merion's skeleton, Juanita Bentham's companion in death, wasn't really his concern. However, Neil had always lived by the principle that if you don't ask, you don't get and he made a call to Colin anyway. But he was to be disappointed.

Colin had sounded genuinely apologetic. Much as he'd have loved to oblige Neil, he was fully occupied with a drowned yachtsman and two road accident victims so he really couldn't fit in a suspected Regency murder. If it had been a present day murder, that would have been a different kettle of fish altogether. As soon as Neil had ended the call he had stood in the vestry, contemplating his next move.

After a few moments the answer came to him. It was so obvious, he didn't know why he hadn't thought of it before. He and Wesley had been at university with Una Gibson – now Dr Gibson. She had specialised in human burials and she'd worked with him on a couple of his past digs. She was a woman who knew her bones. And she was sure to oblige an old friend.

He made the call and, sure enough, Una said she'd drive down from Exeter where she was she was now teaching at the university. She had to take a class at ten thirty but she'd be there that afternoon. She'd sounded keen. Perhaps she'd fancied him after all, thought Neil, although he'd always sensed that she preferred Wesley. Or maybe it was just the bones she was interested in. Neil wasn't getting his hopes up.

It would be a while before Una could make it and, as the delicate work of moving the burials was proceeding smoothly, Neil made a decision. He left his colleagues and the contractors to their grim task and made for the Rectory.

John Ventnor made polite noises, as though he didn't mind at all being dragged away from composing his Sunday sermon. It was only his eyes and the surreptitious glances at his watch that gave away his irritation at having been interrupted.

But Neil's mind was focused on his quest and didn't notice the nuances.

The Rector came straight to the point. 'I hope you've come to tell me you've moved those bones out of the vestry. I want to get the reburials finished as soon as possible and . . . '

'Don't worry. It's all under control,' said Neil, dismissing the clergyman's concern with a casual wave of the hand. 'I just wondered if you knew of anyone who could help me find out more about these "Shining Ones" you mentioned.'

John Ventnor shook his head. 'I only know what I read in that old book I found. You're welcome to borrow it if you like. It's in the study.'

'Thanks. That'd be great. Is there anyone around here who'd know more about them?'

'There's a retired teacher called Lionel Grooby who takes a great interest in the history of the village. When I first came here he was keen to let me know that he'd traced his family tree back to the Amazing Devon Marvel.' There was a slight smirk on Ventnor's lips.

'The what?'

'The Amazing Devon Marvel. He was some sort of child prodigy – did mathematical calculations in public.'

Neil raised his eyebrows. 'So this Grooby's likely to know about these Shining Ones?'

'I'm not sure but it's worth having a word with him. Or you could try Tradmouth library. They've got a large local history section.' He smiled encouragingly, hoping that Neil would take the hint and leave him in peace.

But Neil didn't move. 'Er . . . that book. Can I borrow it?'

'Sure,' said the Rector as he made for the study door, trying to hide his impatience. 'There's not much in it about the Shining Ones, I'm afraid. It just says the sect was started by a local woman and in its heyday, she had a lot of followers around here.'

He disappeared into the study and re-emerged a couple of seconds later holding a dull brown book which he handed to Neil as though it were a hot coal.

'These Shining Ones didn't go in for human sacrifice by any chance, did they?' Neil asked, thinking of the boy whose throat had been cut.

The Rector laughed. 'In Stoke Beeching? I doubt it.' He looked at his watch and suddenly assumed a serious expression. 'I'm sorry, Neil, but I really must get on. You'll let me know when I can . . .'

'Sure. No problem,' said Neil unconvincingly as he wandered off with the book tucked under his arm.

The call came through at one o'clock. A man called Brad Williams wanted a word with someone senior from CID.

Gerry Heffernan, muttering under his breath grudgingly agreed to talk to the presumptuous Mr Williams. It was probably a trivial matter, he thought; something that could easily have been dealt with by uniform. Williams was probably the sort who tried to get let off a traffic offence by claiming to be a close friend of the Chief Constable and Gerry Heffernan had no time for people like that. As he waited for the man to be put through he tried to think up something clever to say – something that would get Williams off his back while at the same time ensuring that he wouldn't be reported to his superiors for rudeness.

He opened the conversation with a wary, 'Hello, Mr Williams. DCI Heffernan here. What can I do for you?' So far so good. Surely the man couldn't take offence at that.

Gerry leaned back in his swivel chair, waiting to hear a sorry tale of a theft of a mobile phone or a trivial theft from the caller's, undoubtedly large, yacht. He took a deep breath and prepared to make soothing noises and standard answers.

But what the man said stunned him into silence for a few seconds.

'Did you hear me? Hello, are you still there?'

'Yes, Mr Williams. Can you repeat what you just said?'

'I don't want to speak too loud,' the man said in a stage whisper. 'They don't know I'm ringing you. But I think you should know. Leah Wakefield's been kidnapped. There's been a ransom demand.'

'Leah Wakefield? The singer?'

'Yes. I'm her manager.' Something, a slight wariness, in his voice suggested that he was holding something back. 'Look, I

80

want this dealt with discreetly. They say they'll kill her if the police are called. Her parents don't want the police involved but I thought . . . '

'You were quite right to call us. The family can't deal with this on their own.' He looked at his watch. 'Can we meet somewhere? Not the house – they could be watching the house.'

Once the arrangements were made Gerry Heffernan put the phone down and sat staring at the instrument, wondering if he had imagined the whole conversation. A kidnapped star. A secret meeting with her manager. The whole thing had a slightly surreal feel about it for a man more used to collaring various representatives of South Devon's rogues' gallery of petty criminals and murdering inadequates. Perhaps it was someone's idea of a joke. Not that he could see the funny side.

He stood up, sending a pile of papers on his desk flying onto the floor. He'd deal with them later, in the meantime he needed to share his strange knowledge with Wesley Peterson. He knew he could rely on his second-in-command to tell him straight if he thought the whole thing was some sort of hoax.

The meeting place was St Margaret's church. As Gerry Heffernan sang in the choir there he knew every inch of the place. And he knew that the flowers were arranged on Friday afternoons, ready for Saturday weddings and Sunday services so any suspicious stranger would stand out in the cool, gloomy interior like a shark in a goldfish bowl.

Wesley said little as they walked together down the narrow streets to the church. Heffernan guessed that he was keeping an open mind, not judging until he knew all the facts.

When they reached the church, Heffernan hesitated for a second before raising the heavy iron latch. The sound echoed through the building, announcing their arrival like a fanfare. They stepped inside and allowed their eyes to adjust to the gloom.

St Margaret's church smelled of wax polish. Several grey-haired ladies were bustling around with bright flowers.

Wesley gave his boss a nudge. He had just spotted a man who looked as though he didn't belong there. Dressed in an expensive soft leather jacket, he lounged in one of the back pews watching the scene of calm industry as an anthropologist might watch the activities of some newly discovered Amazonian tribe.

They began to walk towards the stranger, moving casually so as not to draw attention to themselves. As they approached the man stood up. He looked jumpy, nervous.

'You the police,' were his first words, spoken in an instinctive whisper.

Both men showed their ID discreetly and introduced themselves before sitting down, Heffernan beside the man on the back pew. Wesley sat on the pew in front and twisted round. Gerry Heffernan spotted a lady he knew from the choir carrying a bucket of lilies and he gave her a friendly wave. He waited until she was well out of earshot before speaking.

'So when did Leah Wakefield go missing? What happened exactly?'

'She, er ... walked out on Wednesday evening. Suzy – that's her mum – presumed she'd gone to a friend's or a hotel.'

'How did she leave? Did she drive or ... ?'

'According to Suzy, she'd had a bit to drink. I presume she phoned a taxi or ... '

'OK. We can find that out from her mobile phone company,' said Wesley. If this case was genuine, they'd have to explore every avenue. 'So she just left the house without saying where she intended to go?'

As Williams leaned forward, Wesley caught a whiff of his expensive aftershave. 'That's right. Suzy phoned round all the places she might have been. No luck. Then she got a phone call. Suzy said the voice sounded electronic and she couldn't tell if it was a man or a woman. It said Leah wouldn't be harmed if she did as she was told.' He hesitated. 'And it said not to tell the police.'

'They always say that,' said Wesley, trying to sound as if he knew what he was talking about. The truth was that he had never dealt with a kidnapping before in his life and he felt apprehensive, wary of the unknown. 'Don't worry, we can be very discreet,' he added reassuringly. 'What happened next?'

'Suzy got another call. It told her to go to the old gibbet on the crossroads not far from Derenham. Where the roads to Derenham, Tradmouth and Burnington meet. More a T-junction than a crossroads, I suppose,' he added, his nervousness having rendered him pedantic. 'Suzy and Darren went there and found this note.' He produced a plastic bag containing a plain envelope and a sheet of yellow paper.

Wesley took it from him. In the corner of the bag he saw a

crudely hacked crescent of fingernail immaculately varnished in opalescent blue. 'What's this?' he asked.

Williams swallowed hard. 'They said they'd send proof they had her. Suzy says that's exactly the colour of nail varnish she was wearing when she disappeared. It's an unusual shade. Leah's favourite.' He waved his hand impatiently at the sheet of paper. 'Read the note.'

Wesley read out loud. 'If you love Leah and you want her returned you must pay fifty thousand pounds for her continued survival. We'll say where and when. Wait for instructions and don't tell the police. If you do we'll cut her throat.' He turned to Gerry Heffernan whose face gave nothing away.

Dredging his memory, Wesley tried to think why Leah Wakefield's ransom note seemed so familiar. He had read something very similar recently, he was sure of it. Maybe it was the Marcus Fallbrook case. The notes sent to the Fallbrooks had been on the same coloured paper and he was sure that the wording was similar. He'd have to check it out as soon as he returned to the office. There was always the possibility that he could be wrong.

'Have the family heard anything more?' Heffernan asked.

Williams shook his head. 'They're taking their time. Bastards,' he spat. 'You should see the state Suzy's in . . . '

'I can imagine,' Wesley said quickly. 'Look, we should get all incoming phone calls monitored . . . and someone should be with the family.'

'They said not to call the police. What if they're watching the house?'

'We can do discretion, you know.' Heffernan sounded almost hurt. 'We're hardly going to scream up to the front door with our sirens blazing.'

Williams eyed the chief inspector, unsure whether to believe him. With his large, unkempt frame and his broad Liverpool accent, he hardly looked like the ideal undercover man.

Wesley thought for a moment. 'I presume the Wakefields have tradesmen in . . . cleaners?'

Williams nodded.

'In that case we can fix things so that even if they're watching the place, they won't suspect a thing.' Wesley glanced at his boss. 'We'll use officers who are used to undercover work. OK?'

Williams hesitated for a moment then nodded.

'And you'd better let Mrs Wakefield know the situation. We don't want any complications. Will you do that? Go back now and sit tight.'

Wesley's words seemed to have the right effect. Williams nodded meekly and, after he had written down the Wakefields' address on the back of one of his business cards, he stood up.

'Don't say a word to anyone else, will you?' Wesley reminded him gently. 'We need to ensure that we don't make waves if we want to get Leah back safely.'

'Too right,' said Williams with feeling. 'I've got a lot of money riding on that little cow.'

With that he stood up and sauntered out of the church, letting the door slam behind him.

Acting was one of Rachel Tracey's many talents. She had been at one time a member of the divisional amateur dramatic society and, more recently, her mother had persuaded her to take a small part in a recently discovered Elizabethan play that had been performed at the Neston Arts Festival earlier in the year.

Now she was to tackle the role of cleaner to the Wakefield family and, to convince any malevolent onlooker, she had borrowed a nondescript twelve-year-old Ford Fiesta from one of the young women in the control room, donned a blue nylon overall and scraped her hair back off her face as though preparing to get stuck in to cleaning the Wakefields' many bathrooms.

Fifteen minutes later, by agreement, a dark-haired young man called Tim from scientific support arrived to set up the equipment that would allow them to record and monitor any phone calls. He arrived in a battered white van and ostentatiously carried sections of copper pipe into the house, his electronic equipment concealed in what a casual observer would assume to be a set of plumber's tool boxes.

Once they were both inside the house they each went about their task. Tim set up the equipment quietly and efficiently, testing the system with his own mobile phone and when he'd finished he spent ten minutes telling Rachel how everything worked. She listened intently and repeated the instructions, just to make sure they were fixed in her head.

When Tim was about to leave he gave her a smile and she couldn't help noticing that he was rather attractive. In fact with his longish dark hair, his blue eyes and his infectious grin she found herself wondering why she hadn't noticed him before. Then Tim himself provided the answer. He'd been working in Exeter since he left university and he was new in Tradmouth.

Rachel was summoning the courage to suggest that if he didn't know many people in Tradmouth, maybe she could introduce him to what little there was of the town's night life. Then she realised that she might be stuck there with the Wakefields for the duration and by the time she'd thought of a way of opening up the prospect of a future assignation, he'd gone, taking his copper piping and tool boxes with him. It was the story of her life.

Fortunately, the kidnapper hadn't called before their arrival. This had been Wesley Peterson's chief worry – that they'd be too late and Suzy Wakefield would have hared off to leave a large sum of money at some unspecified destination with no backup, police or otherwise. Desperate mothers aren't renowned for their straight thinking.

Rachel, with her practised blend of sympathy and common sense, was used to putting the families of victims at their ease. But waiting for a call from a kidnapper was a new experience for her. And Suzy Wakefield wasn't making things easy.

As soon as she'd entered the house, she'd discarded the prickly nylon overall and concentrated on gaining Suzy's trust. But Leah Wakefield's mother, fortified by vodka and coke, hardly seemed to notice she was there. Most of the time she sat in brooding silence, lashing out occasionally with bitter comments about her former husband not caring about his daughter and haranguing Brad Williams half heartedly for calling in the police when they'd been instructed quite clearly not to.

Rachel wouldn't have trusted Darren Wakefield an inch and the same went for Brad Williams. But she had to accept that even though she wasn't going to take a liking to any of the ménage, she was there to help them . . . whether they wanted it or not. In the meantime she could only make cups of tea, question Suzy and Darren tactfully, and await the kidnapper's next call.

To Rachel, used to living in a cosy old farm house, the lounge of the Wakefields' neo-Georgian mansion seemed to be the size of a football pitch, thickly carpeted in cream with chandeliers and a huge mirrored drinks cabinet in the corner. As soon as she spotted the cabinet she mentally practised saying the words 'not while I'm on duty, thank you,' with professional coolness. But as a drink was never offered, she didn't have the opportunity to use·them and establish the moral high ground.

As she sank into the white leather sofa, keeping an eye on the telephone, she glanced at her watch. It was four o'clock already and the abductor still hadn't made contact.

Whoever had Leah Wakefield was taking his time. Making them sweat.

Dr Una Gibson bent over the bones, running her fingers gently over the top of the skull.

Una was tall with unruly auburn hair, abundant freckles, an aquiline nose and that elusive quality, charisma. Boudicca in a lab coat, someone had once called her when they were students.

It was several minutes before she completed her examination and turned to Neil Watson. 'You were absolutely right. This poor lad's had his throat cut.' She paused for a few moments. 'At least I think it's a lad. It's sometimes difficult to sex adolescents and I'd put the age as around thirteen from the eruption of the teeth, although he's quite small for his age – poor nourishment during early childhood at a guess.' She stared at the bones for a few more seconds. 'Yes, I'm as sure as I can be that it's a boy although the changes occur gradually during the pubescent years. See the pelvis . . . and the supra-orbital . . . and the sloping frontal bone . . . and the chin looks more square than . . . '

'So it's a boy or a very butch-looking girl?'

Una began to laugh, a hearty laugh that seemed rather inappropriate in the presence of death. A life-affirming laugh. 'Got it in one. But I'd put money on it being a boy. Where did you say he was found?'

Neil frowned. 'That's the peculiar thing. He was in the same coffin as a woman called Juanita Bentham. The plate on the coffin lid said that she died in 1816 aged twenty-seven. No mention of our young friend here.'

'He's unlikely to have been her son then. Mind you, fourteen-year-olds have been known to have babies. Perhaps we should do DNA tests . . . '

'Too late, she's already been reburied in another part of the church-yard. And anyway, I don't think he's her son. A young baby might be buried with its mother but a teenager in the same coffin . . . '

86

'You're probably right,' Una conceded. She had a sudden thought. 'It must have been a big coffin.'

'I didn't look at it very carefully, but now you come to mention it, I think it was a bit deeper than usual.'

'Specially made.' Una raised her finely plucked eyebrows. 'Wasn't there a Sherlock Holmes story about someone being buried underneath a corpse in a specially made coffin? A perfect way to dispose of a body.'

'Wesley Peterson'll know the story. He always liked Holmes.'

'How is Wesley? Do you see much of him?'

'Yeah. He's fine.'

A secretive smile crept across Una's lips. 'I always thought he was rather nice. He married that girl from the English department, didn't he?'

'Pam, yeah. They've got two young kids.'

'Nice,' Una muttered. Neil couldn't decide whether the word was said with envy or contempt.

Neil thought he'd better change the subject. 'So can you tell me any more about how the poor lad died?'

Una returned her attention to the skeleton that lay before them on a clean white sheet. 'In my opinion he was killed with some kind of sharp knife. His murderer probably cut his throat from behind in which case he must have been right handed.' She pointed to the marks on the bone. 'See, the marks are slightly deeper on the left-hand side. A great deal of force was used. The poor lad was almost decapitated.'

Neil shuddered.

'I wonder who he was.'

Una touched his arm. 'Can't help you there, I'm afraid. You could always get Wesley to give you a hand.' She grinned. 'In which case, let me know, won't you. It'd be good to see him again.'

'I reckon he'll be busy at the moment. Some nutcase is going round abducting blondes and chopping all their hair off. It's been in all the papers.'

Una's hand went up instinctively to her own abundant curls. 'So what's your next move? Any thoughts on how we can identify our victim?'

'I'm told there's a retired teacher in the village who seems to be the keeper of the flame as far as Stoke Beeching's local history is concerned.'

'Then it might be worth having a word with him.'

Neil shrugged his shoulders. The retired teacher, Lionel Grooby, probably bored for England but it would do no harm to ask a few questions. 'I'll try and see him tomorrow.' He cleared his throat. 'Fancy a drink?'

Una hesitated for a moment. 'Why not?'

It was a short walk from St Margaret's church to the police station and Wesley had done it in record time, Gerry Heffernan panting behind him, trying to keep up.

'You should take more exercise, Gerry,' Wesley commented as he ascended the stairs to the CID office, two at a time.

Heffernan's reply was mumbled and incomprehensible. Wesley assumed it was something rude.

Once back in the office, Wesley made straight for his desk where the files on the Marcus Fallbrook case had been placed neatly in the top drawer. He took out the top file and opened it up before searching through the papers for the ransom note.

He pulled it out and placed it on the desk before pulling the plastic bag containing the note Leah Wakefield's family had received from his pocket. The two notes lay side by side and Wesley looked from one to the other. He'd been right. The paper was the same and the wording was almost identical. The only difference being the victim's name and the amount of money demanded. The sum had increased considerably: whether this was because of inflation or the perceived financial position of the victims' respective families, he wasn't sure.

His heart was beating fast as he made his way to the office where Gerry Heffernan had taken refuge. He'd want to know about this.

Heffernan was talking on the phone when he opened the office door. When he put the receiver down, he looked straight at Wesley. 'That was Rach. Nothing doing yet. He's taking his time.'

Wesley placed the two notes on the boss's desk. 'Look at these. What do you see?'

Heffernan stared at them, scratched his head and swore softly under his breath. Then he looked Wesley in the eye. 'Are you thinking what I'm thinking?'

'Well the paper seems identical and the wording's similar but it's impossible. It was 1976.'

'So our man was youngish then and he's decided to have another go. Maybe he's been doing the same thing abroad somewhere . . . or he's suddenly fallen on hard times and remembered his nice little earner.'

'But could it be the same man? Has Marcus Fallbrook's kidnapper just abducted Leah Wakefield?'

Heffernan stood up and began to pace up and down the office. 'I've no idea. But I'll tell you what though, Wes. A seven-year-old kid would be a lot easier to handle than that little madam Leah Wakefield. Even if Mark Jones is Marcus Fallbrook and they let him go for some reason, there's no guarantee that they can risk releasing the girl.'

He had just put Wesley's thoughts into words. The spoiled Leah, darling of the album charts and, more recently, the tabloids, would be more of an irritation and a danger to a kidnapper than an terrified seven-year-old prep school boy. Suddenly he was afraid for Leah Wakefield. Very afraid indeed.

He sat down, trying to get things straight in his mind. 'Look, Gerry,' he said after a few moments. 'If this Mark Jones is really who he says he is, he might be able to help us. Perhaps he can give us some lead about the kidnapper . . . if it is the same one.'

'No reason to believe it isn't. If he was in his late teens or early twenties in 1976, he's be in his late forties or early fifties now. And more experienced . . . less likely to cock things up.'

'I presume the wording of the note wasn't publicised at the time.'

'I doubt it. But we can double check with Barry Houldsworth. Why don't you give Mark Jones a ring, arrange to have another chat? The sooner the better in my opinion.'

'Yes, I'll do that.' Wesley looked at his watch. 'It's quarter to four. Remember we're seeing Linda Tranter at four . . . Della's old colleague.'

Gerry Heffernan nodded. 'If this woman knew the Fallbrooks at the time she might be able to tell us something that isn't in the files.'

'Something Barry Houldsworth never got to hear about?'

'I've always had this theory, Wes, that people only tell the police the sanitised version of events. If you know everything's going to be written down and likely to be read out in court, you don't share the gossip and speculation, do you . . . the things people chat about when they're off their guard?'

Wesley grinned. 'And that's what we want, isn't it ... a bit of gossip and speculation?'

A couple of minutes later they were on their way to see Linda Tranter, Della's former teaching colleague, now retired. She lived in the Upper Town, on the road leading to the castle. The Upper Town lived up to its name. Its streets wound round the contours of the steep land that tumbled down to Tradmouth's medieval heart. Seen from the river, the neat pastel-coloured houses looked like toys clinging precariously to the hillside but as Wesley walked along the street, admiring the spectacular view of the river to his left, the buildings seemed all too solid. He passed a terrace of houses which, he guessed would once have housed the families of sea captains, before arriving at a double-fronted detached house, its white stucco façade gleaming like a wedding cake.

As they climbed Mrs Tranter's steep garden path, the fluffy clouds raced away and the sun came out, suddenly turning the river from grey to dull blue with diamond ripples dancing on the surface. But they had no time to appreciate the beauties of nature.

Mrs Tranter must have been watching for them from her window because the door was opened a split second after Wesley had rung the door bell. She ushered them in as if she was anxious to get them out of view before the neighbours saw the police were calling.

Linda Tranter was a large lady with a taste for bright, Indian clothes. A skirt printed with golden elephants swirled around her substantial ankles and an emerald green silk scarf was tied around her steel-grey hair, holding back a long ponytail. The words aging hippie leapt into Gerry Heffernan's mind but in his experience aging hippies were a harmless breed, being too busy with artistic pursuits and New Age activities to hold up banks or commit multiple murders.

'You must be Della Stannard's son-in-law,' she gushed at Wesley. 'She rang me yesterday out of the blue and said you'd be in touch. I'm delighted to meet you.'

Wesley smiled amiably like a good son-in-law should. After he'd introduced Gerry Heffernan, Linda led them into a cluttered living room, filled with souvenirs of travel, mainly, Wesley guessed, to the Indian subcontinent. The two policemen, realising that some things couldn't be rushed, made themselves comfortable on the worn corduroy sofa and awaited the arrival of tea and scones. There were some things you couldn't fight against and the hospitality of a retired widowed lady was one of them.

Once Wesley had consumed his first, surprisingly excellent scone, he came to the point of their visit. 'I understand you were a friend of the Fallbrook family at the time their son, Marcus, went missing.'

Linda raised her hand to her substantial breast. 'It was a terrible business. Tragic. It killed Anna Fallbrook, you know. They say stress can bring on cancer, don't they? I lost touch with Jacob after Anna died although I did hear he'd married again and had another son. The second wife died too, you know, quite recently. And Jacob just last month.' She shuddered. 'It's almost as if there's a curse on that family. Don't you agree, Wesley?'

Wesley had to nod. He guessed it was expected of him.

'Is there any particular reason you're asking questions about poor little Marcus's abduction after all these years?' she asked.

The two policemen exchanged looks. There was no fooling this woman that this was just a routine enquiry. Gerry Heffernan leaned forward. 'Look, love, I'd be very grateful if you'd keep this to yourself . . . '

'I'm not a gossip, Chief Inspector,' she sounded rather hurt.

'Of course not,' said Wesley quickly. 'It's just that it's a rather delicate matter and it's not easy for Adrian Fallbrook . . . that's Jacob's son by his second wife.'

Linda tilted her head to one side expectantly. They'd come this far, Wesley thought, and if they didn't confide in her he suspected she wouldn't confide in them. He took a deep breath.

'A man turned up at the Fallbrooks' house in Derenham.'

'Mirabilis. They called it Mirabilis. Not very appropriate as it turned out. Tempting fate almost,' said Linda solemnly.

'Quite. Well a man turned up at Mirabilis a few days ago claiming to be Marcus Fallbrook.'

Linda frowned and took a shuddering breath. 'Surely he's lying.'

'He agreed to take a DNA test. And he remembers a lot about the house and the family. He even looks like Adrian. There's a definite resemblance.'

She bowed her head. 'Oh dear. If it's true it makes Anna's death more tragic, doesn't it? If he was alive somewhere all the time . . . '

91

'Yes,' said Wesley softly watching Linda's face. She was clearly upset. Grieving for her friend Anna Fallbrook even after all this time.

'You and Anna were close?'

'We'd known each other since we were small. My parents were her godparents and vice versa. We were each other's bridesmaids. She was an artist, you know ... very talented. She used to exhibit at local galleries.' She looked Wesley in the eye. 'Look, if you want to ask me any questions about the Fallbrooks, I don't mind. I'd just like you to get to the truth ... for Anna's sake. She was a very special person.'

'Thanks, love,' said Heffernan, helping himself to another scone. 'Tell us about the Fallbrooks, eh. What kind of family were they?'

Linda Tranter sat in silence for a few moments, as though choosing her words carefully. 'I wouldn't have called them a happy family. Jacob and Anna ... ' She sighed. 'There was something wrong. I could sense it. But Anna never talked about it, even to me.'

'Is it possible Jacob was violent towards her or Marcus?'

'Jacob never struck me as a violent man. But then you can never tell what goes on behind closed doors, can you?'

'You don't think ... ' Wesley hesitated. The question was delicate but it had to be asked. 'Is it possible Jacob was abusing Marcus in some way?'

'You mean sexually?' She shook her head. 'It's not something that ever occurred to me at the time but then in those days nobody ever spoke about that sort of thing. The honest answer is that I don't know. I suppose it could be a possibility.'

'You didn't like Jacob?'

'To be honest, no, I didn't.'

Wesley and Heffernan exchanged glances. The notion that all wasn't well in the Fallbrook household opened up all kinds of new possibilities, none of which had been mentioned in Barry Houldsworth's notebooks.

'Could there had been someone else? Could Jacob have been having an affair?'

'If he was, Anna never mentioned it.'

Wesley thought he saw a flicker of wariness in Linda's eyes – there for a split second then gone. Or it might have been his imagination.

'What about Marcus's relationship with his parents?'

'I think he spent most of his time with his nanny. What was her name?'

'Jenny Booker.'

'That's right, Jenny. She seemed a sweet girl. But I don't think she was the sharpest knife in the box. Anna mentioned she had a boyfriend. She said he seemed rather peculiar . . . but I'm not sure what she meant.'

Wesley's ears pricked up. Barry Houldsworth had mentioned the nanny's boyfriend, Gordon Heather, and that he'd had no convictions at the time. He'd been meaning to find out whether he'd blotted his copybook since but he hadn't got round to it. He put it on his mental list of things to do.

'I suppose it was inevitable that Marcus spent a lot of time with Jenny and this boyfriend?' he said.

'I suppose it was. Jacob was a businessman and expected Anna to support him in the way wives used to in the olden days.' She smiled. 'And Anna was on a lot of committees, and there was her art as well, which was very important to her.'

'You think Marcus was neglected?'

'I wouldn't use the word neglected. Jenny was always there to entertain him.'

'He must have been very attached to Jenny.'

'I suppose he was.' She hesitated. 'Can I meet him? Can I meet this man who's claiming to be Marcus?'

Heffernan cleared his throat. 'We'll certainly ask him . . . see what he says.'

'A sort of test, you mean? If he doesn't want to meet his mother's oldest friend, he's a fraud?'

Heffernan smiled. 'You said it, love.'

'I was thinking more of offering him support . . . a chance to talk about his mother and the family.'

'Of course,' said Wesley. 'We'll try to arrange something, shall we?' he said as he stood up.

'You do know that Jenny died, don't you? She drowned about a year after Marcus disappeared. There was talk that she killed herself but . . . I think the inquest gave an open verdict.'

Wesley gaped at Linda Tranter for a few seconds then sat himself down again.

Chapter Six

From the Reverend Charles Boden to Sir John Bentham, 23rd July
1815

*I met with Matthew Hackworthy this day and he informed me that
his son, Peter, has been displaying the gifts the Lord has gra-
ciously granted to him at The Fisherman's Arms in Tradmouth
which is, by repute, a low tavern frequented by all manner of lewd
and common persons. I reiterate, sir, that a boy of his tender years
ought not to be used like some performing beast for the enrich-
ment of his grasping father and I beg you to put forward the good
offer of my Oxford acquaintance. A little thought will surely convince you of the rightness of this.*

*There is, sir, another matter that causes me concern. I have
heard tell that your sister, Elizabeth, has visited the house of Lord
Penworthy to see the woman Joan Shiner. This worries me greatly
as, in my opinion as a man of the cloth, the woman is nought but
a charlatan and a rogue. Does not the Good Book warn us to
beware of false prophets?*

I am, sir, your servant, Charles Boden

Rachel Tracey was bored. Nothing had happened and the strain of
waiting – and reassuring the Wakefields that everything was under
control – was taking its toll on her nerves. She looked at her
mobile phone. As soon as something happened she would report
in but in the meantime all she had to do was make endless cups of
tea and clear up the half-drunk cups. Suzy Wakefield had a nasty
habit of stubbing out her cigarettes inside her cup and leaving the
stubs floating like surfaced submarines in the cold brown dregs of
tea.

The Wakefields hardly seemed to notice that she had opened some windows to let some fresh air mingle with the fug of cigarette smoke. She worried fleetingly about the dangers posed by passive smoking as she watched Suzy Wakefield clear away the remains of the pizzas she had found in the freezer and cooked for their evening meal. Rachel and Brad Williams had finished theirs but Darren and Suzy Wakefield had only taken a few bites.

Rachel thought of her own bed and sighed. She supposed she'd be comfortable in the Wakefield's spare room – complete with marble tiled en suite bathroom – but she doubted if she'd be able to sleep.

Suzy had returned from the kitchen and was pacing the floor again, cigarette in hand. Darren who had been sitting, head in hands, suddenly jumped to his feet.

'Why don't they bloody ring? What's keeping them?' The question was greeted with embarrassed silence.

Rachel and Brad Williams caught each other's eye and he gave her a weak smile. Rachel had been observing Williams and had come to the conclusion that he either wasn't particularly worried or he was hiding it well. She had seen him reach out a hand to touch Suzy as she passed, locked in her own world of anxiety. She hadn't responded but Rachel sensed there was more between them than she'd been led to believe. Rachel wondered if they were or had been lovers. The slight, almost imperceptible, hostility in Darren's body language certainly suggested it.

Rachel was rather relieved when Suzy switched on the huge plasma screen television that hung on the wall over the fake Adam fireplace. At least it would provide some sort of distraction. But no sooner had the strains of the *EastEnders* theme begun than the telephone started to ring.

For a few seconds everyone froze. Then they all looked at Rachel for guidance. She picked up the remote control from the coffee table and flicked the TV off. They'd need all their wits and their concentration to get through this.

With nervous hands Rachel set the recording machine going, wishing Tim was there to make sure she was doing it right. Then she nodded to Suzy who picked up the receiver and said a breathless hello before her emotions overwhelmed her.

The words came pouring out, gabbled, her voice brittle with fear. 'Is she all right? Let me speak to her. Please . . . '

Then came a stunned silence. And from the crestfallen expression on Suzy's face, Rachel knew it wasn't the call they'd been expecting. She heard Suzy say 'No. No, don't come in tomorrow. I'll let you know.' Another silence. Then a curt 'Yes, of course you'll be paid. Look, I've got to go.'

She replaced the receiver carefully, terrified of leaving it off the hook so the call she was waiting for couldn't get through.

Rachel, who had been listening to the call on headphones, gave Suzy a sympathetic smile. 'Your cleaner?'

Suzy nodded.

'You did the right thing. The fewer people who know about this the better. But, er, perhaps next time it would be better if you just said hello and waited to see what the caller had to say.'

'Yeah. Right. I was in such a state, I wasn't thinking.'

Suzy flopped down on the sofa beside Rachel. She looked exhausted. And it was early days yet. These things sometimes took time – not that Rachel had had any experience in dealing with kidnappers' ransom demands. She was as much in the dark as the Wakefields. And, like them, all she knew came from TV police dramas. But she guessed that kidnappers liked to spin out the agony. To play the long game.

Then a sudden thought hit her. She looked at Brad Williams. 'Money. If they want the money tonight have you got it ready? We don't want to put Leah at risk by leaving a bag full of torn up newspaper. It's Saturday tomorrow. The banks are shut.'

Brad Williams smiled. 'I thought of that. I've brought some cash with me. Forty-five grand in used notes. And, if necessary, I'm sure we can rustle up the extra five grand from somewhere, eh Darren?'

Rachel raised her eyebrows. She had never encountered anybody who could carry around tens of thousands of pounds with such casual nonchalance before. Perhaps she had led a sheltered life.

The time passed slowly. The television had gone on again and the sound of arguing London voices filled the room as Suzy paced to and fro, chain smoking. Rachel had advised her against consuming more vodka and cokes in case she had to drive. Nobody was watching the goings-on on the screen but at least it provided a relief from the oppressive silence.

Rachel looked at her watch. Had something gone wrong? Or

was this just the kidnapper's way of keeping them on edge and desperate. And the desperate will agree to anything.

It was half an hour before the telephone rang again. And this time it was the call they'd been waiting for.

Neil Watson felt a little nervous as he stood on Wesley's doorstep. It was a while since he'd seen Pam. In fact, although he hated to admit it, he'd been avoiding her. Of course Wesley had never found out about the incident with Jonathan and, as far as Neil knew, the problem had gone away of its own accord. Everything had returned to normal and Neil was the only one who possessed the uncomfortable knowledge. But he'd much rather have remained in ignorance.

When Pam answered the door, she gave him a coy smile.

'Hi. Er . . . Is Wes in?'

She stood aside to let him in and touched his arm as he passed her. 'How are you, Neil? OK? We've not seen you for a while.'

Neil wasn't listening to the words she spoke. He was watching her face. Her eyes were pleading with him; pleading for him to say nothing; saying it had been a disastrous mistake. Asking forgiveness. He took her hand and squeezed it. 'I'm fine. You?'

She smiled with relief. 'Yeah. Me and Wes are both fine. And the kids. You know Michael's just started school?'

'Yeah. Wes said.' Being one who followed the advice of W.C. Fields and never concerned himself with children or animals, he was anxious to change the subject. 'I wanted to tell Wes that I've just seen an old friend of ours. I don't suppose you remember Una Gibson, do you? She studied archaeology with us. We used to call her Boudicca because of her red hair. I've just been for a drink with her but she had to get back to Exeter.'

'I think I know who you mean.' She stood aside. 'Go through. Wes is watching something about a shipwreck.'

Wesley stood up as Neil entered the living room, abandoning the murky underwater scene on the TV screen. As the two men greeted each other Pam scurried out to fetch a bottle of wine from the kitchen.

Neil sat down, hoping that sharing his dilemma with Wesley would make things clearer in his mind. He told him about Una and the skeleton that shouldn't have been there. The small adolescent male whose skull had grinned at him from behind Juanita Bentham's.

'Sounds interesting,' was all Wesley could think of to say. 'Let me know what you find out, won't you?'

Neil nodded, slightly disappointed. He had hoped for a little more enthusiasm. 'I'm meeting a bloke called Grooby tomorrow – he's a local historian. I want to check out these Benthams and find out who Juanita was and where she came from. I know the Benthams were squires so I'm hoping their lives were quite well documented. It's the Regency period . . . hardly the dark ages.' He looked at Wesley hopefully. 'Fancy coming with me to see this Grooby. It's Saturday tomorrow. They give you weekends off, don't they?'

Wesley was about to explain why he couldn't commit himself but a sudden attack of discretion stopped him. The less people who knew about Leah Wakefield's kidnapping, the better. Even friends and family might let something slip in earshot of the wrong person. 'I don't know. There's something big going on at work and I might be needed.'

Neil's eyes lit up. 'What is it? A bank robbery or . . . ?'

'Something like that,' Wesley said quickly. 'But if it turns out that I'm free, I'll give you a ring, shall I?'

Pam returned with the wine and three glasses but when she offered it round, Wesley and Neil refused. Neil was driving and there was a possibility Wesley might have to go out later if an expected phone call came. Pam poured herself a glass and took a sip of the ruby liquid, savouring it for a few seconds before telling the two men that there was orange juice in the fridge and water in the tap. Neil noticed the absence of dirty looks and snide remarks when Wesley mentioned the possibility of work disrupting his evening. It would take a while to get used to the new, chastened Pam.

Neil drew a piece of paper from the pocket of his jeans and unfolded it. 'Have you ever seen anything like this before?' he asked passing it first to Wesley, then to Pam.

Wesley shook his head. 'What is it?'

'It was carved on one of the memorials we've been moving. Family called the Benthams – the local squires apparently. The Rector thinks it's the emblem of some sect or cult called the Shining Ones.'

'Never heard of them,' said Wesley. 'Sorry.'

'We could see if there's anything about them on the internet,'

Pam suggested. She walked over to the computer desk in the corner of the room. 'Want to give it a try?'

Neil nodded, wondering why he hadn't thought of that himself. But at that moment the telephone began to ring. Wesley hesitated for a few moments before answering it. He'd been looking forward to doing a spot of impromptu historical research and he just hoped it was someone selling double glazing so he could tell them where to stick their windows, rather than the call he was expecting.

But his luck was out. He put the receiver to his ear and heard Rachel's voice. She sounded strained, as though she was trying to keep calm against great odds. The call, she said, had finally come. An androgynous voice, filtered through some electronic gadgetry, had instructed Suzy Wakefield to go to Whitepool sands where she'd find further instructions left beneath an upturned blue dinghy next to the café. She was to bring the original note found at the gibbet and leave it with the ransom money. The call had been traced to a phone box in Morbay, a different one this time. An unmarked police car had gone straight to the spot but by then the caller was long gone.

He told Rachel he'd be right over.

'I've got to go. Sorry. Don't know what time I'll be back, I'm afraid.'

'I'll let you know what we find out about the Shining Ones,' said Pam calmly, reaching up on tiptoe to kiss him on the lips.

Neil gave him a nervous smile as he made for the door.

The voice had asked whether they had the money. When Suzy Wakefield had answered in the affirmative, she was given clear instructions. She was to put the cash in a waterproof bag and go down to the beach alone at ten thirty. She was to walk straight to the café where she would see an upturned blue dinghy lying to the right of the front door. If she lifted the boat, she would find a plastic bag underneath containing her instructions. She was to follow them to the letter or she would never see Leah alive again. She was to return the instructions and the original note with the money and she wasn't to carry a mobile phone. Under no circumstances were the police to be informed: if they were contacted, Leah Wakefield would die immediately. Her throat would be cut. The last words chilled Suzy's soul. But she had to be brave. She had to do it for Leah's sake.

Her mind began to contemplate potential disasters. What if the tide had come in and swept the dinghy out to sea? What if some kids had decided to have a beach party? They could have moved the dinghy. They could have found the note and discarded it. The beach might be a hive of activity when she got there. The kidnapper might have chickened out if he'd found that there were lots of people about walking dogs or lighting barbecues. All these nightmare scenarios flashed across her troubled mind. It didn't matter that the tide never came up as far as the café or that, as it was nearing the end of September, it was far too cold for beach barbecues: Suzy knew that everything that could go wrong, would go wrong.

DS Rachel Tracey was being very supportive in a practised, professional sort of way. But it wasn't like having a close friend or family member there. All she knew of Leah was what she'd read in the tabloids. Everybody thinks they know a celebrity, she thought, but it's the image they know, not the person.

By nine o'clock everything was arranged. The original note had been photocopied at the police station and returned to Rachel to be dropped off with the money. The kidnapper was clever: he or she knew that, were the police to get their hands on it after Leah's release, it could yield valuable forensic evidence. But at least this precaution suggested that the abductor didn't know that the police were already involved . . . which was good.

Two of Rachel's colleagues had already gone to the car park by the beach to keep watch: Trish Walton and Steve Carstairs had been chosen because it was assumed that a man and a woman at that place and at that time would be taken for a courting – or more likely adulterous – couple and would excite little curiosity. Rachel wondered how Trish felt about this subterfuge – she'd already sampled Steve's dubious charms once and vowed never again. But sometimes you have to take the rough with the smooth in the modern police service.

Rachel wasn't comfortable with the idea of Suzy travelling to Whitepool Sands by car alone, but those were the instructions and they didn't dare to disobey them when a life was at risk. But Rachel was concerned for the safety of a woman too distressed to think straight, even though an unmarked police car would be waiting for her in a lay-by on the road from Neston to Tradmouth and would follow at a discreet distance until she came to Whitepool Sands car park. There the surveillance would be handed over to

Steve and Trish. The car, driven by DC Paul Johnson, would wait further along the road and, at Trish's signal, would follow Suzy wherever she was instructed to go.

The scheme was laid. But Robert Burns's wise words about the best laid schemes, echoed in Rachel's head as she wished Suzy luck and watched her walk out of the front door.

The Barber ran his finger across the shining steel blade and withdrew it quickly. The scissors were sharp. Razor sharp. Such a blade could cut through most things. Hair. Flesh.

He had been on the Internet again and found that the reply had come. Encouraging . . . urging him on. This was something he had to do.

He glanced in the rear-view mirror and pulled the baseball cap down. He had decided to be clean shaven today and he thought with satisfaction that he looked so nondescript, so ordinary. And that's exactly how he wanted to look. The local paper had been issuing warnings to women to be on their guard. But many people took no notice of prophets of doom. It could never happen to them.

He had parked in one of Neston's side streets, just around the corner from Weston Place. From listening to the taxi frequencies on his radio he knew that she called for a taxi most Friday nights . . . Ms Wetherby. He had watched her walk out to the cab and he had watched her slip into the back seat, her short skirt showing a long length of pale thigh. She always called the same firm . . . Neston Cabs. And he had the car prepared. Ready.

He strained to listen to the radio, to hear the call he knew would come. It was perfect. It was meant to be.

Then he heard the voice of the woman in Neston Cabs' control room. 'Anyone free to pick up a fare from Weston Place? Lady by the name of Wetherby. Going to Morbay.'

Then came an answering male voice, gruff, uninterested. 'OK Dawn. I'm just dropping a fare off in Tradmouth. It'll be fifteen minutes.'

'Thanks Les. I'll tell her. It's number five Weston Place.'

The Barber put the scissors and the parcel tape in the glove compartment before starting the engine and letting the handbrake off.

Ms Wetherby's taxi would be early for once.

*   *   *

101

At least the moon was full and Suzy could see where she was going. She parked the SUV, as instructed, just by the path leading down to the beach.

It all seemed vaguely familiar and then she remembered that she'd been there before a long time ago when Leah had been small. They'd come down to Devon on holiday in those far-off, lean days before Brad had spotted her daughter's talent. Then they'd left their small semi in Croydon and stayed for a week in a caravan park on the outskirts of Morbay. It had been a different life back then for her and Darren. A life of loans; of scrimping and saving and worrying. But now they had wealth, the worries seemed greater. Suzy Wakefield had always assumed that money bought happiness. Now she knew it didn't. In the poor times, Leah had never been in danger. In those days nobody had ever threatened to cut her daughter's throat.

She could hear the waves crashing, louder and louder as she walked down the sandy path to the beach. The tide was high and the moon sprayed the sea with shifting flecks of light. She reached the coarse sand and stopped. She could feel her heart leaping against her ribs as she looked round. Whitepool Sands was backed by trees, giving it a Mediterranean feel when the sun shone. The kidnapper could be anywhere, watching her. Making sure she obeyed the instructions to the letter.

Suzy took a deep breath and forced herself to move. She carried the waterproof bag she'd found, the one Leah had used to use to put her swimming things in when she was young. And she'd parcelled the money up into self-seal freezer bags inside it just to be sure.

The flashy black Ford Probe had been parked at the far end of the car park, the couple inside apparently kissing, engrossed in each other, and Suzy wondered whether it was her back-up or just some random courting couple. She hadn't been aware of an unmarked police car following her there, but then she hadn't really been aware of much apart from the pounding of her heart and the feeling of dread in her stomach.

She walked forward, her feet sinking into the damp sand. Three steps. Four steps. The café loomed on her left, a small, white one storey building, little more than a glorified hut. In the summer they sold ice creams, buckets and spades and brightly coloured flags to fly from the battlements of a thousand sand castles. But now it was locked up and deserted. She looked beyond the café to the small blue dinghy, which lay upside down on the concrete in front of the building, just to the right of the door and well out of the tide's hungry grasp.

She squatted down beside it, unsure what to do. It looked heavy but as she tried to lift it, she was surprised to find that it was fairly light. Fibreglass rather than wood. Her hand crept underneath and touched the damp sandy concrete. The relentless noise of the waves seemed deafening now, the vastness of the sea mocking her helplessness.

Then she felt a plastic bag, cold and pliant to the touch. She pulled it out from its hiding place and realised that she'd forgotten to bring a torch with her. She could see an envelope inside, the same as the other; a type available in any stationer's or supermarket. Self-sealing so no tell-tale trace of DNA could trap whoever had Leah in their power. She stood there for a few moments, taking deep breaths. She had to keep calm . . . for Leah's sake. For her little girl.

She began to run back to the car, the soft sand slowing her steps. She had to read the note. She had to know what to do next.

She unlocked her car door and climbed into the driver's seat, flicking on the light above the mirror. She sat there, breathless, reading the words neatly printed in black ballpoint pen on the sheet of pale yellow paper.

'Drive to Derenham and leave your car in the car park near the waterfront. At the jetty turn right and walk along the shore for three hundred yards. You'll see a rowing boat called *The Spider's Web* pulled up on the shore by some old lime kilns. Put the money and both notes inside the boat and walk back. Then drive straight home. You will be watched and Leah will die unless you do exactly as you're told.'

Suzy felt warm tears streaming down her face. How on earth was she going to walk along the deserted shore in the dark?

She sat there, crying for five minutes as Trish and Steve watched helplessly.

When Suzy started the car, Steve lunged at Trish with more enthusiasm than she was comfortable with. He had said they had to make it convincing but she wasn't so sure. Their simulated clinch hid the fact that Trish was talking into her mobile phone to Paul Johnson, stationed near by.

Their target was on her way out. And for God's sake don't lose her.

Wesley Peterson had parked his car some way away from the Wakefields' house and walked the rest of the way. But he doubted whether this subterfuge was necessary. The kidnapper's attention would surely be focused on Suzy, unless he had an accomplice who was watching the house even now. It wasn't wise to take chances.

Rachel's borrowed car had been moved out of sight round the back of the house to fit in with her cover story. Cleaners aren't usually invited to stay the night. Wesley had called her to ask for the battery of security lights to be switched off as he made his approach and, as a result, he had to stumble his way round to the back door in the dark.

Once he was inside the house he coughed as the sudden wall of cigarette smoke hit the back of his throat. Rachel led him to the lounge and introduced him to Darren Wakefield who shook his hand absentmindedly. Brad Williams, lounging on the white sofa, gave him a worried nod and went back to examining his finger-nails.

'Everything's going to plan so far,' Wesley announced, trying to sound positive. 'Your wife picked up her instructions at Whitepool Sands and she's driving towards Tradmouth. We've got someone tailing her in an unmarked car and ... ' He gave Rachel a shy smile. 'Rachel here placed a tracking device on her car so there's no chance of losing her. She doesn't know it's there. We thought it was best.'

He was glad to see that Darren Wakefield looked relieved.

'Good,' he said. 'I was worried that there was going to be a cockup. Just make sure there isn't, eh?'

'We'll do everything we can, Mr Wakefield,' said Rachel softly as Wesley's phone began to ring.

After a brief conversation Wesley took a deep breath. 'Paul's followed Mrs Wakefield to Derenham. She left the car in the car park by the waterfront. He parked on the street and followed her as far as the Ship Inn. He says she walked to the jetty and then she took the path along the shore.'

Darren looked worried. 'All those trees ... He could be hiding in the trees watching.'

'That's why Paul couldn't risk following her ... but he's called the river patrol.'

Brad Williams stood up. 'No,' he shouted with unexpected violence. 'If he's watching and sees a police launch on the river, he'll know the cops are involved and he'll kill Leah.'

Wesley smiled bravely. 'They'll use an unmarked launch. Don't worry. We're not going to take any risks.' He tried his best to sound confident. Someone had to. But the more he thought of this new development, the more he feared that Suzy's impromptu walk along the lonely, tree-lined river bank held all sorts of possibilities for disaster.

But there was nothing for it but to wait.

Chantelle Wetherby sat in the back of the minicab, studying her reflection in her make up mirror. With a job like hers – hostess at Morbay's premier casino – she had to look her best. She took her lipstick out of her bag and pouted, ready to execute some essential running repairs.

Once she was satisfied with the overall effect, she spared a glance for her driver. This one was quiet. They usually chatted you up ... or at least chatted about something even if it was only the weather. New ones usually asked if she was going on a night out and she had to put them right.

Chantelle didn't know about the Barber because she never watched the TV news or read a newspaper. Her casino colleagues' main topic of conversation was the activities and relative wealth of their reptilian punters and who was screwing who in the claustrophobic world of South Devon's foremost gaming establishment: they were hardly the type to swap local news over a cup of tea so the subject of the Barber had never cropped up.

Consequently, Chantelle sat in the back of the cab, oblivious to the possibility of danger, preoccupied with her own thoughts and her own concerns, the chief of which was how to avoid landing up alone with the new boss in his office and being screwed on top of his desk like her colleague, Gigi. He was fat and he looked like an overfed penguin in his cheap tuxedo. He also smelled of sweat and cheap aftershave that had fallen off the back of some lorry or other. He was a creep and there was no way she was going to let his hands wander over her body, thank you very much.

Having worked herself up into a state of indignation at the

thought of this imagined dangerous liaison, Chantelle hardly noticed that the cab had turned off the main road to Morbay and down a country lane. Instead she took out her mirror again and began to adjust her platinum curls.

Paul Johnson had reported that Suzy had returned safely to the centre of Derenham. Unfortunately the river patrol boat hadn't spotted her on the river bank and where she'd left the money was still a mystery. Paul had asked Wesley whether he should speak to Suzy when she returned to her car but Wesley had advised against it. If the kidnapper or his accomplice had been watching her, it was best to lie low. They'd discover all the details when she returned to the house. They had to play this carefully until Leah was back home safe and well.

Darren Wakefield was watching from the window for his ex-wife's return. Wesley hadn't liked to break the news that they had no idea where the money had been left. It was probably best if the police didn't appear too incompetent. When the headlights of Suzy's SUV came into sight, cutting through the darkness, Darren ran to the front door, followed by Rachel.

Suzy collapsed into an armchair. She looked pale and shaken and it took a few minutes and a large vodka and coke before she was able to give a coherent account of what had happened once she was out of Paul Johnson's sight. 'I don't know how I managed that bloody walk. It was pitch dark and I kept tripping over tree roots and rocks . . . and those bloody trees. I'm sure I was being watched. I was bloody shaking,' she said, her voice unsteady. 'But they say you can find the strength, don't they? When your child's in danger.'

The isolated river bank had been a clever touch, Wesley thought to himself. A lot of planning had gone into ensuring that the kidnapper would know if the police were following Suzy. He hoped that none of the officers involved in the ultra-discreet surveillance had done anything to arouse his suspicions.

Suzy's story came spilling out. She had been told to leave the money inside a rowing boat called *The Spider's Web* which had been hauled up onto the bank, round a bend in the river and just out of sight of civilisation. Clever. Before calling Gerry Heffernan to bring him up to date with developments, Wesley made a call to the patrol boat to tell them where the money had been left. But he advised them to do nothing to draw attention to themselves. Their main priority was to get the hostage back safely.

It wasn't until the patrol boat called him to say that, with the aid of night vision binoculars, they had located the probable spot where the drop had been made but there was no sign of a bag lying inside the rowing boat. Did Wesley want them to go ashore and investigate further? After a moment's thought, Wesley declined their offer. There was always a chance that the kidnapper was still around and the last thing he wanted was to put the hostage in any danger.

He decided to call it a day and go home to get some sleep. Rachel was there to keep an eye on things. And he'd trust Rachel with his life.

In the morning he would have to be wide awake and ready for whatever the next day would bring. He only hoped that it would be the safe return of Leah Wakefield. The alternative was unthinkable.

The minicab veered to the left and came to a sudden halt at the entrance to a field, throwing Chantelle forward.

The driver said nothing while she righted herself with a stream of mumbled expletives. He sat, still and upright, breathing deeply before opening the glove box.

'What's the matter? Why have you stopped? I've got to be at work and if I'm bloody late again, I'll get the bloody sack. Come on, my lover, get a move on, will you?' She tried to sound casual but in reality fear was creeping in.

'Did you hear what I said? Start the bloody car, will you?' She looked out of the window, her heart pounding. She'd assumed he was taking some short cut but now the truth was beginning to dawn on her. She was in the middle of nowhere with this silent man. 'Come on. Stop pissing about. Start the bloody engine, will you?'

When no answer came and all she could hear was the man's heavy breathing, panic set in. Chantelle flung herself at the door handle but nothing happened. The bastard had put the child locks on. She started banging on the window, screaming. 'Let me out. Let me out.'

He had got out of the car. Slowly. Moving purposefully as though he hadn't heard her cries, like someone in a trance. The back door swung open and Chantelle instinctively backed away, cowering in the back seat, her legs drawn up, her body pressed against the upholstery as he loomed over her. She could smell sweat and something else . . . a chemical smell she couldn't quite place. He was murmuring something softly – words that didn't make any sense. Babbling nonsense. She hid her face in terror and let out another scream.

She was going to be raped, she knew it. But there was no way she'd make it easy for him. He had something in his hand. Something that looked like a knife. Chantelle kicked out at him but he was on top of her, pinioning her arms and legs so that she was helpless.

Then she saw the blade pointing at her head and she closed her eyes tight. She had heard that your life flashed in front of you when you were going to die but her mind was empty of everything but the need to fight, to survive. With an almighty effort she tried to move her legs but no sooner had she wriggled one free than it was trapped again. She was being bound with something. Tape maybe. She felt tears of rage and helplessness well in her eyes as she pleaded to be released.

'If you let me go I won't tell anyone. Please . . . ' Then she made one final throw of the dice. 'Look, I'll let you . . . I'll let you do it if you promise not to hurt me. Please.'

He was going to stab her. Or cut her throat. She shut her eyes tight. Nothing had worked . . . not pleading, not fighting, not offering sex. She'd played all her cards and this was the end. This was death.

Then she heard the sound of snipping. Scissors, not a knife, she thought. He was cutting her hair. Her beautiful hair. She lay there, bound and helpless, feeling her hair being pulled and tugged this way and that.

Then suddenly, in desperation, she reared up, hoping to unbalance him, to take him off his guard. But she misjudged the manoeuvre badly and she felt something stab into her neck.

And as the blood began to flow, he continued hacking away at her hair.

Chapter Seven

*Letter from Mrs Sarah Jewel of Brighton to Juanita Bentham,
28th July 1815*

My dearest Juanita

*I thank you most heartily for your letter and rejoice to hear that
you are in good health. I know the Devon air is good, as is all sea
air. And yet, in spite of being in Brighton, I still suffer from that
malady that has afflicted me since Charlotte's birth.*

*Mr Jewel has instructed me to travel to Bath to take the waters
with fashionable society and it may be that I shall go. I would that
you could accompany me for I am loath to go alone, but it would
be most wrong of me to take you from Sir John so soon after your
marriage.*

*It is most strange that I came across a name here in Brighton
that you mentioned in one of your letters. The Amazing Devon
Marvel is to appear at a hall nearby. It seems this prodigious child
is able to perform any calculation that is asked of him by his audience and the Prince Regent himself, I hear has commanded him to
perform before him. I am full of curiosity, although I shall not
attend myself of course. How strange that he comes from Stoke
Beeching and that his father is a tenant of Sir John's.*

*And it seems that yet more curiosities come out of Devon. I hear
tell of a woman called Joan Shiner who claims to be a prophetess
and talk of her has spread to us in Brighton. Did you not say Sir
John's sister has met with her? I long to know the truth of it.*

Your most loving friend, Sarah Jewel

He'd panicked. After shoving the hair roughly into a plastic bag,
he'd driven away from that silent lane with the girl slumped in the

back of the car screaming, the blood gushing from her neck. Then the screaming had stopped and the strange gurgling noises she was making scared him.

He brought the car to a stately halt in a side road near to the hospital and undid his seat belt. Her breathing didn't sound good. She was lying on the back seat, her body twisted like a rag doll roughly discarded by some monstrous child. With a great effort he pulled her out, her sticky blood oozing onto his hands, and dragged her towards the hospital entrance, hardly noticing that she had lost both her shoes and the heels of her fishnet tights were disintegrating with the friction of her bare feet on the concrete pavement.

Not daring to go too near the brightly lit hospital, he left her propped up near a bay marked 'Ambulances only.' She was bound to be discovered there and taken care of.

When he considered that she was as comfortable as he could possibly make her, he bent and whispered in her ear. 'I'm sorry,' before disappearing off into the night.

Wesley Peterson was in that strange state between sleeping and waking, when the phone call came. When he put the receiver down he turned to Pam who was lying beside him and kissed her on the forehead. It was the sort of apologetic kiss she had become familiar with over the years.

'Sorry. I'm needed.'

'Must you go in? It's Saturday.' Pam knew that her question was a silly one. But she still asked it, probably out of habit. She ran her fingers down her husband's naked back and he turned towards her and smiled.

'Sorry. The Barber was at it again last night. Only this time the victim's in hospital.'

Pam's hand went to her mouth. 'You said it would escalate, didn't you?'

He nodded solemnly. 'Things like this usually do.'

She gave him an affectionate push. 'You'd better go.'

He turned to her. 'You haven't told me what you found out about those Shining Ones on the internet last night.'

'I haven't had a chance. I was asleep when you got back.'

'Well?'

'It was started in the early nineteenth century by a local woman called Joan Shiner. Now I know where the rhyme comes from.'

'What rhyme?'

'Some of the kids at school have this skipping rhyme. I've never really listened to the words but it starts "Joanie Shiner burning bright." It's most likely a local thing 'cause I've never heard it anywhere else. The kids probably picked it up from their parents and grandparents.'

'So what did you find out about this Joanie Shiner?'

'She claimed that the secrets of the universe were going to be revealed to her and her followers said she could perform miracles.'

'Were there many followers?'

'There were quite a lot around here. She claimed that she was going to give birth to a baby but no baby ever appeared. And when she died she prophesied that she would return and have a Shining Babe at the start of the second millennium.'

'She's taking her time.'

'That's what I thought. There were a lot of strange sects around at that time. For some, claiming to be some sort of prophet was probably a good career choice.'

Wesley climbed slowly out of bed and made for the shower. Much as he'd have liked to involve himself with Neil's little mystery, he'd have to leave the question of the extra skeleton and the presence of the Shining Ones in Stoke Beeching churchyard, to those with more time on their hands.

'Wes,' Pam said to his disappearing back.

He halted and turned around. 'What?'

She hesitated for moment. 'I love you.'

He made his way back to the bed and gave his wife a long, lingering kiss before retracing his steps to the shower. Things were looking up.

As he trudged down the hill to the police station, he wondered what had brought on Pam's forgiving mood. Normally when he had to work unsocial hours in term time she gave him a hard time. But recently – perhaps since Maritia's wedding – things seemed to have changed. Preoccupied with work and grateful for a peaceful life, he hadn't given the matter much thought. But all of a sudden he found himself wondering if something might be wrong; some illness perhaps that Pam was reluctant to mention. But she had seemed fine that morning . . . in fact she'd never looked better. He put the thought from his mind. He had enough worries to be going on with.

111

In the CID office it was impossible to tell that it was a Saturday morning. Rather than being a haven of weekend relaxation, the place seemed rather busier than normal. The Barber enquiry had been cranked up a few notches after last night's disturbing development.

And then there was the Leah Wakefield case. The money had been collected but there had still been no message from the kidnapper about Leah's release and Wesley felt uneasy. The ransom was fifty thousand pounds this time. What was to stop whoever had Leah demanding another fifty, then another?

Gerry Heffernan was already at his desk. He had the look of a man who hadn't slept much, if at all.

Wesley sat down opposite him and leaned across his cluttered desk. 'You OK?'

The DCI gave him a weak smile. 'I went to look at a nursing home with Joyce last night. Sedan House . . . it's on the outskirts of Morbay.' He shook his head. 'I just hope I never end up in a place like that.'

'Bad, was it?'

Heffernan shrugged. 'More depressing than bad. All these old dears wandering about not knowing what day it is and sitting round the walls of this lounge on those upright armchairs. Why do they always have those chairs in places like that?'

'Have you told Rosie about Joyce yet?'

Heffernan shook his head sheepishly and Wesley rolled his eyes to heaven. The boss's fear of his daughter's disapproval was beginning to irritate him.

'Anything new come in?' he asked, scanning the desk as though he hoped to find the answer to all their problems amongst the chaos.

Heffernan scratched his head and yawned. 'Still no word from the kidnappers. Rach is over at the Wakefield place and she'll let us know as soon as anything happens. We've traced the owner of *The Spider's Web* – he has a yacht called *The Spider's Nest* moored a couple of hundred yards out in the river . . . uses *The Spider's Web* to get out to her.'

'So who owns it?'

'Her,' Heffernan the sailor corrected automatically. 'Boats are always she. She belongs to a solicitor – one of the Weltons of Welton, Welton and Brace on the High Street.'

112

Wesley nodded. 'I know them.' Welton, Welton and Brace had ensured the release of many an offender Wesley would have preferred to keep safely behind bars. But, as that was their function in life, he harboured no ill feeling. Everyone had their job to do but his would be easier without Welton, Welton and Brace. 'Where does he live?'

'Derenham. Place overlooking the waterfront.'

'Nice,' said Wesley with a hint of envy. Places overlooking the waterfront in the village of Derenham came at a hefty price. Perhaps, he thought, this Welton lived beyond his means and had had to resort to kidnapping to make ends meet. But after a few seconds of pleasant speculation, he dismissed the idea as fanciful. 'Are we going to have a word with him?'

'I've already sent Trish and Paul over there to catch our Mr Welton while he's in the middle of his croissants or whatever solicitors eat on a Saturday morning. I want to know why his boat was singled out.'

'It was in the right place at the right time?' Wesley suggested.

Heffernan shrugged. 'Probably. Let's face it, if he was involved, he'd hardly use his own boat, would he?'

The chief inspector had a point, Wesley thought. If Welton was the kidnapper, he wouldn't wish to draw attention to himself. It was something Trish Walton and Paul Johnson could deal with on their own, just a matter of taking a statement to the effect that Welton knew nothing. But Wesley would read between the lines of the statement, when it arrived on his desk, examining each phrase for the smell of a lie . . . just in case.

'Are we going to see the Barber's latest victim?'

'She's still in hospital but it's just a precaution. She lost a bit of blood but the quacks say she's not in danger. Mind you, if she'd not been dumped outside the hospital it might have been a different story.'

'It was bad enough when he was just chopping off their hair but this means we've got to find this joker and find him quick. Any CCTV footage from around where she was dumped?'

Heffernan sighed. 'There were a couple of cameras nearby.' He paused before delivering the punch line. 'Trouble is, neither of them had any tapes in.'

'I should have guessed. What was the excuse?'

'Short staffed.'

Wesley rolled his eyes again. 'If she was left at the hospital someone might have found her and dumped her there because he didn't want to get involved.'

'Or our Barber knew he'd gone too far. He'd lost control and felt bad about it. We'd better get over there and have a word with her before she's discharged.' He let out a long sigh and put his head in his hands.

'What's the matter, Gerry?'

'It's this business with Joyce's mum.' He looked up. 'This Sedan House can take her right away so . . . .'

'Difficult decision,' said Wesley with genuine sympathy. He could appreciate Joyce's dilemma. Sometimes guilt is the hardest thing to conquer. It hangs round in the background like a smell from the drains, tainting life, taking the edge off any morsel of enjoyment. He felt sorry for Joyce Barnes. 'What about Leah Wakefield?' he asked, thinking a change of subject was due.

'Someone'll let us know when there's any developments,' said Heffernan optimistically.

Half an hour later, after intense negotiations with a small but fearsome ward sister, Heffernan and Wesley were sitting at Chantelle Wetherby's bedside.

Neil Watson had rung Wesley's home number, only to be told by Pam that he'd had to go into work. There was no resentment in her words – or if there was, she hid it well.

He had tried to call Wesley at the station but he had been out on some unspecified mission, which meant that Neil would have to talk to Lionel Grooby, the local historian, on his own. He had contemplated asking Pam to go with him as she seemed to be interested but he told himself that she'd have the children to look after. Besides, he didn't know if he'd quite forgiven her yet. Even last night, things had been a little strained.

The excavation of the corner of St Merion's churchyard earmarked for the new parish room was continuing, even though it was the weekend. Nobody wanted the graves to be open for longer than was strictly necessary. After checking that everything was going according to plan, Neil set off on his mission. His colleagues could be trusted to deal with things for an hour or so. Neil had always believed in the wisdom of delegation.

Lionel Grooby lived in a most unhistoric bungalow, built in the architectural nadir of the nineteen sixties. It stood on the outskirts of the village, separated from the road by a wide, faux farmgate with a wagon wheel set in its centre in a misjudged attempt give it a hint of rural authenticity. But even this gate and the rustic stone wishing-well in the garden couldn't make the bungalow appear to be anything other than suburban. Neil felt rather sorry that a man with a passion for history should be condemned to live in such a house. But perhaps he had a wife who preferred that sort of thing. In battles of taste, women were usually the victors.

It was the retired schoolteacher himself who answered the door. Grooby – who insisted that Neil call him Lionel – was a sprightly man, in spite of an overhanging gut which strained at the buttons of his checked shirt. Neil judged that he was a youthful sixty-five.

He led Neil though to the lounge, a sunny room with a beige carpet, pink walls and an over-ornate three piece suite and invited him to sit down before hurrying from the room. There was no mention of a wife and no sign of a female presence. Perhaps the choice of the bungalow had been Grooby's own, Neil thought as he looked around. Or the wife had gone long ago – departed for the next life of absconded to pastures new. Neil hardly liked to ask.

After ten minutes Grooby returned staggering under the weight of several folders. He placed them on the coffee table and sat down beside Neil, his eyes glowing with something akin to religious fervour.

'They've cropped up in a lot of my researches over the years,' he began.

'Who have?'

'The Shining Ones. The followers of the Blessed Joan.'

'Joan Shiner? I looked her up on the Internet last night.'

Grooby's face was serious. 'Have you seen the website? The Disciples of the Blessed Joan?'

'Can't say I looked at that one.' The truth was he and Pam had glanced at it and passed it over as appearing too weird. They'd gone for the plain facts of Joan Shiner's life, ignoring anything that looked like New Age mysticism.

'Did you know the Shining Ones used to hold their meetings in the attic of the Bentham Arms. And that one of the Benthams was a leading light in the movement – an Elizabeth Bentham – the sister of one Sir John – was introduced to Joan Shiner by her friend,.

Lady Penworthy, and she came to be one of her most ardent supporters.'

'You mean she gave her money?' Neil had always been of a cynical disposition.

Grooby gave a mirthless smile. 'Even prophetesses need to eat, Dr Watson. You were enquiring about the symbol on the tombs you're, er, digging up, is that right?'

'Yes. John Ventnor told me that you were the person to ask.'

'I suppose I am. It's not much use talking to Mr Ventnor. The church didn't altogether sympathise with the Blessed Joan's claims.'

'A friend who teaches in a local primary school told me the kids have a skipping rhyme about . . . '

'Oh yes. "Joanie Shiner burning bright, Joanie Shiner our true light. Baby, baby where are you? In the stars that shine on you." I'm glad to hear these old rhymes are still going strong in this age of computers and iPods.' He smiled as though congratulating himself on his knowledge of the modern world.

'Tell me about Joan Shiner.'

'Her family were poor and she went into service at the age of ten, finally becoming housekeeper to a popular, if unconventional preacher.'

'Housekeeper? Anything more?'

Grooby raised his eyebrows. 'The Blessed Joan claimed to be pure, Dr Watson. She was examined by seven matrons and found to be so.'

Neil was about to say something flippant but one look at Grooby's face told him that he was treating the subject of the Blessed Joan with deadly seriousness.

'Do you believe she was some sort of prophet, then?'

Grooby looked rather flustered, as though he'd been caught out. 'Oh, I wouldn't say that exactly. But she had a great deal of influence in this area at the time and the support of certain members of the Bentham family, which was probably why she made Stoke Beeching her headquarters, much to the horror of the Rector of the day, a mealy-mouthed gentleman called the Reverend Charles Boden.'

'So the Rector disapproved?'

Grooby nodded.

'And this Joan had influence?'

Grooby hesitated. 'Yes. She seemed to have quite a hold over her followers.'

'So what happened to her in the end?'

'It's rather sad actually. She was convinced that she was going to give birth to a child called the Shining Babe. She'd prophesied its birth, of course and she appeared to be pregnant. But after nine months nothing happened and she died several months later. It might have been a phantom pregnancy ... or some sort of cancer perhaps. Mary the First – Bloody Mary – suffered much the same sort of thing in the sixteenth century of course.'

'So that was that?'

'Not necessarily. According to that website I mentioned, some people think she's been reincarnated ... in California of all places.'

Neil raised his eyebrows. 'Where was Joan buried?'

'In the churchyard at Howsands – the trouble was, the village fell into the sea ... and so did the churchyard so ... ' He gave a theatrical shrug. 'She was supposed to possess the seven secrets of the universe but goodness only knows what she did with them. There was talk of a box of some kind but again, I've no idea where it could have got to ... if it ever existed. I've looked for it, of course ... tried to follow clues but ... '

'Have any of her present-day followers ever turned up in Stoke Beeching?'

'People come from time to time to look at the church and the Bentham Arms where the Shining Ones used to hold their meetings. I met a man a few months ago. He used to live in Devon but he'd been up in Leeds for years ... only just moved back down here. He said he'd seen the website and he was very interested in the Blessed Joan.'

'How interested?'

'I think his interest was more than casual, if you get my meaning.' He paused. 'In fact he seemed a little odd ... But it takes all sorts, doesn't it?' Grooby began to sort through the papers in front of him. 'Look, I've got copies of quite a few contemporary documents. Letters from local people mentioning Joan Shiner. Pamphlets, that sort of thing. And I've got some fascinating stuff about the Amazing Devon Marvel if you're interested.'

'John Ventnor mentioned him. Wasn't he some sort of mathematical genius?'

'Indeed he was.' Grooby blushed. 'His name was Peter Hackworthy and as a matter of fact he's an ancestor of mine – my mother was a Hackworthy.'

'So what did he do, this Marvel?'

'Around the time Joan Shiner was active in the area, the Rector, Charles Boden, discovered that Peter had amazing talents. He could add, subtract, divide or multiply any numbers that were given him. Unfortunately, the Hackworthys were at the bottom of the social pile in those days and the Rector and Peter's father had rather different ideas about how his gifts should be used. The Rector wanted to send him away to a school run by a friend of his in Oxford and pursue the life of a scholar and his father wanted to exploit the lad for financial gain and lift the family out of poverty. There were a lot of children in the family – not unusual for those days – so you can't really blame him. You can't judge our ancestors by the standards of today, can you?'

'So who won? The father or the Rector?'

Grooby smiled. 'The money, I'm afraid. His father hawked the lad round inns and assembly halls until he became quite a celebrity. He even performed in front of the Prince Regent.'

'What happened to him?' Neil leaned forward. The story of the young boy manipulated by his greedy father had caught his imagination.

'It's said that he suddenly lost his powers and from that time on he never went on the stage again and ended his life in obscurity, having lived to a ripe old age. He married and had children and I'm a direct descendant ... Although unfortunately I haven't inherited his talents. According to the burial register, he's buried in the churchyard, but there's no headstone.'

'Perhaps the pressure got too much for him. Maybe the price of celebrity was high even then.' Neil looked at his watch. He had been away from the excavation longer than he intended. But he had one more question to ask. 'Have you ever come across the name Juanita Bentham?'

'I have indeed. In fact I have some of her correspondence in my collection. She came originally from the West Indies – she married Sir John Bentham and died young, I believe. She had one son, Charles, who eventually inherited the estate.'

'Do you know what she died of?'

Grooby shrugged his shoulders. 'I'm sorry, I don't. But I know that she was very much against her sister-in-law's devotion to Joan Shiner. I have copies of some letters she wrote and in one she refers to Joan as a charlatan.' He hesitated. 'It was rumoured that the Shining Ones had something to do with the boy, Peter Hackworthy, losing his remarkable abilities. But I don't see how the two things could be connected, do you?'

'But these odd sects had some nutty ideas, so it's not beyond the bounds of possibility.' He paused before dropping his bombshell. 'We had to disinter Juanita Bentham's coffin and it turned out she wasn't buried alone. There was the skeleton of an adolescent boy in the coffin with her. His throat was cut.'

Grooby looked genuinely surprised. 'Really?'

'Maybe he was abducted by this strange sect for some reason and that's how they got rid of his body. Maybe they practised human sacrifice.'

A guarded expression appeared on Grooby's face. 'Now, now, Dr Watson, I think we're getting into the realms of fantasy here. There was never any hint, even from the Reverend Charles Boden, that Joan Shiner's followers went in for that sort of thing.'

Grooby began to make for the door.

'Look, if you find out any more about Juanita or the Shining Ones, will you let me know?'

'Of course,' was the automatic reply.

Neil knew his time was up so he thanked Grooby and left, with the uncomfortable feeling that the man had some special knowledge that he had no intention of sharing. But Neil's curiosity was aroused. Someone had dumped a murdered boy in Juanita Bentham's coffin and he wanted to find out who that someone was.

He was halfway down the garden path when he remembered the question he should have asked . . . but it would wait for another day.

Wesley and Heffernan had arranged to meet Rachel Tracey at the Ship, a comfortable pub on Derenham waterfront. But it was no social assignation: they wanted to meet well away from Leah Wakefield's house just in case it was being watched by the kidnapper or his associates. The last thing they wanted to do was to let him know that the police had been brought in and put Leah in danger.

Wesley took the drinks over to the table they'd chosen in the corner of the lounge bar. If anybody was watching them, they were just a group of friends having a Saturday pub lunch and they were careful to keep up the façade . Heffernan had ordered a pint of bitter while Wesley, the driver, and Rachel, the nursemaid to the Wakefield family, made do with orange juice.

When the sandwiches had been delivered to their table, they got down to business.

'How are they?' was the first question Gerry Heffernan asked.

Rachel suppressed a yawn. She looked tired, as though the strain was getting to her. 'Suzy took some sleeping pills after she delivered the money. She's been spark out ever since. Darren's getting jumpy, waiting for news. The manager, Brad Williams, is taking it all calmly.'

Wesley looked up. 'Too calmly, do you think?'

Gerry Heffernan immediately grasped the implication of Wesley's words. 'You think he arranged it? You think it could all be an elaborate publicity stunt?'

'Some people would do anything for publicity these days. And let's face it, when this all comes out, it'll hit the headlines with a mighty bang.'

'But we're doing our best to make sure it won't come out, aren't we?' Rachel said. 'And the state Suzy's in – you couldn't fake that.'

'Maybe her and Darren aren't in on it. Maybe it suits Brad Williams better if their reactions are genuine.'

'Williams provided the money,' said Rachel. 'Well, most of it. Darren stumped up the remaining five grand. Neither of them seems too worried about getting it back as far as I can see.'

'Which points to Williams being behind it. If it was his money, surely he'd be wanting it back. Unless he regards that sort of sum as loose change,' Wesley added with what sounded a little like envy.

Heffernan shifted in his seat. 'If it turns out you're right, Wes, we'll throw the ruddy book at that Brad character. Wasting police time'll be the least of his worries.'

'I could be wrong,' Wesley acknowledged. 'But, in view of the similarity to the Marcus Fallbrook ransom notes all those years ago, I think we should have another word with this Mark Jones. Try and pin him down, find some link to someone who was around then who's still around today. It can't be a coincidence, surely. The lab couldn't do proper tests on the Leah Wakefield note because the abductor wanted it back but they reckoned there was a good chance that the paper was the same as the 1976 ones. And the writing looks identical too so it was either done by the same person or someone trying to copy the original.'

Rachel took a long drink of orange juice. 'There is another possibility.'

Wesley and Heffernan looked at her, curious.

'What if it's someone who was involved in the original case – not the kidnapper but someone who knew the contents of the note – has managed to get hold of some similar paper?'

Heffernan leaned forward. 'Who have you got in mind?'

'I know we don't like to think of it but what about the police officers who worked on the Fallbrook case at the time?'

There was a long silence. Both men knew that Rachel's suggestion wasn't altogether outrageous.

Heffernan looked Wesley in the eye. 'Fancy a session at the Bentham Arms?'

'Not particularly. You think Barry Houldsworth might know something about all this, do you?'

'We won't know if we don't go and ask him. And I want to find out why he didn't mention Jenny Booker's death and all.'

'I'd prefer it if he came into the station.'

Heffernan shook his head. 'I think he'd be more willing to reminisce on his own home turf, Wes. We'll put him on our list. But the person I really want to see is Jones. If he is Marcus, he must remember something about who kidnapped him, surely. Give him a call at his guesthouse, will you? Tell him we're on our way.'

Wesley took his mobile from his pocket and called the number, only to be told that Mr Jones was out. He said he was going to see his brother.

'Getting his feet well and truly under the Fallbrooks' table by the sound of it,' was Heffernan's cynical verdict.

'Maybe he's just getting to know his family,' said Rachel, slightly irritated at the chief inspector's lack of trust. Families were important: living away from home for the first time, she was beginning to realise that.

Rachel had to get back to the Wakefields. She had taken an hour's break for lunch, leaving a young policewoman who was

121

new to Tradmouth, to hold the fort and to alert her immediately if there were any developments. Tim had said he was coming over to make some modifications to the recording equipment. And she wanted to be there when he arrived.

'I should have thought the kidnapper would have contacted them by now,' she said as she stood up to leave.' She hesitated, looking Gerry Heffernan in the eye. 'He's not going to let the girl go is he, sir?'

Heffernan didn't reply. He stared into his beer as though expecting to read the future in the disappearing froth on top of the golden liquid.

'We'll just have to hope for the best,' said Wesley, giving her a weak smile.

'You do realise that this is exactly what happened when Marcus Fallbrook was kidnapped, don't you.' Gerry Heffernan spoke quietly, as though he was afraid of tempting fate. 'The parents dropped off the ransom then they heard nothing. Not a word . . . ever again.'

For a few moments nobody spoke. Then Rachel touched Wesley's shoulder lightly. 'I've got to go,' she said, her face deadly serious. She hurried out of the pub, leaving the two men sitting in funereal silence. They both had a gut feeling that this thing wouldn't end well. But they hoped they were wrong.

As soon as Heffernan had taken his last, comforting gulp of beer, Wesley stood up.

'Let's go to the Fallbrook house and have a word with Mark Jones.'

'Mirabilis.'

'What?'

'Mirabilis. That's the name of the house.'

'Odd name that.'

'Optimistic certainly.' Wesley began to walk out of the pub, nodding to the barman as he passed. Heffernan followed, lumbering out into the damp air after his colleague.

Mirabilis wasn't far. Just up the steep incline that was Derenham's main village street, turn right by the church at the top of the hill and down a lane. Gerry Heffernan was puffing a bit by the time they got there but Wesley assured him that the walk would do him good.

When they reached Mirabilis, Wesley rang the doorbell and

waited. The rambling house, covered in Virginia Creeper, had been built, Wesley guessed, in the early part of the twentieth century. He wondered how it had acquired its name. Mirabilis. Wonderful. Perhaps something good had happened there once.

The door was opened by Carol Fallbrook, Adrian Fallbrook's wife and, if Mark Jones was telling the truth, Marcus Fallbrook's sister-in-law. She had the strained look of one who is being put upon by unwelcome guests but is too polite to do anything about it. Mark was there, she said as she stood aside to let them in. Wesley knew by the way she said those three words that she wasn't altogether happy about the situation.

They found Mark Jones and Adrian Fallbrook sitting facing each other like a pair of bookends on two parallel sofas near a fireplace filled with a display of yellow lilies, it being too early in the year for a roaring fire. Both men had the satisfied look of those who had just dined well and they both stood up as the two policemen entered the room. Wesley noticed Adrian glance at Mark with something approaching brotherly affection. The policeman in him hoped that he wasn't in for a disappointment.

Adrian invited the two policemen to sit, a small smile on his lips that hinted at a secret of some sort.

'I don't know whether you're aware that we took a DNA test a few days ago,' Adrian began. 'We've used a private company I found through the Internet which promised quick results. Neither of us wanted there to be any doubt.'

'That's understandable,' said Wesley.

'Look,' said Adrian. 'Will this take long? Marcus and I are taking the boat out this afternoon and . . . '

'Don't worry, sir. We'll try not to take up too much of your time. We'd like to talk to Mr Jones alone if we may.'

Adrian hesitated for a moment, looking at Mark as though seeking his approval. When Mark showed no sign that he was bothered one way or the other, Adrian muttered 'Of course' and hurried from the room.

'Anything you have to say to me, you could have said in front of Adrian, you know,' Mark Jones said with a hint of pique.

Wesley caught Gerry Heffernan's eye. It was time to come to the point. If the kidnapping of Marcus Fallbrook and Leah Wakefield were indeed linked – if Mark Jones was who he claimed to be – he was their best chance of identifying the kidnappers. They knew it was a big 'if' but it was worth a try. Anything was.

It was Heffernan who spoke first. 'We won't beat about the bush, Mr Jones. We need you to tell us everything you remember about the person who abducted you . . . Anything, however small, would be useful.'

Mark Jones looked at the chief inspector curiously. 'You make it sound as if it's urgent.'

'We think your abduction might be linked to a recent crime. It's vital that you tell us everything you know, however trivial it may seem.'

Mark Jones thought about this for a few long moments. 'What recent crime?' he asked eventually. 'Not another kidnapping?'

'I'm afraid we can't go into detail at the moment,' said Wesley, evading the direct question with the skill of a politician. 'But we wouldn't be asking you if it wasn't important.'

Jones issued a long sigh. 'I'd like to help but the truth is, like I told you before, I don't remember very much about the time between when I lived here and when I was in Ireland with the travellers.'

Wesley suddenly remembered something he'd promised to do. 'Anna Fallbrook . . . your mother . . . she had a close friend called Linda Tranter. I've talked to Mrs Tranter and she'd like to meet you.'

It was hard to gauge the man's reaction to the suggestion: his face was a neutral mask, showing neither apprehension or enthusiasm. But then, Wesley supposed, the prospect of meeting an old friend of your mother's would hardly be something that would fill most men with unbridled delight.

'Yeah. Why not?' he said after a few moments. 'I suppose I'll have to get used to having family and friends I don't know from Adam, won't I?'

Wesley smiled. 'I suppose you will. Look, have you remembered anything more, anything at all? You said it was starting to come back and we just wondered . . . '

Jones shut his eyes. 'It's just snatches. Like I see something and then it's gone.' He buried his face in his hands. Then after a few moments he looked up. 'Remember I told you about Jenny with the blue Mini?'

'What about her?' Heffernan asked, trying to hide his impatience.

124

'I remember something about Jenny being there. But . . . '

'But what?'

'I don't know.'

'Try, please,' said Wesley, willing him to remember. 'Just think of what happened that day. You disappeared from school at lunchtime. Did Jenny meet you? Did she take you somewhere?'

Mark shook his head but he didn't look too sure.

'Or was there someone else? Did you go off with someone else?'

Mark looked Wesley in the eye. 'I dunno. I think Jenny was there but . . . '

Wesley waited patiently for him to continue.

'It's all hazy . . . but I think someone else was with her. I dunno.'

Gerry Heffernan leaned forward. 'Who else was there? Was it a man or a woman?'

Mark shook his head. Wesley sensed that he was becoming agitated, as though he was starting to relive memories that were painful but elusive. 'I don't remember any more. I wish I did.' His voice was unsteady and his eyes were glazed with unshed tears.

Wesley handed the man his card. 'If you do recall anything – anything at all – will you ring me?'

Mark Jones nodded. 'Yeah. I'm trying to remember. Believe me, I'm trying.'

Wesley and Heffernan made for the door. When they were on the threshold, Wesley turned. 'Does the name Gordon Heather mean anything to you?'

Jones frowned, as though the name was familiar but he couldn't quite place it. 'Who is he?'

'He was Jenny Booker's boyfriend.'

Jones looked up, his eyes pleading. 'I dunno, I . . . Did he have something to do with it? Is that who you think took me away?'

'That's what we'd like you to tell us,' said Wesley.

'Have you found Jenny? Have you spoken to her? You should ask her what happened.'

'I'm sorry, Mr Jones, but Jenny's dead. She died not long after the abduction.'

Mark Jones couldn't have faked the shock, the devastation, that passed across his face as Wesley delivered the news. It was as if his last hope had gone.

Wesley said goodbye and left the man staring helplessly after them, his arms held limply by his side.

Jenny Booker was dead. She had drowned and it was possible that she had killed herself, perhaps out of guilt that she hadn't taken better care of her young charge. Or perhaps she'd felt guilty because she'd unwittingly led the kidnapper to his innocent victim. Jenny had been seeing Gordon Heather and, as far as they knew, Gordon Heather was still alive.

Had he got close to the young nanny in order to have access to Marcus? If they found him, they could ask him.

He was still out there somewhere.

Leah Wakefield could hear the water lapping outside. She had tried her best to escape the rough ropes that bound her wrists and ankles but the effort had chafed her delicate skin until it was sore and bleeding. The only relief was when her captor came to feed her and unbind her feet so that she could be led to the toilet.

Soon her captor would come with food – a sandwich, ham probably – which he would hold while she ate. Or was it a he? Maybe it was a she, the figure in black wearing a ski mask who never spoke. He had brought her a banana last time. And water. When hunger gnawed at her stomach like a voracious animal, she was grateful for anything to end the pain.

She wondered what day it was. She guessed she'd been there three nights. She'd listened to the sounds outside her windowless prison and concluded that the quiet time when the busy river traffic fell silent and only the hooting of owls and the determined chugging of night-time fishing boats making for the open sea, punctuated the silence. She was near the water, she knew that much. In a place with splintering floorboards and the tide lapping not far away. A boat house perhaps. But wherever it was, nobody but her captor came there. A fine and private place . . . like the grave.

It was still daytime, she could tell. But it was quieter than it had been a while ago. Perhaps it was tea time outside in the real world. In the world she could glimpse through sound but from which she remained separated by a barrier as strong as death itself. She had tried to call out, to scream but it had become clear quite early on that there was nobody there to hear. Sometimes she sang to keep her spirits up. Songs she had recorded, her latest record. Then, more comfortingly, songs from her childhood; cheap pop songs she'd sung along with while she was growing up and sometimes even nursery rhymes that returned her to a time when everything was innocent and uncomplicated.

Her ears were attuned to the slightest sound and as soon as she heard the metallic click of the outer door being unlocked, she froze. He was coming. She longed for him to be there because his presence meant food and physical comfort. But at the same time she dreaded his arrival because she didn't know what the visit would bring. Perhaps one day he'd turn up and kill her. She couldn't be sure.

She began to call out. 'Please, please ... help me. Let me go, please. I won't tell anyone. Please.' She knew she sounded like a whining child but she didn't know what other role to play.

She heard the door open, the scraping of wood on wood as the swollen door caught against its frame. He was in the room, standing there in the darkness. She could feel his eyes piercing her flesh. But she sensed no desire there and again she wondered whether she was mistaken in thinking of her captor as a 'he'. Perhaps it was a woman. It was possible. He – or she – had never spoken.

She heard the footsteps approaching, hollow on the bare, dusty boards. 'Please let me go,' she whined. 'I won't say anything. I promise. I need the loo. Please. And I'm hungry. Please.'

When the hand touched her hair, she jumped as though she had received an electric shock. She felt her hair being stroked, gently, almost sensuously. Then a sudden pain as a strand was wound around the caressing hand before being pulled out violently by the roots.

Leah began to cry in helpless fury as her captor untied her ankles and pulled her to her feet.

Chapter Eight

Letter from Juanita Bentham to Mrs Sarah Jewel of Brighton, 7th August 1815

My Dearest Mrs Jewel,
 I thank you most heartily for your letter and your kind sugges-tion that I accompany you to Bath. I regret, however, that I must decline your most generous offer for the happiest of reasons. For I am with child and Sir John shares this, my deepest delight. He is most solicitous towards me, forbidding me all but the mildest exercise. I miss my walks in this beauteous countryside but I must not be careless of the Lord's blessing.
 How very strange that you should have come upon the Amazing Devon Marvel. The boy's sister, Annie, is a maidservant here in our house and his eldest brother, Joseph, a carpenter on the estate. There are many children in the family and until the boy's talents were discovered, they lived in some poverty. Our Rector, Mr Boden, speaks most eloquently of the boy's brilliance and the avarice of his father who exploits him in such a manner. The brother, our carpenter, Joseph, is much like the father, I think: I have heard that he pours scorn on his younger brother's gifts, saying that such cleverness is of no use to the son of a labourer, although I suspect there might be bitter envy in his words.
 You ask about my sister-in-law, Elizabeth and her unfortunate connection with the woman, Joan Shiner. It is a source of grave concern to me and she speaks most wildly on occasions, urging me to accompany her to meetings held at the Bentham Arms, an inn in the village which, although respectable, is hardly a suitable place for a lady of Elizabeth's station to be seen alone. She tells

me that this Joan Shiner is with child and that the babe will be born in the same month as my own little one. It is all most strange.

Your most loving friend, Juanita Bentham

Saturday night was normally the busiest night of the week for taxi drivers. But one cab lay hidden from the world in a lock up garage in Morbay.

The Barber sprawled across the back seat with a scrubbing brush in his trembling hand. A bucket of soapy water sat on the garage floor and each time he returned to it to clean his brush the water turned a deeper shade of rusty red. He could smell the metallic scent of blood and he was afraid.

Last time it had gone too far. The game had changed. It had become more dangerous.

He thought of the woman in her skimpy clothes, displaying her flesh for all to see. Then the blood had run in scarlet rivulets down the bare flesh and he knew he had stepped over the line. She had been hurt. Thinking about it gave him a disturbing blend of revulsion and excitement and he wondered how he would find the courage to do it again. And to go even further.

Perhaps he should have finished it there and then. But the thing that controlled him wouldn't let him go. He had to carry on – start the cycle all over again until his task was fulfilled.

As he scrubbed at the carpet, he contemplated ringing the hospital to make sure she the woman was all right. But some inner sense told him that would be foolish. If they traced the call they might catch up with him and lock him up again.

And going back to that place was the last thing he wanted.

On Sunday morning Suzy Wakefield awoke, blinking, from her deep drugged sleep. She could hear the bells of Derenham church ringing in the distance as she looked around her white and gold bedroom, her fingers touching the smoothness of the satin counterpane. Her clothes lay, discarded, on the cream shag pile carpet. It hadn't been a bad dream. It was real. Leah had been kidnapped and was still out there somewhere with someone who would cut her delicate throat without a second thought.

She closed her eyes and slithered down beneath the bedclothes. Anxiety had brought on a kind of heavy inertia. Even getting dressed and putting food into her mouth was too much trouble.

129

She knew the police were still there, squatting in the living room with their recording equipment at the ready. Just in case. Suzy hardly dared to hope that he'd ring again. Perhaps her Leah was already dead and that's why she hadn't been returned. She curled up into a foetal ball, eyes tight shut in the dark beneath the duvet. If only she knew one way or the other, she could face it. Or maybe not. At least this way she still had a thread of hope to cling to.

The sharp sound of the telephone ringing made her jump. She uncurled herself and was about to pick up the extension by the bed when she remembered the orders. She was to wait until the police had set the tape running and set the call-tracing procedure in motion before answering. She leapt from her bed, not caring that her night dress was crumpled and her hair wild, and hurtled down the staircase towards the lounge.

When she reached the open door she saw the policewoman, Rachel Tracey, nod to Darren. She had wanted to be the one to take the call but something told her it wouldn't be wise to snatch the receiver from her estranged husband's hand. She stood in the doorway, hardly daring to breathe, watching and listening as the tape began to turn.

Darren cleared his throat before he spoke. He looked terrified.

'Hello.' His voice cracked with nerves.

'If you want to see Leah again, drive to Stokeworthy. Behind the church, up against the wall is the grave of a Thomas Birkenshaw. Your instructions are in the gap between the grave-stone and the wall.' The voice was metallic as before, like some sort of malevolent robot.

Rachel signalled for Darren to keep talking. The longer he talked the more chance they had of tracing the call.

'Hang on, I'm writing that down. Behind the church. Is that the opposite side to the porch?'

'Yes. The grave of Thomas Birkenshaw.'

'What if there's someone in the churchyard?'

'Don't ask stupid questions.' The voice sounded impatient, almost as if he was starting to realise what Darren was up to.

'How do I know Leah's still alive.'

There was a moment of hesitation before the answer came. 'You'll have proof when you collect your instructions.'

'We paid what you asked. Why haven't you let her go?'

130

Another pause. 'You must collect the instructions,' said the inhuman, metallic voice.

Then the line went dead.

Rachel Tracey picked up her mobile phone and pressed the buttons that would connect her with Tim. He answered almost immediately and after a short conversation, she looked up at Darren. Suzy had come into the room and was staring at Rachel with wild eyes. Rachel thought she looked like a mad woman, the type that was locked in attics in Victorian novels.

'The call's been traced to a phone box in Neston. A couple of plain-clothes officers are on their way there now.'

'But he'll get away again.'

'We don't know that,' said Rachel soothingly, knowing in her heart of hearts that Darren Wakefield was right. There was no way the kidnapper would hang around a call box, waiting for the police to arrive. On the other hand, there was no indication that he knew they'd been called in so there might be a tiny flicker of hope. But she wasn't holding her breath.

'So what do we do?' Darren looked at Rachel desperately, like a child in a hostile crowd clinging tight onto the hand of the only familiar adult.

'You'll have to do as he says.' She looked into his pleading eyes. 'I'm sorry.'

Suzy began to cry. 'Why don't you lot do something?' She almost spat the words at Rachel.

'Maybe this is the break we need. Maybe he's about to make a mistake,' Rachel said with more confidence than she felt inside. 'Where's Mr Williams, by the way?'

Darren and Suzy looked at each other.

'He went back to London late last night,' said Darren. 'I thought I'd told you.'

'No problem,' said Rachel as she picked up her mobile again. Gerry Heffernan would want to be told of this new development.

Leah Wakefield could hear church bells in the far distance. Sunday morning. At least it gave her some idea of how much time had passed. Her captor had called in first thing that morning to feed her and untie her legs so that she could be guided to the filthy makeshift toilet that stank like nothing she had smelled before – but then she had led a sheltered life.

She realised now that his – or her – visits were regular, predictable. And this meant that he was unlikely to turn up in between times. Her head still hurt after the assault on her hair last night and she had found it hard to get to sleep on the damp smelling mattress that served as her bed. She had no idea how much hair he'd managed to pull out: it had felt like a lot and she imagined that it had left a bald patch in the right side of her head. She had cried herself to sleep, soaking her face with warm salty tears.

It would be hours before he returned. If she could just loosen the tape around her hands . . .

She began to wriggle and, after what seemed like hours, her heart leapt as she felt the tape around her wrists give slightly with her efforts. She carried on. Nothing in her upbringing and recent life had prepared her for this but she was aware that she was tapping some mysterious hidden resources she hadn't known she possessed. She rocked to and fro rhythmically, singing to herself, not one of her hit songs but a nursery rhyme: see saw Marjorie Daw, Johnny shall have a new master . . . . Over and over again she sung the words, rocking loosening her bonds.

Until at last her hands were free and she scented liberty.

Gerry Heffernan wasn't pleased. Singing, he explained to Wesley as they drove to Stokeworthy church, was good for the body and the spirit and was one of the few ways he managed to relax. He looked forward to his stint in the church choir of St Margaret's church in the centre of Tradmouth every Sunday. And today's anthem was a particular favourite.

Wesley said nothing. He would have liked a lie-in, a lazy Sunday with Pam and the kids. Even a mundane chore like washing the car seemed attractive at that moment.

Heffernan interrupted his thoughts. 'I was supposed to be going to the cinema last night with Joyce but we never made it. Her mum again. She decided to wander off and she had all the neighbours out looking for her. Found her heading for the main road in her nightie.'

'Has Joyce decided about . . . ?'

'I don't think she's got much choice, Wes. She can't cope with all that on her own and the vacancy at Sedan House is still available.'

Wesley made sympathetic noises but he knew they had to

concentrate on the more immediate problem of getting Leah Wakefield back to the bosom of her family. A matter of life and death.

Rachel had relayed the kidnapper's message. The next instructions were to be found behind a gravestone in Stokeworthy churchyard. It seemed their man liked variety – gibbets, beaches, boats and churchyards. Wesley had a nasty suspicion that he was playing games with them.

Both men realised that the message was timed so that they would turn up when the church's congregation was arriving for morning service. They wondered whether this was deliberate or accidental. Perhaps the kidnapper wanted people around. Perhaps it was easier for him to observe Suzy and Darren as they went to pick up the instructions if he could mingle with a crowd – easier to make sure there were no police around. They were going to have to be careful not to give themselves away and put Leah in danger.

When they arrived in Stokeworthy, Wesley parked the car behind a row of others in the lane near the church. According to Rachel, the Wakefields had only just left the house in Suzy's silver Merc. If they made their move now, they would be one step ahead of them. Waiting.

Gerry Heffernan led the way to the church porch, hurrying as if they were late for the service. Wesley walked beside him wondering whether they would fool anyone who was on the lookout for undercover police officers. But they had to try.

As they reached the open church door, a helpful church warden smiled a greeting and held out a hymn book. Gerry Heffernan gave him an apologetic shrug. 'Sorry, mate. Not today, thanks.' The man looked a little puzzled and resumed his seat just inside the door, leaving the two newcomers standing in the porch.

'Perhaps we should have gone in,' Heffernan whispered after a few moments of awkward feet shuffling. 'We're a bit conspicuous out here.'

Wesley touched his arm. 'You're right. Let's make for the pub next door. We'll be able to see the back of the church from the car park.'

The sound of singing began to drift from the church as the two men strolled casually down the church path. There was nobody about who looked out of place. Just a couple of children in the lane, circling aimlessly on shiny bikes and a man coming out of the village store opposite the church with a plump Sunday paper tucked underneath his arm. A picture of lazy Sunday normality: he only wished he could be part of it.

As they walked towards the low, white pub which stood next to the church, the silver Mercedes SUV came into view, driving slowly towards them. It came to a halt behind a row of cars and Darren and Suzy Wakefield got out and hurried up the church path. Suzy hugged a large cardigan round her body, as though for protection. Darren's face looked pale and strained, almost old.

The Wakefields marched straight round to the back of the building as Wesley and Gerry took up their post in the pub car park. The wall between pub and churchyard, between the sacred and the secular, was just over five feet high: perfect for observation. They stood quite still and watched as Leah's parents made straight for their goal; the row of eighteenth-century gravestones standing against the south wall of the church. They began a frantic search, plunging their hands into the gap between the memorials and the rough church wall and after a minute or so Darren pulled something out; a brown padded envelope.

The two policemen looked around and, as far as they could see, nobody was watching from the trees and bushes surrounding the churchyard. But they weren't taking any chances. The Wakefields were hurrying back to the car, tearing at the envelope.

By agreement Wesley stayed in the car park for a while to see if there was any sign of the kidnapper while Gerry Heffernan strolled towards the Wakefields and when he met them by the church gate, he bent down and pretended to tie his shoelace. He hissed at them to follow him to the car and began to walk away while Wesley made his way out of the car park, alert for anyone or anything out of place. If the kidnapper had been there, watching, one of them would have seen him. As it was, they saw nothing suspicious as the sound of singing once more drifted out of the church and over the sleeping dead.

When they reached the car, all the time looking about them, Darren and Suzy slid into the back seat. Gerry Heffernan had taken the envelope from them and they were gazing at it desperately.

'Sorry about the cloak and dagger stuff,' said Wesley. 'But we had to make sure you weren't being watched.'

Gerry Heffernan had put on a pair of plastic gloves and was opening the package carefully. After a few seconds he pulled out a cheap white self-seal envelope and Wesley's heart sank. More instructions or demands. This wasn't looking good.

There was something else in the padded envelope too. Heffernan pulled out a clear plastic bag containing a hank of hair – bright blond – with the roots still attached.

Suzy Wakefield stifled a scream and began to sob hysterically while Darren clenched his fist. 'I'll kill the bastard,' he muttered. 'So help me, I'll kill him.'

'I think we better see what's in the envelope,' said Wesley quietly as he started the car engine.

'Another glass of wine, Marcus?' Adrian Fallbrook hovered with the bottle, like an obsequious waiter.

Marcus put his hand over his glass. 'Ta, but I'd better not. I'm driving.' He smiled up at his half-brother and their eyes met.

Adrian turned and saw that Carol was watching them, her lips pressed together tightly in what Adrian knew after several years of marriage was an expression of disapproval. He wished she'd realise that he'd just found a brother who'd been lost to him. His own personal Lazarus had returned from the dead and he wished she'd rejoice with him.

She'd been polite to Marcus over Sunday lunch, refraining from making barbed comments about his table manners. Adrian knew her politeness had been that veneer of good manners assumed by the middle classes to hide the turmoil beneath. But the DNA results would be with them in a few days and he hoped the confirmation that Marcus was indeed one of the family would make her feel differently. Marcus had been talking about going to see a woman who knew his mother. He said he wanted to find out as much as he could about her, which Adrian thought was perfectly understandable. We all long to know about our roots.

Adrian was starting to suspect that the difference in his own and Marcus's upbringing was likely to cause some difficulties. Certain things Marcus said jarred with Adrian's middle-class sensibilities. He scattered the conversation liberally with four-letter words and made the occasional politically incorrect comment that would be frowned upon in polite society. It was pure ignorance, of course – they had grown up in different worlds. Nothing that couldn't be overcome with time and a bit of tactful brotherly advice. And Marcus possessed a natural charm, an openness, that made it impossible to dislike him.

Marcus strolled out of the French windows into the garden and Adrian followed him, clutching his glass of shiraz by the slender stem, something to occupy his hands. Marcus stopped suddenly at the big oak tree at the edge of the lawn and gazed up into its branches. The leaves were still green; in a month or so they'd turn brown and carpet the grass. Adrian stood beside his brother, wondering what there was about the tree that so fascinated him.

'The tree house was up there, you know.'

'I remember it. It rotted and became dangerous so it had to be taken down.'

'I loved that bloody tree house.' There was a faraway look in Marcus's eyes. He was remembering. Perhaps, Adrian thought, this would help him to remember the day his life changed for ever. He hoped so. He wanted to know the truth about what happened himself.

They stood in silence for a while, paying homage to the past. Then suddenly Marcus spoke. 'Jenny used to meet him there.'

'Jenny?'

'Jenny. She looked after me.'

'Who did she meet?'

'He must have been her boyfriend. The police told me his name but I can't remember it. He had dark hair. He was a big bloke. But I guess everyone would have seemed big in those days.' Marcus turned to Adrian and looked him in the eye. 'I think it was him. I think he took me away.' A spasm of pain crossed Marcus's face. 'The police said she was dead. I bet he bloody killed her.'

Adrian's heart began to beat fast, pounding in his chest. 'You'll have to tell the police,' he said.

But Marcus had turned away as though he hadn't heard and was starting to make for the river.

The money – another fifty thousand pounds – was to be taken to the car park at Bereton Sands the following day. Monday. It was to be in used notes and left in the envelope Leah's hair had been sent in. And it was to be left in a waste bin to the left of the pay and display machine.

The note – again printed carefully on thin yellow paper – was to

136

be returned along with the money like before. Suddenly Wesley felt despondent. This kidnapper had thought things through ... had taken precautions. It was the careless ones who were easy to catch.

After contacting Forensics to request an examination of the note and envelope – with the strict understanding that they had to be returned in time for the drop – the Wakefields were taken back to their car and sent home to await developments in the care of Rachel Tracey. They insisted on phoning Brad Williams who said he'd return to Devon as soon as he could. The money would be obtained from the bank tomorrow and the drop made. All they had to do now was to make sure that nothing went wrong and hope the kidnapper didn't get too greedy. He'd had fifty thousand already and was holding out for the same again.

They decided to go back to Gerry Heffernan's house to grab something to eat. Rosie Heffernan was out seeing friends so they'd have the place to themselves. It was Sunday afternoon and both men were tired. Too tired to hang around the police station on uncomfortable institutional chairs. They walked through the Sunday streets in amicable silence, noting that the tourists with young families had been replaced by retired couples making the most of the period between the end of the school holidays and the onset of autumn.

They decided on a Sunday dinner of beans on toast washed down with tea. Gerry Heffernan made a good cup of tea – much better than the stuff from the machine in the office – and once they were settled, Wesley sinking deep into the comfortable sofa, the chief inspector glanced at his watch. 'Wonder how Joyce is getting on. She's taken her mum to Sedan House for a visit.'

'I'm sure it's for the best.' Wesley knew he'd just uttered a platitude but he was lost for more meaningful words.

After a long silence Heffernan spoke again. 'We never got to see Barry Houldsworth yesterday, did we? Fancy a swift half at the Bentham Arms now? Our man's bound to be there propping up the bar.'

'And this time of day Houldsworth should be reasonably sober,' said Wesley with what sounded to Gerry Heffernan like naive optimism.

Wesley looked at his watch. He didn't want to abuse Pam's newfound tolerance. But Gerry Heffernan was making for the door with steamroller determination and Wesley knew he'd have to follow. He had no choice. Anything that could help them find Leah Wakefield alive had to be followed up. And if her kidnapping was connected in any way to the Marcus Fallbrook case, ex-DCI Houldsworth was the man to talk to. And Wesley suspected that he hadn't yet told them the whole story. There was something he was keeping back.

'So what have we got so far?' Wesley asked as they drove down the winding A roads that led to Stoke Beeching. He wanted to get things straight in his mind, a mind that thrived on order rather than chaos.

'Leah Wakefield's been kidnapped by someone who likes playing games . . . tormenting her family. Someone greedy.'

Wesley nodded. 'She's a celebrity and I reckon that's why he's asking for more money. To some people once you've stuck your head above the parapet and entered the public eye, you cease to be a person and become a commodity. Then there's the ransom notes.'

'Suspiciously like the ones sent to Marcus Fallbrook's parents. Similar paper . . . similar wording. Same writing . . . well either the same or very carefully copied. . .'

'And Marcus has turned up.'

Gerry Heffernan snorted. 'I won't believe that until I see the results of that DNA test they're supposed to have taken. Who's to say this bloke who's just turned up hasn't met someone who used to work for the family or . . . ?'

'You're right of course,' said Wesley. 'But there is a remarkable family resemblance between Adrian Fallbrook and the man who's turned up claiming to be his brother.'

'Half-brother.'

Wesley glanced at the chief inspector. It wasn't like Gerry Heffernan to be so pedantic.

'And what about the Barber?' Heffernan continued. 'I rang the hospital first thing. Chantelle Wetherby's been discharged. We haven't had a full statement from her yet.'

'That can wait till tomorrow. What I want to know is, why is he doing it? What kind of weirdo gets his kicks from hacking off women's hair like that, eh?'

'Blonde women. That must be significant.'

Gerry Heffernan fell silent for a while. The reason why the

Barber did what he did was a mystery to them both. But madmen need no reason – their own twisted minds can supply motive enough.

When they reached Stoke Beeching, Wesley brought the car to a halt outside the Bentham Arms.

As Gerry Heffernan stormed ahead, making for the pub door, his eyes were drawn to the church opposite, to the metal screens and the blue plastic sheeting that was flapping lazily in the breeze. He turned round to address Wesley who was following on his heels. 'Your mate Neil not working today?'

'Shouldn't think so.'

'Has he found out anything about that skeleton yet?'

Wesley shook his head. As far as he knew the identity of the second skeleton in Juanita Bentham's coffin remained a mystery. But although he found it intriguing, he'd been far to preoccupied with his modern-day investigations to pay it much attention.

Once inside the pub the two men made for the corner where they'd first found Barry Houldsworth. Sure enough he was sitting there, as if he'd not moved from the spot since their last visit. The pint glass in front of him was almost empty.

Wesley went to the bar and ordered a pint for Houldsworth, a half for Gerry Heffernan and an orange juice for himself. The middle-aged woman who served him had a dyed blond helmet of hair and looked as though any awkward drunk who crossed her path would come off worst. She also bore a strong resemblance to Barry Houldsworth and Wesley guessed she must be his sister, the landlady of the establishment. When he returned to the table, Houldsworth took the pint without a word of thanks and downed half of it in one gulp.

'Jenny Booker's boyfriend, Gordon Heather,' Gerry Heffernan leaned forward to emphasise the importance of his enquiry. 'What can you tell us about him? Was he in the frame at the time?'

Houldsworth stared at the golden liquid in his glass for a few moments, deep in thought. Then he looked up. 'The simple answer's yes. But we could never prove anything. He had access to the kid. He was his nanny's boyfriend so he had his trust. And he seemed a bit weird to me . . . very odd.'

'But there was no evidence against him?'

'He was a slippery bastard. Made sure he had alibis for the relevant times.'

'Where did he say he was?'

'With Jenny Booker at the actual time of the kidnapping. Shopping.'

'No proof?'

'They said they didn't buy anything. They looked at engagement rings in a jeweller's in Morbay and the assistant remembered seeing them but he couldn't confirm the exact time. It could have been before the kid was taken, or it could have been after.'

'Would you go and look at engagement rings if you were about to abduct a kid?' said Heffernan.

'Unless they saw the ransom money as their key to the future,' said Wesley. 'It would have paid for the deposit on a house in those days . . . put them in a position to get married.' He turned to Houldsworth. 'What did Heather do for a living?'

'He worked in a boatyard. He was a bit of an oddball . . . hardly the type who could charm the birds out of the trees but it seems he charmed the knickers off Jenny Booker somehow.'

'She was besotted then? Under his influence?'

He considered the question for a few moments. 'I'd say so.'

'What was she like?'

'Young. Impressionable. A bit thick. As far as I could see she adored the kid but who was to say she didn't adore Heather more?'

Heffernan scratched his head and took a sip of beer. 'If Heather did a good job of convincing Jenny that the kid would come to no harm, she'd probably have gone along with anything he said.'

'Got it in one, Gerry.'

'Trouble is, we'll never know because, according to an old friend of the Fallbrooks, she killed herself not long after.'

Houldsworth raised an eyebrow. 'I suppose if she'd helped Heather to arrange the kidnapping and when she found out that her boyfriend had a very different agenda to the one she'd imagined and the kid ended up dead, she was so overcome with remorse that she felt she had no choice.'

'Did you know about her suicide?'

'I heard something.'

'Why didn't you tell us she was dead when we were here last?'

Houldsworth shrugged. 'Didn't think it was relevant. It was a while after she left Devon and, let's face it, I wasn't really surprised.'

'Why's that?'

'Like I said, she probably couldn't live with the guilt, poor little cow.'

Something about Houldsworth's attitude annoyed Wesley but he made an effort not to show it. They had to keep the ex-DCI co-operative.

'Did she leave the area right away after the kidnapping?'

Houldsworth shrugged. 'Pretty much . . . went back to her family.'

Wesley looked Houldsworth in the eye. 'But if she had been involved and she knew the child had survived, she'd have had no reason to kill herself, would she?'

'You're thinking of this joker who's turned up claiming the Fallbrook inheritance, are you? If I were you, I wouldn't believe everything you're told, Detective Inspector.' He said the last words with heavy sarcasm.

'How much is the inheritance exactly?'

Houldsworth downed the remainder of his pint. 'Definitely enough to kill for, I reckon. There was family money going back years. The Fallbrooks had something to do with the boat builders across the river. It was thriving at one time . . . used to build light-ships and trawlers there. The business has shrunk over the years and they only repair yachts now. It used to be Afleck and Fallbrook in its heyday but Fallbrook got out before the slump.'

'Afleck's boatyard. I know it,' said Heffernan, the authority on all things maritime. 'They fitted the *Rosie May* with a new keel a couple of years back.'

'Old man Fallbrook – Marcus's father – was a ruthless bastard, so rumour had it. Pulled out when the going got rough and left Afleck in the shit. He's still in business – just. But the yard's a shadow of its former self.' Houldsworth banged his fist down on the table as though he'd just remembered something. 'Gordon Heather – he worked for Afleck's boatyard. And he left suddenly after the kidnapping. Him and Jenny both left the area.'

'Together?'

Houldsworth shook his head. 'Don't think so. But that doesn't mean they didn't meet up again later.'

'Where did you say Jenny Booker's family lived?'

Houldsworth looked at Wesley. In spite of the amount he'd had to drink it was obvious his brain was still sharp. Wesley began to fear he might have underestimated him. 'I didn't. It was some-where near Bristol, I think. Or maybe it was Birmingham.'

Heffernan frowned. 'Well, which is it?'

Houldsworth shrugged. 'You're a detective. You find out. I've retired. Caught my last villain years ago.'

That was it. Houldsworth slumped back in his seat as though the effort of the conversation had exhausted him.

They thanked the man and stood up. They weren't going to get anything more. They'd read through Houldsworth's notebooks and they both suspected that there were a lot of things left unsaid; things the ex-DCI hadn't wanted to commit to paper; things he'd kept locked up in his head. They'd exhausted the lode for now but in a few days, if they still hadn't made any progress, they'd try again.

They began to make for the pub door. Wesley looked at his watch. Three o'clock. If he went straight home, he could still give Pam and the kids a small sliver of his time. Not enough, of course, but at least it was something.

But as soon as he saw Neil Watson at the bar, deep in earnest conversation with the landlady, he knew his best laid plans were about to be scuppered. He hesitated, torn between the natural urge to greet his friend and his domestic duty. The latter won and he was sneaking out of the pub in Gerry Heffernan's wake when Neil spotted him and called across the lounge bar.

It was Gerry Heffernan who turned and made for the bar. 'If you're not down a hole, you're in a pub. Wes, it's your mate Neil.'

There was no way Wesley could escape. He retraced his steps, Heffernan following in his wake, and gave Neil a brave smile. 'I thought you'd be taking the day off.'

'I am . . . sort of. I asked last night if I could see upstairs and May here said to come back when it was quieter.'

Wesley inclined his head, awaiting an explanation. But it was Gerry Heffernan who asked the obvious question. Why did Neil Watson want to examine the upper storey of the Bentham Arms?

Neil didn't answer. After checking that nobody needed serving and shouting over to her brother to keep an eye on the bar, the landlady led the way up a staircase covered with sagging patterned carpet. When they reached the top of the building, she flung open a battered door. 'In there. Turn the light off when you come down,' she said before disappearing back down the stairs.

Neil felt round the corner for the light switch, aware of Wesley and Gerry Heffernan standing behind him, their presence somehow comforting in that strange, unknown place.

The light flashed on, a bare bulb hanging from a grubby wire in the centre of the large attic room.

As they stepped into the windowless room Heffernan said something softly under his breath that Neil and Wesley couldn't quite make out. The floorboards were bare and there was no furniture but the walls made up for the room's plain simplicity. They were covered in symbols, executed in muted vegetable colours that hinted at antiquity. They reminded Wesley of Egyptian hieroglyphics; pictograms that narrated some truth . . . or maybe some fiction.

Neil began to walk around the room, with the casual interest of a visitor to an art gallery doing a circuit of the paintings. The far wall was filled with a large seven-pointed star with a flower at its centre as though it was meant to be the focus of the room. Neil stood staring at it for a few seconds before turning to his companions.

'What do you think?' asked Wesley quietly.

'Probably some sort of code. The Shining Ones would have known what it meant.'

Heffernan looked bemused. 'Shining Ones?'

Neil proceeded to outline the bare bones of what he knew, which, he acknowledged, wasn't much.

'Any good at code-breaking?' Wesley asked.

Neil looked at him and shrugged. 'I know the basics – looking for the most frequently used letters and all that. It shouldn't be hard to crack. I might give it a go.'

Wesley looked at his watch. 'We'll leave you to it then. Pam'll be wondering where I am.'

Neil opened his mouth to reply but he thought better of it. He would have been glad of some company up there. The room gave him a strange feeling and he didn't relish the thought of being there alone. But he knew Wesley had no choice.

Wesley dropped Gerry Heffernan back at his cottage on Baynard's Quay before driving home.

As he approached his front door he heard Amelia exercising her lungs. He was needed. But he thought of Neil in that strange room and wished he was somewhere else.

Somehow Leah Wakefield hadn't expected the door to be locked. She'd imagined that her bonds would have been enough to convince her captor that escape was impossible. She'd managed to free herself from the ropes and, by her reckoning, she had plenty of time before he returned. Plenty of time to find her way out of there somehow.

Her prison was a wooden building, a boathouse or a shed; probably the former because she could hear the lapping of water outside. There were shutters of some kind on the windows so the room was pitch dark. And it must have been well away from civilisation as she hadn't heard the sound of human voices in all the time she'd been there. But she had heard the distinctive whistle of a steam train from time to time which told her that she was somewhere near the steam railway that ran from Morbay to Queenswear. Somewhere along the stretch of river that ran within earshot of the line. The knowledge that she wasn't in the middle of nowhere gave her fresh confidence.

She walked around the room, exercising the muscles, honed for her elaborate dance routines but now stiff with disuse, looking for some way out of the place before her abductor returned. As she walked, her foot came into contact with something hard. She bent down and picked it up and found it was a torch. He'd left his torch there by the door, ready for his visit. She flicked it on and flashed the beam around the room.

There was a cupboard in the corner, roughly made and covered in ancient paint that flaked off the surface like diseased flesh. She walked over to it and as she opened it there was a loud creak. She froze, listening, for a few moments. Then she reached inside and her hands touched paper: a neatly stacked pile of virgin yellow paper; A4 size; typing paper perhaps.

Beside the pile were some loose sheets, slightly crumpled as though they'd already been written on. She drew them out with trembling fingers and began to examine them by the light of the torch. Her puzzlement slowly gave way to horrible realisation. There were three sheets in all . . . drafts of ransom notes, roughly written with crossings out. Someone, her abductor, was asking for money for her return.

But as she read the notes more carefully, she realised that they didn't apply to her. They demanded fifteen thousand pounds for the return of someone called Marcus. She wondered where he was being kept . . . or if his abduction was still in the planning phase. She stuffed the notes back in the cupboard before shutting the door. When she was free she would tell the police about them. Stop the bastard's games for ever.

She walked across the room and kicked at the door experimentally. Then she noticed a section of rotten wood at the foot of the door and after a few hearty blows it yielded a little. Encouraged, she set to work on the spongy wood and soon she had made a hole in the door the size of a cat flap. With more determined kicks the hole expanded.

But just as she knelt down, preparing to make her escape she heard the hollow sound of footsteps on the bare wooden steps outside.

She flattened herself against the wall and held her breath. He – or was it a she? – was back.

Chapter Nine

Letter from Letitia Corly to Elizabeth Bentham, 12th September 1815

Mr Dearest Elizabeth

I thank you most heartily for the remedy you sent with your servant. My mother's trouble is now much relieved thanks to your kindness.

Is not the servant you sent sister to the boy Peter Hackworthy who has been much spoken of of late? She did not have the appearance of one whose brother is hailed as a genius but then appearances often deceive.

I hear Joan Shiner is to be at the Assembly Hall in Tradmouth at the end of this month. I trust you will be there for I am eager to see her for myself. Tell me, can she cast spells? For I am in sore need of some sorcery that would encourage Captain Ross's attentions. At the ball he danced much but only twice with me.

I pray you, write soon and it may be that we shall meet in Tradmouth on the night of Mrs Shiner's performance.

Your affectionate friend, Letitia Corly

'Barber victim hurt.'

He held the local paper at arm's length and read the headlines again.

She'd struggled. It had been her own fault. Stabbing her with the scissors had been a terrible accident but he knew nobody would believe the truth. They judged everyone by their own standards – the standards of the gutter.

Leaving the flickering computer screen, he walked to the drawer and pulled it open. He had added her hair to the rest,

146

although he had washed it, cleansed it of her blood. He wondered whether the blood had rendered it useless, blemished. But on consideration, he'd decided to use it anyway. These things weren't easy to come by.

He sat in front of the mirror and looked at the dark wig. He'd look different this time.

He would darken his face a little to give him an Asian appearance. They weren't looking for an Asian minicab driver and he couldn't be too careful.

His mission was almost accomplished. Soon the car, the car that now smelled of stale cloths and blood, could be abandoned. It would soon be over.

Monday morning dawned bright and Wesley Peterson woke up feeling hopeful. The ransom would be dropped. And with any luck, Leah Wakefield would be returned to the bosom of her not-so-loving family.

At the back of his mind the vague suspicion that it was all some kind of elaborate set-up lingered like an irritating, unforgettable jingle. There's no such thing as bad publicity, so the saying went. And maybe Brad Williams didn't seem to be as worried as he should be.

He watched Pam as she put Michael's shoes on ready for school. He would have liked to ask her opinion; to know whether she too thought the whole case didn't smell right. But there was a news embargo and the subject couldn't be discussed outside the police station in case a careless word alerted the kidnapper to the fact that the police had been called in. It was a precaution worth taking. If the kidnap was for real a girl's life could be at risk.

He and Pam left the house at the same time, their lips meeting for a split second in an absentminded kiss before they went their separate ways. At eight forty-five Wesley reached the police station and was greeted by Rachel who was bearing down on him with the determination of one who has momentous news to impart.

'The Barber tried it on again last night. A waitress at a restaurant in Tradmouth ordered a taxi as usual from Tradcabs. She wasn't suspicious when the taxi arrived. She uses the firm almost every night and she just thought he was a new driver.'

'So what happened?'

'He stopped the car on the road to Whiteley – that's where she lives so he didn't do a detour this time – and when she tried the door she found that the child locks were on. Lucky for her she had her wits about her and as soon as he opened the door she managed to push past him and she ran down the lane ... flagged down a passing car. The fake minicab sped off and that was it.'

'She was lucky. How is she now?'

'Trish took her statement and she reckoned that she was more angry than shocked.' She grinned. 'I think our man met his match with her.'

'Has she told us anything useful?'

'She said he was Asian. Foreign accent.'

Wesley shook his head. 'Either it's a copy cat attack or he's changing his appearance. Does the DCI know about this yet?'

Rachel nodded. 'He thought that woman getting hurt might have put him off for a bit but ... '

'If it is the same man it obviously hasn't.'

'He reckons the whole thing's escalating and it'll only be a matter of time before someone gets seriously hurt ... ' She hesitated. 'Or even killed.'

'I take it she was blond?'

'Oh yes. She managed to scratch his face and she had the presence of mind not to wash her hands so Forensic have taken samples from under her fingernails. They can't be definite yet but it looks as if he used theatrical make-up.'

He looked at Rachel. There were dark rings under her eyes. She looked exhausted. 'Had much sleep?'

Rachel stifled a yawn. 'I was up playing nursemaid to Suzy Wakefield till one in the morning. She's getting jittery about the drop this morning.' She yawned. 'When Jan came to relieve me I thought I'd come here – catch up with what's going on. I'm going stir crazy down at the Wakefield place. Talk about claustrophobia. The Wakefields keep bickering at each other. But at least that Brad Williams has gone – said he had business in London. I was getting sick of him hanging round like a bad smell. I don't trust that man, Wes, I really don't.'

'Think he's got something to do with it?'

'We've had details from her mobile company of the last call Leah made. It was after she left the house and it was to Brad Williams's mobile.'

Wesley raised his eyebrows. 'He didn't mention getting a call from her.'

'No. He didn't,' said Rachel, the words heavy with meaning.

'Publicity stunt?'

'He's made all the right noises but to be honest it wouldn't surprise me. But, mind you, if that's the case I'm sure Suzy and Darren aren't in on it. Their reaction's absolutely genuine.'

'They've got the money together?'

Rachel nodded. 'Darren went to the bank in Morbay first thing. They're driving to Bereton at eleven. We're watching their backs.'

'Not too obviously, I hope.'

'If it's Williams, it hardly matters, does it?'

'If it's Williams, we'll throw the book at him for wasting police time. But there's always a chance it isn't, in which case, we stay out of sight.'

At that moment Gerry Heffernan appeared at the door of his office. 'Wes. A word.'

Rachel touched Wesley's arm gently. 'I'd better get back to the Wakefields' . . . See that everything's ready for the drop . . . Top Suzy up with Valium if necessary.'

Wesley shot Rachel a sympathetic smile and hurried into the DCI's office.

'Thought you might have gone back to the pub last night to give Neil a hand,' Heffernan said as he entered.

Wesley smiled. 'And risk the wrath of Pam? No, I had a long bath and an early night. Thought we might be in for a busy day today. Rach says Darren Wakefield's got the money and the drop's all set up.'

'Let's just hope he lets her go this time. The last thing we need is for this to drag on. I don't know how much longer we'll be able to keep it out of the papers – there's cleaners and all sorts around the Wakefield house who might get the idea something's up if they keep being told to keep away from the place. It only takes one of them to get curious and go to the press . . . '

'Let's not think about that, eh?' said Wesley. 'What about this connection with the Marcus Fallbrook kidnapping?'

Gerry Heffernan scratched his head.

'The notes are virtually identical.'

'And all the detail about them – the paper, the wording and so on – was kept under wraps at the time of Marcus's abduction. Nobody who wasn't involved could have known.'

'What I want to know is where Gordon Heather, the nanny's boyfriend, is now.'

'He's number one suspect, I suppose.'

'Too right,' said Wesley. 'What's to say he's not round here now ... using another name.'

'Something went wrong when he took Marcus Fallbrook and he had to dump the kid. But now he's desperate for money and he's decided to do the same again ... Only he's gone for Leah Wakefield ... someone in the public eye. Someone he knows has a lot of disposable cash. He's going to make sure everything goes like clockwork this time.'

'With age comes experience,' said Wesley. 'We don't even know what Heather looked like. I presume we'll be visiting Jenny Booker's family at some stage. There might be a photo of him amongst her things ... if they've kept them.'

'Let's start a bit closer to home, eh? He used to work at Afleck's boatyard, didn't he? It was a long time ago but there's a chance that someone there might remember him.'

Wesley nodded. 'Have we got time to go over there now ... before the drop?'

Gerry Heffernan shook his head.

Wesley told Heffernan about the call to Brad Williams that Leah had made just before she disappeared but the DCI didn't seem particularly excited by the information. Asking Williams to explain himself was put on their long list of things to do.

Through the glass partition separating the DCI's lair from the main CID office Wesley could see Steve Carstairs sitting at his desk, gazing out of the window. Not that Wesley could blame him: the view from the office window over the memorial gardens and the river was an attractive one and there were times when Wesley had been lured away from the path of duty by it himself. 'We could always send Steve to Afleck's,' he suggested.

Heffernan shrugged. He didn't have a very high opinion of DC Carstairs's skills as a detective but he supposed that even he couldn't go far wrong asking a couple of simple questions at the boatyard. Did anybody remember Gordon Heather and, if so, did anyone have any idea where he was now?

Once Steve had accepted his task with all the enthusiasm of a prisoner being led from the dock to begin a five-year stretch at

Dartmoor, Wesley and Heffernan called the team together for a briefing.

One mistake on their part and Leah Wakefield might die.

The kidnapper had made a wise choice. There wasn't much scope for concealment at Bereton Sands – a mile-long crescent of shingle beach some four miles west of Tradmouth, licked by the unpredictable tides of Lyme Bay. In the summer children played there, running, playing and dipping small limbs in the treacherous waters. During the Second World War hundreds of US troops had died there rehearsing for the D-Day landings. Knowing this last, grim part of its history, Wesley couldn't help thinking of the beach as a sad place – on days out with Pam and the children he avoided it if possible.

He drove down the coast road towards the car park with Gerry Heffernan silent in the passenger seat. He wouldn't stop there. It would be too obvious. Trish Walton and Paul Johnson were doing the undercover work, walking hand in hand along the beach like a courting couple, skimming stones into the sea, laughing and chasing. Paul had even brought his dog along to provide extra cover – a notoriously dopey golden spaniel whose only resemblance to a police dog lay in the fact that it belonged to the same species.

Wesley put his hazard lights on and brought the car to a halt before he took a map from the glove compartment and pretended to study it. It was a map of the London area but the casual observer wasn't to know that. As far as appearances went, they were two men who'd taken a wrong turning and had stopped to get their bearings.

Heffernan looked out of the window and grinned. 'There they are. Love's young dream. The dog's a good touch. Whose idea was that?'

'Paul's.'

Heffernan looked impressed. 'Good lad, Paul. Taking his sergeant's exams, isn't he?'

'I believe so. But it'd be a pity if we lost him back to uniform.' He looked at his watch. 'Five minutes to go. Any sign of the Wakefields' car?'

Heffernan craned his neck to look in the rear-view mirror. 'Looks like them now. Big silver Merc coming up our backside like a bat out of hell.'

'I hope they're ready in the car park.' Two officers in an unmarked van were pretending to mend the pay and display machine. Wesley only hoped they were making a convincing job of it. He started the car and drove slowly past the car park entrance just in time to see a nervous looking Darren Wakefield climbing out of his car, a plastic carrier bag clutched to his chest. He turned to the left and brought the car to a halt in the car park of a small hotel. They could see their quarry from there, standing awkwardly by the Second World War tank that stood as a memorial to the dead. Darren was still holding the bag. And something else; a piece of paper which he studied with a puzzled frown on his face.

Darren Wakefield hadn't dumped the money and he was moving. He had begun to march quickly out of the car park and he was heading for the beach. Something was wrong.

Wesley was about to get out of the car but Heffernan put a restraining hand on his arm. 'Hang on. Let's not do anything hasty.'

Wesley did as he was told. He sat tight while Darren disappeared from view. Trish and Paul were there, he told himself, trying to convince himself that he could safely leave the responsibility to them . . . and not quite succeeding.

'OK,' said Heffernan after a couple of tense minutes. 'Let's have a look, shall we? Casual, like.'

They climbed out of the car slowly, as if they had all the time in the world. By unspoken agreement they walked towards the beach, scanning the golden fringe of shingle for Darren Wakefield. But he was nowhere to be seen. He had either returned to his car or he'd walked up towards the village of Bereton and they'd missed him altogether. Wesley experienced something akin to panic. It had all gone wrong. Leah Wakefield's safety had been entrusted to him and he had blown it.

'Where is he?'

Heffernan hesitated for a few moments. 'God knows.'

Paul and Trish were walking towards them, hand in hand. The dog bounding ahead, making straight for Wesley and Heffernan. Wesley bent down to greet the animal who jumped up at him ecstatically, washing his hands with its lolling tongue.

'What's happening?' Heffernan said to Paul who was making a great show of calling the dog off.

'Wakefield dropped the package in that boat over there, sir. I think he put it inside some sort of waterproof bag,' said Paul quietly, still in role.

There was a boat a couple of hundred yards away, pulled up onto the beach near the water's edge – when the tide came in it would float. There was no sign of anyone else about. Perhaps, Wesley thought, he was waiting until the beach was empty before making the pick up.

'We should go. There's a couple of men undercover in the public car park. When our man arrives, he's bound to park there. They can pick him up when he returns to his car with the package.' Heffernan sounded more confident than Wesley felt but what he said made sense. Their man had to come by car or on foot – probably the former. And when he did, they'd get him.

All of a sudden the gentle lapping of the waves was drowned out by an approaching buzzing, like an angry wasp; a large, furious insect that was getting nearer and nearer. They didn't take much notice at first. Idiots in power boats – the lowest form of marine life in Gerry Heffernan's opinion – liked to exercise their anti-social toys from time to time.

But as the sound increased in intensity, they looked round.

'I hate those things,' Heffernan said absentmindedly as the jet ski skimmed across the waves.

The chief inspector turned away but Wesley couldn't help watching as the machine made a beeline for the shore.

'Hell,' he exclaimed after a few seconds. He snatched the dog's beach ball out of Paul Johnson's hand and threw it with some force towards the upturned boat. 'Fetch,' he said and the dog bounded off. 'That goes for you and all,' he shouted to Paul. 'It's him. The bugger's come on the water. That must be why he changed the drop-off point.'

As Paul and Trish lurched after the over-excited spaniel, the jet ski shot out of the water and came to a temporary halt by the boat before speeding out to sea again, the driver – a blur in a wetsuit – with a waterproof bag slung across his back.

'He's running bloody rings round us,' Heffernan said, turning away.

Wesley didn't reply.

Steve Carstairs edged his shiny black Ford Probe into a parking space. The car park at Afleck's was hardly full so he'd been spoiled for choice. He got out and locked the car door. You could never be too careful, he thought – and the car was his pride and joy after all.

The great bulk of the wooden boat shed loomed before him and he was aware of the river lapping against the gravel shore. The building looked rather neglected; uncared for as though nobody had the money or the inclination to renew its flaking paint or clear away the rubbish and discarded equipment that had accumulated around its base. The same went for the collection of splintering wooden outhouses that huddled round the main shed like children around a mother. To one side of the shed a small, utilitarian brick office building squatted, its brutal 1960s architecture starkly out of place against the green, wooded shore of the River Trad, an angry pimple on a beautiful face. Boats, in various stages of repair lay stranded on a wide strip of concrete between the buildings and the river or on the wide seaweed-covered slipway that had been constructed for larger vessels in more prosperous times.

The water lapped relentlessly against the shore but Steve couldn't be sure whether the tide was going out or coming in – he rarely concerned himself with the ins and outs of nature. A throaty whistle in the near distance told him that they weren't far from the steam railway which ran along the coast from Morbay to Queenswear. But railways were something else that didn't impinge on Steve's life.

Steve took a deep breath, thrust his hands into the pockets of his leather jacket and marched purposefully towards the office entrance. This was a wild-goose chase, he thought, a total waste of time. But he supposed it had to be done. There was a chance, albeit as slim as a catwalk model, that someone here might remember Gordon Heather from all those years ago.

There was no receptionist – it really wasn't that sort of place – just a tall man in oil-stained overalls searching frantically through a box file overflowing with what looked like invoices. Steve guessed that he was about sixty: he was wiry with sparse grey hair cropped short and he had the lined, tanned face of a man who had spent much of his life out of doors.

The man looked up. 'What can I do for you?' He had a mouth that naturally formed itself into an amiable smile and he sounded welcoming which meant he'd probably taken Steve for a boat owner in need of help with vital repairs.

Steve flashed his warrant card with the studied arrogance he'd observed in the more successful TV cops. 'I'm looking for a Teddy Afleck.'

'You've found him. Look, if this is about those stolen outboard motors, I've had someone round already. They've not come my way and if they did, I'd be straight onto your lot.'

The man sounded as though he meant it. But as Steve rarely came across honest men, he was uncertain how to react. It was a few seconds before he collected his thoughts and focused on the reason for his visit. He'd been instructed by Inspector Peterson that, as nobody was supposed to know that Leah Wakefield had been abducted, he wasn't to give too much away. This one wasn't going to be easy.

'It's not about the outboard motors. I believe someone called Gordon Heather used to work here.'

Afleck frowned. 'Now that's a name from the past. What are you after him for?'

Steve drew himself up to his full height. 'I'm afraid I can't tell you that, sir. It's in connection with an ongoing enquiry.'

Afleck's eyes met his. 'You mean you've been told not to tell me. This is very intriguing.' He smiled as if he was enjoying a private joke. 'Fire away, then. What do you want to know?'

'Can you tell me how long he worked here?'

Afleck scratched his head and frowned, putting on a fine show of racking his brains. 'It must have been about a year ... eighteen months. I don't think it was any longer. He went back up north.'

'So how come he ended up here in the first place?'

'Search me. I think he came down here on holiday and liked the place ... decided to stay. Then he met this girl.'

Steve's brain made the connection. 'She worked as a nanny ... name of Jenny Booker?'

'That's right. Little lad she was looking after was kidnapped ... Never found him, poor little sod. His dad and my dad were business partners, you know. Not that I had much to do with old man Fallbrook by then. He was never one to get his hands dirty – he buggered off when the hard times came.'

Steve could detect a note of bitterness in his voice but he decided to ignore it and move on. Old business grudges were irrelevant. 'What happened to Gordon Heather?'

'Like I said, he went back up north not long after the kid disappeared. I don't know if he went off with the girlfriend or . . . '

'She died not long afterwards. There was talk that she killed herself.'

Afleck's face was suddenly solemn. 'That's awful.' He shook his head. 'What a waste of a life. Not that I ever met her of course. And if she fell for our Gordon she can't have been the sharpest rivet in the hull.'

There was a short, heavy silence while both men searched for something appropriate to say. Steve wasn't comfortable with the subjects of love and death. Cars and football were more his thing.

'I must say I'm surprised he's come back here . . . after everything that happened.'

Steve looked up, puzzled. 'How do you mean, come back?'

'I saw him a few weeks back.'

'Where was this?'

'Now was it Tradmouth or Neston?' He thought for a moment. 'Neston, it was . . . near the river.'

'And when was this exactly?'

'I never put it in my diary if that's what you're getting at. But it must have been around June . . . July.'

'Did you speak to him?'

'Didn't get a chance. He was on the opposite side of the road. He got into a car but before you ask me, I can't tell you what make of car it was. They're all the same to me. Now if it was a boat . . . '

'Did he see you?'

Afleck shook his head. 'Shouldn't think so. It was a fine day so there were a lot of people about. And he looked as if he had a lot on his mind.' He gave a small, bitter laugh. 'In a world of his own, he was.'

'But you're sure it was him?'

'Oh aye. I never forget a face. He'd changed, mind . . . his face was a bit chubbier and his hair was longer and he looked like he was going a bit thin on top. Still, it's thirty years since I saw him last and age comes to us all, doesn't it?'

Steve, who hadn't yet experienced the creaking approach of time's winged chariot, said nothing.

Afleck suddenly moved over to a massive oak bureau that almost filled one wall of the office. He opened the top drawer and began to rummage inside, his face a mask of intense concentration.

156

Eventually he seemed to find what he was looking for and extracted something from the drawer's chaotic interior with a triumphant flourish.

'Want to see a picture of him?'

Steve nodded meekly. He'd been about to ask for a description but this was even better.

Afleck thrust a dog-eared black and white photograph into his hand. Eleven men in football kit sat in three rows, arms folded. Their ages ranged from teenage to middle-aged. 'That's me,' Afleck said proudly pointing to a younger self with a shock of longish dark hair. He must have been in his late twenties or early thirties at the time, Steve guessed . . . possibly his sporting swan song. 'And that's Gordon. He didn't play for us long – pub team it was. The Queenswear Arms. We were a man short cause one of the regulars broke his leg so Gordon filled in a few Sundays. But he was no George Best so it didn't become a permanent arrangement.'

Steve looked at the man Afleck was pointing out. He stood at the end of the back row looking like the outsider he was. He seemed young, hardly out of his teens, and he was good looking in a girlish sort of way. 'Mind if I borrow this?' said Steve with the casual authority he had observed in his superiors.

'I want it back, mind.'

'No problem,' said Steve automatically. He looked Afleck in the eye. 'I get the impression you didn't like Heather much.'

'You could be right there. He was an odd bloke . . . something very strange about him.'

'You said he came from up north. Whereabouts?'

'Yorkshire, I think. Leeds.' He leaned forward. 'Look, why are you asking about all this now? Has something happened? Are you reopening the Fallbrook case?'

Steve Carstairs drew himself up to his full height, remembering DI Peterson's instructions. 'It's just routine, sir. Thanks for your time,' he said and hurried out of the office clutching the photograph before Afleck could think of any more awkward questions.

Now that the grisly exhumations were completed and the coffins were all reburied, Neil Watson was looking forward to doing some proper archaeology.

His colleagues had gone to the Bentham Arms that lunchtime

but he'd decided not to join them. He had seen John Ventnor entering the church half an hour earlier and, as he hadn't seen him leave, he assumed that he was still in there.

He tried the church door and found that it opened smoothly and silently. If he'd been so inclined he could have crept up on John Ventnor who was, presumably, in the vestry. Perhaps, he thought, the Rector should be more concerned about his personal safety . . . or maybe he just left that sort of thing to a higher authority.

He gave a perfunctory knock on the vestry's open door and the man at the large oak desk looked round, startled. 'Neil. Come in. You gave me a shock.'

'Sorry. Have you got a few moments?'

Ventnor sat back in his chair. 'What can I do for you?' he asked with a professional sympathy that made Neil slightly uneasy about imposing on the man's time for no better reason than idle curiosity.

'I went to the Bentham Arms last night.'

Ventnor inclined his head. 'Oh yes?'

'I went up to the attic. Ever been?'

The Rector suddenly looked wary. 'Can't say I have.'

Neil pulled a sheet of paper from one of the pockets of his combat jacket. 'Recognise any of this?' He handed the paper, decorated with the strange hieroglyphs he'd copied from the wall of the Bentham Arms's attic, to Ventnor and waited for the verdict.

After a few moments Ventnor handed the paper back to him. 'I've seen something like this before. When Miss Worth's cottage was cleared out they found some framed embroideries . . . samplers I suppose you'd call them. Only instead of the usual alphabets or pious verses, they were full of this stuff.'

'What happened to them?'

The Rector frowned. 'I suppose they went with all the other stuff to the house clearers . . . They'll be in some antique shop by now, I suppose. Could be anywhere.' He hesitated for a couple of seconds then he raised his hand. 'No. I tell a lie. I think someone said they'd been sold separately to someone local. Lionel Grooby might know. He seems to be the fount of all knowledge about that sort of thing around here.' Something in the way he said these last words told Neil that there was some animosity between Ventnor and Grooby. Or maybe animosity was too strong a word . . . irritation perhaps . . . or just a mild dislike.

'I was going to have a word with him anyway,' said Neil.

Ventnor cleared his throat. 'I'm going to bury those bones later . . . '

Neil said nothing. The question of the boy who had been Juanita Bentham's companion in death still nagged at the back of his mind . . . like unfinished business. 'I'll be going then,' he said, picking up the copies he had made of the strange symbols and putting them back in his pocket.

John Ventnor gave him a sad smile and returned to his paperwork.

There had been no sign of the jet ski or its owner. It had vanished around the headland and the money with it. Gerry Heffernan cursed himself for his stupidity, even though Wesley Peterson kept assuring him that nobody could have foreseen that particular development.

After ordering a search of the surrounding coastline with the police launch, they returned to Tradmouth. Heffernan said nothing on the journey back but Wesley could sense his despondency. He felt it himself. They should have been prepared for anything but they weren't. And Leah Wakefield might pay for their failure with her life.

The best that they could hope for was that the kidnapper would be satisfied with the hundred thousand pounds he had already received in ransom and release Leah. Wesley had to cling to this hope. He found the thought of the alternative unbearable.

'Well he's got the money now so he's no reason to keep hold of her. And he's got the notes back so he thinks he's left no evidence. As far as he knows the Wakefields have obeyed his instructions to the letter and we've kept a low profile. He won't know they called us in,' said Heffernan with an optimism he didn't feel.

'Hopefully,' said Wesley absentmindedly. He hated to admit, even to himself, but he'd been impressed by the jet ski stunt. It showed a certain level of panache. Their man was resourceful . . . a formidable opponent. 'I've told a couple of the DCs to check out all the local places that hire out jet skis. We might get lucky.'

'We might.' Gerry Heffernan didn't sound altogether convinced.

He had opened his mouth to say something when Steve Carstairs burst into the office without even a token knock.

'I've been to Afleck's, sir. He gave me a picture of Gordon Heather . . . the nanny's boyfriend. He didn't work there long . . . left after the incident with the kid. But he played for a local football team a few times. Afleck had a team photo.' He produced the picture proudly and handed it to the DCI.

'Well which one is he?' Heffernan said impatiently.

Steve pointed. 'There at the back.'

Wesley leaned over to see. 'Not very clear, is it? But I suppose we can get it enlarged. See to it will you, Steve?' He gave Steve a businesslike smile as he handed the picture back.

'And there's something else. Afleck's sure he spotted Heather in Neston.'

'When was this?'

'Around June, July.'

'Was he certain?'

'He claims he never forgets a face but he did admit he only saw him from a distance.'

'Thanks, Steve. You've done well.' Wesley always considered that a little praise never did any harm.

As Steve disappeared out of the door, he passed Trish Walton on the threshold.

'Sir, Marcus Fallbrook's nanny, Jenny Booker. According to her death certificate she died up in Somerset. Clevedon. After Marcus was abducted she moved back there to live with her family. I've sent for the inquest records.'

Wesley gave her an encouraging smile. 'Thanks, Trish. Let us know what turns up, won't you?'

Trish nodded earnestly and turned to go.

'Any word from Rachel yet?'

Trish turned back. 'No. The kidnapper's not been in touch yet.'

'It won't be long now, surely.' Wesley hesitated. 'How's your new place?' he asked. Trish looked at him, puzzled. 'The cottage you and Rachel are sharing . . . is it OK?'

Trish smiled. 'Yeah. It's fine. We're getting on fine . . . Not that Rachel's been around for the past few days.' she paused. 'I hope Leah Wakefield's all right,' she said before disappearing through the doorway.

'Me too,' Wesley muttered under his breath. 'Why hasn't the kidnapper been in touch with the family? He's got the money now. What more does he want?'

'He'll be counting it,' said Heffernan. 'Then he'll be working out the best way to do the exchange. He'll want to be well away when she's found, won't he?' He stood up and walked over to the ordnance survey map of the Tradmouth area that hung on his wall. 'Wonder where he's been holding her. If nothing happens soon we'll have to bite the bullet and start a proper search of isolated premises. She could be anywhere but I've got a hunch that she's not that far away. Meanwhile, I'd like a word with Mark Jones – or should we be calling him Marcus?'

Wesley considered the suggestion for a moment. But much as he'd like to get out of the office, he thought their priority should be Leah Wakefield. 'I think we should sit tight here in case the kidnapper gets in touch again,' he said. 'I dare say Marcus will be sticking around until the DNA results are back.'

Heffernan sighed. 'If he's genuine he will be. Otherwise . . . .' He walked over to the window and stared out.

'Anything the matter?' Wesley asked.

'I had a call from Joyce before. She's decided on Sedan House. They can take her mum right away. She says it's very nice.' He didn't sound very convinced. 'She's still feeling bad about it.'

'From what you've said it sounds as if her mum needs to be looked after.'

'Oh, I know all that, Wes. But now I'm feeling guilty about wishing her mum was out of the way and . . . '

Wesley said nothing. If he was in Gerry's shoes, if his attempts to establish a relationship with a woman were being hampered by the constant demands of a senile mother in the background of her life, he too might have felt relieved by the old woman's removal from the scene. It might be selfish, but then Gerry Heffernan was only human . . . as was he.

'Does her mum realise what's happening?'

Before Heffernan could answer DC Paul Johnson knocked at the door. 'Sir, a report's just come in – a jet ski was stolen from a lock-up garage in Stoke Beeching some time last night. Thought I'd better tell you, sir.'

'Thanks, Paul. Get over there, will you? You never know, some-one might have seen something.'

Paul nodded in his earnest way and shot off to do the DCI's bidding.

*   *   *

Sedan House just outside Morbay was a large, neo-Gothic pile. The fact that the interior was modern and brightly decorated did nothing to negate the sinister nature of its appearance. It was a house straight out of a horror film but the staff did their best to make it cheerful for the residents, many of whom had little idea of where they were or why.

Edna Barnes touched her daughter's face, her eyes clouded by cataracts and confusion. She muttered something about evacuees: she'd had evacuees on her shattered mind for some time now, as though the events of the Second World War were more real to her than the present day. Edna had once lived on a farm near Neston which had received wartime evacuees from London and now she was back there, talking to the alien children who had turned up with their lice and city ways as though they were in the room. Joyce knew that Edna had no idea who she was. Her daughter had no place in her little world. She was as much a stranger to her own mother as were the nurses and care assistants she had only met that day.

Joyce felt her eyes prickle with unshed tears as she kissed Edna's forehead and assured her that she'd visit tomorrow. She had to get back to work. And she was going to see a play with Gerry that evening . . . his suggestion to take her mind off things. The only thing that might interfere with their plans was his work: he had something big on but he hadn't told her what it was and she hadn't asked. The thought of Gerry Heffernan cheered her a little – a small ray of light in the gloom. He was a straightforward, uncomplicated man. No rose-tinted spectacles could render him handsome but he was decent and after her ex-husband, decent would do nicely. The only shadow on the horizon was his reluctance to tell his daughter, Rosie, about their relationship. But it was early days yet, she told herself optimistically.

She left her mother sitting on one of the high armchairs ranged around the walls of the communal lounge, muttering to herself about how the evacuees needed a good bath. Hard as it was to leave her, she knew it had to be done.

She made for the front door, walking quickly. Then suddenly she felt the pressure of a hand clutching at her arm. She swung round to see a woman standing there, staring at her with confused, pale-blue eyes. She looked considerably younger than her mother but her face was thin and pale beneath her lank, mousy hair.

Joyce smiled as she tried tactfully to free herself from the woman's grip. But the woman put her face close to hers.

'Are you his mother?' she whispered.

'No. I . . . er . . . ' All Joyce could think of was how to get away without upsetting her assailant. She looked around for a member of staff but the hallway was empty.

'I know where he is. I know where your Marcus is . . . '

'Please, I've got to go . . . '

'I said it was wrong. I said it was wicked. That poor little child . . . '

Joyce took her hand firmly and gave it a gentle squeeze. 'Sorry, love, I've got to go.'

At that moment one of the care assistants, a plump girl with wavy fair hair and the round face of a story book milkmaid, entered the hall and saw what was happening. She strode over and took the woman's arm gently. 'Come on, Helen. Let's get you back to your room.'

She flashed Joyce an apologetic look and led the woman away.

Tim had called at the Wakefield house again to make sure the recording equipment was working as it should be. Once more he arrived in the guise of a plumber and Rachel thought he looked rather good in his overalls. But she suppressed the thought. She had to concentrate on keeping Suzy calm during the long wait for news. An hour seemed like a month in the smoke-laden atmosphere of the house. Rachel had long given up worrying about the dangers of passive smoking. If chain smoking calmed the Wakefields' nerves then she had to accept that her lungs were going to be exposed to an unwholesome cocktail of tar and nicotine until the whole thing was over. And she hoped, prayed, that it would be over soon. She couldn't bear watching Suzy Wakefield's pain for much longer.

The arrival of Tim was the high point of her day, her only contact with a world of sanity that lay somewhere outside the walls of her luxurious neo-Georgian prison. But he hadn't stayed long and she soon returned to her routine of helping around the house, making cups of tea and watching the telephone.

She had just settled down with another cup of tea, helping herself to a chocolate biscuit as she watched Suzy pacing the floor, puffing absentmindedly on cigarette after cigarette, when Darren

163

Wakefield burst into the room with a violent energy that alarmed her for a second.

'He's not been in touch.' He turned to Rachel accusingly. 'If he got wind the cops were watching . . . '

'That's not possible, Darren. We were very careful.' She spoke softly, as if calming a wild animal. 'We've done nothing to put Leah in danger, I can promise you that.'

'And Brad's not been in touch. What's he up to, that's what I want to know?'

'He's got business in London. He said he'll be back soon,' Suzy whinged. 'Shut up and sit down, Darren. You're getting on my bleeding nerves.'

Darren did as he was told, landing heavily on the white marsh-mallow sofa with a rush of air like a deflating balloon.

'I don't trust that Brad. He's got something to do with this, I know he has.'

'Shut up. You're talking crap.' She began to chew at her nails. Why didn't the kidnapper ring?

The blackened bones of the old ship – an ancient schooner beached and left to rot when its useful days had come to an end – protruded from the sandy shore like the skeleton of some long beached and decayed whale. It had been hauled above the water line where the tide never reached and it had sat for decades, a slowly decaying landmark for the living who used the river for business or pleasure.

The *Lazy Day*, a white cabin cruiser, the marine version of the family hatchback, bobbed a few yards from the shore. At first her owner, a businessman from London who had sped down the M4 on Friday night for a few days of relaxation on the River Trad, noticed nothing unusual. It was only when he boarded his inflat-able dinghy to row to the shore where his Range Rover was wait-ing to take him to a Tradmouth restaurant, that his long weekend took a turn for the worse.

As he took the oars, he spotted what looked like a bundle of clothing caught on the mooring rope and tutted with disgust at the idea that someone should have polluted the river – a designated area of outstanding natural beauty no less – with their unwanted rubbish. He laid down the oars and clambered back on board the *Lazy Day*, intended to shake the offending object clear of his rope and push it well away from his property.

But as he stood on the deck and looked down into the water, he realised that he'd been wrong. The bundle of clothes had taken human shape: a figure floating face down, arms outstretched. A young woman with long hair that floated like golden seaweed on the surface of the water.

His first instinct was not to get involved, to push the body away with the boathook lying on the deck in the hope that it would float off on the tide. But when he looked round his heart sank as he noticed a yacht nearby, a family on deck wearing bright orange lifejackets. If they saw him . . .

He swallowed hard, pondering his dilemma, before taking his mobile phone from his pocket and dialling 999.

Chapter Ten

Letter from Elizabeth Bentham to Letitia Corly, 20th September 1815

If you have a mind to attend Mrs Shiner's meeting, I will indeed see you at the Assembly Rooms in Tradmouth. Yet I warn you that she is no sorcerer. Rather she is a prophetess, a messenger from the Most High who has been entrusted with great revelations. She is not to be mocked as my sister-in-law, Juanita, mocks her.

There is, we are told, a box in which she has placed seven secrets and it is said that she will open it when her Shining Babe is born. It has been promised that I should be present when it is opened. I do not know whether I am excited or afraid.

Yesterday Juanita chided our carpenter, Joseph (the brother of Peter Hackworthy our Amazing Devon Marvel) for kicking a dog. Joseph is an unpleasant young man who dismisses his brother's talents as the devil's work. Our Rector still urges Peter's father to send him to be educated but to no avail.

I beg you to write soon and tell me if you are to attend Mrs Shiner's meeting.

Your affectionate friend, Elizabeth Bentham

It was Leah Wakefield all right. The body hadn't been in the water long enough for the tide and sea creatures to disfigure the face so she was quite recognisable. The Wakefields had been informed and, according to Rachel, they were distraught.

The pathologist, Colin Bowman, guessed that Leah hadn't drowned, despite being found in the river. Death, he said, had probably been caused by a head injury. But whether this injury was due to a fall or a blow with some kind of blunt instrument, he

166

wouldn't say until the postmortem. But one thing was certain – her abductor hadn't carried out his threat to cut her throat. He pale, slender neck remained unmarked by violence.

The owner of the *Lazy Day* seemed appalled that his weekend of pottering about on the River Trad had been tainted with such brutality. Wesley's gut feeling told him that the man could be eliminated from their enquiries; after all, he had been in London at the time of Leah's abduction. And besides, he'd hardly attach her body to his own mooring rope if he had had anything to do with her death.

After sending the team out to search for witnesses, any boat owners around the creek who might have seen anything suspicious, Wesley slumped down opposite his boss. He needed time to think. 'Any ideas?' he asked.

'Our man's probably local and he knows the river,' was Gerry Heffernan's verdict delivered with the certainty of holy writ.

'Colin reckons she was dead before he picked up the cash. He let the parents go through all that for nothing.' Wesley found the idea repugnant. Whoever they were looking for was cold and heartless. Cruel beyond belief.

'But is it the same person who abducted Marcus Fallbrook? That's what I want to know.'

'Houldsworth was sure that nobody knew the contents of the Fallbrook ransom note, apart from the family and the officers working on the case. If that's the case, we'd better start tracing everyone who was around at the time.'

Heffernan sighed. 'We've already got a list and nobody stands out as a potential murderer. I know some of the blokes who were on the case: they're mostly retired now or working in other stations and there's not a psychopath amongst them as far as I know. As for the family, the ones who were around at the time are all dead. There's always Gordon Heather, of course.' He picked up the photograph of the football team which was lying on the desk. The image was indistinct but it was the best thing they had. Gordon Heather didn't have a criminal record so there was nothing on the police computer about him.

'Afleck told Steve that he thought he saw Heather recently in Neston. He might have been imagining it. But if he wasn't ... ' Wesley let the sentence hang in the air. If Teddy Afleck had been right, Gordon Heather was at the top of their suspect list. He had been on the spot when Marcus Fallbrook had been kidnapped and he could have returned to abduct Leah Wakefield. He had failed with Marcus – the boy had survived somehow and was now back in the bosom of his family . . . if the impending DNA results confirmed that he was who he claimed to be. But what if Heather had decided to try again . . . and this time his victim wasn't so lucky?'

'Why the time gap?'

'Maybe he's been out of the country. Or he's suddenly fallen on hard times and needs the money again.'

Heffernan nodded. 'Is Rachel still with the Wakefields?'

'Yeah. She's bringing them to Tradmouth for the formal identification. They're distraught . . . blaming us.'

Heffernan was silent for a few moments. He was blaming himself, going over in his mind what he could have done differently that would have ensured the girl's survival. But he couldn't find an answer. 'I was supposed to be seeing Joyce tonight,' he said. 'We were going to see a play – the Tradmouth Players are doing some comedy or other and a friend of hers is in it. I wondered . . . '

'What?'

'That greasepaint found under the nails of the Barber's latest victim . . . I've been wondering whether he could be a member of some local dramatic society.'

Wesley shrugged. It was a possibility. But today's developments had put the Barber investigation on the back burner. 'I'm sure Joyce'll understand.' He looked at his watch. 'I'd better ring Pam to tell her I'll be late.' He thought for a few moments. 'I'll get copies of Heather's picture circulated. If Afleck's right and he's still around . . . .'

Wesley left the chief inspector deep in thought, his chin resting on his hands, staring into the space beyond the chaos of his desk top. He returned to his desk, wondering where to start. If the Fallbrook case was linked with Leah's murder, it might be worth talking to Mark Jones – or was he calling himself Marcus Fallbrook these days? – to see if any more memories had returned. He wondered whether to suggest hypnotism. He'd had a case not long ago where it had unlocked hidden traumatic memories and led to the conviction of a killer. Perhaps he'd mention it when he talked to Jones. Test the waters.

As soon as he sat down at his desk, Trish Walton came hurrying in: her purposeful expression suggested that she had vital news to impart.

'I've traced the records of Jenny Booker's inquest,' she said sitting down heavily on the chair beside Wesley's desk as though she needed to rest her weary feet. 'When she went back to live with her family after the kidnapping she became depressed . . . blamed herself for what happened. She left a note saying she couldn't live with the guilt any more.'

'That suggests that she was involved in some way. Or that she'd inadvertently given the kidnapper access to the kid. Any mention of Gordon Heather?'

'Only in passing. I get the impression that she didn't see him again after she went home.' She paused for a few moments, as though she was saving the best till last.

'I rang Jenny's parents . . . talked to her mother. They haven't moved house and all Jenny's stuff's still there – they couldn't bear getting rid of it. There are some letters Jenny sent them around the time of the abduction and she said if it helps us find the truth about what happened to Marcus Fallbrook, she wouldn't mind us looking through them as long as we left everything as we found it.'

Wesley thought for a new moments. 'Clevedon is it?'

Trish nodded.

Wesley sat forward. 'I don't suppose she'd send the letters down, would she?'

Trish shook her head vigorously. 'She said there's no way she'd let anything belonging to Jenny out of the house.'

'Tricky. Thanks, Trish. I'll think about it.'

He watched Trish return to her desk, wondering whether a trip up to Somerset would solve their problems. Or whether it would be a complete waste of time.

A fine veil of drizzle had just begun to fall and Neil was glad that it was four thirty, almost time to finish for the day. He and his colleagues had done some serious digging in the base of the now empty graves in Stoke Beeching churchyard and the knowledge that whatever they found would be archaeology rather than exhumations made the atmosphere lighter.

The discovery of some masonry, possibly belonging to an earlier church, had improved his mood no end and as he walked the short distance to Lionel Grooby's bungalow he felt positively cheerful.

When Grooby opened the front door, Neil noticed that he

looked tired. But the man stood aside to let him in and offered tea, which was refused.

Neil came straight to the point. 'I wonder if I could have a look at that correspondence you mentioned when I last called . . . the stuff concerning Juanita Bentham.'

Without a word, Grooby hurried off, leaving Neil alone in the cramped living room. While Neil waited, he began to look around, examining the collection of unexciting prints of local scenes which hung against the green patterned wallpaper.

Out of idle curiosity, he opened the door which he supposed led to a kitchen or dining room and was surprised to see a well-equipped office. The files on the shelves bore the names of local towns and villages. Grooby took his interest in local history seriously, Neil thought. Maybe too seriously.

Then something caught his eye. Hanging on the wall to the side of the desk were two samplers. Neil recognised the strange symbols that had been embroidered onto the canvas in what looked like pale silk. He had seen something similar before in the attic of the Bentham Arms. He stepped into the office to get a better look and was surprised to see that the silk resembled human hair.

The sound of Grooby's return made him move quickly back towards the door but he was too late. Grooby had caught him in the act of trespass.

Neil did his best to look confident, which he'd found from experience usually did the trick on such occasions. 'Are these the samplers from Miss Worth's house? John Ventnor told me about them but he didn't know you'd bought them.'

Grooby opened his mouth to speak but no sound came out.

'They look as if they're made with human hair.'

'I . . . I don't know.'

Neil looked him in the eye. The man hadn't mentioned his intrusion: perhaps attack was the best form of defence.

It seemed to work. Grooby held out a bundle of letters. 'Here's the correspondence I mentioned. If you'd like to . . . '

'Mind if I take them away and read through them?'

Grooby made no objection and Neil suspected that he was too timid and polite to refuse . . . which suited him fine.

'I checked out the website you mentioned – that woman in California who's claiming to be a reincarnation of Joan Shiner.'

'Did you?' Lionel Grooby looked uneasy.

'Her followers believe that the Shining Babe's going to make an appearance at the start of the third millennium and it needs a shawl made from the hair of the chosen.'

Lionel Grooby said nothing and Neil sensed the subject of Joan Shiner was closed.

He turned to leave. 'Thanks for the letters,' he said. 'I'll bring them back as soon as I've finished with them.

He walked down the garden path towards the road, the letters clutched in his hand. And when he looked round to bid Grooby a final farewell, he was surprised to see that the man looked worried . . . very worried indeed.

Pam didn't utter a word of complaint when Wesley told her that if he had to travel to Clevedon to see Jenny Booker's family, he might be very late home. The fleeting thought that there might be another man in her life flickered briefly into his mind. But he dismissed the idea as quickly as it had arrived. Pam wasn't the sort of woman who went in for deception: she was one of the most open people he knew. And besides, with two young children and her teaching career she simply wouldn't have time. The idea was laughable.

On his return to the CID office he had spent some time studying the ransom notes; those sent to Marcus Fallbrook's parents and the copies they'd taken of the ones sent to Leah Wakefield's family thirty years later. There was no question that they were virtually identical, which couldn't be a coincidence. There was a link and Wesley Peterson was determined to find out exactly what it was.

If Mark Jones – or Marcus Fallbrook – was genuine and if he could remember something about his abductor, Wesley was certain that it would lead them to Leah Wakefield's killer. Gerry Heffernan agreed that it was high time they spoke to him again so at five o'clock, with hunger just beginning to set in, the two men drove out to Derenham – to Mirabilis – down narrow lanes, dark and glistening with recent drizzle. Neither spoke much during the journey. They still hadn't recovered from the shock of seeing Leah's body – from the discovery that their hopes of finding her alive were dead.

Carol Fallbrook greeted them in her usual businesslike manner but Wesley sensed an unease behind her studied politeness. She led them through to the large living room where Adrian Fallbrook

171

sat, completely relaxed, in a sagging armchair. Mark sat opposite him, a glass of whisky in his hand and the two men looked at home in each other's company – brothers reunited. Perhaps the Fallbrook story would have a happy ending after all.

Adrian stood up when the two policemen entered and held out his hand. Mark stayed where he was, staring into his glass.

'You won't have heard the good news,' Adrian began.

Heffernan and Wesley looked rather puzzled. The only news on their mind was the discovery of Leah Wakefield . . . and that certainly wasn't good.

'The DNA test. The results have just come back. There's a ninety-three per cent chance that Marcus and I are half-brothers and that's good enough for me.' He looked at Marcus and smiled proudly. 'We're going out for a meal tonight to celebrate. It's not every day you find a brother you never knew you had, is it?'

'You must be delighted,' said Wesley tactfully, glancing at Carol who was looking anything but delighted. But then she'd just lost half her husband's inheritance. People had killed for less.

Gerry Heffernan lowered himself down onto the sofa and looked Marcus in the eye. 'You won't have heard yet but a young woman's been kidnapped . . . '

Carol sat up, suddenly interested.

Wesley assumed a suitably solemn expression. 'And I'm afraid she was found dead this afternoon. We're working on the assumption that she was murdered.'

Carol's hand went to her mouth.

'That's terrible,' Adrian muttered, Marcus echoing his words after a few seconds' delay.

Wesley looked at Marcus. 'You can understand, Mr . . . Jones.'

'Fallbrook,' he said quickly. 'I'm using my real name now.'

Wesley nodded. 'We'd like to talk to you again about your own abduction. If it was indeed the same perpetrator, you might be able to give us vital information.'

'What makes you think it's the same person who kidnapped Marcus?' Adrian asked.

'There are certain similarities,' said Wesley. 'The notes sent to the young woman's family are virtually identical to the ones sent to your parents, both the wording and the distinctive paper used.'

Marcus stared down at his feet. Then, after a few moments, he

172

looked up. 'I don't remember anything much about it. I'm trying my best and bits keep coming back but . . . '

'We had a case not long ago where hypnotism was used to retrieve a woman's memory of a crime that happened when she was a child. It was very successful.'

Marcus shook his head. 'I've got a phobia about things like that . . . not being in control. I suppose it comes from the time when I was . . . '

'It'll be done properly by a consultant psychiatrist. You'll come to no harm, I assure you.'

Marcus thought about the proposition for a few moments then he took a deep breath. 'OK. If it helps, I'll do it.' He looked up. 'Like I said, I keep remembering things . . . little things. I think it's being back here . . . where it all happened. I keep thinking of Jenny. When I close my eyes I can see her. She was really pretty and . . . '

'She committed suicide about a year after you were abducted. I've seen the inquest findings and it seems that she blamed herself.' Wesley watched the man's face carefully and saw a flash of something that looked like pain in his eyes.

'She was really nice. I . . . I loved her,' he said softly.

'What about her boyfriend, Gordon Heather?'

Marcus frowned. 'I didn't like him. I remember being scared of him . . . wishing he'd go away.'

Wesley drew the picture of the football team that Teddy Afleck had given to Steve out of his pocket and put it on the coffee table in front of Marcus. 'Do you recognise anyone there?'

Marcus picked it up and held it at arm's length. 'Should I?'

'Look carefully. Are any of the faces familiar.'

He stared at the photograph. 'It was a long time ago. I was only seven.' He was silent for a few seconds while he studied each face. 'He had dark hair . . . is that him?' He pointed to a man on the front row who wasn't, Wesley had to admit, dissimilar from the real target on the back row. At least Marcus had picked out someone of the right physical type which wasn't bad after all those years.

'I'm sure my brother wants to help in any way he can,' said Adrian Fallbrook with a hint of priggishness.

'Of course I do,' said Marcus quickly.

'We can make arrangements for you to see that doctor then?' said Heffernan.

Marcus hesitated before giving a nod of assent. Wesley noticed he was fidgeting with the front of his shirt. He'd been telling the truth when he'd said that the idea of hypnosis made him nervous.

Wesley suddenly remembered something else he'd wanted to ask. 'Your mother's friend . . . Mrs Tranter. Are you still willing to meet her?'

Marcus nodded. 'Yeah. Why not?' he replied before draining his glass of whisky.

Rachel Tracey wanted a change of scene. She'd been with the Wakefields since Leah's disappearance and, now the worst had happened, she felt she couldn't take any more. She had talked to Gerry Heffernan and he'd agreed to send someone else to stay with the family while the investigation continued. It wasn't that she didn't pity the Wakefields. But she needed to get out of that gilded cage for the sake of her own sanity.

Since she'd received her reprieve, it felt as if a huge weight had been lifted from her shoulders and when Gerry Heffernan and Wesley Peterson arrived at the Wakefield house, she greeted them with a smile that was inappropriately cheerful.

'How are things?' Wesley asked quietly as he stepped over the threshold.

'The doctor's given Suzy a sedative and she's gone to bed.' She hesitated. 'And the manager, Brad Williams, is back. Says he's here to support Suzy and Darren but if you ask me, he's got his own agenda.'

'Apart from protecting his investment and wanting to get his money back?'

'Mmm. He's looking bloody worried. I'm sure he's hiding something.'

Gerry Heffernan gave her an affectionate slap on the shoulder. 'Thanks, Rach. Well done. WPC Hanwell's taking over from you later so if I were you I'd go home and get a good night's sleep.'

Wesley looked at his watch. It was six thirty and hunger was gnawing at his stomach. It had been a long day. He needed a break himself if he was going to be at his best.

'I suggest we have a quick word with the Wakefields then go back to the station to collect our thoughts. We'll make an early start in the morning.'

The chief inspector barged ahead, Wesley and Rachel following in his wake. Darren Wakefield was slumped on the sofa, a cigarette between his fingers poised over the overflowing ashtray which lay on the seat beside him. He looked as if he'd been punched. The worst had happened and he was in his own private hell. He didn't bother looking up when the policemen entered the room.

Wesley felt Heffernan nudge his arm. It was up to him to do the talking. 'Sorry to bother you at a time like this,' Wesley began. 'But we'd like to ask some questions.'

Darren gave a small shake of the head, indicating that he wanted to be left alone. Wesley and Heffernan looked at each other. Perhaps it would be best to leave it till the morning. It was then they noticed Brad Williams, standing by the bar in the far corner of the room. Slowly, almost nonchalantly, Leah Wakefield's manager strolled over to the sofa and stood behind Darren, arms folded.

'What about you, Mr Williams? Do you mind answering some questions?'

Williams shrugged. 'Why not?' He glanced at Darren. 'Not here, eh.'

He led the way into the gleaming white kitchen and sat down on a high stool. 'I wanted to talk to you actually. There are things you should know and now Leah's . . . '

'Now she's dead?' Heffernan said bluntly, watching the man's face.

Williams looked uncomfortable. 'Yeah . . . er . . . '

'What did you want to tell us?' said Wesley. His empty stomach was making inappropriate noises and he hoped they couldn't be heard.

'A few weeks ago Leah thought she was being watched.'

Heffernan pulled himself up to his full height and glowered down at the man on the stool who was starting to look nervous. 'And you didn't think to report it?'

'That's cause I didn't believe her. She was always saying things like that. Darren was off the scene then and she didn't want to worry Suzy so I dealt with it. I asked a couple of roadies to keep an eye on her while she was in London and I told her to call me if ever she was frightened but she never did. The roadies never saw anything unusual and it all blew over – she never mentioned it again. I didn't think it was important. She was an imaginative girl. An artiste. Highly strung.'

'But now you think she might have been telling the truth?'

'I don't know. But I thought I'd better mention it.'

'Did she describe the person who was watching her?'

'No. But he drove a dark-coloured car. A Ford Mondeo. She called him Mondeo Man. I reckon it might have been some photographer. Paparazzi. She should have been used to it. She shouldn't have let it get to her.'

Wesley and Heffernan looked at each other. 'This man we're calling the Barber – the one who abducts women and cuts off their hair – he drives a dark-coloured saloon . . . possibly a Ford.'

Brad Williams looked Wesley in the eye. 'Well, I don't want to teach you your job, but I suggest you find him.'

Chapter Eleven

Letter from Juanita Bentham to Mrs Jewel of Brighton, 3rd February 1816

My Dearest Mrs Jewel,

I feel I must write for I am most vexed with my sister-in-law, Elizabeth, and her strange obsession with this so-called prophetess, Joan Shiner. She scolds me constantly for refusing to attend the woman's meetings and says I should not listen to our Rector, Mr Boden, who calls Mrs Shiner a false prophet of the kind warned against in the Bible. Joan Shiner has a grip on the hearts and minds of many of the villagers, almost as though she has some power over them. Sir John tolerates his sister's fancies, saying she has always been a silly creature and is in sore need of a husband, but I am worried for her and I would seek your advice.

I find myself in good health as my time draws near and yet there is something that worries me. The relations of that prodigious child known as the Amazing Devon Marvel have been concerning me of late. The boy's sister Annie, a sly girl, is Elizabeth's maidservant and his eldest brother, Joseph, is a carpenter on the estate. This Joseph watches me in a most impudent manner: perhaps he has never seen anybody before with a dark complexion such as mine but I find his stares objectionable. When I chided him one day for beating a dog, he gave me such a look that I feared at that moment for my life. And yet I am reluctant to mention his impertinence to Sir John who would dismiss him at once and deprive him of his livelihood.

I look forward greatly to receiving your good counsel, oh wisest of friends.

Your loving friend, Juanita Bentham

*   *   *

The day began early at Sedan House. The residents had to be got up and dressed. Rather like young children they had to be coaxed and cajoled into putting the correct arm into the correct sleeve. And over the years she had worked as a care assistant, Sheila Lovatt had learned patience because the alternative was unthinkable.

The room smelled faintly of lily of the valley and urine and Helen Sewell was asleep. She slept on her side, her expression serene, her left arm encased in flowered flannelette lay on the duvet, the thumb of her right hand touched her bloodless lips. Sheila stood there for a few seconds watching her.

The first thing she had to do was disturb Helen's slumbers in order to take her to the toilet before washing and dressing her. She was about to touch the woman's shoulder when something caught her eye.

A book lay on the floor; the old-fashioned kind of scrapbook that people used for keeping souvenirs: postcards, rail tickets, invitations. Sheila bent to pick it up and saw that it contained newspaper cuttings. Suddenly interested, she began to turn the pages and she recognised the name that appeared on the yellowed scraps of newsprint.

It wasn't a name that she'd given any thought to for almost thirty years but she knew it all right. A terrible case. A poor child abducted, never to be seen again. Marcus Fallbrook.

She wondered why Helen Sewell had gone to the trouble of cutting the reports of his kidnapping out of the paper and pasting them in a book at the time when the case was in all the papers. It was a mystery. And she knew there was no point asking Helen – she had probably forgotten why she'd done it herself.

Sheila flicked through the pages. Sure enough, they were all about little Marcus's disappearance. No other story featured in this sad tattered book. Poor mite, she thought as she stared at the little boy's face. He reminded her a little of her grandson and the thought made her shudder as she placed the scrapbook on the chest of drawers.

'He's my little boy.'

The sound of Helen's quivering voice made Sheila jump.

'Have you seen him? Do you know where he is?'

Sheila shook her head. Helen was back in the past ... in the time little Marcus had disappeared. But for people like Helen, this was normal. The past was more real than the present.

'Now, dear, it's time we got dressed, isn't it,' said Sheila soothingly.

'Are you here to look for him?' Helen asked, raising herself on
her pillows and staring into the middle distance. 'We've got to
look for him. We've got to find Marcus.'

Wesley Peterson had been exhausted. And even though Pam felt a
stab of irritation when he had fallen asleep on the sofa instead of
listening to her account of the problems she was facing with her
new class – at least three of whom had behavioural difficulties –
she had controlled her tongue.

She had heard about Leah Wakefield – the whole world knew
about it by now. The press hadn't been kind to the police.
According to the papers, they had failed to protect Leah. She
noticed how they always blamed everyone except the bastard who
actually killed her. Wesley had taken the criticism philosophically
. . . which is more than she would have done. She found herself
feeling angry on his behalf.

He went off to work early the next morning because he had a lot
to do before attending Leah Wakefield's postmortem – something
he wasn't exactly looking forward to.

When he arrived in the office he found Rachel deep in conversation with a young man whose face was familiar, but it took Wesley
a few moments to place him – Tim from Scientific Support was
leaning over Rachel's desk, sharing a joke. As Wesley watched
them he realised that at one time he would have felt a twinge of
envy. But he'd put all that behind him. If Rachel had met someone
she liked, he wished her luck.

After checking his messages he made straight for Gerry
Heffernan's office. If they were to catch Leah Wakefield's killer,
they couldn't afford to waste time.

Heffernan looked up as he entered the room. He looked as tired
as Wesley felt. There were dark rings beneath his eyes and his
shirt was unironed as though he had dressed in the dark. He
greeted Wesley with a weary 'hi' and pushed himself out of his
swivel chair with considerable effort, like an old man with
arthritic joints. 'I suppose I'd better muster the troops.'

Wesley looked at his watch. 'Colin's expecting us at the mortuary in an hour.'

The reminder that time was passing seemed to spur the chief

inspector into action. He gathered his team for their morning briefing and, once the day's enquiries and interviews were allocated and a team of uniformed officers sent out in search of possible sites where Leah had been held before her death, Wesley knew that it was time to face the trip to the mortuary. After the postmortem they planned to travel up to Clevedon to see Jenny Booker's family. It was an interview he and Heffernan were keeping for themselves. They both had an inkling, a nagging suspicion, that Jenny might be the key to the whole matter. But how and why, they didn't yet know.

When they arrived at the mortuary they walked through the polished corridors, scented with air freshener to banish the odour of death and formaldehyde, and Colin Bowman greeted them with a cup of Darjeeling and his usual high quality, organic biscuits.

Once the social niceties had been observed he led the way to the postmortem room where Leah Wakefield, small and naked, awaited them on a stainless steel table. Wesley could hardly bare to look as Colin's scalpel penetrated her ivory flesh. She looked almost like the child she had been before she had began her precocious career and encountered the darker side of rock music – although Colin was quick to point out that she was no virgin and that, in his opinion, she'd undergone a fairly recent abortion.

Her last meal had been soup. Vegetable. And crisps. Washed down with lemonade. Hardly cordon bleu but enough to keep body and soul together. Marks on her wrists and ankles suggested that she had been bound with rope during her captivity and it was almost impossible to know whether her head injury was caused by a fall against a hard object or a blow. But one thing was certain; it had been the head injury that had killed her. She had been dead before she entered the water.

Once the postmortem was over, Gerry Heffernan refused Colin's customary offer of refreshment. He was eager to get away from the hospital, walking purposefully like a man with something on his mind. But it wasn't until they were back at the station that he told Wesley what that something was.

Before they confronted Jenny's family he wanted to speak to Marcus Fallbrook again to see if he'd managed to remember any more about Jenny and Gordon Heather. He guessed that Carol Fallbrook was probably sick of having the police turning up almost daily on her doorstep. But it was necessary so she'd just have to get used to it.

They were about to leave when Steve Carstairs, the phone receiver cradled to his ear, began to gesticulate to attract their attention. Heffernan halted. Whatever it was might be important – or not as the case may be. Steve's judgement wasn't always razor sharp.

Steve put the receiver down, his eyes shining with juicy news. 'A witness saw a black Porsche waiting in the car park near the centre of Derenham village on the night Leah Wakefield was kidnapped. There was a man sitting in it and he matches Brad Williams's description. He got out and leaned on the car as if he was waiting for someone.

'Who's the witness?' Wesley asked.

'Teenage lad who'd been hanging around the phone box. He likes cars and he noticed the number plate – BRAO only the O looked like a D. BRAD.'

Heffernan scratched his head. 'Wasn't Williams supposed to be in London when she went missing?'

'That's what he said,' Wesley replied. 'Is this lad sure he'd got the right night?'

Steve nodded. 'It was youth club night. He's sure. And that's not all. We've had Leah's mobile phone records back. She rang Brad Williams's mobile on the night she disappeared. He didn't mention that to us, did he?'

'I think we better have another word with Mr Williams.'

Rachel had already gone over to the Wakefield house to tell them the findings of the postmortem – someone had to do it. Wesley rang her to say that they were on their way.

Wesley didn't trust Brad Williams. He knew more than he'd admitted so far, he was certain of that. Knowledge was power and the Brad Williams of this world kept back information as a matter of principle. But he had been in Derenham on the night of Leah's abduction and she had called him. That made him a suspect.

They found him at the Wakefields', at the house of mourning where he seemed to have assumed the role of guardian at the gate. Wesley had wondered whether he would lose interest in the Wakefields now that the goose who'd laid the golden eggs that paid for his Porsche and penthouse was well and truly dead. But he hadn't taken into consideration the morbid sentimentality of the public. A tragic death at a young age did wonders for the brand – James Dean, Elvis, Princess Diana all proved this point. Leah's latest album was already shooting up the charts. And the Wakefields had to be kept onside if he was to take full advantage of this grim harvest.

Brad Williams was reluctant to let them in at first. 'This is the last thing they need,' he said when he saw them on the doorstep. 'Can't you leave them alone?'

'We haven't come to talk to Mr and Mrs Wakefield. We've come to see you.'

He took a step forward, his body language aggressive. 'I've told you everything I know.'

But Gerry Heffernan stood his ground and after a few seconds Williams led them to a small study near the front of the house. They could hear the TV blaring in a distant room and Wesley visualised the Wakefields sitting, stupefied, in front of the moving images on the screen, trying to blot out the pain in any way they could.

Wesley came straight to the point. 'You were seen in Derenham on the night Leah was kidnapped. You told us you were in London.' He watched the man's face for a reaction.

Williams took a deep breath. 'OK. I admit I was here. I'd arranged to meet Leah but she never turned up.'

'Why did you arrange to meet her?'

There was a long silence, as though he was deciding how much to tell them. 'OK,' he said, slumping down in the deep leather chair that stood by the desk. 'It's ironic really. We were going to stage a kidnapping . . . for publicity. We all need publicity . . . to be kept in the public eye. We wanted to hit the headlines for a few days. Raise her profile.'

'So you kidnapped her and it all went wrong. She had an accident – a fall maybe – and . . . '

'No, no, no.' Williams shook his head vigorously. 'That's not true. She rang to say she was on her way but she never turned up. I never saw her. And when I tried to ring her mobile, it was switched off.' He looked Wesley in the eye. 'When I realised it had happened for real, I played it safe and called you lot in . . . went along with the news blackout like you asked.'

'The Wakefields were in on it?'

Another silence. 'No. We thought it was best to keep them in the dark. If the truth were known, we didn't trust their acting abilities.'

'So if your plan had worked you intended to report her kidnapping to the police for maximum publicity?' Heffernan asked ominously. 'And it would have been all over the papers.'

Williams looked sheepish and nodded.

The DCI put his face close to Williams's and the man backed away instinctively. 'I could do you for wasting police time.'

'But I didn't, did I?' Williams snapped, on the defensive. 'It never happened.'

'That's your story,' growled Heffernan. 'We'll be in touch,' he added as they left the room. It was a threat, not a promise.

'What do you think?' Heffernan asked as they walked to the car.

'I think he's telling the truth.'

'I don't.'

They got into the car and drove the short distance to Mirabilis. It was time they had another word with Marcus Fallbrook.

Carol Fallbrook sat upright on the sofa and stared at her newly acquired brother-in-law. Adrian had insisted that Marcus transfer his things from his Tradmouth guesthouse to one of their spare bedrooms – the actual room he had occupied as a child: Adrian had thought this was a nice touch; a gesture to welcome him; make him feel at home. Marcus's battered red Nissan sat outside on their gravel drive next to Adrian's new Range Rover and her six month old black VW Golf – a thorn between two motoring roses.

Carol looked at the headlines of the paper he was reading – a red-topped tabloid with a naked woman on the front. 'Leah murdered.' That said it all. The poor girl's fame and money couldn't save her. It only took one act of evil to put an end to it all.

She cleared her throat. 'So what are your plans, Mark?' She couldn't bring herself to call him Marcus yet, in spite of the DNA test results.

He looked up from his paper. 'Dunno yet.' His accent – his slovenly way of speaking as she saw it – put Carol's teeth on edge.

'Won't you have to go back to Manchester? There's your job. And what about your girlfriend?'

'Yeah, right.' The words irritated Carol but she tried not to show it.

'I'll have to go back up soon to sort things out . . . maybe bring

Sharon down.' He hesitated, looking Carol in the eye. 'I'm thinking of moving down here for good. Did Adrian tell you?'

'No, he didn't. What will you do? Where will you live?'

Marcus raised his eyebrows. 'Adrian said I could stop here till I've found somewhere.'

It took all Carol's self control to confine herself to polite 'Did he?'

The ringing of the doorbell saved her from saying something that might be reported back to Adrian by his precious long-lost brother and held against her. She hurried out into the hallway, seething with resentment. Why hadn't she been consulted before her husband installed this cuckoo in her well appointed nest?

And the sight of two policemen standing on her doorstep did nothing to improve her mood.

She had met the pair before – the scruffy Liverpudlian DCI and his rather good looking, well-spoken black inspector. They seemed pleasant enough but police were police. After confirming that Marcus was indeed at home, she invited them in and her offer of a cup of tea was accepted with appropriate gratitude.

Carol was determined to stay and hear what Marcus had to say for himself. Once the tea was made and brought it, her natural curiosity made her resume the seat she had vacated. It was her house after all.

It was Marcus who spoke first. 'I rang that lady last night . . . Mrs Tranter. I'm going over to Tradmouth to see her later.'

'Good,' said Wesley.

'She'll be able to tell me about my mum. I feel I never knew her.'

Wesley made sympathetic noises but he was anxious to change the subject. Marcus's psychological need to discover his roots could wait till another time.

'I don't suppose you've remembered any more about your abduction?' Wesley asked tentatively. 'We're on our way to talk to Jenny Booker's parents.' He watched the man's face, looking for a reaction, but he saw none. 'We'd really like to find out more about Gordon Heather, Jenny's boyfriend.'

'Am I going to see that doctor . . . the shrink?'

'We're trying to arrange an appointment. We'll let you know when . . . '

'I'm starting to remember more, you know. Now I'm here

things keep coming back. I remember something about a picnic. Jenny was there ... and her boyfriend. I remember being in this shed place. I couldn't get out and I was crying.'

Wesley and Heffernan looked at each other. It looked as if they'd hit the jackpot. 'Go on,' Wesley said quietly, not wanting to interrupt the flow.

'I just remember being scared. I was on my own and it was dark and I was really scared.'

'Was it Jenny's boyfriend who left you there?'

'Yeah, I think so. I remember Jenny with this big man and ... It must have been him, mustn't it?'

'You're doing well,' said Gerry Heffernan. 'Think hard. Is there anything else?'

Marcus shook his head. 'Bits keep coming back ... sounds and smells. But ... '

Carol frowned. 'What about your parents? Didn't you ever want to find them? Why didn't you try and find out about your background sooner?'

'I didn't remember my parents much. I don't think I had much to do with them. I remember Jenny better ... ' He swallowed as if he was choking back tears. 'But she left me – maybe that's what hurt – maybe that's why I blotted it out. It's only the accident and coming here that's brought it all back and made me want to find out who I really was.'

'We've been wondering about the travellers who found you. What can you remember about them?'

'Not much. I remember Carrie. And going to Aunty Lynne's ... I remember that.' There was something in the tone of his voice that suggested his memories of Carrie were more pleasant than those of Aunty Lynne.

'Did you ever ask Aunty Lynne about Carrie and how you got there?'

Marcus shook his head. 'Yeah but she'd never talk about it. Just said "least said soonest mended". That's what she always used to say ... "least said, soonest mended."'

Wesley stood up. 'Thank you, Mr Fallbrook. You've been very helpful.'

Marcus looked up at him, his eyes anxious. 'Look, I'm going to have to go back to Manchester sooner or later to sort things out. Then I'm moving down here for good.' He glanced at Carol.

'Blood's thicker than water, ain't it? Do you want me to give a statement now or what?'

Heffernan shook his head. 'From what you've told us, we really need to trace this Gordon Heather ... Jenny's boyfriend. He's been seen in this area recently and I don't suppose it'll do any harm to tell you that we'd like to question him about the abduction and murder of Leah Wakefield.'

Marcus looked shocked. 'You think he did that?'

'Do you remember him being violent at all?'

Marcus frowned. 'I just know I was scared of him. Maybe it was Jenny who protected me. Maybe he didn't dare do anything while she was around.' He hesitated. 'I dunno ... wish I did.'

Wesley thought here was something pathetic in the way he clung to Jenny's memory. She must have been the one stable thing in his early childhood and she had probably betrayed him for an unsuitable man.

Marcus's eyes widened, as though a disturbing memory had just flashed into his head. 'He had a knife. He used to clean his nails with it.'

Wesley stood up. 'Look, if you remember anything else that might help us – anything at all – please get in touch. You have my number, don't you?'

Marcus nodded.

Carol Fallbrook waited until the two policemen were out of the house before speaking. 'You did well to remember all that,' she said

Marcus detected the hostility in her voice. He shook his head, hurt and puzzled. Then he looked her in the eye. 'I went through Hell and now I'm home. Right?'

He started to make for the door. 'I'm going to see that old girl who knew my mum ... that Mrs Tranter. At least she wants to see me. At least she sounded pleased that I've come back.'

Carol ignored him and began to clear away the teacups.

Neil Watson had had business in Exeter that morning – a tedious meeting with the planning authority. He had once heard someone describe British archaeology as Indiana Jones and the Local Planning Department – he had laughed at the time but he guessed that this description wasn't so very far from the truth.

As he was in Exeter, he seized the chance to return to his flat for an hour or so, pick up his post and e-mails and grab something to eat.

Switching on the computer had probably been a mistake. There were no e-mails of note, just the usual crop of spam to be deleted, and he soon found himself logging on to the Internet.

His first port of call was the website of the Disciples of the Blessed Joan. As he read, he scratched his head. It was weird – especially the bit about the woman in California who claimed to be Joan Shiner's reincarnation.

After a while he widened his search. There seemed to be a lot on the Internet about strange religious sects that had sprung up in the seventeenth, eighteenth and nineteenth centuries, usually around some self-appointed prophet – or in Joan Shiner's case prophetess – who claimed to have a private hot line to the Almighty. Most had severe, Old Testament overtones: one man up near Manchester claimed to be a prophet who required the assistance of several virgins. It was a pity, Neil thought, that archaeologists couldn't plead the same bizarre necessities – if they did they'd probably be locked up.

He switched off his computer and turned to his notebook. Cracking the coded messages on the walls of the Bentham Arms attic room had been easy. He had discovered at a very early stage that the small pictures represented their initial letters. B for boat. A for apple. J for jackdaw. The more difficult letters like x and z were used as normal. The website of the Disciples of the Blessed Joan claimed that she had devised the 'sacred writing' herself. If this was true, she was no mistress of the art of encryption. A child could have done it.

And once the code was broken, the sayings proved disappointingly banal. A smattering of paraphrased biblical misquotations interspersed with what were probably Joan's own pearls of wisdom. 'The Shining Babe Shall Come', seemed to be a particular favourite. And 'Blessed is she who gives her tresses to the Shining Babe.' But the Shining Babe, by all accounts, had never arrived. The whole affair had ended in tragedy and disappointment.

The thing that surprised Neil most was that there seemed to be such interest in the failed prophetess today. There were those on the website who claimed they were still waiting for the Shining Babe's appearance, not in Devon this time but in the kinder climate of America's west coast. There were several mentions of the seven secrets, whatever they were. Neil doubted if he'd ever get to find out. The Reverend Charles Boden, the Rector of Stoke Beeching who had so vehemently opposed the Blessed Joan's brand of hocus-pocus, must have been a frustrated man.

Beside Neil's notebook lay the letters Lionel Grooby had lent him and, even though he was in a hurry, the temptation proved too great. He unfolded the first letter, careful not to tear the brittle paper, and began to read.

The correspondence was rather jumbled – there were copies of letters Juanita Bentham had sent to a lady in Brighton as well as various letters received by the Bentham family. Neil took particular interest in the correspondence between Sir John Bentham and the Rector, Charles Boden. Peter Hackworthy, the Amazing Devon Marvel, was mentioned a great deal and Neil wondered what had become of the boy. It was possible, of course, that the Rector had got his way and the boy had gone to Oxford, shaken off his humble origins and his grasping family and lived a long, peaceful and scholarly life before being buried in St Merion's churchyard with the rest of his family. Or had he ended up staying in Stoke Beeching and living in obscurity, his early promise stunted by his family's demands? He would have to find out.

In the meantime he'd keep digging.

The man hunt was on. Teddy Afleck had seen Gordon Heather in Neston which meant that he might still be in the area. If he had kidnapped little Marcus Fallbrook all those years ago and collected a ransom of fifteen thousand pounds, it was possible that he'd come back for another try with Leah Wakefield – another pay day, bigger this time. And Gerry Heffernan wanted him found.

The trouble was that Heather didn't have a criminal record – not under his own name at least. There was no picture of him apart from the rather poor image on the back row of some long-forgotten local football team. But the police were working on it; checking on hotels, guesthouses and caravan parks; examining the electoral register in case he'd been living locally for a while without their knowledge. Gordon Heather had to be somewhere. It was only a matter of time before they found him.

Gerry Heffernan had told Rachel Tracey to take the afternoon off – to get her head down and grab some rest after all those hours she'd spent nursemaiding the Wakefields. But she had come into work, pleading boredom, saying she'd rather be at work doing something useful than staring at the walls of her rented cottage. Wesley suspected that she wasn't comfortable on her own, having been used to living on a farm all her life surrounded by a large family.

The phone on Wesley's desk rang and a female voice on the other end of the line said a cautious hello and introduced herself as Linda Tranter. They'd met the other day.

Once Wesley had assured her that he remembered her, she began to sound more confident. 'I've just had a visit from Marcus Fallbrook,' she said. 'It was lovely to see him. He's so like his father but I can see Anna in him as well. I'm just ringing to . . . ' She gave a small girlish giggle. 'I don't know why I'm ringing really . . . probably just to thank you for putting us in touch with each other. Anna was very dear to me, you know. And to have her son back . . . Well, it's like a link with her, I suppose. Something nice after all that tragedy that's dogged the Fallbrooks over the years. The poor boy's had a hard life – oh, I'm calling him a boy but he's a middle-aged man. It'll take him some time to get used to our ways and . . . '

She continued in that vein for some time and Wesley listened politely to the flow of words until Linda Tranter paused to take a breath and he had the chance to interrupt.

'I don't suppose Marcus said anything to you about his abduction?'

'He said he didn't remember much and he was more interested in hearing about his mother, but that's only natural. Poor boy.' It was obvious that Linda Tranter was taken with the idea of her old friend's lost child returning to life. A happy ending at last to a tragic story.

Eventually Wesley, at his most tactful, managed to end the call. Della's old colleague was full of her meeting with Anna's lost son and, living alone, she had wanted to share her elation with someone. And that someone had been him.

He had just begun to go through the transcripts of the kidnapper's phone calls to the Wakefields when Rachel walked over to his desk and perched on the edge. He looked up and smiled. 'How are you feeling?' he asked.

She picked a pen off Wesley's desk and played with it absentmindedly. 'OK. I understand you and the boss are going off to see Jenny Booker's family soon.'

189

'We need to find out everything we can about her and her connection with Gordon Heather.' He looked at Rachel shyly. 'How are you getting on with Tim?'

Rachel's cheeks turned red. 'Who told you?'

'Nobody told me. I just saw you talking to him earlier, that's all.'

Rachel turned away. 'I'd better get back.'

'Any progress on the Barber enquiry?'

She turned around. 'I've had an idea. I seem to be the type he goes for so why don't I act as bait? I don't mind spending a couple of evenings ringing round local taxis as long as I can get it all on expenses and, who knows, I might strike lucky.'

Wesley stared at her for a few moments. He couldn't fault her logic but a slight feeling of unease nagged in the back of his brain. 'We'll have to make sure you've got enough back up ... that you're not put at risk.'

'You've never been a risk-taker, have you Wesley?' she said softly, eyeing the files and papers arranged with almost military precision on his desk and the neatly written list which lay near his hand.

'That's how I manage to stay out of trouble.'

'So you'll ask the boss?' She grinned. 'And if I know Gerry Heffernan, the answer'll be yes.'

She was right, of course. Gerry Heffernan would think it was a great idea to use Rachel to lure the Barber into a trap – in fact he had suggested it a few days earlier. But as he watched Rachel walk away, Wesley wasn't so sure.

No sooner had he thought of the DCI than he appeared, grinning, at the office door, his shabby anorak over his arm, anxious to be off.

Wesley stood up, mentally preparing himself for a two hour drive up the M5. At least it wasn't in the main tourist season which meant, barring accidents or road works, they shouldn't face too many delays.

Marcus Fallbrook's face was solemn as he entered the sitting room. Carol looked up. Something was wrong.

He slumped down in the armchair opposite her. 'What time's Adrian home?' He sounded worried, distracted.

Carol looked at her watch. 'Not till late. He said he had things to see to at the Morbay office.'

190

Marcus put his head in his hands. 'I wanted to see him before I left.'

'You're leaving today?' She tried her best to keep the elation out of her voice.

'I've just had a call on my mobile. It's was from Sharon, my girlfriend. She's been taken into hospital in Manchester, suspected appendicitis. She wants me to go up. And anyway, I've got loads of stuff to sort out if I'm moving down here for good so it'll give me a chance to get things organised.' He looked up at her and smiled awkwardly. 'Look, Carol . . . er . . . thanks for everything. It can't have been easy for you having me landing on your doorstep like that.'

Carol made polite noises of denial. Faced with this barrage of apologetic charm, it was hard to be churlish.

'I'd better pack then.' He stood up and began to move towards the door. Then he stopped suddenly and swung round. 'If the police want to see me, tell 'em I won't be away for long . . . just a few days probably.'

'OK,' said Carol with the best grace she could muster.

It would have suited her fine if her newly found brother-in-law never returned. But she knew he'd be back and probably with Sharon – who would no doubt turn out to be a bottle blonde in a denim miniskirt – in tow.

Who was it said you can choose your friends but you're lumbered with your family?

The motorway was clear. The powers that be, in their wisdom, must have decided to give the motorist a temporary respite from the agony of road works and the traffic jams they spawned. Unexpectedly, Wesley enjoyed the drive. With the pressure of the Leah Wakefield investigation, he was glad of a change of scene, however brief. And there was always a chance that Jenny Booker's family might be able to given them some clue as to Gordon Heather's whereabouts.

Gerry Heffernan sprawled in the passenger seat, his eyes closed as though he were asleep. Wesley was surprised when he spoke. 'Does any of it make sense to you?'

Wesley kept his eyes on the road as he pondered the question. 'How do you mean?'

'A rich kid was abducted in 1976. There was a ransom demand

and the money was picked up but the kid was never returned. The kidnapper abandoned him somewhere in the wilds.'

'Maybe something went wrong and the kidnapper panicked. Or he thought that if he'd left him somewhere close to home, he'd be caught. Or perhaps the message saying where he could be found went astray somehow and the Fallbrooks never received it.'

'Possibly. Then the kid turns up again after thirty years saying he was taken in by some New Age travellers who went across to Ireland. Never an easy lot to pin down, New Age travellers. They'll be dispersed to the four winds by now so they're no good as witnesses.'

'True. However, one of them – Carrie – came back to England and dumped the kid with a woman in Manchester called Aunty Lynne before going off on her merry way. Wonder how she explained away the fact that she suddenly had a kid in tow?'

Heffernan shrugged. 'With these New Age traveller types it wouldn't surprise me if there were quite a few random children wandering about. And they'd hardly go to the authorities if they found an extra one, would they?'

'And they'd be unlikely to listen to the news or read the papers so they wouldn't realise the whole country was looking for Marcus Fallbrook.'

'He said they went to Ireland soon after they picked him up anyway. What do you think of our Marcus? Think he's on the level?'

'Seems to be. And he is who he says he is. The DNA test has proved that beyond any doubt. He went to see Linda Tranter, you know – said he wanted to find out more about his mother.'

'That's understandable.'

'And his story about the accident in Manchester all checks out . . . as does the address he gave. And the existence of Aunty Lynne: there was definitely a Lynne Jones at that address and, according to official records, she died six months ago just like he said. He left a message to say he was going back to Manchester for a while . . . something to do with his girlfriend.'

'So that's that. And he's pointing the finger at Gordon Heather so it looks like he's probably responsible for Leah Wakefield's murder and all. Same MO. Only this time he got greedy. Something went wrong and the girl ended up dead.'

Wesley smiled. 'Teddy Afleck saw him in Neston recently so he's around somewhere.'

'Unless he's already done a runner,' said Heffernan pessimistically. 'And I don't see how Afleck could have been so certain it was him after all these years . . . not if he just saw him in a car. It might have been someone who just looked like him. Or Afleck was lying.'

Wesley didn't answer. He preferred to look on the bright side for the moment until the investigation proved him wrong. They were nearing the Clevedon turn-off. He indicated and pulled off the motorway.

Jenny Booker's parents lived near the waterfront. Wesley, who had never been to Clevedon before, drove slowly, taking in his surroundings. It was a pleasant seaside town, slightly old-fashioned: the sort of place young people leave in search of excitement and the retired flock to in their droves. Jenny Booker had left but her adventure had been her downfall – she had ended up drowning herself.

Wesley drove along the promenade and parked to examine a map. Gerry Heffernan decided to get out of the car and stretch his legs and, after getting his bearings, Wesley did likewise. As the two men strolled towards the entrance to the elegant Victorian pier which stretched out to sea on slender legs, they looked out over the muddy brown waters of the Bristol Channel.

'Let's leave the car here and walk it,' Wesley suggested, hoping for a bit of exercise after two hours spent in the driving seat.

Heffernan seemed content to follow where Wesley led, which was up a side road and to the front door of a Victorian villa. Jenny Booker's childhood home looked solid, respectable. And the young nanny's family clearly weren't short of money themselves; although they probably weren't in the same elevated financial bracket as the Fallbrooks.

They were expected, that much was clear from the speed with which Mrs Booker answered the front door. She had been waiting for them.

The first thing Wesley and Heffernan noticed about Jenny Booker's mother was her monochrome appearance. Her hair was dark grey and so where her clothes. Even her pale flesh had a grey tinge, as though the colour had drained from her life many years ago.

Wesley made the introductions as they were invited in. Mrs Booker seemed nervous. But Wesley thought this was hardly surprising. Their visit must have brought back painful memories. But then those memories had probably never really gone away. He had read the inquest findings. Jenny had been depressed for a while and she had gone out one evening without saying where she was going. Her parents had reported her missing and the next day her body had been washed up on the seafront. They had never recovered from their loss. Nobody could ever recover from something like that.

Why had Jenny Booker taken such a drastic step? The more Wesley thought about it, the more it seemed likely that she had been unable to live with the guilt that must have consumed her. And she would hardly have felt guilty unless she had been involved in some way – even if that involvement had been indirect, such as bringing the kidnapper into little Marcus's life.

They were led into a living room which, on first impression, looked dark and cramped. It wasn't until Wesley looked around that he realised the room was quite spacious: it was only the dark red walls, the highly patterned carpet and the almost Victorian level of clutter that made it appear smaller than it really was. A tall thin man was sitting on the edge of the large velour sofa and he stood up as his wife brought the visitors into the room. He smiled too much as though he was anxious to please.

'We're sorry to bother you like this,' Gerry Heffernan began. 'But I think I explained on the phone that . . . ' He searched for the words but none came out.

Wesley took over. 'There have been some developments in the case Jenny was involved in . . . the abduction of Marcus Fallbrook.' He paused. Mr and Mrs Booker were sitting close together side by side, quite still, hanging on his every word. He felt suddenly overwhelmed with the responsibility. 'Marcus is still alive,' he said softly. 'The abductor abandoned him and he couldn't find his way back home. He was found by some travellers and taken to Ireland.' He could almost read their minds. If the child had been alive, there had been no reason for Jenny to take her own life out of remorse. She had died for nothing. Mr Booker's hand searched for his wife's and clutched it tight.

Gerry Heffernan leaned forward. 'You might have heard about Leah Wakefield . . . .'

'It's been on the news,' Mr Booker said quickly.

Heffernan gave Wesley a nudge. It was his turn to speak. 'We have reason to believe the two abductions could be linked. We've talked to Marcus Fallbrook and we're anxious to trace a man called Gordon Heather. He used to be, er . . . a friend of your daughter's.'

'We met him once,' said Mr Booker, giving his wife a sidelong glance. 'Can't say I liked him much. Don't ask me why; it was nothing you could put your finger on.'

'You wouldn't have a photograph of him by any chance, would you?'

Mrs Booker thought for a few moments and shook her head.

'What was he like?'

She looked at her husband. 'I thought he was a bit odd. Didn't you, dear? He was interested in . . . Oh I'm not sure if you'd call it the occult but something like that. Sorry, I didn't really take much notice of what Jenny said about it. I just wished she'd found herself someone more . . . '

'More what?' Wesley sensed she was on the brink of a revelation.

Mrs Booker shook her head and a curtain of straight grey hair fell over her face. 'More normal, I suppose. We just met him the once when we went down to visit her and I can't say I took to him, did you, John?'

Mr Booker shook his head. 'Wasn't all there if you ask me. Jenny said he worked in a boatyard but he told me he was some sort of historian . . . researching into something. No idea what. He didn't make much sense. I asked Jenny what she saw in him and she said she liked him because he was different. He wasn't boring, she said. Well, she wasn't wrong there, was she?' he added bitterly.

Heffernan nodded. His children had only just made the transition from teens to young adults. He understood only too well how the siren appeal of the unsuitable friend or partner can turn the impressionable young away from the path of reason and common sense. His kids had survived unscathed. Others weren't so lucky.

'You told us on the phone that you'd kept Jenny's things.' Wesley thought he might as well get straight to the point.

Mrs Booker stood up. 'We've touched nothing in her room. Everything's still as it was when . . . ' Wesley and Heffernan looked at each other. This was better than they'd expected. 'The letters she sent us are all up there as well. You're welcome to have a look at them but . . . '

Wesley told her not to worry; they'd do their best to leave everything as they found it. He was only too aware that their daughter's bedroom would have become a shrine to her memory, even after thirty years, and that the situation needed sensitive handling.

They were shown to the room and then left alone, much to their relief. Jenny Booker's room was neat and tidy. A towelling dressing gown hung behind the door and the dressing table was laden with the usual trappings of a young woman's life; make-up and perfume and a few items of cheap jewellery. The thing Wesley found most disturbing was the sight of the red cotton dress laid across the single bed as though its owner had popped down the landing to the bathroom and would return in a few minutes to change her clothes.

Jenny's letters were in the top drawer of the dressing table. She had written in a round, almost childlike hand and her letters were chatty, informal and easy to read.

Wesley was just reading an account of a visit to the cinema with Gordon Heather when Gerry Heffernan spoke. 'Here, Wes, look at this.' He thrust a letter into Wesley's hand. 'What do you think?'

Wesley read the letter and looked up. It was a cheerful letter, full of chat about her charge, Marcus, whom she clearly adored. There were sections about his achievements at school, the things he said. She even wrote that she'd spotted a child who looked so like Marcus that they could have been twins. The girl was obviously devoted to the little boy. Perhaps as devoted as a mother.

'Somehow she doesn't strike me as the sort of girl who'd go along with a plan to kidnap the kid she was supposed to be looking after. What do you think?'

Wesley shrugged. A nagging inner voice told him that he had to agree with Gerry Heffernan's assessment. Jenny Booker wrote so fondly of little Marcus, in her letters home. She told her mother of their outings together; of his little foibles. And behind the loving words Wesley could detect veiled criticism of Marcus's mother, Anna Fallbrook. She seemed, according to Jenny, to take little interest in her son's day-to-day life: that was the preserve of the paid nanny. And there was something else.

Wesley re-examined the letter in his hand. 'They're a strange family, not at all like you and Dad. Mrs Fallbrook – she likes me to call her Anna – spends a lot of her time painting and when she's in her studio she mustn't be disturbed. I felt sorry for Marcus the

196

other day: he'd just got back from school and he really wanted to show her some work he'd done – he'd got ten out of ten and he was really excited. Anyway, he ran over to the studio to show his mum his book but she just shouted at him to go away ... really bawled him out. The poor little thing was in tears and I did my best to cheer him up. I sometimes wonder if people like that should have children. Marcus is such a nice little thing – I don't know how she can treat him like that. Mr Fallbrook's not much better. He took Marcus on the boat and just ignored him and he was clinging to the rail terrified. Then he shouted at me to go and see to Marcus and I had to take him ashore and calm him down. Then yesterday I was in the garden and I saw a woman walking through the trees by the river. I've seen her before a few times but I don't know who she is. I know Mr Fallbrook had been down there messing with the boat so she must have been with him. But I shouldn't really say anything, should I? How the other half live, eh.'

He turned and put the letter down on the dressing table. He was starting to like Jenny Booker. She sounded kind; a gentle girl thrust into an unfamiliar world where parents gave their children everything ... apart from love. He was getting a different picture of the Fallbrooks as well. Jenny painted a picture of a selfish pair, preoccupied with their own affairs. He found himself wondering who the woman walking through the trees had been and why Jenny mentioned that she'd seen her before. Had the woman been involved with Jacob Fallbrook perhaps? Had they had an assignation down by the river? Or maybe the whole thing was innocent and Jenny had just had a vivid imagination.

Gerry Heffernan passed him another letter. He took it and read it. 'Gordon took me to a strange place at the weekend. Howsands was a village that had been washed into the sea years ago. There are still a few abandoned houses standing on the cliff top but it's far too dangerous to get to them. There was one house that had half fallen over the cliff already and you could see the rooms inside ... the wallpaper and the fireplaces. It was really weird. Gordon says there was a church in the village but it's already gone. He says that when the churchyard was falling into the sea you could see the skeletons tumbling off the cliff. I told him to shut up. I used to like Gordon but now I'm getting a bit fed up. The things he's interested in make me uncomfortable and I'm thinking of finishing it. I think it's cooling off anyway so I hope he won't take it too hard. He says he'll meet me for a picnic on Thursday while Marcus is at school. Perhaps I'll tell him then. What do you think, Mum? I feel bad about hurting him but I think it'll be for the best. If it's not right, it's not right.'

Wesley handed the letter to Heffernan. 'This is dated a few days before Marcus's abduction. He went missing on the Thursday. She mentions meeting Gordon but she says Marcus'll be at school. No mention of him coming to the picnic.'

'Maybe Gordon suggested they take him out of school ... give him a treat.'

Wesley shook his head. 'She was going to tell Gordon it was over. She'd hardly want the kid around. And besides, I can't see Jenny taking him out of school unofficially. Perhaps I'm wrong but Jenny Booker sounds like the sort who'd do things by the book. Mind you, Gordon's statement saying him and Jenny were looking at engagement rings hardly holds up if she was planning to finish with him.'

Heffernan sighed. 'You know what, Wes, I think you're right. I've read these and Jenny sounds more like Mary Poppins than the Nanny from Hell. She disapproved of the way the Fallbrooks were treating their kid and she was going to end her relationship with Gordon Heather ... which puts paid to the theory that he had her in his power. And he hardly sounds like an evil genius either. Have we got this all wrong, Wes?'

Wesley shrugged. He didn't know what to think any more.

They drove back to Tradmouth. This time there was an accident on the motorway and the journey took them three hours.

Helen Sewell was dead. She'd died peacefully in her room at Sedan House at four forty-five or thereabouts. Sheila had found her slumped in her chair, her eyes closed, her head bowed over her chest. Sheila had become used to death – peaceful death: falling asleep and never waking up sort of death – and when she looked at Helen Sewell, she knew that her time had come. Helen's sleep was of the permanent kind.

The doctor had been called – discreetly of course – and he had pronounced life extinct, diagnosing a stroke from the appearance of Helen's mouth which had been dragged down at one corner by some invisible force, contorting her still, ash-pale face.

When the body had been whisked away by the undertakers,

Sheila stood in the middle of Helen's room and felt a great wave of sadness overwhelming her. She always felt like this when a resident passed away, even though she would never have claimed to have known Helen intimately. And she certainly knew nothing of her life before she came to Sedan House.

She suddenly remembered the scrapbook she'd seen. It wasn't by the bed so, presumably, Helen had put it away. Sheila walked over to the chest of drawers and began to search.

It didn't take long to find what she was looking for, hidden underneath Helen's underwear in the top drawer. She turned the pages, reading the cuttings more thoroughly this time. Every one was about Marcus Fallbrook's abduction. Helen must have been obsessed with the case, she thought. Either that or she had some personal interest. Maybe she'd worked for the Fallbrook family at one time. Sheila knew nothing about Helen's life so anything was possible.

She went through the book until she came to a picture: the blurred black and white image that had featured on most front pages in the country back in June 1976. Little Marcus Fallbrook standing proudly in his school uniform against a background of leafy rhododendron bushes in full bloom.

She stared at the picture for a few moments before closing the scrapbook and shoving it back in the drawer.

The new resident, Mrs Barnes, had a daughter who was friendly with a chief inspector from Tradmouth. Joyce was a nice, chatty woman and her relationship with this representative of law and order had cropped up in conversation several times. Maybe she could have a word with her that evening when she made her daily visit . . . see what she thought.

At seven o'clock Rachel Tracey made her first phone call. Somehow she hadn't been able to face an evening doing nothing so, after consulting Trish, she'd decided on action. And if she was the one to catch the Barber, it would do her career no harm whatsoever.

She put on her coat and waited for the first cab of the evening to turn up. Trish had already settled down to watch TV and they had agreed that Rachel would keep her informed of her whereabouts at all times. And if anything untoward happened, she would call for back-up right away. Rachel didn't intend to take any chances . . . with her life or her hair.

As she waited, she closed her eyes and thought of Tim. But she realised that she knew very little about him. During their conversations, it had been her who had done most of the talking, telling him about the cottage she was sharing with Trish and the problems of moving away from home for the first time. Perhaps she should have done less talking and more listening, she thought, cursing herself for her stupidity. Tim was nice. So was Wesley Peterson, but he was married and she had long given up hope in that direction. Sooner or later her love life had to look up. Up till now, it had been a sorry catalogue of failure and longing for the unattainable.

She heard a car horn outside. The show had begun. It might be a fruitless exercise but at least she was doing something. And Gerry Heffernan had thought it was a good idea.

Rachel hadn't really taken much notice of minicab drivers before but now, sitting in the back seats of a series of shabby saloon cars, she paid them particular attention.

Dressed respectably in jeans and an anorak to avoid any unwanted attention that might distract her from her goal, she booked cabs to and from her cottage to the centre of Tradmouth, using a pub just round the corner from the police station as a base. This pointless shuttle service had lost its air of possibility and excitement by the fifth ride of the evening.

The journeys were uneventful and the drivers seemed to fall into two categories; chatty or morose. But there were none who made her inner alarm bells ring.

The sixth journey, however, was different. A couple of minutes after she'd made the call to the last taxi firm on her list, a dark-blue Ford Mondeo, turned up, driving slowly like a kerb crawler looking for business. It was ten thirty and the streets were quiet which sharpened Rachel's sense of danger as she stood there, a young blonde woman alone outside a pub, obviously waiting for something. The cab rolled up slowly and the driver seemed to study her before braking and reversing back down the road towards her. He was clean shaven with bushy eyebrows, glasses, a baseball cap and a face that seemed rather plumper than the photo fits provided by the Barber's victims. He wound down the window.

'Cab for Tracey?' The words seemed a little muffled as though the man was chewing . . . but Rachel could see no ruminatory movement of his jaws.

'Yeah,' said Rachel, opening the back door. She got in, gave her address along with brief directions and the driver set off at speed, the force sending Rachel sprawling across the back seat. At last this was it. Her heart began to pound with excitement as she righted herself and sat there, preparing for fight or flight. She pushed the button on her mobile phone that would summon help and held it by her side so the driver wouldn't realise what she was doing.

'Where are we now?' she asked in a clear voice so she could be heard at the other end of the phone line. 'Oh I know, we're just passing the naval college, aren't we?' She kept up the commentary, hoping that the driver would mistake it for chattiness. 'I think you've come too far. That's the Sportsman's Arms on our right, isn't it? This isn't the way, you know. You're turning down the road to Derenham. You've got to go back.'

The man drove, silent, as though he hadn't heard.

'This is the crossroads. You can turn right to Hatbourne and get back on the main road. Don't go straight on. You're taking us right out of our way. We must only be a mile and a half from Derenham. Why are you stopping?'

She looked at the phone. It was lit up. As arranged, the officer on the other end was listening. She only hoped he or she hadn't fallen asleep. She hoped help had been summoned. She felt in her pocket and fingered the handcuffs. At least, unlike the other victims, she was prepared. She tried the door but the child locks were on and for a split second she experienced a wave of panic, like a trapped animal discovering that there was no escape.

The driver had got out and was making his way round the car. There was something about the way he walked, the way he stared ahead like an automaton that made her afraid. When he opened the door she looked him in the eye and said nothing. She could see the glint of metal in his hand. Scissors or a knife – she hoped it was the former: the last thing she wanted was to be expecting the Barber and getting a crazed rapist instead. He was reaching in, stroking her hair. But instead of backing away as he expected, she summoned all her courage and leaned towards him.

'I'll get out, shall I?'

This seemed to stop him in his tracks. He froze.

'If you want my hair it'll be easier if I get out of the car. It is my hair you want?'

He hesitated before nodding, like a child asked whether he wanted a treat, and Rachel breathed a sigh of relief that she hadn't miscalculated.

She closed her eyes. This was it. She could feel the warmth of his body near her. He took her shoulders gently and turned her round, raising the hand holding the scissors.

He caressed her hair for a few seconds before taking a strand between his fingers and rising the scissors. She heard a snipping sound. Then the crinkling of a plastic bag. He was putting the hair carefully into a bag. Then he put his mouth close to her ear. 'Keep still. I won't hurt you,' he whispered. She could feel his hot breath on her face as he gasped like a lover. He pressed his body hard against her and her heart lurched. What if he wanted more than her hair? She stiffened, her heart pounding, her hands numb with fear.

Then she heard the sound of a patrol car in full cry. Distant at first but getting nearer. Closing in.

The Barber froze as if he didn't know what to do, torn between finishing his self appointed task and making his escape. Suddenly Rachel swung round, catching him off balance. She grabbed his wrist and deftly twisted his arm up his back, pulling the handcuffs from her coat pocket with her free hand. He began to struggle but she held on. But with each movement she was losing her grip on the situation.

'I'm DS Tracey, Tradmouth CID, and you're nicked,' she said, aware that the words sounded feeble. He was almost free.

As she clung on, the patrol car came into view. And as she grabbed at the back of his jacket, the fight seemed to go out of him. When at last a trio of uniformed constables relieved her of her responsibility, she sank breathless to the ground.

The man said nothing as the handcuffs went on. Staring at Rachel, he spat what looked like wads of cotton wool out of his mouth onto the ground and his face immediately took on another shape. He looked thinner. And Rachel thought there was something familiar about him although she couldn't tell what it was.

As the Barber was pushed into the patrol car, his eyes met hers again and she shuddered, tears pricking her eyes.

Chapter Twelve

Letter from Elizabeth Bentham to Letitia Corly, 28th February 1816

My dear Letitia,

Was not Mrs Shiner's last meeting at the inn most wondrous? Though I was most afraid when the Blessed Joan prophesied that Cain would rear his head and there would be death and deception. Of all the prophesies she made, this seemed the most urgent, do you not think? Her Shining Babe must be due at any time and I have been chosen to attend the birth and the opening of her wondrous box. Oh how I am truly honoured and blessed.

One strange thing happened yesterday that I must tell you of. Our steward came to my brother, Sir John, with a tale that Joseph Hackworthy, our carpenter, was drunk and had near broke the head of a carter who remonstrated with him. He is eaten with some sickness of the soul and has been seen tearing down bills announcing his young brother Peter's performances. It is most strange.

My sister-in-law, Juanita, nears her time and Sir John prays that the child will be a boy.

Do you attend Mrs Shiner's next meeting on Wednesday? It may be the last before the Shining Babe is born.

Your affectionate friend, Elizabeth Bentham

The Barber had spent the night in one of the cells in the bowels of Tradmouth police station but the experience, as far as Wesley and Heffernan could tell, didn't seem to have bothered him in the least. He sat opposite them in the interview room, the tape running, smiling to himself as though he were enjoying some private joke.

Wesley knew that Rachel had been shaken by her ordeal but she was putting a brave face on it, moaning about the mess the prisoner had made of her hair. Not that it looked much different to Wesley.

Gerry Heffernan had already said that he thought the man was a few ants short of a picnic but Wesley was inclined to be a little more sympathetic. From what the custody sergeant had told him, it sounded as if the man had problems – some sort of psychosis or obsessive disorder maybe. But, whether he was mad or simply bad, they had to get to the bottom of the affair.

The man they had been hunting for the past few weeks sat quite still in the white paper suit he had been given when his own clothes had been taken away for forensic examination. His thin face still bore the remnants of a layer of theatrical make up and one of the bushy eyebrows he had stuck on drooped drunkenly, giving him the look of an aging wild animal who had come off worst in a fight for supremacy.

Heffernan leaned forward. 'You terrified the life out of those poor women.'

'They never came to any harm.' He spoke pedantically, calmly.

'You can't say that. They're traumatised . . . scared to go out of their houses. And what about the one you put in hospital?'

'I didn't mean to hurt her. And you can't prove otherwise.'

Wesley looked him in the eye. There was something familiar about his face but he couldn't tell what it was. They didn't have a name for their prisoner yet. So far he was refusing to reveal it. 'You haven't answered the chief inspector's question. Why did you want to cut their hair? What did you do with it? If you told us, we might understand.'

The gentleness of Wesley's tone seemed to startle the Barber more than any bullying words could have done. He looked up at Wesley. 'It has to be made out of hair . . . fair hair. If it's not ready . . . '

'If what's not ready?'

'The shawl.'

Wesley and Heffernan exchanged glances. 'Whose shawl?'

'I was told to send it.'

'What?'

'The hair.'

'Who told you?'

The Barber looked around, as though he was afraid somebody might be eavesdropping. 'A woman in California is carrying the Shining Babe. It's on the website.' He swallowed. 'You should read it.'

Wesley leaned forward. 'So what have you got to do exactly? Collect the hair and send it to California? I don't suppose you have to send money as well do you?'

The man suddenly looked uncomfortable. 'That's just for her expenses.'

'Whose expenses?'

'The Prophetess Lindy . . . '

Heffernan and Wesley looked at each other. 'Lindy?'

'She's the Blessed Joan reincarnated. She has her sacred box. It contains the seven secrets of the universe.'

Heffernan mouthed something Wesley couldn't quite make out but he decided to ignore him. This was getting more interesting by the minute. 'You're talking about Joan Shiner?'

The answer was a nod.

'She was around at the beginning of the nineteenth century, wasn't she? How did you find out about her?'

The man's eyes lit up. 'Are you a believer yourself?'

Heffernan grunted. 'Every heard the saying beware of false prophets?' he muttered under his breath. 'How did you get sucked in?'

The prisoner drew himself up to his full height. 'I resent your attitude.'

Wesley put up a hand. 'I'm sorry, let's start again. Tell us how you found out about Joan Shiner.'

He looked at Wesley as though he'd found an ally. 'I first heard about her when I lived round here years ago. Then when I was in hospital up in Leeds . . . '

'What was wrong with you?' Gerry Heffernan asked with what Wesley considered unnecessary brutality. The man obviously had problems and his own chosen strategy was softly softly.

The prisoner swallowed hard. 'I'd rather not talk about it.'

'You've not got much choice, mate,' said Heffernan brutally. 'I'll ask again. What was wrong with you?'

After a long silence the prisoner spoke. Quietly, almost inaudibly. 'I've, er . . . had problems. Something happened and . . . '

Heffernan snorted but Wesley got in quickly to rescue the situation. 'Tell us what happened.'

'My girlfriend . . . she died.'

'I'm sorry,' said Wesley automatically. 'You were telling us how you became interested in Joan Shiner.' He tilted his head to one side and waited.

'Like I said, I heard about the Blessed Joan when I lived here and I was drawn to her. Did you know she was buried at Howsands – I went there once but there was nothing to see. Her grave had been swallowed by the sea.' He paused, a faraway look in his eyes.

'Go on,' prompted Wesley gently.

'I've been in and out of hospital a lot over the years and, about eighteen months back, one of the other patients had this old book about the Blessed Joan and her prophesies and . . . I'd known about her before but this time her prophesies seemed . . . really spoke to me. And when the box containing the seven secrets of the universe came into the possession of the Prophetess Lindy, she started the website. As soon as I left hospital, I went on the internet in the library and typed Joan's name in. That's how I found the Disciples' website and . . . '

Wesley nodded. He could just see the Prophetess Lindy, using the old story of Joan Shiner and her strange cult, preying on the vulnerable like the man sitting there in front of him . . . no doubt getting them to send money. Some people, he thought, should be locked up.

'Why the disguises? How did you get hold of the theatrical make up? What gave you the idea of the bogus taxi?'

The prisoner smiled at his own cleverness. 'Last time I was in hospital I read a book about a serial killer who used a different disguise each time he killed. And he made his car look like a taxi . . . used false number plates and copied the signs of local taxi firms. I copied the idea. Only I never killed anybody. Killing's wrong. It's a sin.'

'Well at least we agree on something,' Wesley said. 'You were going to tell me about the make-up?'

'I used to have a flat in Leeds. It was above a theatrical shop and when it closed down the manager said I could help myself to anything I wanted. It was all there . . . greasepaint . . . false beards . . . .' He gave a childish little chuckle as if this part of his escapade had been rather fun. Then the smile suddenly disappeared. 'The hair I collected . . . I can send it, can't I?'

Heffernan opened his mouth to speak but Wesley got in first.

206

'We'll have to see,' he said gently. 'We don't know your name yet . . . or where you live. You wouldn't tell the custody sergeant . . . or the arresting officer, DS Tracey.'

'She hurt me.'

Wesley decided to ignore the last comment. 'What is your name? We'll find out sooner or later, you know.'

The prisoner thought for a few moments. Then he pressed his lips together in stubborn defiance.

Then, to Gerry Heffernan's surprise, Wesley took a photograph from a folder and laid it on the table in front of him. 'Recognise this? You were a lot younger then. How old would you say? Eighteen? Nineteen?'

Tears began to fill the prisoner's eyes.

'I know your name already,' Wesley said in a low voice. 'It's Gordon Heather, isn't it? And your girlfriend who died was called Jenny Booker.'

Gerry Heffernan's mouth fell open. He picked up the photograph and looked first at the man then at the image of the young footballer.

'Changed a bit, hasn't he?' Heffernan said as though the prisoner couldn't hear him.

'Times change,' was Wesley's soft reply.

'So we're going to let him stew for a bit?' Wesley climbed into the driver's seat, wondering why Heffernan had cut the interview with Gordon Heather short. He was their prime suspect after all; for the abduction of Marcus Fallbrook and the murder of Leah Wakefield. The trouble was, now that he had met him, he found it hard to see him as Leah's ruthless, calculating kidnapper. Even Gerry had his doubts as to whether money featured much, if at all, in Heather's strange inner world.

Heffernan nodded. 'He's been charged with the taxi abductions and with assault. He'll keep.'

Paul Johnson and Trish Walton had gone to the address Heather had given – a run down bed-sit on the wrong side of Morbay. There they'd found the victims' blond hair, lovingly tied, ready for dispatch to California. There had also been a box filled with theatrical make-up and various disguises, along with a computer. It all fitted with the story he gave. But there was nothing in that sad little flat to connect Heather with the abduction of Leah Wakefield.

207

Heffernan looked at his watch. 'It's eleven already. We've been down there with Heather for two and a half hours. I've started to wonder if he's really as daft as he's trying to make out. All this Shining Babe stuff might be an act . . . maybe he wants to plead insanity.'

That possibility had occurred to Wesley. The Barber abductions had taken a great deal of planning. And Heather had admitted himself that he took his MO from a book about a serial killer. Who was to say he didn't emulate the plot in more ways than one?

'Perhaps he intended to do more to his victims than give them a haircut. Perhaps he chickened out at the crucial moment. Or perhaps if he'd carried on, the violence would have escalated until he killed.'

'Do you think he could have killed Leah Wakefield?'

'He could certainly have abducted her. And as for killing her . . . If something went wrong or if he lost control, why not?'

Wesley thought for a moment. 'You could be right. And you've got to admit that he's the best suspect we've got at the moment. In fact, he's our only suspect.'

'Leah's manager, Brad Williams – I reckon he's still hiding something.'

'Now you're clutching at straws.'

Wesley started the engine. 'So where are we're going?' Gerry Heffernan had been rather mysterious about his plans and Wesley was curious.

'Sedan House . . . the nursing home Joyce's mum's in. I had a call from Joyce before we started interviewing Heather. She says it might be nothing but one of the nurses had a word with her last night. She's a bit worried about something she found.'

'What?'

'Joyce didn't say. But it's something to do with an old lady who died yesterday.'

'Suspicious death?' That was all they needed.

'Apparently not. But something was found in her room. Joyce said the nurse mentioned the name Marcus Fallbrook.'

Wesley said nothing. He started the car and the DCI sat back in the passenger seat, perfectly relaxed.

Neither man said much for the remainder of the journey. Wesley concentrated on the road while Gerry Heffernan admired the view from the window; the fields, bare after the harvest or dotted with grazing cattle or sheep.

208

'Are they expecting us?' Wesley asked as he turned the car into the drive of Sedan House. The drive was lined with thick rhododendron bushes which made the approach to the house dark and oppressive. Wesley didn't really know what to expect when they got there. But life is full of surprises.

They were met by Sheila, the care assistant who'd spoken to Joyce. She seemed to be a placid woman, plump and patient. She didn't strike Wesley as someone who'd let her imagination get the better of her.

'I hope I'm not wasting your time,' she said. 'But it just seemed a bit strange, Helen having all that stuff about that little boy's kidnapping ... and I read in the paper that you think it could have something to do with that Leah Wakefield's murder so I thought ... '

'You did the right thing, love,' was Heffernan's reply as she led them along a thickly carpeted corridor to a door bearing Helen Sewell's name, written on a piece of card and secured with a pair of drawing pins ... easily replaced.

'Helen had Alzheimer's,' Sheila said matter-of-factly as she unlocked the door. 'She'd been getting worse recently and she started talking about a little boy. As far as we know she had no kids of her own but she kept asking where he was and started asking for Marcus ... asking women if they were his mother. It didn't click until I saw the scrapbook that the Marcus she was talking about was Marcus Fallbrook.'

She walked across the room, took the scrapbook out of the top drawer and handed it to Heffernan who began to flick through it.

'She was looking at it the morning before she passed away. I didn't really know what to do and I knew you were a friend of Mrs Barnes's daughter so ... '

Wesley and Heffernan exchanged looks. 'You were right to let us know,' Wesley said. 'Thank you.'

Sheila looked at Heffernan slyly. 'Joyce Barnes speaks very highly of you.'

Heffernan felt himself blushing. 'Er, thanks ... er, Sheila. We'll just have a look through her stuff, if that's OK.'

She took the hint and left them to it.

'Nice woman,' the DCI said to Wesley as he watched her disappear through the door. Then he suddenly swung round. 'Right. Let's have a look, shall we.'

Helen Sewell's room was neat and clean. Not a thing out of place, just how Wesley liked it. It made searching a place so much easier if the occupier had a tidy mind.

Gerry Heffernan put the scrapbook on the bed and they began to search the room. In the wardrobe Wesley found a pack of official documents at the back of the shelf above the clothes rail, wrapped in what looked like an old tablecloth.

They made themselves comfortable on the bed while they went through the papers. They learned that Helen Caroline Brice had been born in Plymouth in 1936 and that she was a widow – her husband's death certificate telling them that he'd died of a heart attack in 1995 – and by the absence of birth certificates and photographs, they surmised that the marriage had been childless.

With the official documents was a birthday card, yellowed with age, signed 'your sister, Jacqueline'. There were no other letters in the drawers or wardrobe so perhaps Jacqueline was dead. Or the sisters had simply lost touch.

Wesley called over to Gerry Heffernan who was sifting through a pile of bank statements he'd found in the bedside drawer.

'She had a sister called Jacqueline.'

'Mmm,' Heffernan replied, not particularly interested. 'The matron should have details of her next of kin.' He thought for a few moments. 'You don't think this woman, Helen, could have been one of them New Age travellers who picked Marcus up, do you? What if she sent him to stay with her sister.'

'Aunty Lynne? Jacqueline? It's possible. And the birth certificate says that Helen's middle name was Caroline . . . Carrie? He said he was picked up by a Carrie.'

'Don't jump to conclusions, Wes.'

Gerry Heffernan opened another drawer and took out a framed photograph. Two women. Helen Sewell and another, younger, woman. Between them sat a child aged around nine or ten. His heart began to race as he stared at the picture. 'Hey, Wes. Do you reckon this kid's Marcus Fallbrook?'

Wesley took the picture from his boss's hand and studied it. 'It certainly looks like him. But on the other hand it's not a good picture. Maybe we're clutching at straws, Gerry.'

'Jacqueline . . . .Aunty Lynne?'

'It would explain why Helen Sewell had the Fallbrook case on her mind. If it was something she never talked about – a secret

210

between her and her sister that had bothered her for years – the Alzheimer's would have removed her inhibitions. First chance we get we should talk to Marcus again. He might know if Aunty Lynne's real name was Jacqueline.'

They left Helen Sewell's room, shutting the door quietly behind them – it was a quiet sort of place.

Matron's office was near the front door and, from the casual way they were greeted, the matron was used to death and used to the police turning up on her doorstep.

The details of the residents' next of kin were kept in a tall grey filing cabinet in the corner of the room. Matron, a tall, angular woman with short dark hair, took out Helen's file and placed it on the desk. Wesley opened it and discovered that Helen's next of kin was a Pauline Vine who lived in Tradmouth. There was no mention of her relationship to Helen.'

'Did you know Helen Sewell had a sister?'

Matron raised her eyebrows. 'No. There was never any mention of a sister.'

'This Pauline Vine . . . ?'

'She's a cousin of Helen's late husband . . . visited her about once a month.'

'It looks as if the sister could be dead then.'

Matron smiled. 'Or they haven't spoken for years.'

With this cynical conclusion, they left. They had Pauline Vine's address and they wanted a chat with her as soon as possible . . . preferably over tea and biscuits. Wesley called Trish Walton on his mobile and asked her to give the woman a call.

With the photo of young Marcus and the two women safely in Wesley's pocket, they left Sedan House. The place was getting them down.

'Could Helen have been Marcus's kidnapper?' asked Heffernan as they drove back to Tradmouth. 'Is it possible?'

'If Marcus Fallbrook's kidnapper is the same person who killed Leah Wakefield, that rules out Helen Sewell. She's been in here all the time and she didn't even know what day it was, never mind riding round on jet skis.'

'Colin Bowman said that a woman could have done it.'

Wesley shook his head. He couldn't see it somehow. But then stranger things had been known to happen.

'As soon as Marcus gets back we'll show him this photo – ask

211

him if this is really him. And if it is, who he's with. I want to know more about the women in his life.'

The woman who was waiting in reception for them on their return to the police station was almost as wide as she was tall. Her lank grey hair was tied back with a sparkly hair slide of the sort Wesley had only seen before worn by teenage girls on a night out. In her favour she had a pretty face with delicate features. She must once have been beautiful. But three score years and a lifetime of overeating had put paid to all that.

The desk sergeant said something to her and she stood up.

'Is it Chief Inspector Heffernan?' Her voice was high pitched and sweet with a slight Devon accent.

'That's me, love. What can I do for you?'

'My name's Pauline Vine. I had a call from a policewoman . . . about Helen Sewell. I live nearby so I told her I'd pop in right away and have a word. My late husband was a policeman, you know. Jack Vine . . . he was a sergeant.' She looked around. 'I've never been inside the police station before.'

Heffernan gave her his most encouraging smile, showing a row of uneven teeth. 'That's what comes of living an honest life, love. Come on, follow me. I'll get someone to bring us a cup of tea. This is Inspector Peterson, by the way.'

The woman nodded to Wesley and gave a little giggle. Wesley suspected she was enjoying herself.

'So you're related to Helen Sewell?' Heffernan began when they were sitting in the interview room with tea in front of them. China cups had been ordered. Nothing but the best.

'By marriage. She married my cousin Harold. And we worked together in a children's home . . . Raleigh House in Morbay. It's closed down now, of course – change of policy. They like children to be in foster homes now. I was a house mother there for five years and Helen worked as a care assistant.'

'What was she like?'

Pauline Vine went on to catalogue Helen Sewell's virtues. She was a nice woman, she told them: so tragic about her developing Alzheimer's. Still, she was in a better place now, she said piously, dabbing her eyes with a clean tissue. Helen had been so nice to her when her husband, Jack, had died. She had no idea why she should have been in possession of anything to do with that poor

212

little boy who was abducted. The idea of Helen having anything to do with something like that was absolutely ridiculous, she said with conviction.

Helen hadn't been able to have children which was a shame because she'd loved kids. Harold died about ten years ago which was very sad.

'We found a card amongst her possessions from her sister, Jacqueline. Do you know anything about her?'

'I knew she had a sister up north but she didn't see anything of her. They lost touch.'

'Why was that?'

Pauline Vine shook her head.

'Did Helen ever talk about her past – before she met your cousin, Harold?'

Pauline considered the question for a moment. 'Come to think of it, she didn't. Her and Harold didn't get married till they were in their forties and I remember she said she travelled a lot when she was younger but that's all. She didn't go into detail.'

Wesley glanced at his boss.

'You wouldn't know if the sister's still alive?'

'I've no idea. I'm sorry. Helen never talked about her. I got the impression there'd been some sort of falling out.' She looked Heffernan in the eye. 'The policewoman said this is something to do with the murder of that singer, Leah something.'

'We're keeping an open mind at the moment,' Wesley said, afraid he was sounding rather defensive.

The truth was that they were still floundering about. They needed a lucky break and they needed it fast.

There was something they were missing. Something obvious. And Wesley needed to think. Gerry Heffernan was beginning to believe that the Helen Sewell business might be irrelevant. Perhaps she'd worked for the Fallbrooks at one time and that's when the photo was taken. Perhaps the other woman was a fellow worker, not her sister. Jenny Booker might have known. But Jenny Booker was dead.

Wesley favoured the possibility that Helen may have once been a New Age traveller before going on to lead a more conventional existence with Pauline Vine's cousin, Harold. He had no evidence whatsoever that Helen had such a colourful past but stranger

213

things had happened. And if she had been in the group that had found Marcus wandering – if she had taken him up north to stay with her sister, Jacqueline, who was known as Lynne – that would explain everything. Including why Helen had taken such an interest in the case. Maybe she had decided to keep Marcus because she couldn't have children of her own and she panicked about her decision later, hiding her crime by leaving the child with her sister. It was the only theory that seemed to fit.

Now they had Gordon Heather in custody, he hoped that Marcus would identify him as his kidnapper once and for all. They needed a lucky break ... and it was so close he could feel it.

He'd contacted the Garda over in Ireland on the off chance that they might have been aware of the travellers who took Marcus under their wing but he'd received a negative answer. It was all a long time ago and no child matching Marcus's description had ever come to their attention. It had been a long shot.

He sat at his desk playing with his pen, turning it over and over in his fingers. He looked at his watch. It would be another late night. He picked up the telephone on his desk. It might make things easier at home if Pam was warned that he'd be late again. Although in recent weeks she had seemed to accept it with a sympathetic smile rather than the resentful snarls he had had to endure during previous investigations.

When she answered the phone, he began to apologise but she cut him short. It was OK. She understood. But Michael was asking for him. He wanted to show him his new reading book. If anything was guaranteed to make Wesley feel bad, it was the thought of being a neglectful father. He put the phone down with a heavy heart. He'd make it up to Michael, he promised himself. When the case was wrapped up he'd help him with his reading book, take him out for the day.

His thoughts were interrupted by Gerry Heffernan's large hand on his shoulder. 'Fancy a trip to the Bentham Arms?'

'I thought we were going to have another word with Gordon Heather.'

'He can wait. The longer we keep him, the more he'll want to talk.'

Wesley looked doubtful. He was keen to interrogate Heather again, to hear his version of Marcus Fallbrook's abduction. But no doubt the boss had reasons of his own for the delay.

214

'I want to ask Barry Houldsworth what he knows about the father, Jacob Fallbrook. I've had an idea.'

Wesley sat back. 'And what's that?'

'What if Fallbrook arranged his son's kidnapping for some reason ... in cahoots with the nanny and her boyfriend. What if something went wrong?'

'And the kid wandered off? So you reckon Gordon Heather was just obeying orders?'

'Let's face it, Wes, can you see him as a ruthless kidnapper? He's in cloud-cuckoo-land ... away with the fairies. And there's no evidence in his flat or his car that he had anything to do with Leah's kidnapping. He didn't kill her.'

'I wouldn't be too sure of that. He could have got rid of the evidence and only left the Barber stuff to throw us off the scent. Think how organised he was with the bogus taxi business. All this Blessed Joan stuff could be an elaborate act. I still think he's our star suspect, Gerry.'

Gerry Heffernan shrugged. 'He'll keep. Are you coming or what?'

Half an hour later they were sitting in the saloon bar of the Bentham Arms, facing Barry Houldsworth across a polished table. Gerry Heffernan was drumming his fingers impatiently on the glossy wood. He had a pint of bitter shandy in front of him. Wesley, the driver, had had to make do with an orange juice again. He was sick of orange juice but he was too preoccupied, or lazy, to think of a suitable non-alcoholic alternative.

'So you're still having problems?' Houldsworth sounded annoyingly smug.

'We're getting there, Barry, we're getting there.' Gerry Heffernan did his best to sound positive. In more exalted circles they referred to it as 'spin'.

Houldsworth looked at Wesley. 'So why do you need my help if it's all going so well?'

'We've arrested Gordon Heather,' Wesley replied. 'You know this "Barber" business?'

'Bloke who fancies himself as a lady's hairdresser? Yeah. It's not him is it?'

'As a matter of fact it is. He's been in and out of mental hospitals for years ... ever since Jenny Booker did herself in. He got conned by a group in California who claimed to be the followers of Joan Shiner. You've heard of her, of course?'

'She had something to do with this pub . . . her cronies met in the attic.'

'That's right. Gordon Heather claimed he was collecting hair to be woven into a shawl for the baby some self-appointed prophetess is expecting. At least that's the official story. The trouble is, with the hair he had to send money.'

Gerry Heffernan shook his head. 'There's one born every minute.'

Wesley put down his orange juice carefully on the nearest beer mat. 'Marcus Fallbrook reckons it was Heather who abducted him.' He watched Houldsworth's face for a reaction.

Houldsworth rolled his bloodshot eyes. 'You mean the person who's claiming to be Marcus Fallbrook? You're sure he's not an impostor?'

'He remembers things only the real Marcus would know. And the clincher is that a DNA test has confirmed it. He's Marcus Fallbrook all right.'

Houldsworth took a long drink from his pint glass. 'We had Heather in for questioning but we could never prove anything.'

'You think he did it?'

'Oh yes, I'm sure he did . . . him and the girl.'

'Anybody else in the frame? The father, for instance?'

'I didn't like the father . . . he was a cold bastard. But he wasn't a serious suspect.'

'Anyone else?'

'There was Teddy Afleck, the father's ex-business partner. Fallbrook treated him like shit and there was a lot of resentment there. I suppose it could have been for revenge as well as hard cash.'

'It's taking revenge a bit far to abduct their seven-year-old son.'

'But, according to you, he wasn't killed was he? He was taken somewhere and dumped. Afleck – if it was Afleck – might have thought he'd be found and taken home. He didn't reckon with a load of travellers with no sense of responsibility.'

Wesley and Heffernan looked at each other. What Houldsworth said made sense. And Heather worked for Afleck at the time so he might have been used to do some of his dirty work.

'But what about Leah Wakefield? Are you absolutely sure the details of the Marcus Fallbrook ransom notes didn't get out somehow? Some officer working on the case with a loose tongue perhaps or . . . '

Houldsworth smashed his glass down on the table. 'Nothing's impossible. You've worked on major investigations so you know that as well as I do. There's always some bright spark who can't resist impressing his girlfriend or his mates with his inside knowledge.'

Heffernan sighed. Houldsworth was absolutely right.

Wesley leaned forward. 'Do you remember a sergeant at Tradmouth called Jack Vine?'

'Jack. Oh aye. He worked on the Fallbrook case just before he retired. Why?'

'It's just that we came across his widow recently.'

Houldsworth grunted as though the conversation was starting to bore him.

Wesley changed tack. 'Was Jacob Fallbrook one for the ladies? Only we've seen some letters Jenny Booker wrote to her parents and there's a hint that there was a woman about. Or maybe I was reading too much into it. She didn't say anything specific.'

Houldsworth's eyes widened. 'I did hear something to that effect. But we didn't consider it relevant at the time.'

'So the Fallbrooks' marriage was rocky?'

Houldsworth shrugged. 'Are you charging Gordon Heather with the Fallbrook kidnapping?'

'Possibly.'

'What about Leah Wakefield's murder?'

Gerry Heffernan shook his head. 'We need to discover where she was held – get some forensic evidence that'll clinch it once and for all.'

'Best of luck then. I'd lock him up and throw away the key,' said Houldsworth, standing up. 'I need the gents,' he said as he edged his way unsteadily round the table.

'I think we're being dismissed,' Heffernan whispered in Wesley's ear.

They drained their glasses.

'You seen your mate Neil recently?'

Wesley put his hand to his forehead. 'I knew there was something I wanted to do. Neil was interested in Joan Shiner and her followers because the symbol of her cult was carved on some of the graves he was excavating. I wonder if he's managed to find out anything more about her. It might help us to be armed with a few facts when we interview Gordon Heather.'

'Where is he?'

'Should be in the churchyard.'

He began to walk towards the door and Heffernan followed. Soon they found themselves outside in the late September sunshine. It was warm and Wesley took off his jacket before strolling in the direction of the church.

The high barriers had been taken down now that the exhumations were finished and Wesley spotted Neil immediately, working in the deep trench getting his hands dirty.

'Found anything interesting?' he asked from the side of the hole.

Neil looked up. 'Hang on a minute.' He climbed up the ladder at the head of the trench, leaving three colleagues to carry on the good work, and placed the trowel he'd been using neatly in a black plastic bucket.

'I think I'm getting there,' he said, his eyes alight with enthusiasm.

'Getting where?' Heffernan asked. He'd never really known whether or not to take Neil Watson too seriously. In his opinion archaeologists didn't really belong to the real world.

'My murder investigation. A bloke called Grooby has this sampler . . . embroidered using human hair. I've translated the symbols and it says "Cursed be the Cain in our midst". What do you make of that?'

Wesley raised his eyebrows. 'If I remember rightly from my Sunday School days, Cain was the first murderer so it could mean that one of Joan Shiner's followers had killed someone. But it doesn't tell us who the murderer was . . . or the victim.'

Neil looked vaguely disappointed. 'I've found out all about Juanita Bentham, the woman buried with the mystery skeleton. And I've looked at various records to see if any local boy went missing at around the time of her death. But I couldn't find anything.'

'Now you know what I've got to put up with,' said Wesley, turning away. 'Good luck.'

He needed it. And so did they.

'I think we've kept Gordon Heather waiting long enough,' said Gerry Heffernan as Neil climbed back into his trench.

'You've taken your time.' Gordon Heather stared ahead, as if he was past caring.

'We've had things to do,' said Heffernan as he landed heavily in the wooden chair. 'I've had someone looking up the Prophetess Lindy on the Internet. Nice little scam she's got going. We've been in touch with the police in California too. They're going to look into it and if they find her she could be facing charges of obtaining money by deception or whatever they call it over there.'

'I don't believe you.'

'Suit yourself.' Heffernan pretended to consult his notes. But Wesley could see the pages were blank apart from a few doodles, pictures of boats mainly.

'I think we should have a little chat about Marcus Fallbrook.'

Heather flinched as though someone had hit him. 'I've told you. I had nothing to do with that. I was with Jenny when he disappeared.'

'I'm sorry about what happened to Jenny,' said Wesley softly, his eyes on the man's face. 'I suppose she blamed herself for not watching Marcus more closely. Is that why she did it, Gordon? Is that why Jenny killed herself? Did she feel responsible?'

The answer was a nod, accompanied by a stifled sob. Gordon Heather was crying.

Heffernan leaned forward. 'According to Marcus you were involved in his abduction.'

Wesley touched the chief inspector's arm, a gesture of warning. The last thing he wanted was to drive Gordon Heather over the edge. He was close enough to breaking down as it was.

But Heffernan carried on. 'You kidnapped him, didn't you? And Jenny helped you.'

Heather let out another sob and wiped away the tear that was dribbling down his cheek with the back of his hand.

Wesley leaned forward. 'It's all right, Gordon. Take your time. Would you like a cup of tea?' He could hear Gerry Heffernan's muffled snort of derision but he ignored it. In his opinion Gordon Heather needed coaxing rather than bullying.

'Yes please,' replied Heather, meek as a frightened child.

Wesley nodded to the young constable who was sitting by the door who quickly got the message and hurried out. 'We could do with one too,' Wesley called after his disappearing back. His mouth was dry and he needed something to sustain him.

He smiled at Gordon. In his opinion nice cops always learned far more than nasty cops. 'Why don't you tell us everything you know about the Fallbrooks? Jenny must have talked about them a lot.'

He inclined his head politely and awaited the answer. Gerry Heffernan next to him shuffled his feet impatiently. As far as he was concerned, Gordon Heather was a grade one nutcase and anything he said could hardly be relied upon to be the truth. Not that he'd be lying deliberately – it was just that he considered that Gordon's truth was unlikely to be the same as anyone else's.

'She told me things . . . lots of things.'

Wesley leaned forward. 'What things?'

'About him. About the father. There were secrets in that house.'

'What secrets?'

Gordon Heather hesitated for a few moments before he began to speak.

Chapter Thirteen

Letter from Mrs Sarah Jewel of Brighton to Juanita Bentham, 20th March 1816

My dearest Juanita,

I rejoice to hear the news that you are safely delivered of a fine son and pray that you and the babe are well. It may be that Mr Jewel and I shall visit Devon soon for I long to be reunited with you and to see your sweet little Charles.

News of Joan Shiner's confinement has reached Brighton and some say that she was not with child at all but rather that she suffers from dropsy. I did hear tell of a box of secrets. Have you any news of such a thing?

Your Rector's protégé, the Amazing Devon Marvel, appears in Brighton on the eleventh of next month and all society is to attend. I await his performance with eagerness for I have heard much of the phenomenon and long to see him with my own eyes, as I long to see you, my dearest friend.

With my kindest love to you and your little one. Sarah Jewel

'She used to go away ... Marcus's mother. She used to go to London and leave Jenny to look after Marcus. Jenny thought she had a man ... heard her talking on the phone to him. She felt sorry for Marcus. She said it wasn't right. It upset her.'

'What did?'

'Fallbrook's whores walking around as if they owned the place.'

'Fallbrook had women? Who were they?'

Heather suddenly looked unsure of himself. 'Don't know. Never saw them. Only know what Jenny told me.'

After a few more minutes of fruitless questioning, Wesley and Heffernan left the room. Both men thought that they'd learned all they could from Gordon Heather for the moment. And somehow neither could see him as Leah Wakefield's murderer.

'Think any of that is relevant?' Heffernan asked as they walked back to the CID office.

'If he's telling the truth it means that the Fallbrooks weren't as squeaky clean as they wanted everyone to think at the time. This business about Jacob Fallbrook's women friends and Anna's calls to her fancy man isn't in any of the police reports so they obviously succeeded in fooling Houldsworth into thinking that they were a happy, united family. But we've only Heather's word for all this. I wouldn't take everything he said as gospel, Gerry.'

'True. And as for any of it being connected with what happened to Marcus . . . '

'Do we tell him what Heather's saying about his parents' private life?'

Heffernan shrugged. 'I don't know. What do you think?'

'I don't know either. But I do think that whoever kidnapped Leah is walking around with a hundred thousand pounds burning a hole in their pockets. Sooner or later they won't be able to resist spending it.'

'So we keep an eye out for anyone who's spending money they shouldn't have? It's as good an idea as any. But if our man has any sense, he'll stash it away until the fuss dies down.'

'Luckily for us, people don't always act rationally,' said Wesley.

Rachel was waiting for them back in the CID office, fanning herself impatiently with a piece of paper.

Wesley asked how the search for the place where Leah was held was progressing.

'No luck yet,' she said with a sigh. 'They've just started on the area near Afleck's boatyard.' She paused. 'Afleck's got the builders in apparently.'

Gerry Heffernan was suddenly alert. 'I thought Afleck was supposed to be broke.'

'Maybe he's taken out a loan,' Rachel suggested.

Heffernan shook his head. 'Teddy Afleck's been struggling ever since Jacob Fallbrook pulled out of the business. I reckon he's kept it going on a wing and a prayer . . . and a sympathetic bank manager. Maybe we should have a word with our Mr Afleck . . .

see where the money's suddenly come from. The hundred grand ransom the Wakefields paid for Leah has to be floating around somewhere – and if someone's got it, it's my bet they won't be able to resist spending some of it. Especially if there's an urgent need like in Afleck's case. I can tell you from experience that half his equipment's knackered and there's yards on the Trad that can do the work twice as quick and undercut him for price and all.'

'You think Afleck kidnapped Marcus ... and now Leah? But Marcus said Gordon Heather abducted him.'

'Heather might have helped Afleck. He was working for him at the time after all. Perhaps they used to be closer than they'll admit.'

'We mustn't forget the possibility there might be two kidnappers. Who's to say that the similarity of the notes isn't intended to confuse us? Someone got to know about the original note somehow and decided to use it to muddy the waters?' Wesley considered the options for a few moments before coming up with an idea that had been nagging at the back of his mind for some time. 'I'm wondering, in view of what Heather told us about Jacob Fallbrook's extra marital affairs and Anna's attitude to her son, whether Jenny organised it all to give the Fallbrooks a jolt ... got her boyfriend to help her. Perhaps things got out of hand.'

'And somehow her and Heather managed to lose the kid. It all went wrong.'

Wesley nodded. This sounded a possible scenario. Perhaps Jenny did it for the noblest of reasons and it all backfired and then afterwards she couldn't live with what she'd done. 'I need to have another word with Marcus. When did he say he'd be back?'

'He didn't. I've tried to get him on his mobile but I've had no luck. I'll get onto the Greater Manchester force – ask someone to go and see him and find out what his plans are and ask him to get in touch. We can't have our most important witness going walkabout.'

'Mind you, with everything that's happened I can understand why he wanted to go and sort things out back home. And he mentioned a girlfriend ... name of Sharon.'

Heffernan grinned. '*Cherchez la femme*.'

Wesley frowned. He felt more confused now than when the case first began.

*   *   *

Neil Watson was getting distracted. Looking through the micro-film records of the *Tradmouth Echo's* back copies – way back in this case – he came across reports from the time when King George III had suffered attacks of porphyria which had been diag-nosed by the doctors of the day as madness. The time when the fat, debauched Prince Regent had ruled in his father's place; when America had already been lost and the Brighton Pavilion was brand spanking new. Neil read every article, every advertisement for strange and wonderful things, with the rapt fascination of one discovering a strange new universe. But he told himself that he had to concentrate on the matter in hand – to look for any refer-ence to Stoke Beeching or Joan Shiner.

Several of Joan Shiner's meetings were reported, as was a protest by the Reverend Charles Boden and some of his parish-ioners, who were objecting to Joan's activities in the area. It seemed, reading between the lines, that they weren't having much success – Joan's claims being so much more exciting than the prospect of matins and a lengthy sermon. Joan's star was in the ascendant but it had vanished from the skies as quickly as it had appeared. It had all ended in tears and she had been exposed as a charlatan.

Then a headline caught Neil's eye. 'Devon Marvel unwell. Miraculous powers fade.' He glanced at the date – a month or so after Juanita Bentham's death – and read on. It seemed that the Devon Marvel's prodigious talents had failed him during an evening at an assembly hall in Brighton. The calculations he had once performed with effortless ease now proved beyond his cap-abilities. He had hesitated and made the most basic errors, earning himself the boos and jeers of the audience. It seemed that it had been an embarrassment all round.

Neil scratched his head, wondering what had caused this dra-matic fall from grace. Perhaps the boy had just had enough; per-haps he had been suffering from exhaustion brought on by the schedule imposed on him by his avaricious father. Neil continued his search but he found no further mention of Peter Hackworthy, the Amazing Devon Marvel, who must have sunk back into obscurity after his brief brush with the world of celebrity. But the papers did record Joan Shiner's demise in 1817 – a full year after her Shining Babe had failed to make an appearance – with what seemed like inappropriate glee.

He switched off the machine. Much as he was enjoying his sojourn in the Regency period, he had things to do.

It was four o'clock by the time Wesley steered the car down the corkscrew lane, overshadowed by greenery, that led to Teddy Afleck's boatyard. The reports of the commencement of building work hadn't been exaggerated. A builder's van stood next to the offices and the sound of drilling and hammering drifted over, masking the hypnotic lapping of the waves.

Afleck himself was working on the propeller of a small cabin cruiser, beached on the concrete slipway. The tide had receded, leaving little islands of seaweed. Wesley breathed the salty air in deeply as he climbed out of the driver's door. Gerry Heffernan was already making his way over to Afleck who had stood up to greet him. Obviously recognising an old customer, he extended his hand to Gerry who shook it with distant politeness rather than his usual bonhomie. Afleck was a suspect after all.

'Good to see you, Gerry,' Afleck said with what looked to Wesley like a forced smile. Once the introductions were made, he led the way into the office and invited them to sit.

'I was wondering if I'd see your lot again after that lad came here asking about Gordon Heather.'

'We found him.' Wesley and Heffernan looked at each other.

'Er, how is he these days?' It was impossible to tell from Teddy Afleck's expression whether he thought the rediscovery of Gordon Heather was a good or a bad thing.

'He's been having problems . . . '

'Sorry to hear that,' Afleck said with what sounded like sincerity. 'He was a strange lad but . . . You'll let me have that picture back, won't you? I told the officer who came . . . '

'Of course,' said Wesley. 'You're having some building work done I see.'

Afleck smiled. He didn't look like a man with something to hide but then, in Wesley's experience, it was often hard to tell. 'Long overdue, I'm afraid. There were things that needed doing if I was to stay in business. Equipment I needed to buy.'

Gerry Heffernan sat back in the hard wooden office chair and looked Afleck in the eye. 'I know this is a cheeky question, Teddy, but where's the cash coming from?'

'It's no secret.' There was a small pause before Afleck continued, as though he was thinking of what to say. 'I've, er, come into a little windfall. Uncle of mine died and left me the lion's share. He was quite well off. All things come to those who wait.' He grinned, pleased with himself . . . and the providence of rich uncles.

'We'll have to check it out,' said Gerry Heffernan, sounding more than a little embarrassed.

'Be my guest. Cup of tea?'

They both declined. Wesley looked at his watch. They planned to visit the Fallbrooks after this and time was tight.

'Just one thing I wanted to ask you,' Wesley said. 'We've been hearing stories that Jacob Fallbrook had affairs.'

A smirk spread across Teddy Afleck's face. 'Jacob was a randy old bugger. I always felt a bit sorry for his wife. Mind you, she was no angel.'

'Was there any woman in particular?'

Afleck looked away. 'Me and Jacob didn't talk much after he left me in the shit. Anyway, it was no concern of mine if he'd got himself into a mess, was it?'

'A mess?'

'Going with other women and keeping it from his wife. That's mess enough for any man in my book.'

Wesley and Heffernan looked at each other, wondering if there was a Mrs Afleck.

Wesley had a sudden thought. 'Does the name Helen Sewell mean anything to you. Or Jackie . . . that would be her sister?'

There was a flicker of recognition in Teddy Afleck's eyes, gone in a split second but unmistakable.

'Have you heard the names before? Could Jacob have known one of them?'

Afleck looked undecided for a moment, then shook his head. 'Look, Jacob wasn't squeaky clean . . . not in his love life and certainly not in his business life. But I've told you everything I know. OK?'

Gerry Heffernan gave Wesley an almost imperceptible nod. There was nothing more Teddy Afleck was willing to tell them. And it was about time they found out more about Jacob Fallbrook's secret life.

Half an hour later they were driving through the gates leading to Mirabilis, their car tyres crunching on the gravel drive.

'Is this any use, do you think? It all happened before Adrian was even born. There's no way he'll know if his father had other women. It's hardly the sort of thing he'd have been told, is it?'

But Wesley looked determined. 'There's more than one way of finding out family secrets. He might have come across a letter or he might have heard something.'

Heffernan had to concede defeat. He said nothing more as they got out of the car and rang the doorbell.

'How do you think we should play this?' Wesley asked, suddenly racked by doubt. Asking a man about his late father's illicit love life would hardly make for the easiest of conversations.

'You're supposed to be the clever one,' was Heffernan's only reply. Wesley thought he detected a hint of resentment but he told himself he must be mistaken. Gerry Heffernan hardly went in for that sort of thing.

Both the Fallbrooks were at home and they received them with cool civility before leading them into the drawing and offering tea, which was declined. Neither man felt inclined to spend longer than necessary there.

They began by telling Adrian and Carol that they had questioned Gordon Heather about Marcus's abduction and Adrian expressed some relief that something was happening at last. Marcus, he said, had been robbed of his childhood and he needed some degree of closure. Wesley wondered where he had learned the vocabulary of counselling. He wouldn't have imagined it to be Adrian Fallbrook's thing. Perhaps he'd been reading up on it since Marcus's return.

'There's one thing I've got to ask,' Wesley said, realising he couldn't put the embarrassing question off for much longer. 'Did you know that your father, er, was unfaithful to Marcus's mother?'

Adrian's mouth fell open and Carol, who was sitting, upright and tight lipped next to him on the sofa, let out a faint gasp.

'I'm sorry if it's come as a shock to you but . . . '

'No, no. I realise you have to ask awkward questions. The truth is, I did know.'

'Did you? How?' Carol squeaked. He had obviously not shared the information with her, much to her chagrin.

'I found a letter amongst his papers when he died. Rather an, er, explicit letter.'

'Do you remember the name of the woman who sent it?'

Adrian shook his head. 'She just signed it something like "your own little S". Whatever that meant.'

'S? You're sure about that?' Adrian nodded. 'You wouldn't still have the letter, would you?'

Adrian shook his head. 'I burned it. I thought it was for the best. Why rake up something like that? What's the point?'

'And you know nothing about this woman?

Adrian glanced at his wife whose lips were still clamped firmly shut with disapproval, and shook his head. 'Nothing at all. But then if their affair was over before I was born, I wouldn't, would I?'

'No, I don't suppose you would,' said Wesley, glancing at his watch. He couldn't see any point in prolonging the interview. There was nothing much to learn and it was unlikely that Jacob Fallbrook's sexual conquests had anything to do with the case in hand. 'Have you heard from Marcus? Has he said when he'll be back?'

'No,' said Adrian, earning himself a hostile look from his wife. 'His girlfriend's not well and he has a lot to sort out. He's going to stay here when he gets back. Until he can sort himself out with a place of his own.'

'We've been trying to get him on his mobile. Had to ask the police up there to get in touch with him and ask him to contact us. We badly need to talk to him again.'

'Sorry about that,' Adrian said. 'If he calls, I'll get him to ring you.' He stood up and walked over to the chest of drawers in the corner of the room. He took some photographs out of the top drawer and returned to the sofa.

'I took these the other day,' he said, handing them to Wesley. 'You can see how alike Marcus and I are, can't you?' he said with a hint of pride. 'I can't tell you what it's like, discovering that you've got a brother after all these years.'

Wesley handed the pictures back but before Adrian could put them away Heffernan spoke.

'Mind if we keep one. We don't have a recent picture of Marcus and . . .'

'Help yourself. I've got another set,' said Adrian with a casual wave of the hand. Carol rolled her eyes. All this brotherly devotion was getting her down.

Wesley smiled. 'Thanks for your help. We'll leave you to it,' was the only thing he could think of to say.

* * *

In a grey Manchester suburb, a stone's throw from the airport, the gateway to warmer and sunnier climes, a young uniformed constable opened a rotting wooden gate and walked up a narrow garden path, thinking that a dose of weed killer sprinkled on the grey crazy paving would do the trick. Not that the weeds growing in the cracks between the slabs was the only problem with the front garden of the little brick council house. The grass was overgrown and a plastic garden chair – once dark green but now faded to olive – stood against the front wall of the house balanced on three spindly legs.

PC Blunt adjusted his stab vest for comfort and raised his hand to knock on the door. Two wires sprouted from the wall like weeds where the doorbell had once been but the constable wasn't going to risk electrocution by touching them. As he waited he consulted his notebook. He'd got the right address; the one Devon and Cornwall police wanted him to contact. Someone at the station had said it was something to do with the death of Leah Wakefield. He'd quite fancied her at one time ... before she'd begun to look like trash.

He raised his hand and knocked again. Maybe there was nobody in. Maybe the man he wanted to see was at the shops or down the pub. All he knew was that Mark Jones was a vital witness rather than a suspect. With the characters he usually had to deal with, this reassurance came as a relief. He looked up at the house. A dump. Neglected. But some people didn't mind living like that. Each to his own.

He could hear footsteps now, shuffling towards the door. They sounded like the steps of an old man. But the constable knew from experience that first impressions can deceive.

Someone was trying to open the door but was having difficulty because the wood was swollen with the Manchester rain. The constable had the impression that the door wasn't opened often. The person who lived here either had reclusive tendencies or used the back door.

The door opened a few inches. 'Afternoon, sir. My name's PC Blunt.' He displayed his identification as he'd been taught to do. 'I'm looking for a Mr ... ' He consulted his note book again. 'A Mr Mark Jones. Is he in?'

The door opened a little wider. 'I'm Mark Jones. What is it?'

'Nothing to worry about, sir. We've been asked to contact you by Devon police – Tradmouth Police Station. They've been trying to reach you but they can't get through on your mobile.'

The door opened wider still. The man scratched his unbrushed mop of hair. He looked as if he'd just got out of bed. 'Devon?' he muttered, a look of complete puzzlement on his face.

The constable frowned and consulted his notebook for a third time.

Chapter Fourteen

Taken from the Brighton Gazette, *15th April 1816*

On the eleventh of this month fashionable society in Brighton was sorely disappointed by the failure of the boy known as the Amazing Devon Marvel to perform any of the prodigious calculations for which he is noted. Each sum posed to the boy by the audience was answered wrongly and he left the stage to boos and the throwing of missiles. The boy's father stood before the angry crowd and stated that his son was ill which calmed the mob a little but did not prevent them from demanding back the money they had paid to enter the meeting hall.

Letter from Mrs Sarah Jewel of Brighton to Juanita Bentham, 28th April 1816

My Dearest Juanita,

I was most distressed to receive your letter. Sir John must be told of what you witnessed while visiting your tenants. You say that you may be mistaken and you wish to confront this person but I beg you to take care. And you must remember that there is someone in your household who could do you harm if they wished and you have your innocent babe, little Charles, to consider.

Please have a care and confide in Sir John. You fear that he may have to act because he is a Magistrate and you may be condemning a blameless man to the gallows but I beg you to reconsider. You have a heart that is too tender. I beg you to be wise in this matter for your safety and that of your son.

Your most loving and concerned friend, Sarah Jewel

*   *   *

231

When Neil had finished at the library he made the snap decision to return to Stoke Beeching and ask Lionel Grooby a few pertinent questions. But first he called at the church. He needed to examine the registers. And he hoped that John Ventnor would be understanding.

He needn't have worried. Ventnor was in the vestry immersed in some paperwork and Neil's request to see the church registers didn't seem to bother him in the least. The door to the huge oak cupboard stood open and Neil's eyes were drawn to the old box with the letters JS carved on the lid that sat on the bottom shelf.

As he bent down to examine it Ventnor looked up. 'Nothing in there, I'm afraid. Just a few old hymn books and some sheet music.'

Neil opened the lid which was stiff with age. Ventnor had been right: there was nothing exciting in the box. However, as he closed the lid he had the vague feeling that something was wrong. But he couldn't think what that something was so he turned his attention to the reason for his visit.

John Ventnor unlocked the safe, took out the burial register and placed it on the table, assuming that this was what the archaeologist would want. But Neil walked over to the safe and took out another book instead.

Ventnor frowned. 'You know that's the baptism register, not the burial . . . '

'It's baptisms I want.'

Ventnor said nothing and let Neil get on with whatever he felt he had to do. No doubt he'd find out what he was up to in due course. He was a patient man.

Having found what he wanted, Neil said goodbye to the rector and made for Lionel Grooby's bungalow, halting briefly to see how the dig was going, After sorting out a couple of minor problems and examining the range of unexciting finds that had just emerged from the trench, he continued his journey. He hadn't warned Grooby of his arrival but then he always considered that the element of surprise gave him the psychological advantage.

Sure enough, when the door was opened, Grooby looked surprised.

Neil came straight to the point. 'I think I know who the body in Juanita Bentham's coffin belongs to.'

Grooby looked round anxiously, as though he was afraid that

the neighbours might have overheard what Neil had said. 'You'd better come in.'

Neil was vaguely amused by the worried expression on the man's face. He was the self-appointed local historian, the guardian of Stoke Beeching's past. But even so, Neil found it hard to see how he could be taking it so personally ... unless some sort of professional pride was rearing its head. Maybe he was annoyed that he hadn't got there first.

'I've been looking at old newspapers. I hadn't realised the *Tradmouth Echo* was that old.'

'It was started in 1793,' said Grooby as though the date was engraved in his head.

'Just in time to report on Joan Shiner and her shenanigans.' He grinned. 'And the Amazing Devon Marvel of course.'

'Yes.' Grooby looked decidedly nervous and Neil wondered why.

'I've also been looking at the church registers. The baptism register's very interesting. I hadn't realised Peter Hackworthy was a twin. I presume he was identical.'

'How should I know?' Grooby sounded defensive. Definitely professional pride.

'Just thought you might have come across it while you were researching your family tree. Peter Hackworthy and Paul Hackworthy. Twins.'

'Well?' Grooby looked nervous, as though he longed for the interview to end.

'I came across a report in the *Tradmouth Echo*.' He took a notebook from his pocket and read. 'Devon Marvel unwell. Miraculous powers fade.' He looked up at Grooby. 'Now why should Peter Hackworthy suddenly lose his ability to do mental arithmetic? It's not something that'd leave you suddenly, is it? Not when you're in the habit of doing it.'

'I don't know. Perhaps he was ill.'

'I think it was because it wasn't Peter who gave the abortive performance, it was Paul. For some reason Hackworthy made Peter's twin brother take his place. Peter was his milch cow, wasn't he? What he earned from being hawked round all these inns and assembly halls was making that family rich. But what if Peter couldn't do it any more?' He paused for effect. 'What if Peter was dead?'

233

He was surprised to see something akin to panic in Grooby's eyes. 'There's absolutely no evidence . . . '

Neil decided to make a wild guess. The worst thing that could happen is that he could make a fool of himself. 'You know the truth, don't you?'

'What makes you think that?'

'You're related to the Hackworthys. You've done the research.'

Lionel Grooby turned away. And suddenly Neil knew for certain he'd guessed right. 'All this stuff about Joan Shiner has nothing to do with it, does it? It's something much closer to home. I've got a friend in Exeter who works in the archives. I can ask her to look up the court records of the time.' He said the last words almost as a threat.

Grooby shook his head. 'You won't find anything there.' He stared down at his feet as if he found their appearance somehow fascinating

'I've read the letters you lent me – the Bentham correspondence.'

'Have you finished with them? I'd like them back.'

'Don't worry. I'll let you have them soon. There were a couple of letters that intrigued me. There was one from a Mrs Jewell of Brighton to her friend Juanita Bentham dated a couple of days before Juanita's death, advising her to tell her husband about something she witnessed while she was visiting her tenants. I found the letter to Juanita from Mrs Jewel but no copy of the one Juanita sent to her which was strange because she was a very organised lady and kept copies of her correspondence which people often did in those days.'

Grooby looked uneasy. 'What's the point of all this?'

Neil carried on. 'Then there was another letter from Mrs Jewell to Sir John Bentham suggesting that Juanita was in danger. Sir John replied that his wife died of a fever and he would be obliged if Mrs Jewel would refrain from making such outrageous accusations. I wonder if these tenants Juanita visited were the Hackworthys and she discovered what really happened to Peter.'

Grooby looked down. 'You can't prove any of this.'

Neil looked Grooby in the eye. 'I've just been wondering whether you came across the letter from Juanita to Mrs Jewel . . . Whether it somehow got, er, mislaid. You've always made a thing of being descended from the family of the Amazing Devon Marvel

234

but if it turns out that they were involved in something unsavoury like murder, it's hardly something you'd want to make a song and dance about, is it?'

Grooby pressed his lips together. 'I think you'd better go, Dr Watson. And I'd be grateful if you'd return the Bentham correspondence as soon as possible.'

Neil left Grooby's bungalow with the uncomfortable feeling that he'd gone too far.

Wesley arrived home a little earlier than usual. He found Pam in the living room sitting on the sofa with Michael, both bent over his new reading book. Amelia was playing contentedly with her duplo, constructing what looked like a house, a look of earnest concentration on her face. There was no sign of his mother-in-law, Della, so it seemed they were in for a peaceful evening. Wesley paused in the doorway for a moment, unwilling to disturb the scene of domestic bliss.

Pam looked up. 'Hi. What do you fancy for supper?'

'I'll make it,' he offered, taking off his jacket.

'No, it's OK. You hear Michael read.'

Wesley didn't need to be asked twice. He sat down heavily on the sofa and put his arm around his son's shoulders. 'Where are you up to, then?' he asked.

Michael began to read immediately, a small finger underlining each word as he spoke it. He was good. No problem there, Wesley thought with a swell of paternal pride.

Ten minutes later he called through to the kitchen. 'He's finished the book. He's brilliant.'

'He's not supposed to finish it. He was only meant to do two more pages.'

Wesley grinned at Michael who grinned back as Pam hurried into the room. 'Neil phoned. He wanted to talk to you about an exhumation if that makes any sense.'

'I'll call him later. I take it you haven't eaten yet?'

'I was waiting for you,' Pam said with a shy smile.

It was eight o'clock when he finally spoke to Neil. And what he said didn't seem to make much sense.

Neil came straight to the point, asking him whether he remembered the extra skeleton that had been found in Juanita Bentham's coffin. Wesley remembered it all right; he had even been intrigued by it temporarily before the abduction and murder of Leah Wakefield got in the way.

Then Neil proceeded to tell a strange tale of a child prodigy who had disappeared mysteriously and the prodigy's twin who'd attempted to take his place on the circuit of fame with embarrassing consequences. Then Juanita Bentham had died shortly after alerting a friend to the fact that she was in danger. Neil had thought all along that it had had something to do with Joan Shiner and her weird cult but now it seemed that there was no connection. That had been a separate thing altogether . . . or at least that's what he believed.

It was mostly guesswork, Neil explained. He had gathered up snippets of information and come to his own conclusions. Wesley refrained from saying that he often worked in the same way . . . only he had to get his evidence to stand up in a court of law against lawyers paid vast sums to prove he was a fool or a liar.

'So what exactly are your conclusions?' Wesley asked, a little impatient.

'Not sure yet. But I think Juanita knew something about the swap and she was killed to keep her quiet.'

'And the boy in the coffin with her?'

'The real Peter? The Amazing Devon Marvel?' Neil didn't sound too sure of himself.

'This is all very interesting, Neil, and I'd love to see your evidence but we've a lot on at the moment and I really can't . . . '

Neil grunted at the other end of the line. 'Suit yourself. I'll be in Stoke Beeching till the weekend. We've almost finished at the church now and they're anxious to get the building started. Call me on my mobile if you're free for a drink.'

When Wesley said that he couldn't make any promises, Neil put the phone down without another word. Wesley felt strangely empty. There had been several times since joining the police force when he had harboured a nagging suspicion that the job was too much for him, and this was one of them.

But the fact that Pam had begun to treat him with sweet reason allayed his doubts for the moment. If his home life was OK then he could face most things. He thought of Gerry Heffernan, losing his wife and living with a daughter he was terrified of upsetting by admitting he was seeing Joyce who, in her turn, had problems of her own with her senile mother.

Wesley felt tired. He was hardly able to stay awake for the weather forecast at the end of the ten o'clock news. And once he was in bed he slept soundly.

Until he began to dream.

He saw Neil's Juanita, smiling at him. She reminded him of his sister, Maritia, and he wanted to warn her she was in danger but he couldn't move. Then, in the way of dreams, she suddenly metamorphosed into Leah Wakefield. She was singing to him. *Joanie Shiner burning bright. Joanie Shiner our true light. Baby, baby, where are you? In the stars that shine on you*. He heard the pounding of feet on a hard playground floor and the swish of the skipping rope, rhythmical, hypnotic. Then the words going through his head changed. *Peter, Peter, where are you? Gone away into the blue*. Only Peter hadn't gone away. He was lying there, small and vulnerable in a coffin his throat slit, red and gaping like a second mouth.

Then Peter sat up and his features changed to those of the young Marcus Fallbrook, the boy he knew from those old photographs. He turned to Wesley, his eyes blazing like fire, and smiled.

The smile of a skull. The smile of the dead.

'You look knackered,' was the greeting Wesley received from Gerry Heffernan the next morning.

'I didn't sleep too well.'

Heffernan raised his eyebrows but before he could say anything he was interrupted by Rachel. As she popped her head round the door Wesley noticed that she looked different somehow. Almost radiant.

'There's been a call from someone at Greater Manchester Police – a PC Blunt. He wants to talk to whoever's in charge of the Leah Wakefield case. And that thing you wanted me to check . . . Teddy Afleck's inheritance. It turns out he's telling the truth. He inherited seventy thousand from his late mother's brother. The money wasn't from Leah Wakefield's ransom.' She placed a sheet of paper on Heffernan's cluttered desk and smiled.

The chief inspector thanked her and when she was out of earshot he looked up at Wesley. 'Someone's got out of bed on the right side this morning.'

The words 'Whose bed?' leaped unbidden into Wesley's head but he didn't voice them. In fact he felt a little ashamed of himself. Rachel's private life was her own.

Heffernan looked down at the sheet of paper Rachel had given him. 'I suppose I'd better give this PC Blunt a ring . . . See if he's managed to contact Marcus.' He sighed. 'I want to get this sorted out, Wes. Leah Wakefield's family have been on to the Chief Super and he's told me he wants results.' He put his head in his hands like a man under pressure. And Gerry Heffernan didn't like pressure from above. He liked to do things in his own time in his own way.

'I'll speak to this PC Blunt if you want.'

Gerry Heffernan looked up at him gratefully. 'If you could, Wes.'

Wesley took the details from his boss and was about to return to his desk. But he hesitated for a second. It was still on his mind, the dream that had caused him to wake, sweating and terrified at four in the morning. It had triggered something; some memory; some connection. It was as if he'd seen the truth in those strange images. But he was being ridiculous, overimaginative. It had been a nightmare, nothing more. Stress probably.

'You OK, Wes?'

'Yeah. It's nothing,' he said confidently before making his way back to his desk and picking up the phone.

Five minutes later he wandered into Gerry Heffernan's office, looking worried. 'Gerry, I've just spoken to that PC Blunt from Greater Manchester. It doesn't make sense.'

'What doesn't?'

'He called at the address we gave him for Mark Jones and he found Jones in.'

'And?'

Wesley frowned. 'Mark Jones didn't know what he was talking about. He said he'd never been to Devon in his life.'

'Is he sure he talked to the right man?'

'Oh yes. He produced his passport and everything. And his Aunty Lynne lived at that address until she died last September. He fits the approximate description but he denies knowing anything about why we'd want to contact him.'

Gerry Heffernan put his head in his hands.

'I think we'd better get up to Manchester, don't you?'

It normally takes around five and a half hours to travel from Tradmouth to Manchester. But, thanks to road works on the M5 and an overturned lorry on the M6, it took Gerry Heffernan and Wesley Peterson an extra hour to complete the long and arduous journey. By the time they'd pulled into the car park of Mark Jones's local police station, they felt as if they'd crossed the Sahara on a pair of camels, hot, tired and dry. But all the police station had to offer in the way of refreshment was tea out of a machine which closely resembled heated dishwater.

Wesley looked at his watch. It was half four already. He'd warned Pam that he would have to spend the night away and she'd taken the news remarkably well. However, she had said that her mother would come round and keep her company. Perhaps an evening of Della whispering poison into her ear would make things revert to how they were before. Good things rarely lasted.

After a brief chat with PC Blunt, they asked him to take them to Mark Jones's address. They had to see the man for themselves . . . and find out why he'd been lying to the local police.

'Bit different from the Fallbrook place,' Heffernan commented as they walked up Mark Jones's garden path.

Wesley looked around, noting the scrubby, littered patch of grass that hardly merited the title of garden and the flaking paint-work on the doors and widow frames. 'All it needs is a car on bricks,' he said with a grin.

'Yeah, you're right, Wes. Come to think of it, where is his car?'

But before Wesley could contemplate the answer the front door opened and PC Blunt was starting to make the introductions. A middle aged man stood framed in the doorway wearing faded jeans and a sweatshirt proclaiming his enthusiasm for a gruesomely named death metal band. On paper he probably would have fitted the approximate description of Mark Jones – or Marcus Fallbrook as they now knew him – but, faced with the reality, the two men looked quite different. This man's nose was more bulbous, his cheek bones higher and his hair thinner. There was no strong resemblance to Adrian Fallbrook here – he rather resembled a child molester from central casting.

Gerry Heffernan stepped forward. 'We're looking for a Mark Jones. Is your name really Mark Jones or are you having a laugh?'

The man took a step backwards, intimidated by Heffernan's direct approach. 'I kept telling him.' He jerked his head towards the bemused PC Blunt. 'I'm Mark Jones. I showed him my pass-port and everything. You've got the wrong man.'

'We were given this address.'

'That's not my problem,' the man said sulkily.

Wesley stepped forward. 'Look,' he said, meeting the man's resentful eyes. 'It's obviously just a misunderstanding. The Mark Jones we're looking for isn't in any trouble. We're just trying to contact him on behalf of relatives, that's all.'

The man's expression softened a little. He even began to look a little curious.

'Look, can I just ask you if you've been in hospital recently, if you've had an accident that resulted in a head injury?'

The suspicion returned to Jones's face. 'Yeah, I have. Why?'

'When did this happen exactly and which hospital were you in?'

When the man had recited the facts, Wesley looked at Heffernan. This matched exactly what they'd been told by the man who had been proved to be Marcus Fallbrook. But why had he lied? And why had he assumed this man's identity to do so?

Fortunately, Gerry Heffernan had thought to bring the photograph of Marcus they'd borrowed from Adrian Fallbrook. As soon as he showed it to Jones they saw the flash of recognition in his eyes.

'This is Joe. The old bugger. Has he been giving you my name? Bloody cheek.'

'Joe?'

'Joe Quin. We both work at the garden centre. Only he's not been in work for a couple of weeks. What's he done? Why's he given you my name? Come on, I want to know what's going on.'

He wasn't the only one, Wesley thought. But he stayed silent, listening, thinking.

'Sorry, we don't know ourselves yet, mate,' said Gerry Heffernan, putting on the old pal's act. 'That's what we'd like you to help us find out. Tell us about Joe. What kind of a bloke is he?'

'OK. I work with him and we go for a drink occasionally but I wouldn't say we were bosom buddies.'

'Has he got a girlfriend?'

'Yeah, Sharon. But he hasn't mentioned her recently so I don't know if it's still on or . . . '

'What else can you tell us about him?'

'He used to be a roadie . . . for bands, like . . . travelling round. But he gave that up about eighteen months ago. Dunno why. Must be better than heaving bags of peat around all day.'

'The car he drives is registered in your name.'

'Yeah, I sold him my car a few weeks ago. With this head injury the doctor says I can't drive and . . . '

'So he's never sent his details off – the car's still registered to you?'

Jones shrugged as though such matters didn't concern him.

'Has he ever mentioned Tradmouth in Devon?'

Jones shook his head. 'I don't think so. Him and Sharon used to go to North Wales quite a bit . . . Abersoch. But I don't remember anything about Devon.'

'Did he ever mention a family called the Fallbrooks? Or anything at all about finding his real relatives?'

The answer was a firm shake of the head. 'Never. I would have remembered.'

'What about his family?'

Jones shook his head. 'Never talked about them.'

'What about his dad?'

'Didn't have one.'

Wesley guessed that Jones had told them all he knew. And some instinct told him that what he'd said was the truth. Marcus – or Joe – had assumed his work colleague's identity. Perhaps it was acquiring the car that had given him the idea or perhaps he had planned it all from the start. But as to why he hadn't used his own name, Wesley could only hazard a series of guesses, each wilder than the last. 'Do you have his address?' he asked, suddenly longing to be away from that shabby house and on the trail again.

'It's a couple of miles away. Heald Green. Yarm Road. Number seventeen. But don't tell him I said . . . '

'Like I said, Mr Jones,' said Wesley at his smoothest. 'As far as we know Joe's not done anything wrong. We're just trying to trace him, that's all.'

They were glad to have PC Blunt to act as their native guide. He led them to Yarm Road – number seventeen – and, once they had reached their destination, he hung around expectantly. Gerry Heffernan hadn't the heart to send him away. He might as well do the bloke a favour by diverting him away from Greater Manchester's crime for an hour or so.

Number seventeen was a small semi-detached – a reasonably respectable house in a respectable road – the epitome of the ordinary. It looked rather better kept than Mark Jones's. The net curtains in the window could have benefited from a good wash and the grass in the front garden was in need of a mower but apart from that it looked fairly clean, if a little bland and featureless, as though someone did the minimum amount of maintenance required but took no further interest. They let Blunt, as the local lad, ring the doorbell. But when there was no answer and no sign of life round the back of the house, it was Gerry Heffernan who broke the pane of glass in the back door to gain entry. 'You didn't see that,' he said to Blunt with a theatrical wink. Blunt looked the other way and smiled.

Once they were inside the narrow kitchen Wesley looked around. It was the house of a man, although a vestige of female influence could still be seen in the dusty silk flower arrangement on the windowsill.

Without a word they wandered through into the hall, then into the living room where the bland and unloved theme continued. The carpets were beige with swirling patterns that had been fashionable once but Wesley couldn't remember when. The walls were magnolia and the only picture hung above the tiled fireplace; a cheap framed print of a harbour scene.

'I recognise that,' said Gerry Heffernan, pointing at the picture. 'That's Tradmouth.' He turned to Blunt. 'That's where we've come from.'

Blunt looked at the print of Tradmouth Harbour and made appreciative noises.

'Let's have a look around, shall we?' Heffernan began to make for the door.

'Shouldn't you have a warrant, sir?' Blunt was starting to sound worried.

Heffernan turned, an innocent expression on his chubby face. 'I'm worried about this bloke, aren't I? He's gone missing and we're all losing sleep over it aren't we, Inspector Peterson? We're trying to find something that'll tell us where he might be.'

Blunt hesitated. 'If you put it like that, sir . . . '

'Look away if you're squeamish, Constable,' said Wesley with a grin as Heffernan opened the lid of the oak bureau in the corner of the room and began to search through its contents. 'Or better still, go upstairs and see if you can find any letters or documents . . . Anything that mentions the name Fallbrook. And check out exactly who lives here, will you?'

As Blunt disappeared, Heffernan handed Wesley a folder with the logo of one of the larger high street banks emblazoned on the front. Joe Quin was obviously a man with a tidy mind. His bank statements were in order, Wesley was relieved to see, and told a story of a man with a modest income and frugal spending habits. The only outgoing over the past weeks that could have been described as extravagant was the five hundred pounds he had paid Mark Jones for his old car. All the transactions since then would be on the latest statement, as yet unreceived. That would make for interesting reading, Wesley thought.

There were more bank statements, this time in the name of Mrs Jacqueline Quin. And credit card statements in both names. And there was something else.

'Have a look at these,' Heffernan said as he handed Wesley a buff envelope. Inside there was set of photographs, some in colour, some in black and white.

Wesley examined them, then he went through them again, trying to make sense of what he was seeing. Amongst the photographs was a copy of the picture they'd found in Helen Sewell's room at Sedan House. Two women – Helen and a woman they had assumed was her sister, Jackie – with Marcus Fallbrook.

And there was more.

'This is the Fallbrooks' garden. There's the tree house Adrian was talking about. And here are some shots of the interior. It's not changed very much. What do you think it means?'

'I think these were taken by whoever kidnapped Marcus … reconnaissance. This woman in the photograph. She looks a bit like Helen Sewell but a lot younger. I bet she's the Jacqueline who sent the birthday card. She must have had some connection with the Fallbrook family … a dismissed servant maybe.'

Heffernan stared at the pictures for a few moments, turning the possibilities over in his mind. 'She might have worked for the Fallbrooks. She might have had some sort of grudge against them and decided to kidnap the child.'

'Then she couldn't give him up? Her sister, Helen, must have been in on it.'

'Well, Pauline Vine knew nothing about it and Helen can't tell us now. Do you reckon Marcus found these pictures and started to remember what had happened?'

Wesley thought for a few moments. 'It's possible.'

'I think it's about time we found Marcus, don't you, Wes?'

He opened the second drawer down and began to rummage. 'No sign of a passport yet. Hope he's not decided to fly off somewhere.' As if on cue, a jet thundered overhead, shaking the house.

'Bit noisy round here,' said Wesley calmly. 'I can't see him going very far. He's set to inherit a fortune. And what about Sharon? If we can find out what hospital she's in . . . '

'I want to know why he used a false name. Why pretend to be Mark Jones, his mate? What's the point unless he had something to hide?'

Wesley shrugged. There were all sorts of possibilities. 'Perhaps he wasn't happy about the Fallbrooks knowing his true identity until he knew for certain that everything was OK. Or maybe it was to protect the woman who had brought him up . . . the woman he had always thought of as his mother.'

'Jacqueline?'

'Probably.'

'Maybe he knew all along that she had been involved in his abduction and he couldn't bear the thought of her being exposed as a criminal so he pointed the finger at Gordon Heather to put us off he scent.'

'But where is she?'

'Dead?'

'Or she's lying low somewhere. And there is another possibility: Marcus might have wanted to hide the fact that, as Joe Quin, he's been on the wrong side of the law. Let's face it, a criminal record would hardly go down well with the Fallbrooks.'

Wesley took his mobile phone out of his pocket. 'While I'm on to the station I'll ask them to check if Joe Quin's got a criminal record.'

Heffernan nodded in agreement and Wesley went into the small kitchen to make the call to Tradmouth.

A few minutes later he came back into the room and Gerry Heffernan looked up from his search of the bureau. Seeing the expression on Wesley's face, he froze. PC Blunt, who had just provided the news that the occupants of the house were Jacqueline and Joseph Quin, hung around in the doorway, suspecting that something momentous was about to happen.

Wesley spoke quietly. 'Gerry, we've got to get back. There's been a development.'

'What is it?'

'I'll tell you on the way,' Wesley said, giving Blunt an apologetic look. 'We can leave you to see to everything here, can't we, Constable?'

But Gerry Heffernan was still rooting in the bureau. He had found another photograph. 'Well, well, well,' he said as a slow grin lit up his face. 'That's a turn up for the books. Look.' He handed the picture to Wesley.

'Isn't that . . .?'

'Yeah. Jacob Fallbrook and the woman in the other photo with Helen Sewell – the one we're presuming is Jacqueline. And look, there in the background. Is that who I think it is?'

'Yes, you're right.' He turned to Blunt. 'Have you looked upstairs, Constable?'

'Nothing much up there, sir. All neat and tidy – a woman's room and a man's. He's got quite a few car and boating magazines . . . not much else.'

Wesley's grin widened. 'Thanks, Blunt. You've been very helpful.'

Five minutes later they were on their way, the photograph safely tucked away in the glove compartment. It would be dark when they got back but some things couldn't wait.

Wesley had rung Pam from a motorway service station on the way back to tell her that he'd be home that night, albeit after midnight. He felt exhausted after his marathon drive and he knew he had to get some sleep if he was to be alert first thing. They had a killer to catch.

It was fifteen minutes to midnight when the two men sat in the interview room, the tape machine ready, waiting for Gordon Heather to be brought up from the cells.

As Heather sat down, Wesley took a sip of strong coffee. He noticed a hint of aggression in the prisoner's manner that hadn't been there before.

'I didn't kill her,' were his first words. 'I didn't kill that Leah Wakefield. I want that on the tape.'

Heffernan said nothing. He slid the photograph towards Heather; the image of Jacob Fallbrook with the woman they were assuming was Jacqueline standing close to him on one side and Gordon Heather a little further away on the other.

'Teddy Afleck told us that Jacob Fallbrook wasn't as squeaky clean as he made out, in his business dealings or in his private life.'

A sly look came across Heather's face.

'Tell us about this woman in the picture,' said Wesley.

Heather shrugged. 'Her name was Jackie. Jenny found them together. She was a bit of an innocent was Jenny – she was shocked. He was a randy old bugger was Fallbrook. I told Jenny to watch out or she'd be next.'

'When was this picture taken?'

Heather thought for a few moments, his face screwed up in concentration. 'Mr Afleck was taking a picture of a boat we'd just finished refitting. He took one of Mr Fallbrook and Jackie just to finish off the film.'

'Mr Afleck said he didn't know her name.'

Heather gave Wesley a smile that sent a shiver up his spine. 'He would say that wouldn't he? He'd been having it off with her and all.'

Wesley looked at Heffernan. 'So who was Jackie?'

'She was a secretary ... worked for one of the suppliers. She used to make fun of me. I saw them once at the boathouse and she told me to piss off.' He clenched his fists, as though he was trying to squeeze the throat of the woman who'd humiliated him all those years ago.

'So this Jackie was having an affair with both your bosses?'

Heather said nothing.

'Do you know what happened to her?'

'Dunno.

'Where is this boathouse?'

Heather let out a long breath and frowned. 'Near Stoke Raphael ... where the railway viaduct crosses the inlet. I haven't been there for years,' he said, looking Wesley in the eye, willing him to believe he was telling the truth.

Wesley viewed his last statement with some scepticism but he carried on. 'Did you tell Jenny you'd seen Fallbrook with this woman?'

His face reddened. 'I might have done. Can't remember.'

'Oh come on,' said Heffernan impatiently.

'All right. I probably did. Not that she believed me at first ... not till she'd seen them with her own eyes. She always believed the best of everyone, did Jenny.'

'Can you take one of our officers to the boathouse tomorrow?'

Heather looked uneasy. 'Why?'

'Humour us,' Heffernan said with a mirthless smile.

'I'll try,' said the prisoner half-heartedly.

'And there's one more question I want to ask you . . . '

Once they had their answer they took their leave.

'Shall we pay the Fallbrooks a call now?' Wesley asked as they made their way back to the CID office.

Gerry Heffernan examined his watch and shook his head. 'It's after midnight. It can wait till the morning.'

Wesley grinned. 'I asked Paul to speak to Carol Fallbrook earlier.'

'I presume there's been no word from Marcus?'

'No. But Paul says she was surprisingly co-operative. I told him to tell her that we think we know where Leah Wakefield was held and we'll be continuing the search tomorrow.'

Heffernan looked puzzled. 'Why?'

Wesley didn't answer the question. 'First thing in the morning then. Eight o'clock?'

'Can't we make it half past?'

Wesley hesitated before nodding in agreement.

'I'll set my alarm clock then.'

Wesley slept fitfully and when the alarm went off at seven, he had difficulty opening his eyes and facing the world.

But he made it to Gerry Heffernan's in time, picking the chief inspector up from his cottage on Baynard's Quay where the boats bobbed at anchor on the high tide and the seagulls shrieked their own alarm calls to the sluggards of Tradmouth.

Heffernan looked annoyingly alert, like a hound on the scent. 'Keeping you up, are we, Wes?' he quipped as Wesley stifled a yawn. 'Why do you want to see the Fallbrooks exactly?'

Before Wesley could give an answer his mobile phone rang. After a short conversation, he turned to his companion. Heffernan could tell that the news was good. 'That was Paul Johnson. He took Heather up to Stoke Raphael and they've located the boat-house. He said there was a new padlock on the door but fortunately he had the good sense to smash it. Want to know what he found inside?'

'What?'

247

'Evidence that someone had been held there . . . .tied up. And what looked like blood.'

Gerry Heffernan reached for his own mobile. 'We'd better get Forensics up there right away.'

'There's something else. There's an old cupboard there and Paul found some yellow A4 paper just like the kidnapper used for the notes. And, even more interesting, he also found drafts of the Marcus Fallbrook ransom notes. The kidnapper must have copied them.'

'Marcus said he was locked in some sort of shed . . . could have been a boathouse. Leah's kidnapper might have found the place and discovered the draft ransom notes. Maybe that's what gave him the idea.'

'Let's get the place sealed off, Wes. What are we waiting for?'

'If the kidnapper's left stuff, presumably he or she intends to go to go back there to get rid of the evidence. I've told Paul to watch the place – he's going to let us know as soon as anything happens.'

Heffernan sighed. 'If anything happens.'

'Let's get round to the Fallbrooks' shall we?' Wesley said with a confidence he didn't feel.

They said very little as they drove out to Mirabilis. Gerry Heffernan wasn't sure what they'd find there. Word hadn't come that Marcus had returned to the family fold . . . but that would only be a matter of time. He was family after all. Even if he had lied about the name he'd been living under.

As they drove up to the front door they were surprised to see Marcus's battered red car standing in front of the living room window. But the Fallbrooks' cars were nowhere to be seen.

'He's back,' said Heffernan with some satisfaction. 'Just the man we want to see.'

'Mmm. But a couple of convictions for burglary when he was young doesn't mean . . . '

'No. But it means he lied to us. Just like he lied about his identity. Mind you, Wes, that's probably why he lied. He didn't want his new family knowing he'd been in trouble. It'd hardly go down well in a place like this, would it?'

Wesley said nothing. 'Let's have a word with him in private, shall we? Looks like Adrian and Carol are out.'

They knocked on the door and it was a while before it was opened. Marcus Fallbrook – also known as Joe Quin in another life – looked a little sheepish as he stood aside to let them in.

'I only got back last night,' he said. 'Carol's gone up to Exeter and Adrian had a phone call . . . said he had to go out but I don't know where to.'

'That's OK,' said Wesley, making for the living room. 'As a matter of fact we'd like a chat with you on your own. We've been up to Manchester. We must have just missed you.'

There was no mistaking the worry on Marcus's face. 'I was staying at my girlfriend's. She came out of hospital yesterday.'

Heffernan sat down heavily on the sofa. 'Come on, Joe, don't mess us about. We know you're not Mark Jones. We saw Mark Jones. He told us who you were. And we went to your old house. We know the woman you lived with – the woman who presumably brought you up – was called Jacqueline and we know she was a friend of Jacob Fallbrook's. Where is she, Joe? Where's Jacqueline now?'

Marcus put his head in his hands and when he looked up, Wesley saw that there were tears in his eyes. 'You're right. Jackie brought me up but she wasn't my mum. Anna Fallbrook was my mum.' He shook his head. 'And I did lie. But only because I'd been a bad lad at one time and I thought Adrian and Carol wouldn't take kindly to having a convicted burglar in their nice posh house. I thought it was much easier if . . . I knew Mark wouldn't mind and . . . ' The tears began to trickle down his face. 'Look, I didn't want anything to spoil it. My mum – I mean, Jackie – told me everything before she went.'

'Went where?'

'Abroad. She's gone to France . . . to Provence. She met this man and . . . ' He hesitated, as though making a decision. 'And you're right. She did know my father – they had a thing going. And when I went missing she went looking for me . . . everyone was looking for me. She found me wandering somewhere.' He hesitated. 'She said it was on impulse. She couldn't have kids of her own so she decided to keep me; to go up north and change her surname . . . bring me up as her own. She took me on a train to Manchester where she used to live . . . told me it was an adventure.' He looked at the two policemen, defiant. 'Look, Jackie cared for me more than my own mum ever did. She's been bloody good to me and I don't want her to be in any trouble.'

'So you thought you'd make up a story about having an accident and getting your memory back in order to protect her?'

249

'I didn't want Jackie involved 'cause I think of her as my real mum. Can you understand that?'

'What about Jackie's sister, your Aunty Helen? Did you see much of her? She lived in Morbay. Just died in a nursing home there. Did you ever come down here with Jackie to visit her sister?'

Before he could answer Wesley's phone rang and he answered it. After a brief conversation he stood up. 'That was Paul. There's been a visitor at the boathouse.'

Heffernan's eyes lit up. 'Who?'

'Adrian Fallbrook. They're taking him to Tradmouth Police Station. He claims he had a call telling him to go there.'

The look of triumph on the chief inspector's face was unmistakable. 'Well I never had him down as our man. But I suppose it makes sense . . . copying the ransom notes to make us think we were after the same person who abducted his brother. But why?'

Marcus shuddered. 'That's one of the reasons I was glad to get back to Manchester. I had a feeling something was up . . . that I could be in danger. If Adrian considered me a threat . . . '

'Did you really think he'd try and harm you?'

Marcus looked embarrassed. 'I didn't at first, of course. But Carol . . . '

Heffernan nodded. He'd always had Carol Fallbrook down as the Lady Macbeth type.

'But I had to come back. I don't know why I should run away. I've got as much right to everything as Adrian has.' He buried his face in his hands again.

'So who actually abducted you, Marcus? Who was it?'

'I told you. Jenny's boyfriend.'

'He denies it.'

'Well he's not going to admit it, is he?'

There was a long silence. Wesley sat there staring at Marcus who began to play with the tassels of one of Carol Fallbrook's gold brocade cushions. He looked nervous. But that was hardly surprising.

'We'd better get back to the police station. I take it you're staying here?'

'Adrian said I should but . . . It might be best to stay in a guesthouse and look for somewhere to rent when Sharon comes down.'

'Yes. That might be for the best.'

As Wesley stood up, Gerry Heffernan's phone began to emit a tinny version of 'The Ride of the Valkyries'. It irritated Wesley who was no great Wagner fan: he wished he'd change it.

After a short conversation, Heffernan looked up. 'There's been an accident. They were taking Adrian Fallbrook in for questioning. Steve was driving Fallbrook's car and he crashed it. He's been taken to hospital.'

Wesley turned slowly to Marcus Fallbrook. 'I think we should go for a little drive, Mr Fallbrook.'

The child locks were set on the back doors. A routine precaution.

When one of their own was injured, the station grapevine worked overtime and they had been kept up to date with the minutiae of Steve Carstairs's condition. He had a broken arm, fractured in two places, and he was concussed. Wesley, who disliked Steve, tried to summon up some sympathy . . . and found himself wanting.

He had driven to Neston, taking the long way round to avoid the car ferry. Now they were bypassing the outskirts of Stoke Raphael, following the narrow lane that led to the railway line. A train was passing. A steam engine puffing asthmatically down the track like something out of a children's story book. The line was popular with tourists but locals also used it to travel from Queenswear to Morbay: the Trust that ran the railway allowed locals to travel at reduced rates.

'Where are we going?' asked Marcus from the back seat. He sounded vaguely worried.

Heffernan turned and grinned at him. 'You're being abducted, mate. Scary, isn't it?'

Marcus looked uncomfortable. Wesley glanced at his boss – one day he'd go too far.

'We're going to the place Adrian was told to go. You were there when he got the call were you?'

'Yeah, but he just went straight out. Didn't say where he was going.'

They had reached the overgrown track that led to the boathouse. It was time to get out and walk. As Wesley opened the back door to let Marcus out, his phone rang. When the conversation was finished, he turned to Marcus again. 'That was Forensics. They say Adrian's brake pipes were cut.'

Marcus looked shocked. 'Who'd do a thing like that?'

Wesley didn't answer. He led the way, Heffernan bringing up the rear. Soon he saw it, the little wooden boathouse. It was next to the shore and he could hear the gentle lapping of the waves. The boathouse itself was windowless and the green-painted door stood shut, its padlock lying smashed on the rocky ground.

Wesley opened the door and stepped back as the smell hit his nostrils. The scent of excrement – animal or human – still hung in the air, although there was no evidence of it now apart from an empty bucket in the corner of the room that gave off an unpleasant odour.

Wesley's phone rang again. He answered it but nothing was said apart from a perfunctory thanks.

'What is this place?' Marcus asked, absorbed in his own world, oblivious to Wesley's icy stare. He started to shake and the colour drained from his face. 'I'm sure it was here. He kept me here or somewhere very like it. Is that possible? Did he keep me here?'

There was a long silence before Wesley spoke. 'Let's go inside, shall we?'

Marcus stood quite still, reluctant to enter the place of his imprisonment. Wesley held the door open and he crossed the threshold, looking around fearfully as if it brought back terrifying memories.

'Go inside. Sit down.' He took a torch from his pocket and flicked it on before shutting the door behind him. Marcus's breath was coming faster.

'Frightened?'

'Please, can we go?'

'No, I don't think that's possible. Because you were never abducted, were you? You've been lying to us all along.'

Marcus opened his mouth to protest. Wesley could see his face in the torchlight and the panic in his eyes.

'Copying the Marcus Fallbrook ransom notes when you abducted Leah to make us think we were looking for the same kidnapper was clever, I'll give you that. The last person we'd suspect would be the seven-year-old victim.'

'I don't know what you're talking about.'

'Joseph Quin. I'm arresting you for the abduction and murder of Leah Wakefield. You do not have to say anything which might harm your defence . . .'

As Wesley recited the rest of the caution, the man they had known as Marcus Fallbrook looked around in panic, searching for an escape route. But Gerry Heffernan was leaning on the door, blocking the way. Like the real Marcus Fallbrook and Leah Wakefield after him, he had walked into a trap.

Quin swallowed hard. 'Prove it,' he said with feeble defiance.

And Wesley knew he was right. That was the challenge . . . proving it.

'Not very nice in here, is it? Don't worry, the Forensic team have already been here so we've no need to worry that we're contaminating anything.' He stood opposite the prisoner who occupied the stained plastic seat that had been used by Leah Wakefield. He had toyed with the idea of taking Quin back to the station and questioning him there but he sensed that here, where it had happened, was the best place to find the truth.

'Jackie was your real mother, wasn't she?'

Quin looked uneasy. 'She wasn't. She looked after me. It was like I said – she found me and looked after me.'

'You used to visit her sister, your Aunty Helen when you were young.'

'No. Jackie wouldn't take the risk of me being recognised.'

'Helen used to talk about Marcus Fallbrook.'

'Well?'

'Sometimes people remember incidents from the past . . . they remember them better than yesterday. You visited Aunty Helen, didn't you? There's a picture to prove it – you with Jackie and Helen. There's one at your house in Manchester. Where's the money?'

'I don't know what you're talking about.'

Gerry Heffernan had been silent up to now, staring at Quin, noting every movement, every nervous tic. 'You must have done something with it. Where is it?'

Quin looked at Heffernan as though he were stupid. 'How should I know?'

'There were boating magazines at your place in Manchester. Like boats do you?'

'Not really the sort of thing you do in Manchester. It's forty miles inland.'

'Your friend, Mark Jones, said you spent quite a bit of time in North Wales.'

'So what? Sharon likes Abersoch.'

'Lots of boats there. Ever used a jet ski?'

'No.'

Heffernan put his face close to the man's. 'I don't believe you.'

Gerry Heffernan gave Wesley a small nod. They were a double act and it was his turn.

'You kidnapped Leah Wakefield, didn't you? You kept her here. You tied her to that chair you're sitting on.'

'The answer was a snort of derision. 'I've already got a fortune coming to me. Why would I want to take the risk of kidnapping some . . . '

'But you knew Leah, didn't you? The real Mark Jones said you'd once worked as a roadie so we've been doing a bit of checking. That call I had was from a colleague whose just spoken to Leah's manager, Brad Williams. You worked as a roadie for Williams. Leah knew you and you followed her. And when she went to meet Williams in Derenham you seized your chance. And you used exactly the same MO that had been used for the kidnapping of Marcus Fallbrook.'

'I'm Marcus Fallbrook.'

Wesley ignored him and carried on. 'Only the motive for Marcus's kidnapping wasn't money, was it? The money was collected but it wasn't the main reason he was abducted. That was hatred . . . jealousy.'

Quin's hand tightened into a fist. 'I don't know what you mean.'

'Jenny Booker wrote a letter to her parents. I read it but I didn't take much notice at the time. She mentioned she'd seen a woman with a little boy and that he was the image of Marcus. She said they could have been twins. It was an innocent remark . . . Jenny didn't know the truth. But when I spoke to Gordon Heather he told me he saw Fallbrook with a secretary from one of his suppliers. Her name was Jacqueline. Jackie. Then I got one of my officers to check up on any births to a woman named Jacqueline Brice – we confirmed it was Helen Sewell's maiden name. A Jacqueline Brice had given birth to a son on the 3rd October 1966 . . . father unknown. But she knew him all right, didn't she? And he gave her money because he already had a wife, a wealthy one who was providing most of the money. And the affair carried on, didn't it? Jackie couldn't give up seeing Fallbrook because she had to fight for her son, the son she'd had by Fallbrook. You.'

254

He looked at Quin who was shaking his head. 'No, you're wrong.'

Wesley carried on. 'She was so enraged at the way he treated her and his son – his own son – that she decided to take her revenge. By that time Fallbrook was just using her; seeing her when it was convenient; treating her like some sort of prostitute: he was paying for her after all.'

Quin looked as though he wanted to land Wesley a punch then he took a deep breath and stared at the ground.

Wesley continued. 'She wanted to teach Fallbrook a lesson so she kidnapped his son, Marcus. Oh she didn't intend him to come to any harm. She wrote the letters and collected the money; made him pay. But then something went wrong and Marcus died so she didn't dare contact Fallbrook again. Whatever happened gave her such a shock that she disappeared from the scene altogether. She went up to Manchester and changed her name to Quin . . . got well away from Tradmouth. I doubt if Fallbrook ever suspected it was her. I expect he just thought the kidnapping had changed things and she'd decided to get away.'

Quin jumped out of the chair and banged his fist on the wall, the sudden noise, thundering in the silence, made Wesley jump. 'You're wrong about Jackie. It wasn't her.'

'But she was your mother?'

There was a hesitation then a shake of the head.

'You're Jacob Fallbrook's son all right . . . but you're Marcus's half-brother. It wasn't the DNA that lied, it was you.'

'Prove it.'

'We can get a DNA sample from Jackie when we find her.'

'I told you, she's abroad.'

Heffernan leaned forward. Well her sister, Helen Sewell hasn't been buried yet. We can get a DNA sample that'll prove she's your aunt.'

Quin sat back, uncomfortable.

After a few moments Wesley spoke again. 'Did you ever meet Marcus?'

He shook his head vigorously. 'Never. I could never go to the house when the family was there.'

Wesley and Heffernan looked at each other. 'You went to the house?'

'Mum used to take me there. She had a key. She'd taken it from

my father's pocket and had a copy made. We used to look round
... pretend it was ours. She said it would be one day. I used to play
on my own in the tree house. She used to say it was really mine. It
was all to be mine when ... '

'Only there was the small problem of Jacob Fallbrook's wife
and his son, Marcus.' Wesley spoke softly, sensing that Quin was
about to confide in them. He had no choice. Nowhere to go now.
He knew that they knew. It was just the details that were missing.
'I presume you told the truth when you said Jackie was abroad.
We'll need to speak to her. Where can we find her?'

Quin shook his head. 'She said she was travelling round for a
while – I haven't heard from her yet.'

'Did she tell you the truth before she left?'

Quin nodded. 'She'd had an affair with Fallbrook for years – he
was my father. He was married but he said he'd leave his wife.
She believed him. But when his wife got pregnant he didn't want
to know. He just paid mum to keep my existence quiet. Nobody
had to know she had a kid. Helen looked after me some of the
time. Mum hung around, living in a flat he paid for – only the
price of the rent was her silence. He'd pay the bills as long as she
didn't rock the boat. His other son got everything he wanted while
we were treated like shit. That hurt.'

'I imagine it did,' said Wesley.

'The night before my mum left for France she said there was
something she had to tell me. She hadn't mentioned Fallbrook for
years ... not since I was a kid. I had vague memories of my trips
to Mirabilis but that was it. She showed me drafts of the ransom
notes she'd written. It was like she wanted to get everything off
her chest. Confession, like in church.'

Wesley took a deep breath, breathing in the smell of smoke and
seaweed ... and something else. Death. 'So what did she tell
you?' he asked gently.

Gerry Heffernan was shuffling from foot to foot. Wesley could
tell he was anxious to get back to the police station to continue the
interview in a more formal setting but he was reluctant to break
the spell. The man was talking. A car journey might give him fresh
courage to keep his mouth shut ... to rethink his decision to con-
fess all.

'What did she tell you?' Wesley repeated.

Quin looked up at him. 'She planned it all. She went to

Marcus's school and persuaded him that his dad had sent her to fetch him.'

'Were you with her?'

Quin nodded. 'That's why he trusted her . . . 'cause she had a little boy with her.'

'And she brought him here to the boathouse?'

'She told him it was a game. She said his father would come looking for him. We sat in here playing I spy. Then she said we had to go and his father would be along to fetch him soon. She locked him in here and we left him.'

'What happened then?'

'She sent me to stay with Aunty Helen. I suppose that's when she sent the ransom note and all that . . . '

'She collected the ransom money.'

Quin shook his head. 'Yeah, but he was dead by then. She told me that she unlocked the door one morning and she found him dead. He was epileptic or something. She said he must have died of a fit.'

Wesley and Heffernan looked at each other. 'So where is he now? Where's he buried?'

Quin took a deep breath. 'She said she'd buried him near here. By the railway line. There's a stone near the entrance to a tunnel. She put him there.'

'Whose idea was it that you came here pretending to be Marcus?'

'My mum's. She saw in the paper that Jacob had died . . . said I should come down here and claim what's mine.'

'What about Leah? Why kidnap her?'

'Money,' he said bluntly. 'I needed money and I didn't know how long it'd take to get my hands on what the Fallbrooks owed me.'

'So you killed her.'

'It was an accident. I didn't mean to kill her.'

'You're lying. You couldn't let her go cause she'd recognised you. You had to kill her.'

He shook his head vigorously. 'She tried to escape and she fell and hit her head. And she couldn't have recognised me: I always wore a ski mask so she couldn't have known who I was. She didn't know me that well in the first place. I was just another roadie to her. She treated everyone like trash.'

257

'That's why she died, isn't it?'

'I told you, I didn't kill her. I panicked when I saw she was dead and dumped her in the river. That's the honest truth.'

'Where's the money?'

'In Manchester.'

'With Sharon?'

Quin looked up. 'There's no Sharon.'

'How do you mean?'

'I mean there never was a Sharon. I made her up.'

'Why?'

Quin didn't reply.

Then Wesley suddenly remembered something. 'The real Mark Jones knew all about her. She existed all right.'

'Like I said, I made her up.'

There was something in the way he spoke that made Wesley uneasy. He looked at his watch. 'We'd better get back to Tradmouth. Can you show us where Marcus is buried?'

'Don't know. I'll try,' said Quin meekly.

Wesley took his mobile phone from his pocket and called for back up. Somebody had to dig up Marcus Fallbrook's mortal remains and Wesley's first thought was Neil. He had helped them in his professional capacity before and he knew how to deal with delicate evidence as well as any scenes of crime officer. He'd get him called out – from what he said about the Stoke Beeching dig, he'd be glad of the distraction.

As they walked out into the weak sunlight, Quin turned to Wesley. 'The Fallbrooks owe me. I only wanted to claim what was mine by right.'

'Is that why you tried to kill Adrian Fallbrook? Is that why you cut his brake pipes?'

Quin didn't answer. He began to lead the way, climbing upwards, scrambling through the trees towards the railway line with the two policemen following; Wesley close by and Heffernan panting in an effort to keep up. Wesley spotted the large stone near the yawning tunnel entrance, moss covered like some gigantic grave stone in an ancient churchyard. If Quin was to be believed, this stone marked the grave of Marcus Fallbrook. The story of Marcus was almost at an end.

Quin pointed. 'I think that's it.'

They stood there while Heffernan got his breath back. They

could hear the throaty whistle of a steam train approaching, probably in the tunnel.

'Let's get back.' Wesley started to walk. He wanted to contact the French police and ask them to trace Jackie. If she had bought or was renting a place, they would find her eventually. He could hear the puffing of the steam engine now. It was getting nearer. Much as he would have liked to stay and watch it pass by on its stately progress towards the viaduct, he had more pressing matters to attend to.

He began to retrace his steps, allowing Quin to go first. The bank was steep and Quin was steadying himself with one hand. Then all of a sudden he sprang up the bank again, taking Wesley by surprise. He was heading back to the railway track, moving fast. Gerry Heffernan made a futile grab at the man as he shot past but he grasped at air. Quin was too quick for him and he shouted to Wesley who was caught off balance so it took him a second or two to turn. He began to run. He could see Quin ahead and he was gaining on him slowly. But then he stopped and shouted. 'No,' the word echoing into the smoky air.

Joe Quin had intended to cross the track a second before the engine passed, thinking he could make his escape while his pursuers were held up by the passing train. Only he miscalculated badly. No longer having the speed and agility of a young man, he went beneath the great metal wheels with a terrible cry of startled anguish like someone who had seen the gates of Hell opening before him in a cloud of fire and smoke.

Wesley fell to his knees and hid his face from the sight of the mangled body that lay quite still on the track after the train had passed, like a half-eaten carcass spewed by some gigantic predatory beast.

'I knew it.' Carol Fallbrook's lips formed into an expression of unbearable smugness. Adrian felt like hitting her but he didn't because he had never been that sort of man.

Wesley sat perched on the edge of their sofa and took a sip from the cup of Earl Grey that Carol had provided. He had set the wheels in motion, asking the Manchester police to check Sharon out, and he had contacted the French authorities about tracing Jackie Quin. But he had an uncomfortable feeling that it wasn't over just yet.

He gave Carol a half-hearted smile and turned to Adrian. 'I'm sorry you've had to discover all this about your father's relationship with this Jackie woman. I hope it hasn't come as too much of a shock.'

Adrian opened his mouth to speak but Carol got in first. 'From what I know of my late father-in-law, it's come as a surprise. I never thought of him as a lady's man. Money always seemed to be his driving passion rather than sex.'

'His affair with Jackie and the loss of Marcus probably put him off for life.'

'So this Joe was really my half-brother. At least he was telling the truth about that.' Adrian sounded grief stricken and Wesley wondered whether he had really grasped the situation.

Carol gave a contemptuous grunt which her husband ignored.

'He'd no need to lie. He could have told me the truth. I would have accepted him even though he was ... '

'Oh do shut up, Adrian. He tried to bloody kill you ... cut your brake pipes.'

'Now we don't know that for sure.'

'He was a criminal. He kidnapped that girl ... the singer. He murdered her. He was a murderer,' she said as though spelling an unpleasant fact out to a child.

'As a matter of fact our pathologist did say that Leah Wakefield's injuries were consistent with Quin's account of her death. It could well have been a tragic accident.'

'Just like Marcus's.'

Carol gave another snort. 'You don't believe that story about Marcus being epileptic, do you? There's never been any mention of it before. To paraphrase Oscar Wilde, one accident is believable, two look highly suspicious.'

Wesley smiled. He didn't particularly like Carol Fallbrook but in this case he had to agree with her. He stood up. 'Thank you for the tea, Mrs Fallbrook. As I said, I really only came to bring you up to date with developments. I really must be off.'

It was Adrian Fallbrook who saw him out. 'You will let me know when Joe's funeral is.' He spoke softly so that his wife couldn't hear. 'I'd like to go. He was my brother after all.'

'Of course,' Wesley said, suddenly feeling a wave of sympathy for the man. He'd found a brother and now he'd lost him. And a brother is a brother ... your own flesh and blood.

Wesley took the car ferry over the river. It was a fine early autumn day and the dense foliage of the trees that lined the river was just starting to show the first hints of red and gold. He remembered the way to the place where Quin had claimed Marcus Fallbrook lay buried. Neil would already be there with a couple of his colleagues and some SOCOs. These things needed to be done carefully and methodically without destroying evidence.

When he arrived Neil didn't look up. He was too intent on what he had discovered in the shallow grave at the foot of the rock.

'Well? Have you found him?'

Neil looked up. 'He wasn't very far down ... I'm surprised animals didn't get him. Want a look?'

'Not really,' Wesley replied. 'But I'd better have one all the same.'

The small bones lay there in the damp earth. Hair clung to the skull and rags to the bones.

'What's that?' asked Wesley, pointing to the skull.

Neil began to work on the skull area with a small leaf trowel. This was delicate work. After a few minutes he looked up at Wesley again. 'The skull's badly fractured. At a guess someone hit him on the head with something small and heavy like a hammer ... probably several times.'

Wesley bent down to get a better look at the bones. The sight of them made him feel slightly sick. But he had a job to do. 'So all that stuff she told Joe about him dying of an epileptic fit was a lie,' he said softly. 'She killed him after all.'

Neil looked up and smiled. 'Looks like it ... and violently.'

Wesley straightened himself up and stood for a while, deep in thought. After a few moments he spoke. 'That theory you had about Juanita Bentham's murder? Did you ever find any proof?'

Neil shook his head. 'No. That's what it'll have to remain ... a theory. Why?'

'No reason.' He stared down at the bones. 'Is Colin Bowman on his way?'

'Yeah. You OK, Wes?'

'Course I am.'

'How's Pam?'

'Fine. Why don't you come over for a meal now this case is wrapped up?' He hesitated. 'We miss seeing you, you know.'

Neil gave him a sad smile. 'Yeah. Why not?'

Before he could say any more, Wesley's phone began to ring. When he answered it, he heard Rachel's voice on the other end of the line. 'I've had that nursing home on the phone ... Sedan House. Helen Sewell's room was being cleared out for the next resident and they've found something hidden at the back of her wardrobe. They said we might be interested.'

Wesley didn't know why his heart began to beat a little faster but it did. 'OK, Rach, I'll be over right away.'

'Do you want me to go?' Rachel asked tentatively.

'No, it's OK. I could do with a change of scene,' he said glancing at the small bones exposed against the soil ... at the smashed skull.

Wesley pressed the button that would end the call and stared at the phone for a few seconds, wondering if the belongings Helen Sewell had been so careful to hide would prove once and for all that her sister, Jackie, was a child murderer ... the lowest of the low. Maybe it was a good thing that her son wasn't alive to discover the truth about his mother.

Two of the SOCOs were talking while Neil continued his meticulous excavation. Wesley didn't take much notice at first; it was just a casual chat between colleagues. Then one word made him listen intently.

'I gave it to Tim. You know, the new bloke in Scientific Support. He started at Exeter just as I left and my wife knows his wife – they met at antenatal class when she was expecting our Matthew. It's a small world. He says she's staying up there with the kids till they sell the house.'

Wesley turned away. It was time he got back to Tradmouth.

It was Joyce's mother who greeted Wesley Peterson and Gerry Heffernan in Sedan House's entrance hall with a blank stare and an enquiry about the whereabouts of a Vera. Heffernan knew from what Joyce had told him that Vera had been on her mind a great deal. The trouble was, Joyce hadn't the faintest idea who Vera was.

Gerry Heffernan was never quite sure how to behave when he came face to face with Joyce's mother. There's no time-honoured etiquette that tells you how to greet your lady friend's mother when she is hardly aware of her own daughter's existence. So he took the easiest option and smiled, saying nothing about who he was or why he was there. However many times they met, Gerry was destined to remain a stranger.

They found the matron in the office. She was talking on the telephone with the smooth sympathy of the professional carer. From what Wesley could hear of the conversation, she was trying to reassure an anxious relative that their mother had settled in well. When the call was over she turned to the two policemen and smiled.

'Thanks for calling us,' Wesley began. 'You told DS Tracey that you found something hidden in Mrs Sewell's room that might interest us.'

The matron stood up and bustled over to the grey metal filing cabinet. She opened the top drawer and took out a large brown envelope. 'It's all in here. One of the staff was sorting out Helen's room and came across a loose plank in the wardrobe floor. She lifted it and found these letters underneath.' Her eyes suddenly glowed with suppressed mischief. 'I'm afraid I couldn't resist having a look.'

Gerry Heffernan grinned back. 'We're not going to arrest you for it, love. Aren't you going to let us in on the secret?'

She handed the envelope to the chief inspector. 'Why don't you see for yourself?'

Heffernan emptied the contents of the envelope onto the tidy desk in the middle of the room. A trio of small white envelopes lay there, addressed to Helen at Raleigh House in Morbay – the children's home where she used to work with her husband's cousin, Pauline Vine, who would, no doubt, be horrified to hear about the skeletons which were emerging from the family closet. Wesley picked up the nearest envelope and extracted a letter written on yellow paper – the same paper as the ransom notes. Jacqueline Quin must have had a job lot of the stuff.

'I've got to tell someone or I'll go mad and I know I can trust you,' it began. 'You'll think I've done something really stupid. But I just wanted to get my own back. I've taken the kid . . . Jacob's kid. I thought that if he wasn't going to leave her at least I could get some money out of him and hurt him at the same time by depriving him of his precious brat. Why does he prefer to stay with her and her brat when he could be with me and Joe? Every time I think about the way Jacob's treated me and Joe, I feel like killing him but I reckon this way's better – inflicting maximum pain for maximum gain. Jacob always called me his little S . . . his little secretary. I didn't mind when I was infatuated with him but now I just think, how patronising can you get? Why oh why did I fall for that bastard?

'The kid's quite happy. He's in the flat, sleeping in Joe's room and I've told him that his mum and dad said he had to stay with us for a while. I've already sent Jacob's wife a note saying he'd be returned when they pay me fifteen thousand. Jacob can afford it easily and it's the only way I'm going to get anything out of him. The main problem will be getting the kid back home once I get the money. I think the best thing is to leave him somewhere where he'll be found and get out of Devon quick. I think I'll go up to Manchester again and change our name. Don't think too badly of me, Helen. I'm desperate and the kid'll come to no harm. Jacob will get the fright of his life, I'll get the deposit for a house for me and Joe and the kid'll have an adventure, that's all. I'll keep in touch, I promise. Don't judge me too harshly. I'm doing it for Joe . . . for our future. It's only right that he gets something from his father. Your loving sister, Jackie.'

He handed it to Heffernan who scanned it quickly. 'Doesn't sound as if she was planning to kill Marcus.'

But Wesley had started on the second, dated a day later.

'I wish I hadn't started this now. The neighbour in the downstairs flat started asking questions last night. I said the boy was Joe's cousin – they're so alike. But he's really different from Joe – you know the trouble I've always had with him – he's so good, does everything you tell him. I'm sure the neighbour sensed something was wrong – she's a nosey old bag and she's always moaning about Joe's behaviour. I've decided to move the kid to the boathouse where me and Jacob used to meet. Nobody ever goes there so there's no one to ask any awkward questions. I can lock him in there. I feel bad doing it but I've got to think of me and Joe. A lot of the time he'll have Joe with him for company so I hope he won't get too scared. Please don't think badly of me. It's the only way I can think of to get what's owed to me.'

'This one's dated a few days later,' said Wesley as he began to read the third and final letter.

He read it in silence. And when he had finished he looked up.
'She didn't kill him,' he said softly. 'Jackie didn't kill him.'
Heffernan snatched the letter and began to read.

Chapter Fifteen

e-mail from Rev John Ventnor to Dr Neil Watson

Neil, you remember that old box in the vestry cupboard? It's been there for years and I've always assumed that it belonged to the Rev. Singleton, a former incumbent, as his initials were carved on the lid. Well, I was planning to show it to an antique dealer, to see if it's worth selling it for church funds, so I emptied it out. When I looked at it carefully, I saw that it was a good deal bigger on the outside than the inside so I started to investigate and, to my surprise, I found that it had a false bottom.

Of course I didn't suspect for a moment that it was the box mentioned on that Joan Shiner website but in the false compartment I found some material relating to Joan Shiner including a rather odd manuscript headed 'The Seven Secrets'. On reading I was rather amused to discover that Joan's 'seven secrets' were related to local goings on rather than the mysteries of the universe.

The first 'secret' was that the landlord of the Angel in Tradmouth was bedding the wife of a sea captain. The second was that Sir John Bentham had had a love child by one of the maidservants . . . and so on and so on. All little scandals which makes me wonder whether our Joan was practising a bit of blackmail in her spare time: perhaps that's why she had so little local opposition.

Her seventh 'secret', however, was serious stuff. Murder no less. And it makes me wonder whether Joan was killed herself in order to keep her quiet. Accounts of her death suggest she might have been poisoned but this is pure supposition and as her grave has, I am told, long ago toppled into the sea, we shall never know. I'm attaching the relevant section for you. Interesting how she came to know all these things in such detail, don't you think?

Perhaps she had special powers after all … or more likely good informants. Speak to you soon, John Ventnor.

Extract from Joan Shiner's 'The Seven Secrets'.

'*Know the Seventh Secret: The boy Peter Hackworthy was done to death by his brother, Joseph, who, being eaten up with envy, did kill the boy and caused Paul, his twin brother to take his place in his noted performances. Know also that Peter's sister, a maid-servant at the hall, did poison Lady Juanita who, by chance, discovered the truth and was about to reveal it to all, and did bury the said Peter with my lady, Joseph, the carpenter, making a coffin large enough for two corpses.*'

'I left him with Joe … it couldn't have been for more than five minutes while I went to empty the bucket he'd been using into the river. The money was due to be dropped and I thought I'd take the kid some food before I picked it up. He was crying when I went in saying he was scared but I kept telling him it was an adventure, like camping, and he'd be home soon. To be honest, I just wanted to pick the money up, get him back home and get ourselves up north ASAP. I locked the two boys in together but when I got back to the hut and opened the door the first thing I saw was Joe standing there with a strange look in his eyes. I don't know how to describe it. Sort of cold, like he looked when he killed that white mouse he had. I looked down and the kid was on the floor. I rushed over to see what was the matter with him then I saw the blood on his hair, all sticky and matted. By this time I was panicking. I shook him but he was floppy so I tried to give him the kiss of life. All the time Joe was standing there watching me and it was only then I saw he had a hammer in his hand. He must have found it in the boathouse. He's only ten and I want to think that he didn't understand what he'd done but I know I'm kidding myself. I should have seen it coming. He said he hated Marcus and he kept asking why Marcus had nice things and he hadn't. I've never seen a child so eaten up with envy but maybe that's my fault, the way I've gone on about Jacob and the way he owes us. Perhaps I'm to blame but when we say things we don't always think of the effect they're having on children, do we? We had to get away so we came right up here to Manchester. I know I can trust you not to say anything. It'll be our secret. It's all over now and Joe has to be protected at all costs. If they took him from me, I'd kill myself. Please, Helen, understand. The kid'll never be found, I've made sure of that. I'll be in touch soon and let you know when we get somewhere permanent to live.'

Gerry Heffernan buried his face in his hands. 'We got it all wrong.'

Wesley said nothing. He stared at the words on the yellow paper.

'He had us both fooled. I wonder how many other times he's killed.'

Wesley looked up. 'I keep wondering what happened to the girlfriend, Sharon.'

'Maybe we should get onto Greater Manchester again and suggest they make some enquiries.'

'I've already done it.' Heffernan looked impressed.

'Joe didn't reckon on his mum confiding in her sister, did he?'

'He probably didn't know. If he did, I've a feeling Helen wouldn't have lasted long. I suppose Jackie felt she had to confide in someone and Helen was the only one she could trust. It must have preyed on Helen's mind. She made that scrapbook.'

They put the letters carefully back into their envelope. Wesley wondered why Helen hadn't destroyed them. Perhaps she had kept them because she suspected her nephew might be a danger one day, to her or to someone else. Perhaps they were her ammunition . . . until she had become too confused to use it. But even when she had descended into second infancy, she had kept them close but well hidden, as though somewhere in the back of her poor, befuddled mind, she was aware of their importance.

'Let's get back to Tradmouth,' Heffernan said.

As they made for the front door Joyce's mother was still doing shuffling circuits of the hallway, muttering words that made sense only to her.

'Do you still believe Leah's death was an accident?' Rachel asked. In view of what Wesley had told her about Joe Quin and the way he committed cold-blooded murder at the age of ten, she had her doubts.

'According to Colin Bowman, Quin might have been telling the truth.' He looked at her. 'But it seems very convenient. Maybe he pushed her against the wall. We'll never know now, will we?'

'So why are we going to the Wakefields to tell them a story we don't believe ourselves?'

'We promised to keep them up to date with any developments. That's what we're doing.'

Rachel fell silent and gazed out of the car window at the fields they were passing. Harvest was over now and the season of harvest festivals and harvest suppers was in full swing. Living at the farm she had been in the centre of it all but now that world seemed distant. She looked at the clock on the dashboard. 'You don't think we'll be long, do you? I want to be off early tonight. I'm going out?'

'Anywhere nice?'

Rachel felt her cheeks burning. 'I'm going out for a meal with Tim. You know . . . from Scientific Support.'

Wesley's foot nearly slipped on the accelerator. He said nothing for a few moments, wondering how to tell her what he had discovered . . . if indeed he should tell her. Perhaps it was none of his business. He opened his mouth only to find he was lost for words.

Rachel carried on. 'We're going to try the Angel – they do good bar meals there and . . . '

'Rach, he's married.' When he'd blurted the words out, he immediately regretted his bluntness. He could have put it more tactfully, phrased it in a way that would cushion the blow a little.

Rachel didn't speak for a few moments. Then she said 'What makes you think that?'

'I overheard someone talking. I'm sorry but I thought you should know.'

As the car swept through the Wakefields' gates Rachel remained silent. And on the journey back to the station, Tim's name wasn't mentioned again.

The bodies were found three feet down in the garden of 17 Yarm Road. The decomposing corpse of an female in her sixties. And the recently buried body of a blonde woman in early middle age, identified from a handbag buried near by as Sharon Carr.

The graves had been easy to find. It was obvious that the ground had been disturbed and a retired neighbour who fancied himself as a one-man neighbourhood watch had told tales of nocturnal digging.

According to the neighbours, the mother, Jackie, had disappeared suddenly a few weeks back – Joe had said she'd gone off to France with an unknown man. And Joe's lady friend, the blonde who had been such a regular caller, hadn't been seen for a couple of weeks.

But Joe was such a nice, unassuming chap, always ready to pass the time of day. He'd led an exciting life before settling down in the suburbs – he'd been a roadie for various rock stars until a year or so back. But in spite of these exalted connections, he wasn't at all stand-offish.

He was the last person you would have thought. He simply wasn't the type.

Suzy Wakefield sat alone with a gin and tonic in her trembling hand. The two police officers had been nice, full of sympathy and gentle words even though the woman, Rachel, had looked as if she had something on her mind. But their sympathy only made it worse. She almost wished they had been nasty. She deserved nasty.

Darren was still hanging about. She wished he'd go. If he knew the truth he'd walk out of the door and never come back again.

She dabbed her nose with a crumpled tissue. It would be her secret. She'd take it with her to the grave and, now he was dead, there was no way anybody could find out. She'd have to live with the dreadful knowledge that she'd destroyed her own flesh and blood for the rest of her days. She wished Brad would come round with the white powder that took the pain away for a while; she was running short. But she knew that, after a while, even that wouldn't work. Nothing would. Only death.

She cursed the day she'd met Joe by chance in Neston. She'd recognised him at once – Joe the roadie – always friendly – always ready to oblige. They'd gone for a drink and she'd poured her heart out to him. Fool. Then he'd suggested staging the kidnapping. She'd suspected Brad was going to do it as a publicity stunt – she'd overheard Leah talking to him on the phone – but what if she'd got in first? What if they all thought it was for real? Why shouldn't she get her hands on some of the money, the money Brad had cheated out of them, after all her efforts? Darren didn't need it. He was very cosy with his new tart. But she did. She not only needed it, she deserved it.

She'd told Joe what she'd found out – how Leah was going to

meet Brad who was to stage the kidnap and take her to a cottage belonging to some friends of his from London until her dramatic reappearance a few days later. Leah was doing it for the publicity. It was all planned. Until Leah didn't turn up for the assignation in the car park and Brad began to panic.

Suzy had called Joe, just to make sure everything had gone to plan and Leah was all right. Then she'd heard those words that made her heart plummet in her chest. Joe hadn't got her. He'd been late going to the meeting place and she hadn't been there. He'd assumed Suzy would contact him to make fresh arrangements if she still wanted to go through with it.

Then the calls had come . . . and the notes. Leah had been kidnapped for real. The joke had backfired.

And now they were saying Joe, nice unassuming Joe who always had such a cheerful smile, was some kind of psychopath. They said Leah's death had been an accident – but she knew that it wasn't. Bodies had been found buried in Joe's garden up in Manchester. It had been on the news.

As she absentmindedly popped the third paracetamol tablet, then the fourth, then the fifth, then the sixth, into her mouth, she closed her eyes.

It would soon be over and the pain would be gone for ever.

'They found the money in a holdall in his loft,' said Wesley.

Heffernan nodded. 'It was bound to turn up sooner or later . . . like the bodies of his mum and girlfriend. I reckon he was a psychopath. Classic case.'

Wesley said nothing. Maybe the DCI was right. Joe Quin – alias Mark Jones, alias Marcus Fallbrook – had had a certain charm and complete plausibility with no empathy for the feelings of others. And from what Wesley had heard about the psychopathic personality, this was par for the course.

'But why did he need to kill his mum and Sharon?' Heffernan asked, puzzled.

'Maybe Jackie found out what he was planning and tried to stop him. Perhaps after all those years of shielding him, she thought enough was enough. Maybe Sharon found out that Jackie was buried in the garden so she was sent to join her. Let's face it, we'll never know.'

'He was a ruddy good liar, Wes. He had us fooled.'

Wesley didn't answer. He felt angry with himself for having been taken in. He looked at his boss who'd just taken a cracked mirror out of his desk drawer.

'I'm getting off early, Wes . . . Taking Joyce to see her mum.'

'Talking of secrets and lies, have you told Rosie about Joyce yet?'

Heffernan's face turned red. 'I'll do it this weekend. OK?'

'Coward.'

'Why don't you get off too? You look knackered.'

Although Wesley suspected that he was being dismissed because Gerry wanted to avoid the subject of Rosie's wrath, he didn't need telling twice. He left the police station and drove to Tradmouth Primary School. Perfect timing.

He parked the car a little way away from the school entrance, not wanting to become entangled with the mothers on the school run. They scared him more than hardened criminals.

As he made his way to the school gates he realised that he was the only father there amongst the gaggle of mothers with pushchairs exchanging the news of the day, which he thought rather surprising in this day and age.

Suddenly the children emerged like young animals released from captivity. He could see Michael charging out of the school door armed with a painting that looked almost as big as he did and he stepped forward with a glow of paternal pride.

Then he noticed a group of girls, aged around eight or nine, were skipping obsessively as though their lives depended on it. 'Joanie Shiner burning bright. Joanie Shiner our true light. Baby, Baby, where are you? In the stars that shine on you.'

He smiled. Neil had called him that afternoon to tell him about the e-mail he'd received from the Rector of Stoke Beeching. Joanie Shiner may have been a charlatan but her attempts to black-mail and control her followers had led them to the truth about what happened to the Amazing Devon Marvel, Peter Hackworthy. His elder brother had been eaten up by jealousy at his rare gift and his success. Just as Joe Quin had resented Marcus Fallbrook – the boy who had everything his father had to offer while he was left with the crumbs from the table, the dregs of material comfort, the dregs of affection. Jealousy. A corrosive envy that had led to murder.

Pam had come out of the school door and was trotting across

the playground, hugging her cardigan around her against the chill in the air. To his left a large woman was breaking up a fight between her two sons who had emerged from school spoiling for a scrap. She saw Pam approaching and rolled her eyes. 'They're always at it, Mrs Peterson. Fight like cat and dog.'

Pam smiled. 'They're no trouble in class,' she said reassuringly as the woman dealt with the fracas.

Michael, now halfway across the playground, had spotted his father and was thundering towards him, a look of delight on his face.

Wesley took hold of his son's hand and gave Pam a shy smile. Order had been restored.

Historical Note

In the late eighteenth and early nineteenth centuries – perhaps due to the social upheaval and bloodshed of the French Revolution and visionary, William Blake's yearning in verse for the New Jerusalem – certain sections of English society became receptive to the claims of a few self-appointed prophets. I have tried to make my fictitious Joan Shiner reflect the spirit of this particular age.

Joanna Southcott was born in Devon in 1750 and in 1792, when she was in service in Exeter, she began to make prophesies. In 1802 she moved to London. By this time she had many followers and she did a roaring trade selling 'seals of the elect' which guaranteed entrance to Heaven. About 14,000 of her followers were 'sealed' but trade fell off when one of the 'elect' was hanged for murder at York. In 1814, at the age of 64, she claimed to be pregnant and that her baby was the 'Shiloh' (an obscure messianic figure mentioned in Genesis). Her followers prepared eagerly for the miraculous birth but Joanna died – her 'pregnancy' having been a case of dropsy. Joanna left a box containing, she claimed, something that would save England in her hour of trial and should only be opened in the presence of twenty-four bishops. Several boxes have been claimed as Joanna's original. One likely candidate was opened in 1927 but was found to contain, amongst other things, an old horse pistol, a purse and coins, some earrings and a dice box.

One of Joanna's better known followers (having joined the Southcottians in Leeds in 1820) was another self-appointed prophet called John Wroe who went on to set up his own church in Ashton-under-Lyne near Manchester in the eighteen twenties, believing that Ashton was to become the New Jerusalem. His attempts to walk on the waters of the River Aire near Leeds, and later the River Lyne near Manchester failed hilariously but, ever resourceful, Wroe made the excuse that he had been undergoing public baptism. He appointed seven virgins to accompany him everywhere and when one of them became pregnant, he claimed the baby would be the Shiloh and great preparations were made for the birth. However, much to everyone's disappointment, the baby was a girl and Wroe was forced to leave town. He travelled widely and his sect survives today in some parts of Australia.

My 'Amazing Devon Marvel' is also loosely based on real events. In 1806 George Bidder was born in Moretonhampstead, Devon, the son of a stonemason. His father found it profitable to exploit his rare talent with numbers and exhibit him as 'The Calculating Prodigy' at fairs and shows, travelling further afield as his fame grew. He performed all round the country in halls and inns and he was even invited to appear before Queen Charlotte. Happily, this prodigy was far more fortunate than the fictitious Peter Hackworthy: in 1819 he travelled to Edinburgh and attracted the attention of Sir Henry Jardine who undertook his education. He became a student at Edinburgh University – becoming a friend of Robert Stephenson, son of the famous engineer, George Stephenson – and went on to follow a distinguished career in civil engineering. He prospered greatly, brought property in Dartmouth, Devon, and retired there, one of the town's most noteworthy residents.

It's good to know that at least this 'Amazing Devon Marvel' had a happy ending.

THE PLAGUE MAIDEN

When a letter arrives at Tradmouth police station, addressed to a DCI Norbert it causes quite a stir. For though DCI Norbert has long since moved on, the letter claims to have evidence that the man convicted of murdering the Rev. Shipbourne, Vicar of Belsham, during the course of a robbery in 1991, is innocent. Despite having a full case load, including investigating a series of vicious attacks on a local supermarket chain, DI Wesley Peterson is forced to at least follow up on the letter writer's claims.

Meanwhile archaelologist Neil Watson is excavating a site in Pest Field near Belsham church. He discovers a mass grave that leads him to conclude that the site – earmarked for development – is one of an ancient medieval plague pit. But, more disturbing, is the discovery that the grave is home to a more recent resident…

Praise for Kate Ellis:
'detective fiction with a historical twist – fans…will love it'
Scotland on Sunday

978-0-7499-3461-3

THE SKELETON ROOM

When workmen converting former girls' boarding school, Chadleigh Hall, into a luxury hotel discover a skeleton in a sealed room, DI Wesley Peterson and his boss, Gerry Heffernan are called in to investigate.

But within minutes they have a second suspicious death on their hands: a team of marine archaeologists working on a nearby shipwreck have dragged a woman's body from the sea. And it becomes clear that her death was no accident.

The dead woman's husband may be linked with a brutal robbery of computer equipment but Wesley soon discovers that the victim had secrets of her own. As he investigates Chadleigh Hall's past and the woman's violent death, both trails lead in surprising directions and matters are further complicated when a man wanted for a murder in London appears on the scene, a man who may know more about Wesley's cases than he admits…

978-0-7499-3376-0

A PAINTED DOOM

Teenager Lewis Hoxworthy discovers a disturbing painting
in a medieval barn; a discovery which excites archaeologist
Neil Watson who is excavating an ancient manor house
nearby. But when former rock star Jonny Shellmer is found
shot through the head in Lewis's father's field and Lewis
himself goes missing after contacting a man on the internet,
Detective Inspector Wesley Peterson and his boss,
Gerry Heffernan face one of their most intriguing cases yet.

It seems that the Devon village of Derenham is not only full
of resident celebrities seeking the rural idyll, but full of
secrets, ancient and modern. Lewis's distraught parents seem
to have something to hide. Then the mysterious owner of a
new age shop is silenced before she can reveal what she
knows about Jonny Shellmer. Is Jonny's death linked to
Lewis's disappearance? And does Jonny's best known song,
'Angel' contain a clue?

As Neil Watson uncovers the story of Derenham's medieval
past, it becomes clear that the Derenham Doom – a painted
portrayal of hell and judgement more than half a millennium
old – holds the key to the mystery. And as events reach a
terrifying climax, Wesley Peterson has to act swiftly if he is
to save a young life.

978-0-7499-3756-0

THE BONE GARDEN

An excavation at the lost gardens of Earlsacre Hall is called to a halt when a skeleton is discovered under a 300 year old stone plinth, a corpse that seems to have been buried alive. But DS Wesley Peterson has little time to indulge in his hobby of archaeology. He has a more recent murder case to solve. A man has been found stabbed to death in a caravan at a popular holiday park and the only clue to his identity is a newspaper cutting about the restoration of Earlsacre.

Does local solicitor Brian Willerby have the answer? He seems eager to talk to Wesley but before he can reveal his secret he is found dead during a 'friendly' game of village cricket, apparently struck by a cricket ball several times with some force. If Wesley is looking for a demon bowler this appears to let out most of the village side. But what is it about Earlsacre Hall that leads people to murder?

978-0-7499-3269-5

THE FUNERAL BOAT

When young Carl Palister unearths a skeleton on a Devon smallholding, DS Wesley Peterson and his boss Gerry Heffernan are called in to investigate. Heffernan is convinced that the remains are those of Carl's father, a local villain who vanished from the Tradmouth area three years before. Wesley isn't so sure – he discovers evidence that suggests the skeleton is a good thousand years older than they first thought. A keen amateur archaeologist, Wesley is intrigued by the possibility that this is a Viking corpse, buried in keeping with ancient traditions. But he has a more urgent crime to solve – the disappearance of a Danish tourist.

At first it appears that Ingeborg Larsen may just have gone away for a few days without telling her landlady, but Wesley finds disturbing evidence that the attractive Dane has been abducted. Gerry Heffernan believes that Ms Larsen's disappearance is linked to a spate of brutal local robberies and that Ingeborg witnessed something she shouldn't have. But is her disappearance linked to far older events? For it seems that this may not have been Ingeborg's first visit to this far from quiet West Country backwater...

978-0-7499-3701-0

AN UNHALLOWED GRAVE

When the body of Pauline Brent is found hanging from a yew tree in a local graveyard, DS Wesley Peterson immediately suspects foul play. Then history provides him with a clue. Wesley's archaeologist friend, Neil Watson, has excavated a corpse at his nearby dig – a young woman who, local legend has it, had been publicly hanged from the very same tree before being buried on unhallowed ground five centuries ago.

Wesley is forced to consider the possibility that the killer knows the tree's dark history. Has Pauline also been 'executed' rather than murdered – and, if so, for what crime? To catch a dangerous killer Wesley has to discover as much as he can about the victim. But Pauline appears to have been a woman with few friends, no relatives and a past she has carefully tried to hide...

978-0-7499-3700-3